**Forge Books by
Larry Bond and Jim DeFelice**

LARRY BOND'S
Red Dragon Rising

SHADOWS
OF
WAR

LARRY BOND AND
JIM DeFELICE

FORGE®

A TOM DOHERTY ASSOCIATES BOOK • NEW YORK

This is a work of fiction. All of the characters, organizations, and events portrayed in this novel are either products of the authors' imaginations or are used fictitiously.

LARRY BOND'S RED DRAGON RISING: SHADOWS OF WAR

Copyright © 2009 by Larry Bond and Jim DeFelice

A Forge Book
Published by Tom Doherty Associates, LLC
175 Fifth Avenue
New York, NY 10010

www.tor-forge.com

Forge® is a registered trademark of Tom Doherty Associates, LLC.

ISBN 978-0-7653-6098-4

First Edition: November 2009
First Mass Market Edition: October 2010

Printed in the United States of America

0 9 8 7 6 5 4 3 2 1

This past spring, we were honored to visit the Center for the Intrepid and the Brooke Army Medical Center at Fort Sam Houston in San Antonio. We were humbled by the men and women we met there, veterans who have sacrificed themselves for our freedom and way of life. Some of them were badly wounded in the flesh, yet all were steadfast in spirit.

This book is dedicated to them.

Third world countries, especially those in Southeast Asia and Africa, will feel the brunt of the unpredictable climate changes. Abrupt shifts in long-standing weather patterns will bring turmoil and chaos to already strained economies and societies. . . .

—International Society of Environmental Scientists report

Major Characters

United States

Josh MacArthur, scientist

Mara Duncan, CIA officer

Peter Lucas, CIA station chief, Bangkok/Southeast Asia

Major Zeus Murphy, former Special Forces captain, adviser to Vietnam People's Army

Lieutenant Ric Kerfer, SEAL team platoon commander

President George Chester Greene

CIA Director Peter Frost

National Security Adviser Walter Jackson

China

Lieutenant Jing Yo, commander, First Commando Detachment

Colonel Sun Li, commando regiment commander, executive officer Task Force 1

Premier Cho Lai

Vietnam

Premier Lein Thap

*General Minh Trung, head of the Vietnam People's
  Army*

Other

Jimmy Choi, Korean mercenary

February 2014

Commodity Prices—Chicago Board of Trade

COMMODITY (trade units)	PRICE	1 YEAR AGO	5 YEARS AGO (2009)
Crude Oil	$735.87	$700.13	$74.86
Corn	$1,573	$1,234	$723
Wheat	$3,723	$1,534	$812
Rough Rice	$896	$310	$20.20

Average February Temperatures (Celsius)— Major World Cities

CITY	HIGH	LOW	2009 (average high)	2009 (average low)
Washington, D.C.	13	3.2	8.2	-1.2
Beijing	30.2	5.0	4.2	-7.0
Tokyo	12.3	3.0	9.2	0.1
Rome	16.5	5.2	13.5	4.7
Johannesburg	19.1	7.5	24.8	14.7

FRESH RIOTS SUPPRESSED IN
NORTHWEST CHINA

WULUMUQI, NORTHWESTERN CHINA (World News Service)— Unofficial sources reported today that government forces had suppressed a riot near the town center, the third report of a disturbance in northwestern China over the past week.

While food riots have subsided with the selection of China's new premier, Premier Cho Lai, Western analysts say Cho Lai faces a difficult task as China confronts devastating food shortages brought on by a third consecutive year of record drought. With food and other commodity prices soaring and the country already battered by the worldwide depression, an estimated forty percent of the Chinese male working-age population is out of work.

In Chinese-occupied Tibet, six persons were shot to death by soldiers during . . .

Housing Prices Hit New Record Low in U.S.

WASHINGTON, D.C. (AP–Fox News)—The FDIC today released a report showing that house prices in the

U.S. had reached their lowest point in fifty years, when adjusted for inflation.

Analysts caution, however, that the statistics are somewhat misleading, as rampant inflation in the food sector over the past two years has skewed inflation numbers skyward. The unprecedented rate of inflation is due to decreased crop yields throughout much of the world, and the consequent pressure on American farm prices.

"If we were in a period of normal inflation, say only three or four percent," said John Torano, analyst for the HSBC-Key-Banco, the world's largest bank, "then the decline in house prices would be only about twice what we saw in early 2009."

Still, Torano and others admit that the downward pressure on housing prices will put more families in jeopardy. The bankruptcy reform laws passed last year failed to lower the number of filings . . .

BRIGHTON BEACH RENAISSANCE CONTINUES

LONDON (Reuters–Gannet News Service)—Sally Smith frowned as she pulled into the parking lot B of the new Brighton Motor Park. The sign at the entrance flashed "FULL," even though it was only half past eight.

"Balls," said Smith in frustration as her two little girls complained sleepily in the rear seat that they wanted to get swimming. "It's getting so you have to come an hour before dawn to get a parking spot."

Smith's problem is cause for celebration among the

owners of hotels and tourist spots in this seashore town, which until two years ago was a boarded-up ghost, fifty years past its glory.

Now, thanks to a climate shift that has raised the average year-round temperature in southern England to a balmy seventy-eight degrees, Brighton is booming. In March, where once the average high temperature was a damp 8.3 Celsius, or 47 degrees Fahrenheit, sunbathers must be careful in the afternoons to avoid sunstroke. Last week, the temperature peaked at 32 Celsius, or 89 Fahrenheit—which would have been a near-record for August just two years back.

Scientists say the warm-up is due to a number of factors besides the general trend of global warming. In Brighton's case, the combination . . .

PERSONAL CHRONICLE:
LOOKING BACK TO 2014 . . .

To my beloved grandson Markus:

Here is the continuation of our family chronicle I promised, picking up in the winter of 2014. It seems like only yesterday that this all took place—and yet the time before it seems buried further in the past than ancient Rome. So much has changed, and nearly all of it caused by the conflicts that erupted that year.

*

In the year 2014, the violent changes in the weather and climate began to take their toll on the world in ways that many had feared, but few had spoken of. Violence increased everywhere—in the cities, in the suburbs, even in farm country, where our family lived. But it was the violence between nations that came to dominate our thoughts and nightmares that year.

Our family had been one of the lucky ones. Like most of our neighbors, we had benefited greatly from the rising crop prices. Our corn was worth twice what it had been less than five years before, and the yields, due to the latest genetic advances, were practically three times as high per acre. Best of all, there were ready markets for anything we could grow.

Prices for nearly everything were shooting up fast, but we were still far ahead of the game, especially when compared to the people on the East and West Coasts. My parents had cut back quite a bit, but mostly on things that as a kid you hardly notice—eating out, new clothes, extras. For us, the fact that we couldn't go see friends after school was probably the biggest impact. They cut back on the gas they used, though our four-year-old hybrid got what was considered decent mileage then. The real savings came with the fuel cell engines that had only just come out; we couldn't afford one yet.

We saw on television and read on the Internet about what was going on in Europe and Asia. There were riots in Europe, but Asia seemed to be hit even harder. I remember downloading pictures for a class project that showed more than a hundred bodies floating in a narrow stream—or what looked like a narrow stream, since according to the caption it was really a road. The picture had been taken in China, of a flash flood in a village in a northwestern province. If I remember correctly it was particularly ironic, because the area hadn't seen rain in several months. Then suddenly in two days there was a deluge, twenty-some inches inside forty-four hours.

What I didn't know then, being only ten, was that China was in much worse shape than those pictures revealed. Their rice-growing regions in the north and east—for centuries the mainstay of the population—had been racked by devastating typhoons. The overcrowded population in the smog-filled cities near the coast was suffering tremendously. Unemployment was nearing 50 percent, a sharp contrast to just four or five years before, when China's rapid industrialization had transformed the old Communist society into one of the most productive on earth. Every day there were food riots, though news of them got out only by chance. The Chinese were in free fall.

I doubt I would have understood all of that then, even if I'd known it. A ten-year-old's world has very strict boundaries, and mine were at the edge of our farm. So when my older cousin Joshua—the man we call your Uncle Josh—told the family he was leaving for Vietnam, it was as if he were going to outer space. In fact, I probably knew more about outer space and some of the planets there than I did about Vietnam, or even its neighbor China. But what happened in China and Southeast Asia, to Josh and to the people there, would affect our family greatly in the end, and the whole world. Ignorance, it turned out, was anything but bliss. . . .

Opportunity

危险

1

Northwestern Vietnam,
near the border with China

The sneeze rushed him out of the dream, squeezing away the black shadows he'd been running through. It didn't quite wake Josh MacArthur up, however—the second sneeze did that, shaking his body so violently that he knocked over the small radio near his sleeping bag. He rolled over and slipped to the edge of the mattress before the third sneeze, trying to bury his face in his arm to muffle the noise. This was only partly successful, and Josh, worried that he would wake the rest of the team, grabbed the cover of his sleeping bag and stifled the next sneeze, and the next.

When he was finally able to take a good breath without sneezing, Josh rose to his knees and crawled to the side of the tent, looking for the small plastic box with his antihistamines. After a bit of patting around he found it, but it was too dark inside the tent to sort through the pills—he carried two types, of similar sizes but different strengths. He wanted the one more powerful at nighttime, not caring that it would make him drowsy.

His flashlight had rolled away somewhere when he knocked over the radio, and he couldn't see it. Finally he decided to go outside and walk to the clearing, where the moonlight might be strong enough for him to tell the difference between the blue and green pills; it would also give him a chance to relieve himself. He grabbed his jeans from the edge of the cot and pulled them on. Remembering the snakes he'd seen during the day, he shook out his boots before putting them on, then took his sweatshirt from the base of his camp bed and went outside.

The moist mountain air provoked another sneeze.

Josh cursed his sinuses silently and walked over to the open area where they'd made a fire the previous evening. It was reduced to dead ashes now, but there was enough open space for the moon to shine full; he could see not only his hands but the cuts across his palm. He opened the pillbox and sorted through its contents, worried he would sneeze again and spill them in the dirt, where they might be lost forever. Finally he found one he was convinced was green—one of the strong ones—and popped it into his mouth.

He swallowed, grimacing at the bitter taste the pill left in his throat. Then he moved toward the bushes and trees a few yards away to find a place to pee.

Northwestern Vietnam was not the best place for a man with allergies, but MacArthur hadn't considered his body's foibles when he decided on his career as a weather scientist, nor had he thought about it much when he chose his doctoral thesis topic, the impact of rapid climate change on Asian mammals. Vietnam was not only a good place to study his subject; there was actually money available to fund the research, since few scientists wanted to go to such a distant place when there were ample topics in the developed world. These days, one could study the effects of climate change and still sleep in a hotel bed at night.

But Vietnam, snakes and all, offered other consolations. The mountains and valleys of the north were breathtakingly spectacular. And while they had been greatly affected by the rapid changes in the world's weather that had occurred over the last five years, the changes were much more benign, and even beneficial, than those elsewhere.

One of the changes meant it was slightly wetter and warmer in February than it ordinarily would have been just five years before. But warmth was relative—MacArthur pulled on his sweatshirt and rubbed his hands together, trying to ward off the chill as he looked for a suitable place to relieve himself.

The young scientist had just found a large rock when he heard something pushing through the scrub to his right. He froze with fear.

A tiger!

Ordinarily they didn't range quite this far west, but they too had suffered the consequences of climate change, and were expanding their range.

What was he supposed to do? Crouch? Freeze? Run? What had he been told during orientation?

Before his mind could supply an answer, he heard another sound, this one farther away. There were two, no three animals moving through the brush.

A fourth.

They couldn't be tigers. The cats didn't hunt in packs.

But this realization didn't comfort him. Something was definitely there, moving through the vegetation toward the camp.

Thieves?

Someone shouted. MacArthur spoke very rudimentary Vietnamese, and what he heard didn't match with the words he knew.

There was another shout, and then a very loud and strange popping noise, a bang that seemed unworldly. The whole mountain shuddered, then flashed oddly white.

Then came a noise he *did* recognize, one he'd heard long ago as a child, a sound that had filled his nightmares ever since—an automatic weapon began rattling behind him, its sound the steady, quick stutter of death. Another joined in, then another and another.

Without thinking, without even looking where he was going, Josh MacArthur took off running in the opposite direction, dodging through the thick brush in the moonlight.

2

Northwestern Vietnam,
near the border with China

Lieutenant Jing Yo stiffened as Colonel Sun Li strode up the hill.

"What happened here, Lieutenant?" said the colonel.

"The intelligence was not good. There were Vietnamese soldiers in the camp. The regular troops panicked and began to fire. We came up from the road as soon as we heard the gunfire. By then, of course, it was too late."

"They killed them?"

"Yes," said Jing Yo. "As best I can determine, there were only two Vietnamese soldiers in the camp. The rest were unarmed. It appeared to be a scientific expedition."

"Science?"

"There are different instruments. It was a UN team."

Sun frowned. Killing Vietnamese was one thing; murdering international scientists, quite another.

"An expedition?" The colonel's expression changed as he considered this. "So they were spies."

Jing Yo shook his head. "Their equipment—"

"They were spies, Lieutenant. If the matter should ever be raised later on. Something that is very unlikely. In the meantime, we still have operational secrecy. That was maintained, for better or worse."

Jing Yo knew better than to disagree. Colonel Sun

was Jing Yo's superior as head of the commando regiment. More important as far as the present operation was concerned, he was the executive officer to General Ho Ling, the commander of Group Task Force 1, and thus the second-in-command of the army at the spearhead of the campaign to subdue Vietnam. Though still in his early thirties, Sun was as politically connected as any general in the army, as his position with the commandos demonstrated: he was the nephew of Premier Cho Lai—the favorite nephew, by all accounts.

Still, Jing Yo was not a toady or yes-man; Sun would not have had him as a platoon leader and personal confidant if he was.

"I sense from your silence that you disapprove," said Sun when Jing Yo didn't answer. "You consider this attack a sign of poor discipline."

"It does not signify achievement."

Sun laughed. "Well said, my understated monk." The colonel practically bellowed. "Well said. But what do we expect of these ignorant peasants? We've worn out our tongues on this."

Sun had, in fact, argued against using regular troops rather than commandos for the secret border mission before the invasion. But General Ho had countered that the tasks could be conducted by regular troops with some guidance. The argument became moot when the central command decided to allocate only one commando platoon—Jing Yo's—to the mission. They blamed this on manpower shortages, but in truth the decision had much more to do with army politics: central command wanted to limit the commandos' influence by limiting their glories.

"We'll have to wipe these idiots' noses for them before it's through," said Sun. "But Vietnam is not Malaysia, eh? We won't be fighting the CIA here."

"No," said Jing Yo. "But we should not underestimate our enemy."

One of the regular soldiers rushed up from the side of the hill. It was Sergeant Cho, one of the noncommissioned officers who had presided over the massacre.

"Colonel, Private Bai believes he heard someone running up the hill in that direction," said Cho.

"Lieutenant, investigate," said Sun. "We do not need witnesses."

Jing Yo bowed his head, then turned to Cho. "Which way?"

"I will show you."

"No, you will tell me. My men and I will deal with it."

**Northwestern Vietnam,
near the border with China**

Josh felt his chest tighten into a knot, the muscles stretched across his rib cage. He knew better than to give in to the pain—he had to flee, escape whoever was pursuing him. The sound of the bullets slashing through the air, the metal thump that shook both sides of his skull, had turned him into something less than human: an animal, scared; a rabbit or something smaller, a mouse.

He ran and he ran, maybe in circles, pushing through the thick brush without a plan. He pushed through thin stalks of growing trees and wide fern fronds, jostling against thicker trees. The pain in his chest spread inward, gripping his lungs, squeezing until he couldn't breathe.

And still he ran.

The ground tipped upward, sloping in the direction of the mountains. Somewhere beyond Josh the rain forest gave way to bamboo, the elevation climbing to 2,400 meters. But the jungle still ruled here, and the thick, closely spaced trees would have been a hazard even in full daylight. Josh hit against them repeatedly, bouncing off mostly, pushing to the right or left, until inevitably he fell, his balance and energy drained. He rolled on the jungle floor, the cold, damp earth seeming to climb around him.

His heart pounded furiously. He gulped at the air, desperate to breathe. He tasted the leaves and thick moss deep in his lungs. His eyes watered and his nose was full, but he managed to keep himself from sneezing until he could raise his arm to his mouth and muffle the sound with the inside crook of his elbow. He coughed and wheezed, rising to his haunches. Sweat ran down both temples, and his back was soaked. It felt as if every organ, every blood vessel inside his body, had given way, the liquid surging through his pores.

And then he began to retch.

For Jing Yo, each step was critical. To move through the jungle—to move anywhere—was a matter of balance. The difficulty was to make each move lead to another, to choose a step that would lead inevitably to the step ten paces later. When Jing Yo was moving properly, this was how he stepped; when he went forward with the proper discipline, the hundredth step was preordained.

He had spent years mastering this, learning with his mentors as his practice of self-awareness in the days before his induction into the army.

The trouble was not moving through the dark, but moving with the other men, who knew little of balance, let alone *Ch'an* or the Way That Guides All, often known as kung fu outside China. The commandos on his team were elite soldiers, carefully selected and trained to be the country's best warfighters, but even so, they were not *Ch'an* monks nor indoctrinated like them. They walked as soldiers walk, not as ghosts balancing on the edge of the sword.

Jing Yo was the fourth man in the team, the center of a triangle, with Ai Gua at point fifty meters ahead, Sergeant Fan to his left, and Private Po directly behind him. This was not commando doctrine—a spread, single-file line was preferred in this circumstance—but Jing Yo had his own way for many things.

Ai Gua stopped. Jing Yo froze as well, then turned and held out his hands, trying to signal to Po, who didn't see him until he was only a few meters away; at that point the private fell quickly—and noisily—to his knees.

"Wait," Jing Yo whispered. "Quietly."

He slipped forward to Ai Gua. Raised in south-western China, Ai Gua had hunted from a very young age, and had the judgment of a much older man.

"In that direction," said Ai Gua, pointing to his right. "Going up the slope."

"How many?"

"I cannot tell. Just one, maybe. But a noisy one."

Jing Yo stared at the forest. One man could be more difficult to apprehend than an entire squad.

Sergeant Fan crept close on Jing Yo's left.

"Where?" Jing Yo asked.

Ai Gua pointed. The sergeant adjusted his night-vision goggles as he scanned the area.

"I see nothing," he told Jing Yo.

"They are there," said Ai Gua.

Without even looking at him, Jing Yo knew the sergeant was frowning. In his midthirties, a career soldier from a poor family, Sergeant Fan was a practical man, skeptical by nature.

"Sergeant, take Ai Gua and move in this direction. Private Po and I will go this way and flank our prey."

"Yes, Lieutenant."

"Remember, we want them alive."

"Alive?"

"Until we get information from them, yes."

J osh steadied himself over the small pool of vomit and mucus. He'd finally caught his breath, but his heart still raced and his whole body shook.

He knew he had to move. He pushed himself upright, then rose unsteadily.

Move! he told himself. *Move! You're not a five-year-old anymore. These aren't the people who killed your parents. Go! Go!*

They weren't the same people, but they were just as dangerous—different incarnations of the same evil, he thought to himself as he started to move.

The memory of his childhood horror—never fully repressed, never fully confronted—rose from the dark recesses of his consciousness. He tried to ignore it, focusing on the forest before him, feeling the leaves that snapped and slashed at his fingers as he started to move again. He heard a noise behind him, below—he was running upward, he realized for the first time, climbing the mountain.

They were after him.

The boy whose family had been murdered hadn't panicked, entirely; in the end, he had acted very rationally—and very much like a boy. He had started running out of fear. But then something else took over, something stronger. He began to act as if he were a character in one of the games he often played, *Star Wars Battlefront.*

He became a clone trooper on Dagobah, dodging through the dense swamp and jungle as he hid from the crazy men who'd come to shoot his family. The cornfield, its stalks bitten to the earth by the harvester, became the large swamp at the center of the battlefield. Old Man's Rock—the marker at the corner of their field and the neighbors'—became the landing port for the Federation reinforcements. And the Johnsons' cow field became the portal he had to escape to.

It was not like the game, exactly; he had no weapon, nor options to alter his character. But the boy became the player, dodging through the field, careful to get away. As long as he was the player, rather than the boy, he could survive. He'd done it before, countless times, playing with his older brother.

And he did it again.

Josh slowed, began to walk rather than run. Running only helped his pursuers—it made him easier to hear. His steps became quieter, more purposeful. His breathing slowed. His eyes, nearly shut until now, opened and let him see as well as any cat.

Gradually, a strategy occurred to him, coalescing around questions that began to form in his mind.

How many are after me?

It couldn't be many, because they were difficult to hear.

Which direction are they coming from?

The camp, now to his right. Southeast.

Did they see me, or only hear me running through the forest?

It must have been the latter; if they'd seen me, they would have shot immediately.

The questions continued, as did the answers. Josh moved very slowly now, so slowly that at times he felt that he was sleeping standing up.

What do I have with me? A weapon?

Nothing of use. He had the little Flip 5 video camera in his pocket, left there after the evening campfire when he'd amused his colleagues by interviewing them. He had a lighter, Tom's, which he'd used to light the lantern and failed to give back. He had a guitar pick, from Sarah, a token of good luck she'd slipped into his hand at the airport.

No weapon, no gun.

The noises he'd heard drifted away. But he sensed they were still hunting him, just as long ago the killers had followed. They had wanted to kill him not because he was a witness; their twisted minds didn't care about that. To them there was no possibility of being caught, let alone punished. They wanted him the way a hungry man wants food. Killing his family had whetted their appetite, and now they were insatiable.

He saw rocks ahead. Slowly, he walked to them.

The outcropping was just at the edge of a slope of bamboo stalks.

Hide in the bamboo?

No. It was too thin—someone with a nightscope could see him.

Move through it. There would be another place to hide somewhere.

Josh began moving to his left. There was something to his right, something moving.

He lowered himself to his haunches slowly, crouching, not even daring to breathe.

Perhaps I'm already dead, he thought. *Perhaps these are the last thoughts that will occur to me.*

Jing Yo stopped and turned to Private Po, waiting for the rifleman to catch up. While splitting his small team up made tactical sense, it carried an inherent risk. There was no way for the groups to communicate with each other. Like in every other unit in the Chinese army, none of the enlisted men were supplied with radios.

Officially, this was due to equipment shortages. The real reason was to make it more difficult for the enlisted men to organize a mutiny. The fear was well warranted; Jing Yo had heard of two units rebelling against their commander's orders over the past few months. One of these actions amounted to only a few men who balked at being transferred from the northern provinces where they had been stationed for years. The other was much more serious: two entire companies refused to muster in protest of their failure to get raises. Both cases had been dealt with harshly; the units were broken up, with the ringleaders thrown into reeducation camps.

Their officers suffered more severe punishment: execution by firing squad.

"Our quarry has stopped somewhere," Jing Yo told

Private Po. "See what you can see in that direction there."

The private raised his rifle and looked through the scope. The electronics in the device were sensitive to heat, and rendered the night in a small circle of green before the private's eyes. Unfortunately, the thick jungle made it difficult for him to see far.

"Nothing," whispered Private Po.

Jing Yo became an eagle in his mind's eye, rising above to view the battlefield. The mountain jutted up sharply ahead; the jungle diminished, leaving vast swaths of bamboo and rock as the only cover. A skilled man trying to escape them would stay in the deep forest.

But was their quarry skilled? There were arguments either way. On the one hand, he had made enough noise for an otherwise incompetent soldier to hear him. On the other, he had left no obvious trail in the thick brush, and was now making no sound that could be heard.

There is no silence but the universe's silence.

His mentors' words came back to him. On the surface, the instruction was simple enough: One must learn to listen correctly; hearing was really a matter of tuning one's ears. But as with much the gray-haired monks said, there was meaning beyond the words.

"Are we in the right place?" asked Private Po.

"Ssshhh," replied Jing Yo.

His own breath was loud in his ears. He slowed his lungs, leaning forward. The jungle had many sounds—water, somewhere ahead, brush swaying in the wind—a small animal—

Two footsteps, ahead.

Barely ten yards away.

"Your rifle," Jing Yo said to the private, reaching for it.

Josh tried to hold his breath as he slipped forward. They were very close, close enough for him to have heard a voice.

He stepped around a low rock ledge, edging into a thick fold of brush. He wanted to move faster, but he knew that would only make more noise. Stealth was more important than speed. If he was quiet, they might miss him.

Something shifted nearby. A cough.

They were much closer than he'd thought—ten yards, less, just beyond the clump of trees where he'd paused a moment ago.

Move more quickly, he told himself. *But just as quietly.*

He took two steps, then panic finally won its battle, and he began to run.

It was not sound but smell that gave their prey away. The smell was odd, light and almost flowerlike, an odd, unusual perfume for the jungle, so strange that Jing Yo thought at first it must be a figment of his imagination.

Then he realized it was the scent of Western soap.

He turned the rifle in the scent's direction, then heard something moving, stumbling, running.

He rose. A body ran into the left side of the scope, a fleeting shadow.

It would not be useful to kill him, Jing Yo thought. But before he could lower his rifle, a shot rang out.

The bullet flew well above Josh's head, whizzing through the trees. There was another, and another and another, just as there had been that night when he was a boy.

He'd had many nightmares of that night. His sleeping mind often twisted the details bizarrely, putting him in the present, as a grown man trying to escape, changing the setting—often to the school or even his uncle's house, where he'd gone to live—and occasionally the outcome: once or twice, his father and mother, both sisters, and his brothers survived.

But Josh knew this wasn't a dream. These weren't the two people who'd chased him when he was ten, and he wasn't able to end this ordeal simply by screaming and opening his eyes. He had to escape. He had to *run*!

He bolted forward, tripping over the rocks, bouncing against a boulder that came to his waist and then rebounding against a thick tree trunk. Somehow he stayed on his feet, still moving. There were shouts, calls, behind him.

Panic raged through him like a river over a falls. He threw his hands out, as if he might push the jungle away. A tree loomed on his right. He ducked to his left, hit a slimmer tree, kept going. He pushed through a bush that came to his chest.

More bullets.

A stitch deepened in his side. His chest tightened, and he tasted blood in his mouth. The trees thinned again, and he was running over rocks.

Run, his legs told his chest, told his arms, told his brain.

Run!

S ergeant Fan had fired the shot that had sent their quarry racing away. Jing Yo yelled at him, calling him an idiot, but then immediately regretted it. Upbraiding an inferior before others, even one who deserved it as Fan did, was not his way.

"Don't let him escape," said Jing Yo, springing after the runner. "But do not kill him either. We want to know what he knows."

The forest made it hard to run. Jing Yo realized this was a problem for the man they were pursuing as well as for them, and conserved his energy, moving just fast enough to keep up. Ai Gua and Private Po had moved to the flanks; they had good position on the man if he decided to double back.

He wouldn't. He was panicked, a hare racing from the dragon's claws.

An odd man, to be able to move so quietly, under such control at one moment, only to panic the next. Jing Yo could understand both control and panic, but not together.

His own failing, perhaps. A limit of imagination.

Sergeant Fan fired again. Jing Yo turned to confront the sergeant. This time there was no reason not to speak freely; on the contrary, the circumstances called for it, as the sergeant had not only been careless but disobeyed his direct order.

"What are you doing?" demanded Jing Yo.

"I had a shot. He's going—"

Jing Yo snapped the assault gun from the sergeant's hand. Stunned, and wheezing from his exertion, Fan raised his hands, as if to surrender.

"Sergeant, when I give an order, I expect it to be followed. We want the man alive. I said that very specifically. When we return to camp, you will gather your things and report to division. Understood?"

Without waiting for an answer, he spun back to the pursuit.

Josh didn't hear the water until he was almost upon it. His first thought was that he would race through it—the soft sound made him picture a shallow brook coursing down the side of the mountain. Then he thought he would wade down it, throwing the men off his trail.

With his second step, he plunged in above his knee. Josh twisted to the left, but he'd already lost his balance. He spun and landed on his back. Everything was a blur. This was no gentle, babbling brook. Josh fell under the water, bumped back to the surface, then found himself swirling out of control in the current.

He flailed wildly, rolling with the water, spinning and alternately sinking and rising up, thrown into a confused maelstrom, gripped by the ice-cold water. He felt dead; no, beyond dead, sent to the frozen waste of some Asian afterlife as a doomed soul forced to endure eternal tortures.

Jing Yo pulled his handheld from his pocket and punched the GPS preset. The stream did not exist on the map, the cartographers not able to keep up with changes wrought by the rapid climate shifts. Snow in these mountains was a rare occurrence as late as 2008, when a one-inch snowfall in February made headlines. Now the mountain averaged nearly a foot and a half in winter, most of it in late January, a product of shifting wind, moisture, and thermal patterns. The snowmelt produced the stream, and Jing Yo supposed that the streambed would be rock dry or at best a trickle within a few weeks.

Right now, though, it was as treacherous as any Jing Yo knew from his native province of Xinjiang Uygur, where such seasonal streams had existed since the beginning of time.

"He fell in," said Ai Gua. "He is a dead man."

Between the swift current and the frigid temperature, Ai Gua's prediction was probably correct. On the other hand, it was just possible that he had made it to the other side.

Jing Yo turned to Sergeant Fan. "Sergeant, take Ai Gua with you and head upstream. See if you can find a good place to cross. Then come back west. Private Po will come with me. This time, do not fire except under my direct order. No one is to fire," Jing Yo repeated. "No one."

Jing Yo began walking to the west, paralleling the bank of the stream. The water cut a haphazard channel, at some points swallowing trees, giving them a wide berth at others. It moved downhill, curving into an almost straight line within thirty meters of the spot where they believed their target had gone in.

Jing Yo took the rifle from Private Po, then stepped into the current where he could get a good view downstream. Ignoring the chill that ran up his legs, he moved carefully in the loose stones and mud. Within three steps the water came to his knees. Its pull was strong, trying to push him down; he tilted his entire body against it as he raised the rifle and its sight to see.

The heat of a body should show up clearly if on the surface of the water, but only there. There was considerable brush on both sides of the stream as it continued downward.

Nothing.

Jing Yo nearly lost his footing as he turned to come back out of the water. Only the sense of balance built up by years of practice saved him. He moved silently forward, climbing up the short rise to where Private Po stood.

"Perhaps he is dead already," said Po as he handed back the rifle. "I hope so."

"Do not wish for a man's death, Private."

"But he's an enemy."

There was no difference between wishing a man's death and wishing one's own, but there was no way to explain this to the private in terms that he would understand. Telling the enlisted man about *Ch'an* was out of the question; were the wrong official to find out, even such a simple gesture could be misinterpreted as proselytizing to the troops, a crime typically punished by three years of reeducation.

Unless one was a commando. Then he could expect to be made an example of.

They worked their way down fifty meters to a stand of gnarled trees. The vegetation was so thick they couldn't pass without detouring a good distance to the south, moving in a long semicircle away from their ultimate goal. Finally the terrain and trees cooperated. Jing Yo tuned his ears as they turned back toward the stream, listening to the sounds that fought their way past the sharp hiss of the water. He heard frogs and insects, but nothing large, nothing moving on or near the water, no human sounds.

Perhaps their quarry was a truly clever man, who'd only pretended to panic. Or maybe in his panic he had found the strength to cross the stream. Fear was a most powerful motivator, stronger than hunger or the desire for love and sex.

Western soap. Unlikely for a Vietnamese soldier, who would be paid as poorly as he was fed. So he must be a scientist.

A good prize then.

They returned to the stream at a large, shallow pool. It was longer than it was wide, extending for nearly twenty meters, acting as a reservoir and buffer. This was just the sort of place where a body would wash up. Jing Yo checked the surface carefully, scanning with the private's rifle sight. When he didn't see anything, he headed downstream. The pool grew deeper as he went, until at last the water was at his waist. Once again he used the scope to scan the area; finding nothing, he reluctantly waded back to shore.

He was just handing the rifle back to Private Po when his satellite radio buzzed at his belt.

"Jing Yo," he said, pushing the talk button.

"Lieutenant, where are you?" demanded Colonel Sun.

Yo pressed the dedicated GPS button, which gave his exact coordinates to Sun's radio. As a security measure against possible enemy interference, the location of each unit could not be queried; it had to be sent by the user.

"Have you found your man?" asked Sun.

"We've tracked him to a stream."

Jing Yo started to explain the situation, but the colonel cut him off.

"Get back here. It seems the idiots in the 376th Division have made yet another blunder."

Jing Yo could only guess what that meant.

"Lieutenant?"

"I'm not positive that the man we were following died in the water," Jing Yo told the colonel. "If I could have an hour to find the body—"

"Leave it. I need you here."

"We will come immediately."

4

Washington, D.C.

"No doubt about it," said CIA Director Peter Frost. "A regiment of tanks, right on the border with Vietnam. And there's more. A lot more. Give them three days, maybe a week, and they can have a full army inside the country."

President George Chester Greene folded his arms as the head of the CIA continued. Over the past two weeks, the various U.S. intelligence agencies had been piecing together the repositioning of a significant Chinese force along the Vietnamese border. At first there had been considerable debate; the evidence was thin. But it was thin for a reason—the Chinese had taken every conceivable step to conceal the movement.

"The question is what they do with the force," said National Security Adviser Walter Jackson, the only other man in the Oval Office. "Threaten Vietnam, or invade. This may just be muscle flexing."

"You don't flex your muscles in secret," said Greene drily.

Carried out in the area traditionally assigned to the Thirteenth Army Group, the buildup involved elements of at least two other armies. It had been very carefully timed to avoid overhead satellites, and the units remained far enough from the border to avoid detection by the few Vietnamese units nearby. The

Chinese had been so careful that the analysts had no definitive word on the strength of the buildup, and no images of tanks moving, let alone posted on the border. Their estimates depended on inferences gathered mostly from a few photos of support vehicles and units, signal intelligence, and the disappearance of units from their normal assignments.

Nearly ten years before, the PLA had built vast underground shelters in southeastern China about two hours' drive from the border. They had been abandoned, seemingly forgotten, until just a few weeks ago. Command elements of the Thirteenth Army had deployed from their headquarters to one of the underground shelters. They wouldn't have moved alone, and Frost believed there could be as much as a regiment of armor in the shelters, invisible to satellites.

"A regiment of armor," said Frost. "That could be two hundred and forty, two-seventy tanks. With scouts, and some mobile infantry. And then look there—within a day's drive, maybe two or three if they're conserving fuel and get confused on the directions—a mechanized division. And then up here, three to four days—two more infantry divisions, with their armor, and two other regiments of tanks. That's the entire force of the Thirteenth Army, all four divisions. And, we're tracking command elements of several other divisions not ordinarily attached to the Thirteenth Army positioning themselves just a little farther away. This is going to be immense."

Greene stared at the globe at the far side of his office, barely paying attention. He could see Hanoi's five-pointed circle in the northern corner of the country.

He'd been released from a POW camp there more than forty years ago. He'd felt like an old man then, though he was only in his twenties. Now he really *was* an old man, and he still felt far younger than he had on that day.

Every day away from that hell was a day blessed.

"George?" said Jackson.

The president snapped to attention, as if woken from a dream. "I have it."

"Clearly, they're intending an invasion," said Frost. "There's no other explanation."

"State thinks it's posturing," said Jackson, criticism obvious in his voice.

"The question is what we should do about it," continued Frost.

"We can't do anything about it," said Jackson. "It's just Vietnam. That's the trouble. The American people don't care about Vietnam. And the few who do care would like to see it crushed. Payback for what happened to their fathers and grandfathers."

Greene pushed his chair back and rose from his desk. If anyone in America had reason to hate the Vietnamese, it was he. And yet he didn't. Not the people, anyway.

"It's not Vietnam I'm worried about," he said, walking to the globe in the corner of the room.

And if anyone in America had reason to sympathize with the Chinese, it was Greene. He spoke fluent Mandarin; he'd served there for several years as ambassador and had lived in Hong Kong before that. He still had good friends in Beijing.

China was being affected by the worldwide depression and the violent climate changes more severely than many countries across the globe. After recovering from the recession of 2008–2009, the industrialized West had slipped back into deep recession over the past eighteen months. Consumers and businesses had stopped purchasing Chinese goods. The overheated Chinese economy had literally collapsed. Worse, droughts in the north and a succession of typhoons and overly long monsoon seasons in the west had caused spectacular crop failures.

The combination was several times worse than what had occurred in 2009 and 2010, and even made the Great Depression look mild. The Chinese people didn't know what had hit them.

The country's disruption had helped bring a new premier, Cho Lai, to power. Clearly, the buildup was part of Cho Lai's plan to solve China's problems.

Ironically, the severe weather changes had, on balance, helped the U.S. Its northern states suddenly found themselves in great demand as agricultural centers. So much so that suburban backyards in places like Westchester, New York, and Worcester, Massachusetts, were being plowed under and turned into microfarms.

At the same time, the demise of Chinese imports had led entrepreneurs to reopen factories shuttered for decades. Not surprisingly, items related to the environmental crisis were in great demand. A garden hoe fetched nearly seventy-five dollars at Wal-Mart, and the managers claimed never to be able to keep them in stock.

Of course, there had been considerable disruption in the U.S., and much more was expected, but the country's size and diversity had so far enabled it to avoid catastrophe. For the first time in two generations, the balance of payments with foreign countries, including China, had turned in America's favor.

A good thing, considering the country's massive debt.

"Telling the Vietnamese what's going to happen will reveal to the Chinese that they haven't succeeded in fooling our sensors," said Jackson. "Long term, that will hurt us. If they improve what they're doing, then we'll never see them poised to hit Taiwan. Let alone Japan. Vietnam is just not that important. I'm sorry, but that's a fact."

Frost said nothing, silently agreeing. Vietnam just wasn't important in the scheme of things.

And yet, if China wasn't stopped there, where would it be stopped?

"When will they be ready to attack?" Greene asked.

"Just a guess." Frost shook his head. "Several days at a minimum. A week. Two weeks. Honestly, very hard to say—what else are they doing that we can't see?"

"This will just be the start," said Greene.

"Probably," admitted Jackson. "But we have to preserve our options for the next attack."

Greene frowned, not at his advisers, but at himself.

He wasn't sure what to do. In truth, he seemed to have no choice but to let the Chinese attack. The U.S. was powerless to stop an invasion. And yet it was wrong, very, very wrong, to do absolutely nothing.

"Good work, Peter," said Greene. "Let's get the Joint Chiefs up to date."

5

Northwestern Vietnam, near the border with China

A hundred men beat their drums in the distance, pounding in a staccato rhythm that didn't quite manage a coherent beat. It was maddening, torturous—there was almost a pattern, but not quite. The drumming built, settling toward a rhythm, only to disintegrate into chaos.

Josh rolled over. He tried pulling the blankets closer, but they were wrapped so tightly that he couldn't move. Sweat poured from his body, so thick that he began to choke.

I'm drowning.

Drowning.

He twisted over again, grabbing for his pillow. He remembered the dream, the nightmare memory of the homicide that had changed his life irreparably.

He was choking to death, drowning.

With a sudden burst of energy, Josh jerked upright, pulling himself back to full consciousness. He rose, stepping out of the bushes where he'd dragged himself, exhausted, a few hours before.

His mind emptied of all thought, all emotion and sensation. Josh didn't, couldn't, think. He couldn't even feel the presence of his toes or legs or arms. He simply floated in a void, a vacuum within a vacuum.

And then he felt his legs stinging.

His toes were wet and cold. His ankles felt heavy with fluid. He'd wrenched his right knee, and it throbbed. His right thigh felt like it had been punched by one of the trees he'd run into. His sides burned, as if physically on fire. His right lower rib ached, the pain growing, then easing, with each breath. The muscles at the side of his lower chest—the external oblique anterolateral abdominal muscles, a name he knew because he'd torn them in high school playing lacrosse—sent sharp bolts of pain shrieking across the ribs. His right arm felt numb, his shoulder senseless, his fingers cramped stiff. His neck was wrenched to one side. His jaw had locked closed, his back molars grinding against each other.

Oh, God, I'm alive?

What the hell do I do now?

It was light, either just before or just after dawn. The clouds and thick jungle to the east obscured the sun, making it hard to tell.

Josh pushed himself backward, trying to raise himself into a seated position. His hands slipped into mud and he fell backward, dropping into the water behind him. Caught entirely by surprise—he hadn't thought he was anywhere this close to the creek—he fell below the surface. He rolled and pushed himself up, gulping the air.

Up. Get up. Move. See what's really hurt.

He rose, then stepped to a small apron of smooth stones at the edge of the stream. The water was calm here, the current very gentle. He looked behind him and saw that the stream had flooded a wide area, a nook between two low hills on the ridge. The area didn't look familiar, which *might* mean it was north of their camp. Or it could mean simply that his brain was too scrambled to remember passing it.

Rubbing his thighs with his hands, Josh looked around, belatedly searching the area for his pursuers. Who were they?

Thieves was the only possible answer, and yet it seemed impossible that anyone would want to rob a scientific expedition. Foolhardy, too—the Vietnamese government had endorsed the project, and even sent two soldiers along with the guides.

Thieves were a rarity in Vietnam, and this wasn't supposed to be a dangerous area: Dr. Renaldo had said the soldiers were along not as protection, but so the Vietnamese could justify the fee they took from the UN's grant for administration. "The price of doing business," said the scientist philosophically before they left Hanoi.

So if it was so safe, who had come and killed most of his expedition?

The Vietnamese themselves? It made no sense.

But then, who would kill an Iowa farm family in a murder apparently patterned after the *In Cold Blood* killings decades before?

Looking for logic from human beings was illogical and often futile. Josh knew that by heart.

There was a knot in his stomach. He was hungry. He tried to remember what Kerry, the flora specialist, had told him about some of the plants. He'd been far more interested in the curve of her hips and the way her small breasts poked at the light muslin shirt than in the nutritional value of the local grasses and brush.

The nearby bushes were thick with green and pink berries. Josh reached for a bunch of the pink ones, then stopped. They might be poison, or simply unripe.

He could wait, he decided. He wasn't that hungry.

Josh began walking along the bank of the flooded stream, following the ripples in the water as it moved downstream.

Was it the right direction? He reasoned that as long as he moved downhill, he would be heading toward people, but whether that was really a good thing or not he couldn't say. The Vietnamese tended to be generous toward strangers, but what if the stream brought him to the people who had killed his friends?

Moving was better than sitting.

He was bruised terribly, and his knee hurt, but none of his bones seemed to be broken.

After an hour or so, the sun battered its way through the clouds and the air turned sweet. After another hour, his aches and bruises melted. Except for the insects and the shape of the trees and bushes, he could have been back at school, taking a summer's hike in the woods.

Josh figured he'd been walking for nearly three hours when he spotted a small bridge made of bamboo and tree trunks spanning the creek. The bamboo on the bridge was bright yellow, relatively new—maybe in place for only a week or two. One of the posts was new as well, a rough-hewn tree trunk stuck into the ground at a slight angle, brown rather than gray like the others.

The bridge connected to a narrow path on both sides of the stream. The jungle was thick on the left, but light filtered through the trees on the right; there was a field beyond.

Josh climbed up the incline to the path, trying to muster his small store of Vietnamese words:

Xin chào!

Hello.

Vâng.

Yes.

Tôi không hiểu.

I don't understand.

He knew other words. What were they?

Grandfather—*Ông.* It was an honorific, a title that the Vietnamese used all the time. It was like saying "sir."

Other words.

Josh tried to stoke his memory, dredging up full phrases and sentences. Vietnamese had tones that went with the sounds, dramatically altering their meaning— a word could mean a ghost, or a rice plant, or a horse, depending on how it was pronounced.

Ngon. Very tasty. The food is very tasty. Can you call for help.

Can you call for help?

Công an. Công an.

Police.

Depending on whom he met, Vietnamese might be of little use. Most of the residents of the valley were Hmong natives, who didn't speak much Vietnamese themselves. They were poor mountain people, still very close to their roots as nomadic, slash-and-burn farmers.

The trail looped back around the side of a hill, then continued through a patch of jungle. Josh walked steadily, sticking to the side of the trail so he could jump into the grass and hide if he heard anyone. As he turned a corner, he saw a cluster of thatch-roofed huts on the opposite slope. They were about a mile away, across a steep, rock-strewn ravine.

Josh ran his hand over the slight stubble of his morning beard. Would the people help him?

Yes, he decided. They must. They would. He began trotting down the path, trusting that it would curve back toward the hamlet.

6

Bangkok, Thailand

Mara Duncan was engulfed in a human tidal wave as she stepped out the side door of her apartment building, swept along on the sidewalk with literally hundreds of other Bangkok residents making their way to their morning posts. The entire city seemed to be flooding to work or school, and a good portion of the population seemed to be using the small side street where she lived.

It was always like this, not only here, but all through Bangkok and the close-in suburbs, where the population had gone from an unofficial fifteen million to nearly thirty million in less than a decade. Bangkok—known to most Thai-speaking locals as Krung Thep—was the unofficial poster city for the Third World's population explosion. The streets were perpetually crowded and a thick shroud of pollution hung over the city. But it was a place of great wealth and commerce as well, a twenty-first-century boomtown that justifiably evoked comparisons to America's Chicago or even New York in the early twentieth.

No fewer than five new skyscrapers were being built in the city; each was over one hundred stories tall. One of the buildings, Thai Wah V, was planned to top 455 meters—a height that would make it, not coincidentally, about a yardstick taller than Malaysia's

Petronas Towers I and II. The tower's foundation was considered a modern engineering marvel, due to the wet ground that characterized so much of the city.

Mara glanced around as she joined the line to the escalators up to the skytrain. Bangkok was home to hundreds of spies from nearly every nation on earth, and it was not unusual for them to try to keep tabs on interesting Americans, whether they were known CIA officers or not. Two weeks before, Mara had been followed for several days, apparently by a Russian freelancer who bought her cover as a local sales rep for an American medical-equipment manufacturer and was trying to hunt up information for a Swiss firm. Either he'd lost interest or figured out who she really was; in any event, he'd disappeared without making an approach.

She missed him, in a way. He'd added a little spice to her mornings. Things had been dull since she'd come back from Malaysia.

The escalator moved swiftly. People stood only six or seven deep on the skytrain platform, a sign that there would be at least a five-minute wait for the next train. Mara wedged her way through the crowd, once again looking to make sure that she wasn't being followed or observed.

The CIA's Thailand bureau, traditionally one of the agency's biggest in Asia, had grown exponentially over the past four years, and with space at the embassy at a premium, many of the officers worked in one of the "outbuildings"—secure suites rented by the CIA nearby. Mara's office was in a building two blocks from the embassy; the agency leased five whole floors, but the offices were located in only two. While security was tight—the elevators had been rigged so that they couldn't stop at the floor at all, and the stairwells were guarded by armed men—the "annex" had a much looser atmosphere than the embassy. The jokes were bawdier, and the coffee was better.

Or so the annex's unofficial mayor claimed. He was in rare form when Mara arrived.

"You look just mah-valous," Jesse DeBiase bellowed as she stepped out of the stairs. "Come taste some of the best joe this side of Seattle."

"I don't think I can drink another cup today," said Mara.

"But dah-link, you must. Think of your fans."

"All right, Million Dollar Man. If it'll make you happy."

DeBiase bowed. Just about everyone in the station called him Million Dollar Man, though most had no idea where he'd gotten the nickname. A few thought it was a reference to an op he'd run years before. In reality, he'd been awarded it decades before because his last name sounded the same as Ted DiBiase's, a pro wrestler popular at the time. Why the CIA had ever hired a wrestling fan remained one of the agency's most perplexing mysteries.

DeBiase was one of the deputy station chiefs, in title the annex supervisor, though he claimed his authority barely entitled him to order stationery. Mara had no idea what the Million Dollar Man did beyond telling stories to his officemates; he had never given her an assignment nor mentioned any of his. The latter might not have been particularly surprising, except that the Million Dollar Man talked so much about everything that it was hard to imagine that he would be able to resist at least hinting, indirectly, about things he had done in the distant if not recent past. But DeBiase never talked shop that way, and never seemed to have any appointments that had even the vaguest possible connection to espionage, real or potential. He was either very old-school about keeping secrets, or an officer who'd spent his career being promoted sideways and had never had anything real to do.

Probably the former, but you never could tell.

Today's topic was his upcoming hernia operation, as yet unscheduled, but planned for the first week or maybe second after he returned to the States.

"Why not here?" asked Mara. Thailand had world-class medical care, and in fact many Americans flew there for so-called surgery vacations.

"No," he said. "No. Some things—I was made in America. I'll be fixed in America. So to speak."

"So when are you going?" asked Mara.

"Soon," said DeBiase. It was the same answer he'd given when they were introduced weeks before.

"What the hell's keeping you here?" asked Tai Lai as he stirred creamer into his coffee. Alone among the annex denizens, Lai preferred powdered dairy substitute to the real milk and cream the Million Dollar Man managed to have delivered fresh twice a week.

It couldn't be for his health; Lai, who was on his second tour in Bangkok, stood about six feet and weighed all of 140. A good wind would push him over—though not break him, as he was a karate expert and in excellent shape.

Or so the certificates and trophies he kept in his office claimed.

"Duty, young Mr. Lai," said the Million Dollar Man expansively. "The same thing that keeps us all here. Except Ms. Duncan. She is here because she sinned rather badly in her past life, and must now atone for it."

"So Bangkok is the Buddhist hell?" Mara poured her coffee.

"Worse."

"I go through this and in my next life I come back as a butterfly?"

"The Buddhist concept of hell is separate from reincarnation," said DeBiase. "There is not necessarily any escape."

"Describes Bangkok perfectly," said Lai.

"Actually, there are many different strains of Buddhism," said DeBiase, "and talking about specific beliefs can be highly contradictory."

He was now in professor mode; there would be no interrupting his discourse until he had completely dissected the various strands of Buddhist belief, a process which could take hours. Mara took her coffee and slipped down the hall to the small office she shared with another officer exiled from the field, Roth Setco.

Roth was a dark and moody man; it was not unusual for him to sit at his desk staring at the blank wall in front of him for hours on end. Not yet thirty, he had thick scars on his right leg and both arms, and two small ones on his right cheek. His nose looked as if it had been broken several times, and the lobe of his right ear was either deformed or had been torn off and then poorly repaired. His long hair covered his ear, and possibly other scars on his neck. He wasn't in this morning—neither a surprise nor unwelcome.

Mara flipped on her computer. As she was waiting for it to boot, her secure satellite phone vibrated, indicating that she was receiving an instant message from the bureau's secure paging system. It was from Peter Lucas, the station chief, and consisted of one word: *Come.* He wanted to see her over at his office in the embassy.

She killed her computer and reversed course, gliding past the Million Dollar Man, still holding court.

Peter Lucas checked his watch as he passed into the secure communications suite. He was due to have lunch with the ambassador at the British embassy at noon; his counterpart from MI6 would be there, and while no agenda had been mentioned, the Brits would surely want to discuss the situation in southern Thailand, where the rebel movement was a growing concern to both countries.

The recent discovery of oil along Thailand's southern coast would complicate things further. The world might be rapidly shifting away from oil as a fuel source, but the commodity's value still seemed to double every other week.

They'd also be talking about Myanmar and Vietnam, as well as Malaysia. Lucas's portfolio had been expanded beyond Thailand and Malaysia three days before; he was now in charge of operations in Vietnam, Myanmar, Laos, and Cambodia as well. Officially, the move was temporary, due to a pending reorganization of the CIA's Southeast Asia section; unofficially, Lucas was going to head whatever permanent arrangement resulted.

The shuffle was widely known inside the agency, and it was no secret to MI6, either. But the *real* reason for the reorganization was that the CIA's Vietnam bureau had been compromised.

The counterintelligence people were trying to sort out exactly what was going on. The office's main focus over the past two years had been drug smuggling, and it was clear that at least one officer there had been taking money from an Asian gang. But the NSA eavesdropping programs indicated that some elements of the top secret daily intelligence summaries prepared by the office were being read in Hanoi as well. The counterintelligence people were trying to trace the leak and see who exactly was involved. In the meantime, the office was essentially unusable.

Which was why he had called Mara over this morning.

She was waiting in the antechamber of the suite. Sitting in one of the leather club chairs—Lucas had personally ordered them installed upon his arrival the year before—she fidgeted nervously, clearly anxious and probably excited at the prospect of a new assignment. He remembered that feeling well—he'd felt it himself dozens and dozens of times, maybe hundreds, when he was a young stud.

Not that he didn't feel enthusiasm now, at age fifty, but it was tempered, respectful of the pitfalls and problems that inevitably accompanied a job for the CIA. Too respectful, maybe.

"You're looking good," said Lucas, sliding down into the seat across from her. The secure suite was isolated from the rest of the building by a number of systems that made it impossible to bug. "How are you feeling?"

"You know your message could be considered suggestive," said Mara.

"Suggestive?"

"*Come?*"

"Excuse me?"

"That's what you wrote, Pete."

"I was just being terse."

She cocked her head slightly, still smiling, her body openly flirting. It was all subconscious. Tall and large-boned, Mara had an almost playful nature, a natural outgoingness that Lucas always associated with jocks. Her personality would have made her an excellent recruiter, though it wasn't hard to guess why she had been moved out of that area—she was far from ugly, but she wasn't a knockout either, and her height would be considered a negative by old hands, especially in Asia. Spies wanted to be seduced, or so the theory went; few men were attracted to a woman who could just as easily whip them as seduce them.

As it was, she'd proven herself an excellent PM, or paramilitary officer, though at times a bit aggressive, as her last supervisor in Malaysia had written.

Lucas preferred the word "rambunctious" to aggressive. She was still young; she'd grow out of it. Not too much, he hoped.

"Refresh my memory," he told her, backing into her assignment. "How good is your Vietnamese?"

"It's fantastic."

"I'll bet."

"*Xin chào. Toi hiêu.*"

Hello. I understand.

The tones—there were six in Vietnamese—were off a bit, but the words were intelligible.

"I won't embarrass you," said Lucas. "You won't need very good language skills on this."

"What do we need?"

"It's not really a very important job, or very complicated. You fly into Hanoi and meet a Belgian national in our employ."

"Okay." She nodded.

"Talk to him, then come back."

"Great."

"His name is Bernard Fleming. He speaks English."

"When do I leave?"

Lucas couldn't help but smile. Most of his people would have asked a few questions before taking the job, masking their enthusiasm even if it was already a foregone conclusion that they were going.

"There's a flight this afternoon. You're already booked," Lucas told her. "I suppose you'd like to hear what this is all about."

Fleming was a UN observer on a scientific survey team. They'd been sent to northern Vietnam to gather data on biological changes connected with the recent dramatic shifts in the weather. She would go to Vietnam as a journalist working for Voice of America; she was doing a story on climate change, and was talking to Fleming because he was the only one authorized by the UN to talk about the mission.

Not really, of course.

The area where the survey team was headed was near the suspected crash site of an Air Force F-105 during the Vietnam War; the pilot of the aircraft was still officially listed as MIA. Mara was to ask Fleming if he'd seen any sign of the plane.

That wasn't really what she was doing, either. She would bring that up, but the matter was really a second-string cover story, to be used to placate the Vietnamese if they got very nosy. His real assignment was considerably more delicate.

The agency wanted to plant listening devices in the area to spy on the Chinese—without Vietnamese cooperation—and Fleming had been asked to survey possible sites. Mara was supposed to see how things were going.

Though planned months before, the mission had taken on extreme significance because of recent Chinese troop movements nearby. The intelligence about those movements was so sensitive that Lucas couldn't even tell Mara about them. If he did, and she somehow was captured, by the Chinese or the Vietnamese, America's intelligence-gathering capacities would be severely compromised.

That wasn't going to happen, Lucas thought to himself. Basically, the assignment was a long, late dinner, with maybe some cocktails later on. Fleming would be in Hanoi for only a day, dropping off some snail mail and picking up supplies before heading back by truck to the survey area.

"The border area between the two countries is sensitive, as always," added Lucas. "So ask him about it. The more information you can get, the better. Check in when you get there. Yada yada yada; you know the drill."

"Don't talk to locals?"

She was referring to the CIA bureau in Vietnam. Lucas hesitated. He trusted Mara, and knew she was connected to the problems there, but wanted to tell her only what was absolutely necessary.

"You should not talk to the locals, no," he told her.

"Not at all?"

He shook his head.

"Okay. If I have problems I check in here?"

"Absolutely. You think you can handle all this?"

"In my sleep."

"Let's try it awake, just for practice."

7

Northwestern Vietnam, near the border with China

The path Josh had taken swung back into the jungle for roughly a mile before starting to descend along the valley. It wove a zigzag path downward, the cutbacks easing, though not completely eliminating, the angle of the slope. The bottom of the valley was not a river as Josh had first supposed, but rather a road; though not paved, it was much wider than the path, with tire tracks that looked relatively fresh. Yellow dirt and silver-white rocks lined the bed; the shoulders were rutted grass and occasional ditches.

He couldn't see the village from where he was, and had lost his sense of which way it would be.

A monkey screeched in the distance. Another joined in, then another. The sound rattled Josh, seemingly vibrating in his teeth. He decided to go left.

What was the word for hello?

Xin chào!

Can you speak English?

They would know right away that he was an American, smell it before they even saw him—Americans and Europeans smelled like the soap they washed their bodies with. His clothes, his haircut, his face, his manner—everything about him would make it obvious.

They would know he was an American and they would help him get back to Hanoi.

Good God, had it all been a dream? How could it be possible that robbers had come in and murdered the whole camp? What strange twist of fate was this, to have to endure two massacres in a lifetime?

What luck was it to have escaped both times?

Josh heard chickens clucking ahead. His heart pounded even harder.

"I need help," he mumbled to himself, rehearsing. "My friends have been killed."

He started to run.

"I need help," he said louder. "I need help."

He turned the corner. The chickens, a dozen of them, were scattered in and along the road. When they saw him they moved toward him excitedly.

The buildings sat above an elbow in the road at his right. Josh began running toward them, looking for people.

"Help!" he shouted. "I need help!"

Two cottages sat very close to the road. Both were one-story, windowless structures made of wood. Their steeply pitched roofs paired wood and sheets of rusted tin in a patchwork that seemed more artistic than functional. A slanted fence used for drying clothes stood to the right of the closest one; two large sheets and a man's pants hung on it, flapping in the wind.

"Hey!" yelled Josh. "Help! I need help!"

He ran up the path, along the front of the house to the open door.

"Please," he yelled. "Please."

He slowed as he neared the door, then stopped.

"Help!" he shouted. "Hey! Hey!"

Inside, the house was dark. There was a table and chairs on his left, a primitive stove beyond them. Bedding was laid out on the right.

A loud moo startled him—the only inhabitant was the family's cow, its long oval eyes blinking at him from the corner.

Josh had been raised on farms, but the cow being in the house unsettled him. The animal mooed again, and Josh took a step backward, unsure of himself.

Perhaps everything was a dream, a nightmare that extended all the way back to his childhood.

Moooo.

The sound was more grunt than moo. The animal followed him out. It wasn't a cow but an ox.

It wouldn't be unusual for a family to keep their animals in the house with them if they were very poor.

There was a noise behind him. Josh swung around, expecting to see a person. But it was a monkey.

The animal made a face at him, then ducked past into the house. It ran into the shadows at the side, scampering around among some furniture, then emerged with what looked like a potato, its white flesh revealed by the animal's chiseled bite mark. The monkey shot by and scampered into the jungle, chattering as it ran.

"Hey!" yelled Josh. "Is anybody around? Hey? Hey!"

No one answered. The ox looked at him quizzically.

"Hello? Hey! Hello! Where is everyone!" shouted

Josh, twisting around. "Can you help me? I need to get in touch with the authorities. I've been robbed."

There was no one in the house next to the first, either. Walking up to a second cluster of buildings, he found a small shack set just off the clearing, at the side of what appeared to be a garden. It reeked of dung. He stuck his head inside, saw nothing except for a pile in the corner, then retreated, gasping for fresh air.

Josh wondered whether it might be market day. The people didn't seem to have left in a hurry; there were no plates on the tables, no food in the pots, no possessions seemingly left for the moment. He walked in a circuit around the settlement, calling, expecting someone to answer at any second. As each minute passed, he became more optimistic, more set in the opinion that the villagers had gone off to either their chores or some nearby event. Finding them was only a matter of time.

The hamlet was wedged into the hillside, and his circuits took him up and down the incline flanking the road. Cleared but unplanted fields lay above and below the houses.

He was hungry. If the people didn't mind a monkey stealing their food, they surely wouldn't begrudge him. He'd pay them back, as soon as he was rescued.

Josh walked to a hut next to the lower field. It was built directly into the slope at the back, but otherwise was just like all the others, its large roof extending below the walls. He ducked his head to get through the door, then stood just inside the threshold for a few seconds as his eyes adjusted.

The area to the left was used by the family to sleep; the bedding was disheveled, piled haphazardly. Some of the blankets were rolled against the wall. There were clothes nearby. Josh walked over, staring at the dark shapes.

A set of sandals sat neatly at his left, next to a folded pair of pants and a cone-shaped hat. Josh bent to examine the hat. As he did, he glanced at the corner of the room. The shape of the blankets caught his eye, and for a moment he thought they were a body. He turned away quickly, but then curiosity forced him back.

It's not a body. It's just the weird way the blankets are.

There was definitely a blanket; the shape had a fold and curled furls. But it did look like a body.

He took a step toward it, his mind insisting his eyes were wrong.

It's not a body.

And then his mind admitted what it saw: a dark black stain in the middle of the tan covering. It was definitely a body, wrapped in the blanket where it had been shot, thrown against the side of the house by the force of the bullets striking it.

Josh bolted from the house, his stomach turning.

8

Carlisle, Pennsylvania

Zeus Murphy gunned his Corvette away from the
sentry post, spitting gravel as he exercised the classic
Chevy's engine.

"They don't make 'em like this anymore," said his
passenger, Steve Rosen.

Murphy laughed. He'd heard people say that at
least a hundred times since his assignment at the War
College began, and he'd been here only a few weeks.

It was literally true: they didn't make Corvettes anymore, or any other car that got less than fifty miles to
a gallon of gas. Even if the law hadn't forbidden it, gas
cost $14.39 a gallon; between that and the annual pol-
lution surtax, few people wanted to pony up for a new
sports car, especially when used ones could be pur-
chased at bargain prices. Everyone said that in four
or five years hydrogen-cell vehicles would match the
"classics" in acceleration, top speed, and handling, but
they'd been saying that for years.

Murphy wasn't sure how much longer he could
keep the Vette, a gift from his dad. Even after the raise
that went with his promotion to major, paying for the
gas was tough. It was quickly eating up the store of
money he'd earned from combat pay as a Special Forces
trainer in Ukraine.

Oh well—easy come, easy go.

Or not so easy come. There'd been a few times when he didn't actually expect he'd make it home.

Zeus leaned on the wheel and turned hard onto the interior road, then swung into the parking lot in front of Building B-3, the prosaic name of the War College's newest structure. Built with so-called green construction techniques, its entrance sloped upward from the earth, jutting out from under a moss-covered roof. The building's geothermal system handled all of its heating and cooling; electricity was supplied by a farm of solar electric panels that flanked the northern side of the building.

The panels could not supply all of the building's electric needs; there wasn't enough space for panels or battery capacity to compensate for Pennsylvania's cloudy weather. Even the high-efficiency windmills at the far end of the property couldn't quite generate enough electricity to satisfy the hungry computer servers in B-3's basement. Nonetheless, the building showed how serious the Army was about energy initiatives. It had been the subject of stories by nearly every media organization when it had opened a year before. Some of the techniques used in its construction would set the standards for years to come.

"Another day, another ass-kicking," said Rosen, unsnapping the seat belt as Murphy turned off the engine. "How long will the U.S. last today?"

"Give them six months," said Murphy, unfolding his six-eight frame from the low-slung car.

"Perry was *pissed* Friday when you bombed San Francisco at the start of the simulation."

"Hey, it's allowable under the rules."

Rosen laughed. Known as Red Dragon, the simulation they were running pitted the U.S.—Blue—against China—Red. Neither country's name was ever mentioned in the game, of course, but everyone who played knew who was who.

"They may change the rules if you keep this up," said Rosen. "They'll take away your advantage."

"The rules are already lopsided in Blue's favor," said Zeus. "The simulation underestimates Chinese abilities."

"Most of their army is way undertrained."

"That's reflected in the game. It's overstated, really. China is like the U.S. in the late thirties. Capacity to kill."

Zeus waved his pass in front of the card reader, which took the biometric data on its chip and compared it to the image before it, as well as the one stored in its own database. It took a few nanoseconds to make sure everything matched, then opened the door and let Zeus inside. Rosen had to wait to do the same—the system would not let more than one person pass at a time. Once inside, the two men passed through an eight-foot-wide by twenty-foot-long chamber; as they did, chemical and radiation sensors "sniffed" them to make sure they weren't carrying anything dangerous.

Then came the live checks. The sentry in the vestibule inserted the ID cards into his own reader, then had them open their bags and empty their pockets for inspection.

"Sergeant Jacobs, you do this every day," said Rosen. "Don't you know us by now?"

"Sir, I do this every day because I know you."

"If you didn't, you'd strip-search us?"

"If necessary, sir."

"You want to see us in our undies, don't you, Sergeant?"

"Not so soon after breakfast."

Finally waved through, the two officers walked down the hall past a wall of glass that looked out on a man-made pond and waterfall (part of the heating and cooling system), then took the stairs to the lower level. They were a few feet from their assigned office when Colonel Doner, who ran the simulation section, called out to them.

"Majors, good of you to show up this morning."

"Colonel, we're ten minutes early by my watch," said Rosen.

"Ten minutes early is twenty minutes *late* by my watch, Rosen." Doner scowled at him. "Come and talk with me, Zeus."

The colonel spun on his heel and walked down the hall to his office. Murphy gave Rosen a shrug and followed.

"Maggie, get the major some coffee, please," said Doner briskly as he passed through the outer office into his lair.

Murphy smiled at Maggie. She had a round, exotic face and perfect hips, but unfortunately had only recently married, and was therefore officially out of bounds according to Murphy's sense of duty and honor.

Not to mention the fact that her husband was a

Special Forces lieutenant colonel who not only out-ranked him but knew even more ways than he did to kill with his bare hands.

"Just a little milk, Major?" she asked, getting up from her desk. The coffee was located down the hall in a small lounge.

"Just a little," said Zeus. He watched her walk out the door, then went into Doner's office.

"See something you like?" said Doner. He frowned, though not as severely as he had at Rosen.

"I know the boundaries, sir."

"I'm sure you do. Hang on just a second."

Doner had four different workstations lined up on the table behind his desk. Two showed simulations in progress. He made sure each was working properly, then pulled out his seat and sat down. Besides his personal laptop, a simple Dell open at the corner of his desk, he had no less than twelve working CPUs in the office, most of them in a double bank against the far wall. There were also a number of laptops stacked on a trolley in the corner.

Doner was not the typical hands-off military supervisor Zeus had expected from his tours before Special Forces. The colonel was an unabashed geek who had hand-assembled several of the larger computers in the office, and written parts of the software that ran the war games simulations he oversaw.

Doner liked to claim that when he had joined the Army, the only thing he knew about computers was how to turn them on; while it was a slight exaggeration, the forty-year-old colonel had truly learned on the job.

"All right," said Doner, returning to his desk. "How was your weekend?"

"Real fine, Mike. Yours?"

"The ten-year-old needs braces. I didn't know they put them in braces that early."

"Neither did I."

"I don't think I even knew there was such a thing as braces until I was sixteen or seventeen," said Doner.

And by then it was too late, thought Zeus—though he didn't say it. That was the difference between him and Rosen. His friend didn't know when to shut the hell up. Not very important for a captain, but critical for a major, and all ranks above.

"You probably didn't need braces, did you?" added Doner.

"No, actually I didn't."

"Charmed life." Doner smiled—it was a crooked smile, with a bit too much enamel missing on the front teeth—then leaned back in his chair. "Zeus, I need a favor from you."

"A favor?"

"We have some visitors coming today. They're interested in seeing Red Dragon."

Murphy felt his face flush. The colonel was going to ask him to throw the simulation and let Perry win.

Could he agree to that?

It wasn't simply a matter of ego. Though they operated like very sophisticated computer games, the simulations were very serious business. The results were recorded and analyzed, then integrated into various war plans and strategy papers prepared by the Army staff. The results from *one* simulation might not make that big a difference in the overall scheme of things . . . and then again, they might. Especially if he threw the simulation to let the U.S. win.

But was this a request he could turn down?

Before he could ask, Maggie returned with the coffee. Glad for the interruption, Zeus took the cup, then fussed over how hot the liquid was, waving his hand over it.

"As I was saying, we have a few VIPs coming today, and we'd like them to see the simulation in action."

"Ordinarily General Cody deals with VIPs."

"Yes, but the general won't be here today. He has business elsewhere."

So I have to take one for the team, thought Zeus. He sipped his coffee, waiting for Doner to drop the other shoe. But Doner didn't say anything.

"Well, okay," said Zeus finally, standing up. "Guess I better go get myself ready then."

"There is a little more to it."

Here it comes, thought Zeus, sitting back down.

"We're going to use Scenario One—Lightning War."

"Okay," said Zeus. The scenario called for war in the very first round, a condition that generally favored Red.

"Thing is, I'd like you to take Blue."

"You want me to be Blue?" said Murphy. He tried to keep his voice level, but his relief still came through.

"General Perry is pretty much convinced that there's no way for Red to lose. I don't blame him, given the results over the past year."

"A year? I thought we were the first to use it."

"Officially, yes. But I had it in beta before you got here. I've run this scenario for a while, Zeus. In different guises. If Red plays smart, it takes over Asia. The other scenarios are much more balanced, but this one always stacks the deck."

"And here I thought I was a brilliant strategist."

"You're not bad." Doner gave him another of his crooked smiles. "You're good, in fact. But the deck is stacked. Not on purpose," the colonel added hastily. "Red Dragon is as close to real life as we can get. Except for that bit you pulled about San Francisco."

"I think the Chinese would definitely try that," said Zeus.

"Maybe. But they'd never get into the harbor that easily."

Murphy had used civilian airplanes and cargo ships—allowed under the game rules—to sneak an advance force into the city, paving the way for a larger conventional attack. Neither side was theoretically at war yet, which made the surprise tactic even easier to pull off. It was *exactly* the way things might start, Murphy knew—the twenty-first-century equivalent of Pearl Harbor.

"So I'm today's sacrificial lamb, huh?" Murphy got up. "I'll go down quickly."

"No, no, play hard. Play as hard as you can. Play to win. Definitely play to win."

"But the deck is stacked, right?"

Doner shrugged. "Play as hard as you can."

Even with the most conventional strategies, Blue's position in Asia was hopeless if war was declared in the first round. There was simply no time to get troops there, and no reliable ally to stop Red early enough to keep it from achieving its objective. No matter what Red's immediate tactical goals were—Taiwan, Japan, Indochina, even Australia—Blue could never rally its forces quickly enough. In fact, any response in force ran the risk of leaving it so weak that Red was positioned to launch a successful invasion of the U.S. mainland.

"Complete naval blockade, Day One," said Rosen, whom Murphy had tagged as his chief of staff, by rule his main collaborator in the day's session. "You build up the walls on the West Coast, and hang on."

"That loses. They get whatever they want, game over."

Murphy rose from the console. The simulation played out on a large 3-D map projected from a table in each game room, as well as smaller laptop devices all interconnected through a wireless network. The table was really a very large computer screen that made use of a plasma technology to create stunningly realistic graphics; a viewer watching troops move through the map display could easily believe he was sitting in an airplane.

"Preemptive strike is suicide," said Rosen. "Griffin

tried that against Cody the first week I was here. Led to a nuclear exchange in Month Two."

Another loss, according to the rules of the scenario.

"Wasn't what I was thinking."

"Our best bet is following doctrine, right down the line," said Rosen. "Be the graceful losers. And make sure winners buy. Who are the VIPs, anyway?"

"Who cares?" Zeus pulled out one of the workstation seats and sat down. The Red Team was across the hall, undoubtedly putting the finishing details on the plan. General Perry would be off with the VIPs, but his chief of staff was Major Win Christian—the valedictorian at West Point Major the year Murphy graduated. Murphy had been in the top half of his class, but nowhere near Christian.

Which suited him just fine. Staying away from Christian had been his basic game plan his four years at the Point, after an unfortunate run-in with his fellow plebe during orientation. Christian was already a favorite of the staff because his father was a graduate *and* a general, and the incident had given Zeus exactly the sort of reputation no cadet wanted. He survived that first semester, but just barely.

Every time his path crossed with Christian's following that, whether it was in sports, academics, or social life, inevitably Zeus came off on the losing side.

It would be *really* nice to clock the SOB today.

"What are you doing?" asked Rosen.

"There's got to be a solution."

"That's what Perry's been telling his people for the

past week and a half, and we still cleaned his clock. Perry has tried everything."

"Yeah."

"If there was a solution, Doner would have told it to Perry by now."

"Maybe he doesn't know it."

"Oh, he knows it. He knows everything."

Zeus pulled up the statistics panel, checking to see the average length of hostility—the amount of time Blue usually hung in before the game was lost by the computer. It was only three months.

Three months.

China would defeat America in an Asian war in three months.

Without nuclear weapons.

If it were World War II, America would be out of the war by March 1942. No reinforcements for the Soviets, no invasion of Africa, Italy, and then Normandy. No atom bomb on Hiroshima or Nagasaki—Hitler would have gotten the bomb and used it on London after taking Moscow and confining the tattered remains of the Russian army to eastern Siberia.

Maybe he wouldn't bother using the bomb; he could just starve them out, assuming the U.S. abided by whatever terms the peace treaty with Japan provided. And if the U.S. didn't, then he'd use it on New York and Washington, D.C., instead. Before turning it on the Japanese.

Correlating simulations to real life was a dangerous and fruitless exercise; the simulations were set up to test different theories and situations. Even if they were supposedly neutral, there was no way to accurately account for all of the variables in real life. Once the shooting started and the fog of war descended, even the best plans usually went out the window.

Still, if real life was even remotely this hopeless, America ought to sue for peace right now.

What would he do if this were real?

Try to get Red to attack the Russians.

"You coming to lunch?" said Rosen.

"Huh?"

"I just asked you twice: *Do you want to go get lunch?*"

"What we need is a proxy," said Murphy. He jumped up and walked over to the table. "Someone weak at the beginning of the simulation whom we can build up secretly."

"Then let Red use as a punching bag?"

"Something like that."

"Let's eat."

"You go. I have to look at the rules."

"Hell, you're going to read the rules? I thought you wanted to win."

Northwestern Vietnam,
near the border with China

Finally, there was nothing left for Josh's stomach to give up. He rose shakily, furling his fists under his arms.

There were no illusions left for his mind to fool itself with, either. Optimism was absurd. Survival itself might even be out of the question.

Blundering into the village was a mistake, a stupid mistake. Whoever did this could have been waiting. Why did I do it? Do I want to die?

Hell no. I won't. I won't.

So do something right. Find a weapon. Find a way out.

If he was going to survive, if he was going to make it through this, he had to act like a scientist. He had to be detached, unemotional, take each step carefully.

Josh alternately scolded and encouraged himself as he searched through the hamlet for things he could use. He told himself to act like a survivor, and a scientist. He went back to each hut, forcing himself to look more thoroughly inside. He didn't find any more bodies, but he saw more evidence of shootings—blood clotted on the dirt floors, bullet holes. Things he'd missed or ignored earlier—like the broken furniture—were obvious to him now, and told a consistent tale: the hamlet had been attacked, probably massacred, and then hastily cleaned up.

Josh looked for weapons in the huts. He found a pair of hunting knives, and ammunition for a rifle, but not guns. He took the bullets, hoping he might find the gun, and continued his search. It was difficult to be as empirical as he wanted—his fingers trembled just clutching the box of loose shells. But he was calmer than before, more aware of his surroundings and himself.

At some point, he slipped his hand into his pocket and took out the camera that had been in his pants since the night before. He began videoing everything, beginning with the person in the darkness of the empty cottage. At first he narrated what he was doing, giving the date and the rough location. Then he just let the camera record.

After ten minutes, the memory was full. He turned the camera off and put it back into his pocket, continuing to look around the village and the nearby fields.

Maybe there hadn't been a massacre here—maybe the villager had been killed by someone in the village. That might explain why everyone had fled.

He doubted it was true, but it was a plausible, or at least possible, explanation. Josh continued walking around the village and nearby fields, looking for more evidence.

It wasn't until he had stared at the upper field for a few minutes that he realized part of it had been turned over, while the one below had not.

Who would work a field in February?

Josh sank slowly to his knees. There were footprints—boots. He traced one of the boot marks with his index finger. It was a man's boot, about his size, perhaps one or two sizes smaller.

Evidence of what had happened.

He didn't need it; he'd seen enough.

There was doubt, though. Just one body.

If this were a weather event, he would gather as much data as he possibly could. He would leave nothing to chance.

Josh put his hands into the earth. His heart began throbbing. He pulled the dirt toward him. It resisted. He dug deeper and pulled again.

After his fourth or fifth pull, the dirt came away easily. Sweat ran down the sides of his neck as he worked.

Five minutes after he started digging, Josh's left hand pushed against something that felt like a stick. He pushed a little more, then scooped upward, removing the dirt but not revealing the object. He took as slow a breath as he could manage, and began to dig again, gently though steadily. He moved the dirt around the object like he thought an archaeologist would, bringing it slowly to the surface.

A thick tree branch.

An old shirt on a stone.

An arm, with fingers rolled into a ball.

Enough.

Josh took out the camera and erased one of the files he had shot the night before, giving himself about a minute and a half more of video time. He panned the area, then closed in on the arm, focusing on the hand.

Done, he replaced the dirt with his foot, eyes closed, tamped it back down, and returned to the village.

National Security Situation Room, White House

"Let's see the video," said President Greene.

A screen rose slowly from the middle of the table of the secure situation room. Over in the Pentagon, the Joint Chiefs turned their attention to a similar display at the front of the large secure room there.

A news clip began to play. China's Premier Cho Lai was speaking to a crowd of over one hundred thousand packed into Tiananmen Square. His face was red, his hand motions emphatic.

His words were translated in English subtitles on the screen. Though literally correct, the translation did not quite catch the nuances of venom and racism.

Greene caught it all. His Chinese was fluent, and he needed no help in deciphering the full implication of Premier Cho Lai's words. The message could be summed up in one word: *war*.

Though that was a word the premier never used.

"We must recover the dignity of the Chinese people, sullied too long by those inferior to us, those with despicable agendas, those with goals we cannot share," declared Cho Lai. The premier paused to listen as the crowd erupted in applause.

Greene shook his head. Despite what his critics and late-night comics sometimes implied, the president wasn't old enough to have heard Hitler's speeches firsthand, but he knew they sounded something like this.

"You can turn it off. Peter, review the intelligence, please," Greene told CIA Director Peter Frost.

Frost began speaking, detailing the Chinese buildup as he had earlier for the president and national security adviser. Everyone sitting in on the briefing, both at the Pentagon and at the White House, had heard or seen at least some of the intelligence Frost reviewed. Nonetheless, the CIA director's pithy summary placed the situation in stark relief, and to a person they seemed surprised, and deeply troubled.

"We're looking at World War III here," said the chief of staff, Army General Clayton Fisk. "First Vietnam, then the rest of Asia. India—they won't stop."

Fisk gets it, thought Greene. *Finally.*

One American convinced. Another 350 million to go.

"Maybe they take the country in a few months," said the Air Force chief, Tarn Washington. "Or maybe they get bogged down there like we did in the 1960s. Maybe they don't even attack. The Chinese have a habit of moving troops to their borders. Look what they did at Myanmar a couple of years ago. They're bullies, but they don't actually want to stub their toes, let alone get bloodied."

"The question is, how can we stop them?" said Admiral Nancy Gilead, the Navy head. "If that's what we want to do."

"We can't," said Fisk quickly. "We can't get troops there. And frankly, the American people would never stand for it. Never."

Secretary of State Theodore "Tad" Knox nodded his head vigorously.

"How long before they invade?" asked Fisk.

"*If* they invade," said Washington.

"The analysts' best consensus is that they're a week away, maybe two, from being in a position where they can attack," said Frost. "It's a guess though."

"It could be sooner?" asked Fisk.

"Possibly."

"With all due respect, I have to disagree," said General Peter Shoemaker. Shoemaker headed the Army. "The Chinese are a notoriously slow-moving army. They could take months getting into position—and a half a year going over the border. Especially in western Vietnam. Their history is against them."

"They've been studying Shock and Awe for years," said Jackson.

"I've studied piano just as long, and I still can't play 'Mary Had a Little Lamb,'" replied Shoemaker.

No one laughed.

Frost continued his briefing. The Vietnamese seemed completely unprepared. Their defenses were situated in the northeastern portion of the country, where

China had attacked in the 1970s.

The questions that followed made it clear that even if the U.S. was in a position to stop the invasion, the chiefs would be less than unanimous in support of it. They didn't want to reward the Chinese, but Greene sensed that they would be only halfheartedly in favor of sanctions. There was more lingering resentment against the Vietnamese than he'd expected. And more admiration of the Chinese.

But he was the one making the decisions.

"I want a military plan to go with UN sanctions, if there's an invasion," he told them when the conversation died. "I want something with teeth. I want options."

"They're very limited, sir," said Shoemaker.

"Let's not decide that before we've examined it carefully."

"Mr. President, stopping China—it's just not possible," said Fisk. "If they invade, we can't stop them. And helping the Vietnamese will only make us look weaker in their eyes."

"And why should we?" asked Washington. "We don't owe the Vietnamese anything. Absolutely nothing."

Washington had lost his father in the Vietnam War. But he spoke for most Americans.

"We don't owe them anything, that's true," said Greene. "But this isn't about them. We must be prepared for the worst, and we have to do what's right."

11

Northwestern Vietnam, near the border with China

To Lieutenant Jing Yo, the Chinese army seemed both fitful and petulant, often harsh, and even, at times, maddeningly paranoid. But it could be benevolent and even generous as well—was not the breakfast it was issuing to him this morning an emperor's feast? Hard-boiled eggs, a large piece of bread, fresh cheese, two apples—a poor man in the countryside could live a week on such a meal.

The cook had apologized that there was no rice. He had done the same the day before—and the day before that, and the week before that. The apology had become a pro forma ritual, repeated every morning. Rice was an incredibly expensive commodity, far too precious to be given to common soldiers in the field—let alone soldiers who'd been assigned to a dangerous mission outside the country and might never return.

Jing Yo couldn't remember the last time he had had rice, except when visiting Beijing. China without rice—the very notion seemed impossible. And yet it was now a fact of life.

"Lieutenant, you are lingering when there is work to be done," said Colonel Sun behind him.

Jing Yo rose silently, leaving his half-finished meal on his plate.

"The matter last night?" said the colonel.

"Completed."

"Good. You believe there are others?"

"Certainly."

A dozen different regular army companies, most without direct supervision, were operating in the area, securing it or preparing for the mission. The troops had been taught to hate all enemies, but especially the Vietnamese, considered a mongrel race.

Sun frowned. He did not harbor any particular compassion toward the Vietnamese; his concern was only for the operation.

"Further steps?" asked the colonel, in a tone that sounded like a warning.

Jing Yo considered how to answer. There really was no easy way to deal with the problem, short of recalling all of the troops, and that wasn't going to happen.

"I believe the general's order will be sufficient," he said finally.

Sufficient to prevent further massacres? Or to cover up those that had already occurred but not been seen by Sun?

Most likely the latter rather than the former, but Sun did not ask for elaboration.

"Finish here. Then move on," said the colonel. "I must return to the task force. You deal with division and the staff there as necessary. If there are further problems, report to me."

Jing Yo bowed his head, and turned to go to work. As he walked down the path from the mess area, he fixed his gaze on the far hill. They held the hill, as well as the one beyond it to the east. There were a few scattered Hmong settlements in the valley, but otherwise no Vietnamese.

At least not alive.

The sun bathed the jungle in bright golden light. Jing Yo followed the path downward, leaning slightly to keep his center of gravity positioned properly. Though not trying to be quiet, he walked so silently by habit that he surprised Sergeant Wu, who was leaning against a tree lighting a cigarette instead of supervising a nearby work detail. Wu, the commando platoon sergeant, wore the look of mild disdain typical of commando noncoms, but otherwise would not have fit the stereotype—he was on the short side, a little heavy. His chin was in need of a shave. Unlike most commandos, he had been born in Shanghai, the son of a relatively well-off father and mother whom he never spoke of or to.

Wu's service record, on the other hand, was the envy of the regiment; he had been in Malaysia, though not at the same time or place as Jing Yo.

"Sergeant," said Jing Yo, nodding as he stopped.

"Have a good breakfast, Lieutenant?"

Jing Yo ignored the question, and its implied criticism of the privileges an officer was afforded. The enlisted men were issued only two meals a day—a small roll in the morning, and a bigger one at evening. Sometimes meat was added.

"So, Sergeant Fan is no longer with us?" asked Wu.

"The sergeant had difficulty following orders," said Jing Yo.

Wu was not a friend of Sergeant Fan's—in fact, Jing Yo suspected he could not stand the other commando. Another man in his position might have said something flattering to Jing Yo, earning easy points at his enemy's expense. But Wu was not like that. If anything, Jing Yo suspected his opinion of Fan had changed because of his conflict with his commander.

"Have the things from the science camp been gathered?" Jing Yo asked.

"They've already started to bury them."

"Bury them?"

"Captain Ching said Colonel Sun wanted his people to get rid of them. I sent Po and Ai Gua down to watch the donkeys and make sure they get it right."

"Did *I* tell you to bury them?"

Wu pursed his lips. Shaking his head, Jing Yo started away, jogging a few steps before breaking into a run.

Privates Po and Ai Gua were about a hundred meters away, watching as a pair of regular army soldiers dug a trench on a flat rift in the hill. They had not gotten very far; the dirt was filled with roots and stones. The items from the camp they had overrun the night before, including the clothes the dead men had been wearing, were piled on the other side of the dirt.

"Help me with this," he told Po and Ai Gua. "Look through the clothes. See if there's information that will be of use."

The two privates went to the clothes and began rifling through them. Jing Yo looked at the soldiers who were digging the ditch.

"You'd be better off putting the dirt on that side there," he said, pointing. "It will be easier for you to push these things in. You won't have to climb over the rocks and soil."

The men looked at him as if he had just described the formula for solving binomial equations. They nodded, then went back to work.

Jing Yo walked to the pile of equipment and began looking through it. Colonel Sun had considered salvaging the gear and selling it in Shanghai. But Jing Yo had pointed out that the equipment was bound to be traceable, and if it ever turned up on the world market—something almost sure to happen if it was sold in Shanghai—very possibly their mission would be compromised. The colonel's face had shaded pale, and he had quickly agreed it should be buried with the rest of the remains from the camp.

There were several boxes of instruments, most of which could be only vaguely identified. The expedition had been gathering soil and vegetation samples, and had placed a number of rain gauges near their camp. The documents on their laptop computers—none protected by passwords—indicated that they were studying changes in the climate and local plant and animal life.

"Hey, Lieutenant, look at this," said Private Ai Gua, holding up a satellite phone. "It was in a pocket."

Jing Yo walked over and took the phone. They had found three the night before; all had already been crushed.

"Why did we miss this?" he asked.

"*We* didn't miss it," said Sergeant Wu, answering before Ai Gua could open his mouth. Jing Yo turned to him. Wu's cigarette had been replaced by a smug look Jing Yo associated with most veteran commando noncoms, who generally felt superior to any officer they served under. "The donkeys searched the tents."

"We should have searched them ourselves," said Jing Yo.

Wu scowled. It was obvious what he was thinking: they couldn't be everywhere, or do everything that needed to be done.

Jing Yo turned on the phone. Like the others, it required a PIN. He tried a punching a few buttons in sequence—0-0-0-0, 1-2-3-4, 9-8-7-6—before getting a message saying he was locked out for too many failed ID attempts. Disgusted, he held the phone in his hands and snapped it in two.

Ai Gua whistled. Wu tried to hide his surprise with a frown.

The phone was small and well constructed, but snapping it in two was merely a matter of leverage, a parlor trick as far as Jing Yo was concerned. Any of the novices who had trained with the monks could have done the same in their sixth month there.

"Make sure the clothes are checked carefully," Jing Yo said. "If there are any more phones, they must be destroyed before being buried. Anything with an identity must be burned."

Jing Yo walked to the pile himself and began sorting

through the things patiently, holding each piece for a moment as he considered what it told him before putting it aside.

Trousers—a fat, short man. *Thick fabric*—a man of reasonable means. *Frayed at the heel*—a man who held on to comfortable clothing, possibly out of frugality, but more likely out of habit.

"Are you looking for a new wardrobe?" asked Sergeant Wu behind him.

"If you want to know a man, start with his tailor, then go to his laundress," said Jing Yo.

It was a maxim one of his teachers had taught him, but Wu thought it was a joke and laughed. Jing Yo continued sorting through the pile. Each item varied from the others as its owners had varied in life, and yet they told a single story: Westerners, men of learning, trying to understand something in a country foreign to them.

It was regrettable that they had had to die. But at least their deaths had been swift.

The clothes told more. The scientists were well off, able to afford sturdy wear. They were also relatively well fed, thicker around the waist than even the older officers in the army.

So what the premier said in his speeches *was* true—the West was hoarding the planet's food, depriving China and the rest of the world of its share. Jing Yo regretted the deaths a little less.

"Something wrong, Lieutenant?" asked Private Ai Gua.

"Maybe he saw a ghost," said Sergeant Wu, laughing.

Neither private joined in. Both men, Jing Yo knew, were deeply superstitious.

"The Westerners are enjoying the fruit of our labors," he told them. "They do not have to struggle as we do for food. This war will restore balance and equity. Bury everything well."

Northwestern Vietnam, near the border with China

The huts had dried meat and some stores of vegetables, but the only food Josh trusted was the potatoes. He considered cooking them, but dismissed the idea as too dangerous. They tasted horrible raw, but he ate them anyway, devouring them as he walked up a path that started at the field above the hamlet and cut north, paralleling the road at the valley's base. Going north made the most sense, he reasoned, because there would be soldiers at the border with China who would be able to help him. The border was only a few miles away, a day or at most two of walking.

The winding trail moved in and out of the jungle, cutting back against the slope as it went. Josh thought he would find a vantage at the top where he could look out over the surrounding countryside and get his bearings, but he was disappointed; the hill was dwarfed by its neighbors on all sides except the east, and there the trees were too narrow to support him as he climbed. After a few minutes, he couldn't even see down to the village, let alone the road below.

Josh found another path heading east at the top of the hill. As he began down it, a large animal darted to the left, running through the trees into a small meadow about twenty yards from the path. He followed, thinking the animal was part of a grazing flock, maybe a small oxen or goat. Josh stepped warily, slipping among the trees as he got close to the field. There were three animals, about the size of deer though fatter, and with straight horns like goats might have—*saolas*, or Vu Quang oxen, native to northern Vietnam.

They looked at him warily, certainly aware that he was there, but apparently not afraid of him. When at last he rose and took a step from the woods, they darted away.

Back on the trail, Josh began thinking of the others on the expedition. He hadn't known any of them for very long, but now they seemed like close friends. He thought of Ross, and Millie, the girl who was helping Dr. Renaldo. Fleming, the Belgian with the loud laugh. Phillip, a Chinese-American who preferred Scotch to beer and had taught him several Chinese curse words during a long night at a bar while trying to prove his point.

Dr. Renaldo himself, slightly cantankerous, especially in the morning before his third coffee—he always had four—yet generous to a fault.

All dead.

Grief rose in his chest, a physical thing, pain that eroded his bones and pricked at the underside of his skin.

How can I go on without them?

It was his parents he thought of, not the other scientists. He was a child again, afraid without his mother and father, alone.

No time for grief. Time for action. Move.

The pain was so intense Josh had to stop for a moment. He forced himself to move again, stopped, felt tears streaming down his cheeks.

I've gone through this already, he told himself. *I will survive.*

He tried to distract himself by repeating the facts he knew about Vietnam's weather. He recounted, by rote, the average rainfall, and high and low temperatures of each month. He considered what the consequences of these were, as if he were delivering a lecture or discussing the matter with his doctoral advisers.

Sometime in late afternoon, with the sun sinking below the hills, Josh heard a helicopter. The sound shoved his thoughts about science away. His first reaction was to hide: he plunged into the jungle beyond the road, taking cover between the trees.

As he crouched against a trunk, he realized that hiding was not the thing to do. On the contrary, whoever was in the helicopter would probably help him, perhaps even fly him to safety. But he stayed back.

His sense of danger increased as the rotor of the

chopper pounded heavier and heavier toward him. Finally it appeared, streaking down from the north, a long, dark machine, with a black cockpit and a thick tail. Missiles were stacked beneath the stubby wings, and a large round disk sat atop the rotor. To Josh, the aircraft looked like an American Apache, with a gun hanging beneath its pointed nose. But a star was painted in dull red on the side of the fuselage, faint but still visible to the naked eye.

The chopper skimmed so close to the trees that Josh thought it was going to crash. It thundered past, shaking the ground for more than a minute.

The path looped out of the trees onto a ridge. As he walked along it, Josh could see across to the hills on the other side. He continued a little farther and saw the road below—*the same road I was on earlier*, he thought, though of course now he was several miles farther north.

He could also see a faint glow in the distance where the road curved into the hills.

A village.

He wanted to run, but the glow was too far away to make that worthwhile. Instead, Josh picked up his pace, moving quickly, trying not to get too anxious.

His pants began to sag at his waist. He put his hands in the loops and held them as he went.

The path looped back into the jungle. The sun had gone below the ridge, and the ground before him was gray, filled with shadows. Josh kept moving, bending forward a bit and rehearsing his small store of Vietnamese.

The jungle became darker with each step, until finally he couldn't see more than a few feet in front of him. The winding lane dipped to the left, then climbed so sharply that Josh had to use his hands to help him scramble upward. Finally it leveled out, and the thick jungle canopy gave way to a purple-blue sky. Once again, Josh picked up his pace, moving along the edge of the trail as it skimmed yet another ridge.

A highway came into view down to his left. Nearly straight ahead, about a half mile away, he spotted a double fence topped by barbed wire. Lights played on the fence, cutting through the growing shadows.

It was the Chinese border.

13

Hanoi, Vietnam

Another American arriving at Noi Bai Airport outside Hanoi might have noted the irony of the terminal's westernization in the decades since the end of the war. But Mara Duncan was too focused on her mission. Clearing customs—she was traveling on a regular passport, in keeping with her journalist cover—she walked through the relatively small terminal to the taxi queue. The cab was a brand-new Indian-made REVA, the recently introduced four-door hatchback model of the Standard, an electric car. It was eerily silent as it pulled away from the airport terminal building; only when they reached the highway and the driver floored it did she hear any noise, a high-pitched flutter that sounded more like an overachieving fan than the motor of a car.

Hanoi had grown over the past several years, but compared to Bangkok it looked like a sleepy Asian backwater, especially on the outskirts, where colonial-era buildings shouldered against plain-box new structures four and five stories high, with the occasional ancient historical building plopped incongruously in the middle. The traffic was not anywhere near as bad as elsewhere in Asia, but it still took nearly an hour on the two-lane highway for the taxi to reach center city, where her hotel was. She'd been booked into a new hotel called the Star; rising on the ashes of several much humbler structures, it boasted fifteen stories and a white stone facade turned turquoise by the evening light. Mara paid the driver and went inside.

They gave her a suite with a king-sized bed and a soaking tub lined with tiny bottles of perfumed oil. The bath looked tempting, but she was on too tight a schedule; there was barely enough time to check the room for bugs before going out.

Sure enough, she found a device embedded in one of the lamps in the sitting room, where it ran off current from the wall. It also appeared to use the electrical circuit to send its signal. While Mara hadn't encountered the specific device before, she had considerable experience with other members of its family.

The bug didn't mean that the Vietnamese security apparatus had taken an interest in her specifically, much less that it suspected she was with the CIA. Industrial espionage was a growth industry in Asia, routinely practiced by a number of governments, including several with long historic ties to the U.S. Data was mined and then offered to various customers; while local businesses were generally favored, selling information to overseas competitors was usually more lucrative.

Mara left the bug in place—removing it would only arouse her eavesdroppers' interest. She changed her clothes and went down to get a cyclo to take her to her appointment.

Cyclos were a kind of bicycle with a cushioned passenger seat at the front. They were popular with tourists, who tended to view them as an exotic touch in a place that was rapidly becoming a lot like the rest of the world. Mara liked them because they made it easier for her to see what was around her—and whether she was being followed or not.

As she stepped toward the curb, the driver looked at her face and gave her clothes a quick glance. Deducing that she was an American, he addressed her in broken English.

"Lady, I take you where you want. Best travel. Where you go?"

"Alfresco," she told him, naming a well-known tourist restaurant in the center of the city. "You know it?"

"Restaurant. Very nice."

"How much?"

"Ten U.S. dollar."

"You think I'm rich?"

"Five dollar."

"Two hundred dong," she said, naming a price that worked out to about fifty cents at the current exchange rate. They went back and forth for a while more before settling on five hundred dong.

It was a little lower than the going rate, but the driver didn't seem offended by her hard if good-natured bargaining.

"Good, good, very good," he clucked, putting his foot to the pedal and nudging the cyclo gently toward her as she turned to sit.

After Bangkok, Hanoi's seventy-degree evening seemed cool, even to Mara, who'd been raised in Wisconsin winters. She curled her arms around her chest, keeping warm while she glanced around the street the way she imagined a journalist would: perpetually curious, fascinated by everything. A cluster of Western travelers caught her eye—two families, one with a pair of small children, the other with a young teenager. The little kids were cute, even with the fatigue showing on their faces.

Mara felt a pang of jealousy, and for just a moment wanted to push her life along, move ahead in her career to the time when contemplating a family was not impossible.

The idea evaporated as the cyclo turned the corner, sliding into a knot of traffic. She came back to the present, focusing on the task at hand.

She got out of the cyclo a few yards from the front of the restaurant. After a few steps toward Alfresco she stopped, turning as if she had forgotten something, though really she was checking to see if she'd been followed.

It didn't seem as if she had. Even so, Mara moved back into the shadows near the building, surveying the people around her—almost exclusively tourists. None seemed to notice her, or make too much of a deal out of not noticing her. She made a U-turn and walked to the end of the block, then turned the corner before doubling back. She saw an empty cab and trotted toward it, flagging it down.

"Old City," she told the driver, getting in. "Okay?"

"Okay, lady."

The restaurant where she was to meet the scientist was in the Old Quarter, the center of the city. Called Massalli, it had been open for several years and served Mediterranean cuisine. One of its best features was its wine list; knowing the Belgian was something of a connoisseur, Mara made sure to get the list after she was shown to the table.

She took a travel guide for Angkor Wat—the ancient capital of Cambodia—from her purse and laid it on the table, angling it so a passerby could easily spot it from across the room. The guide was unusual, but not so out of place that it would call too much attention to her; the scientist would look for it as an initial recognition symbol. Mara, of course, had studied his picture and would know who he was when he asked if she was going there.

She glanced at her watch. She'd aimed to be there a half hour early; she'd made it with five minutes to spare. She ordered a bottle of water, and began thumbing through the book, pausing every so often to scan the crowd.

An hour later, she was still waiting. None of the dozen or so diners, all Westerners, looked remotely like the scientist.

Mara ordered some dinner, then took out her cell phone and called the hotel where the scientist was supposed to be staying. He hadn't checked in.

That didn't necessarily mean anything bad. He was coming a considerable distance from the northwestern jungles, and might not consider a meeting with a CIA officer his top priority. But she didn't like it. Deciding the restaurant might be a little too crowded for a detailed discussion, she left her napkin on the chair and got up, walking to the hall where the restroom was. Spotting a door to the side alley, she went over and stepped outside. Except for some neatly stacked wooden boxes and several steel garbage cans, the alley was empty. Mara tried to ignore the smell as she dialed his sat phone from hers.

She got his voice mail service.

"Missed you for dinner," she said cheerfully, not giving her name. "Hope to see you for cocktails."

Back inside, Mara ate slowly, then nursed a Saigon beer. Two and a half hours after she was to have met the scientist, she paid her bill and went to the bar. It was a small, narrow room between the dining area and the entrance, and very crowded. Everyone, even the bartender, was a foreigner. Mara ordered a beer and stood near the door, considering what to do next.

Was the scientist in trouble? Had the Vietnamese or even the Chinese figured out he was in the agency's employ? Or was he just being a scientist, with many other things on his mind?

Maybe he'd gotten cold feet. Maybe he'd decided meeting with her was too dangerous.

Maybe, maybe, maybe.

The bartender came over and leaned over the counter, smiling. Two Australians wanted to buy her a drink. Mara let them. One was cute—about her age, tall, with a soccer player's slim body. He had a two- or three-day beard that softened the hard lines of his chin. His friend, shorter, rounder, did most of the talking. They were techies, installing some sort of machine in a factory at the outskirts of town. Lonely, obviously, and a bit drunk. She flirted with them while waiting to see if Fleming might show up after all.

Mara managed to sip her beer so slowly she still had half a glass when the bartender signaled last call an hour later.

"We can continue this party down the street," suggested the shorter Aussie.

Mara glanced at his friend, who smiled shyly.

"Be fun," he said.

"I don't think so. Thanks though," she said. "Too much work in the morning."

She touched his hand, then walked out with them, let them hail her a cab. A small part of her wondered if they were spies as well, but she'd already dismissed the possibility; something about the way they held themselves told her they were civilians. It had nothing to do with the short man's talkativeness, or the taller man's shyness. They lacked the coiled, just barely contained intensity that a covert agent or spy needed to survive.

Just in case she was wrong, she changed cabs at a second hotel before going to Hien Lam, where the scientist was supposed to be staying. Hien Lam was popular with Asians in Hanoi on business. Though the building dated from the early 1950s, it had recently been renovated to modern Western standards. Gleaming glass and polished aluminum walls greeted Mara as she entered the lobby. There was a video camera watching at the desk, and Mara decided she didn't care to have her face attached to the scientist's name. So she slipped into the lounge at the right to try another call.

The mostly male crowd raised quite a din as they struggled to converse over the music, but neither conversation nor the music was the attraction. Two girls in strategically applied pasties writhed on platforms at either end of the bar, wiggling their surgically enhanced body parts at the crowd. Such a display would have been unheard of in Hanoi a decade before, but apparently was an accepted by-product of the latest push to entice business to the country.

Mara slipped through the crowd. There were only two empty tables; both were far removed from the stage. She took one. No less than a minute later a man came over and asked if he could sit down. He was middle-aged, Japanese, overly polite and slightly nervous.

"You can sit down if you want," she told him in English.

"Thank you."

"I'm waiting for a friend," she told him as he pulled out the chair. A look of disappointment crossed his face. "But he's late, and I don't have a cell phone. Do you mind if I borrow yours?"

He handed it over. Mara had come to Hanoi with a mobile as well as a sat phone. She also had two untraceable SIM cards that would allow her to give the cell phone a new number and account. But why burn a clean SIM card when a phone with a perfectly innocent pedigree could be had for the asking?

She called the hotel; Fleming still hadn't checked in. He didn't answer the sat phone either.

She started slipping the phone into her purse. The businessman stopped her.

"My phone."

"Oh, I'm sorry," she said. "I thought it was mine. I'd forgotten. I'm so used to having one."

Her attempted theft was the last straw for the man, who after a shallow nod excused himself and left. Mara waited a minute, then got up and went to the bar, sidling in near a man who'd left his wallet and cell phone next to his drink. He glanced at her, then turned his attention back to the girl writhing on the stage nearby. A minute later, she was outside the hotel, his cell phone in hand.

Mara found a quiet lobby in the hotel across the

street, then used the man's phone to call every hotel in the Hanoi tourist guide. Fleming hadn't checked into any of them.

Returning to the girlie lounge across the street, she couldn't find the man whose phone she'd stolen.

"I believe one of your customers left this," she told one of the bartenders, holding up the phone. "I found it on the floor beneath the stool."

By now it was after two. Mara's check-in with Thailand was well overdue. She walked several blocks before finding a minihotel off an alley. So-called minihotels were small budget hotels that generally catered to backpackers and other budget travelers, something like a Vietnam version of Motel 6, without the cute advertising or free soap. The clerk, a sleepy-eyed young man barely out of his teens, yawned interminably, then asked for her passport to make a copy—standard procedure in Vietnam.

"I have a copy already," said Mara, producing one from her bag.

This, too, was common procedure; the clerk took it without checking against her actual passport, which had a different number and name.

"Do you have other Western guests?" she asked as he fished the key from its cubby behind him.

"A few."

"A friend of mine sometimes stays here. He's Belgian."

The clerk began shaking his head even before she gave him the name or his country. "No Belgium, no."

"He might seem French."

"Don't know. Your bag?"

"The airline lost it. I have to pick it up in the morning."

The clerk's expression made it clear he didn't believe her. Mara shrugged.

"That's what they told me," she said.

"Maybe it will come."

The room was smaller than even the bathroom at the Star, but it was clean, and the bed had fresh sheets. Mara checked for bugs. When she didn't find any, she sat in the creaky wooden chair and took out her sat phone.

To her surprise, Jesse DeBiase, the Million Dollar Man, picked up. "Well, hello, darling," he answered her. "About time you checked in."

"I was looking for the duty officer."

"Found him."

"This late?"

"I'm a night owl."

"You're doing real work for a change?"

"Will wonders never cease? I expect pigs to be flying next," he said. "Actually, I'm listenin' to Charlie Daniels," he added conspiratorially. "He's gonna fiddle with the devil at the crossroads for his soul."

"There's a contest you'd win."

"You assume I have a soul he'd be interested in. So how is Mr. Fleming?"

"Didn't show."

"Hmmmm."

"'Hmmmm' as in something? Or are you humming a song with Charlie?"

"Neither one. Listen, darling, something may be going on." The Million Dollar Man's voice shifted slightly; though his tone was still light, Mara knew he was suddenly much more serious. "We've heard reports that the Vietnamese are testing the Chinese borders."

"What?"

"Doesn't make any sense," added DeBiase quickly. "But the rumors are flying. Several of our people in Beijing have heard it."

"Beijing?"

"Something to be aware of. You haven't heard anything?"

"Not a peep."

DeBiase was silent for a moment. Talking to the scientist was now ten times more important than it had been that morning; Mara worried that they would decide to send someone more experienced to deal with him.

Not better—just more *experienced*. That's how Lucas would put it.

"Are you staying at the Star?" said DeBiase finally.

"I am. I'm not calling from there, though. The room is bugged."

"Of course. Make sure we can contact you."

"Obviously." She felt a surge of relief—she wasn't going to be replaced. At least not yet.

"Don't take any unnecessary risks, darling," DeBiase added. "Stay close to the hotel. I wouldn't want you getting hurt. There'd be no one left to enjoy my coffee."

"You're sweet."

"Not really. I'm a lecherous old man. But harmless, at least until my hernia is fixed."

They both laughed uneasily, then hung up.

14

Northwestern Vietnam, near the border with China

Josh's first impulse was to tear through the jungle straight at the border, but in the dark that would be foolish. Much of the land close to the fence was mined— he could easily blow himself up in the dark. Besides, he didn't want to climb the fence; he wanted to find someone near it who could help him, soldiers or a customs official. They'd be near the road.

He took a few steps sideways along the trail, keeping the fence in view, until finally he couldn't see it. Turning and walking properly, he followed the path as it swung across a cleft in the mountain and met a narrow and uneven ancient road. Though used by traders and travelers for millennia, the roadbed had never been paved, and over the last forty or fifty years had seen less and less traffic. The hard-packed dirt and rocks had nonetheless successfully held off the jungle, trees and brush clustering at its edges but getting no farther.

As Josh began walking along the road, he heard a chain saw start up and buzz in the distance. The sound baffled him: who would be using a chain saw after dark?

There were dozens, if not hundreds, of potential answers, but before he could think of any, the road before him began to glow with approaching headlights. Josh stepped to the middle of the road, but as the lights grew stronger he remembered how he had blundered dangerously into the village. Rather than taking a chance on the truck, he decided to stick with his original plan of looking for a border guard, and so he slipped back into the nearby woods.

The lights grew stronger. So did the noise of the truck's engine. There was more than one; he could hear at least three or four, maybe many more.

They seemed to take forever to arrive. The first plodded along at barely five miles an hour, going so slowly that Josh felt as if he were watching a slow-motion replay of reality. The second followed almost on the other's bumper, without lights, its driver clunking the gears as he shifted to take the incline. Then came the third truck, and for the first time Josh noticed the yellow star on the door panel. They were military trucks—identical, in fact, to the trucks that had taken the scientific team out from Hanoi.

That couldn't be, though—the trucks were coming from China; they must be Chinese.

But the insignia on the doors, the yellow star in a red field, was absolutely Vietnamese. China's army used a red star. These *had* to be Vietnamese.

What would they be doing in China? And why didn't they have their headlights on?

Twenty trucks passed, kicking up a cloud of thick dust in the night. Then the road was empty, and silence gradually returned to the countryside.

Jing Yo saw the headlights of the first truck as it wove down the old mountain trail roughly ten kilometers from the border. Immediately he felt a surge of anger—strict orders had been given for the vehicles to move south *without* using their lights.

The lieutenant could not let this pass by. He strode to the middle of the road and raised his arm as the vehicle approached.

The truck jerked to a stop so close to him that its bumper grazed his leg. Jing Yo walked around to the driver's side, where a nervous private had rolled down the window. Like everyone else, including the commandos, he wore a Vietnamese army uniform, but was in fact Chinese.

"What are you doing?" Jing Yo asked the driver, keeping his voice even.

"Excuse me, Lieutenant." Jing Yo's ersatz uniform included his proper rank. "I didn't see you in the shadows."

"You should not have had your lights on. That was the order, was it not?"

The driver didn't answer.

"Private—you should not have had your lights on," repeated Jing Yo. "What is your explanation?"

"Without the lights, I would not have seen you at all." The man's voice cracked.

Without the lights, Jing Yo would not have been in the road. But explaining that was a waste of time. Jing grabbed hold of the door handle and pulled himself onto the running board. The driver recoiled.

"Turn off the lights, and drive on," said Jing Yo.

He glanced at the line of trucks behind them, then tightened his grip as the driver put the vehicle in gear.

"There's a switchback to the right in another ten meters," Jing Yo warned the driver as they approached it. "The road drops sharply to the left. Be very careful."

"Yes, Lieutenant. Thank you."

The driver moved the truck so far to the right side of the lane that brush scraped against the fender, then lashed at Jing Yo's side. He held on silently, concentrating on the view ahead. The moon was full and the sky clear, but even the comparatively light jungle canopy did a good job blocking out the light. Jing Yo strained to see.

Before he had begun to train at the monastery, Jing Yo had heard stories of monks who could see through blindfolds. Like much of what was said of *Ch'an*, the tales were apocryphal; the adepts were human, not gods. But a man could see many things others missed if he trained his eyes to observe, and his other senses to do their jobs well.

"Slow down," Jing Yo told the driver. "The highway is just ahead."

The truck jerked as the driver downshifted. Two of

Jing Yo's men—Privates Po and Ai Gua—stood on the highway, waiting.

"Halt!" yelled Po. He raised his rifle.

Jing Yo jumped off the running board as the truck ground to a halt, its brakes squealing as furiously as a stuck pig.

"Is there traffic on the road?" he asked Ai Gua.

The private grinned. "Nothing, Lieutenant."

"Get in the cab and guide them up to the staging point," Jing Yo told him. He looked over at Po. "Go to the tenth truck back," he said. "Sit with them and guide them if they get lost. And make sure they don't use their headlights."

"They'd have to be imbeciles to be lost here," mumbled Po, but he did as he was told.

Jing Yo walked to the highway. Sergeant Wu stood in the middle of the road with an unlit cigarette in his mouth. He was watching a signal light flashing from the scout team about a kilometer down the road.

"All clear," said Wu. He took a lighter from his pocket and lit the cigarette.

Jing Yo waved the truck onto the road. It climbed up over the drainage ditch at the side, across the shoulder, and onto the macadam. The driver turned the wheel so hard as the tires reached the pavement that the truck tipped. For a moment it hung in midair, suspended. Then it flipped onto its side.

Jing Yo sprang into motion, running forward. Wu, throwing the cigarette from his mouth, was right behind.

Fearing the truck would burst into flames, Jing Yo

jumped onto the frame and grabbed at the door handle. He pulled the door up on its hinges; Sergeant Wu grabbed it and held it open behind him. Jing Yo threw his hand against the roof and leaned inside, reaching to kill the engine. He got it off, then curled his head back, looking for the buckle on the driver's seat belt so he could unhook it. But the man hadn't been wearing the belt. The accident had thrown him across Private Ai Gua, who was wedged against the opposite window. Jing Yo turned himself around, draping his legs over the windshield, then reached down into the cab. He could smell gasoline.

"Take my hand," he told the driver. "Hurry—before the truck catches fire. The explosives will blow us all up."

The driver was in shock and didn't react

"Come," Jing Yo told him, leaning in farther. He grabbed the driver by the back of his shirt and raised him straight out, snatching him like an apple from the bottom of a barrel. He pushed him over to Wu, then reached back in for Ai Gua. The commando, still dazed, apparently didn't remember that he had his seat belt on and flailed against it.

"The belt, Private," said Jing Yo, reaching for the buckle. He unlocked it, and helped Ai Gua climb up over him, getting several bruises in the process. Then he pulled himself out of the truck and jumped down. Ai Gua was already staggering up the embankment to the road.

"You idiot! Months of preparation, ruined by your carelessness!" Sergeant Wu had pulled the driver away from the truck and begun berating him in the middle of the road. "You are an imbecile. I should shoot you right here."

"I don't disagree with your assessment of his intelligence," Jing Yo told the sergeant. "But this is not the time to share it. And your solution is not useful."

"He is an ass."

"Very truly. We have to get these trucks past quickly."

"The explosives!" said Sergeant Wu. "Shit."

He left the driver and ran to the trucks stopped behind the one that had crashed, waving at the men who'd gotten out to see what was going on.

"Get back in your trucks!" yelled the sergeant. "Get going! Go, come on. Get on the highway! Quickly."

The charges, rigged to make the vehicle look as if it had been destroyed in a firefight, were not yet connected to their detonators, and it was obvious to Jing Yo that they were safe—otherwise they would already have gone off. But he let Wu go.

"Are you all right?" he asked Ai Gua.

"Yes."

The commando, a blank look on his face, held up his right wrist. Jing Yo took hold of the hand gently. Fixing his eyes on Ai Gua's face, he began to squeeze the wrist, twisting slightly as he increased the pressure. Within a second or two, the private winced, though he did not call out.

A sprain, most likely. Not worth going back to Beijing for—especially since the injury would result in his being removed from the commando corps.

The second truck slipped past the rear wheels of

the one that had flipped, the driver gingerly finding the road.

"Try not to use it," Jing Yo told Ai Gua. "Go with the driver. Make sure he wears a seat belt."

The private went to the truck without saying anything else.

They stopped the last truck to use it to right the crashed vehicle. Sergeant Wu rigged a chain to the rear axle, then stood back with Jing Yo as the driver maneuvered to give his vehicle a good foothold. The slight scent of an orange mingled with the harsher smells of sweat and cigarettes on Wu's uniform. He mumbled something to himself as the truck started.

"Faster," he said finally. "Move!"

The fallen truck rose back up about fifteen degrees before the wheels began to slide. Something from the side caught against the pavement and began to screech. The driver in the vehicle with the tow line jammed on his brakes. The truck yawed to the side, the upper frame bending under its own weight.

"He should have jammed the pedal, not stopped," said Sergeant Wu disgustedly. "These drivers know nothing."

Jing Yo walked over to the truck, straining against the chain. Something clicked—Jing Yo sprang back just in time as one of the links gave way and the truck fell back over.

"Let's try this again," said Jing Yo.

They needed to attach the chain to a higher spot. The only thing strong enough looked like the A-pillar at the side of the windshield. Coiling his leg on the bumper, Jing Yo hopped up to the roof of the truck; there, he composed himself for a moment before whirling down to the hood, kicking out the windshield in the process. He cleared the glass—it was bound by a layer of plastic, and came off in a panel—then took the chain from Sergeant Wu and tightened it around the pillar.

"One more thing," he said to Wu. "Help me with the tree trunk."

Jing Yo had seen the trunk on the ground earlier. About a half meter in diameter and nearly two meters long, it was heavy and difficult to carry between them. Wu told him he needed to let go and rest when they reached the road.

"We'll just roll it from here," said Jing Yo, and they let it drop.

Jing Yo rigged the tree at the corner of the rear wheel, hoping to use it as an anchor or fulcrum, fixing the lower half of the vehicle in place so it could be pulled upward. It was only partly successful—the vehicle dragged against the pavement as the other tugged. Still, the truck began to tilt.

"Go!" Sergeant Wu said to the driver. "Give it gas."

The driver did—but too much. His motor stalled. The vehicles strained against each other, as if playing tug-of-war.

"I'll do it," said Wu, his disgust as evident as his impatience. He climbed up into the cab, shoving the driver aside. After starting the engine, he gunned the truck forward, then jammed on the brakes. The other truck jerked back onto its tires.

"See if it will start," Jing Yo told the driver who'd crashed it originally.

Until now, the man had stood, frozen and silent, at the side of the road where Sergeant Wu had left him earlier. Now, sensing that he might win a reprieve, he sprang forward. Inside the cab, he pumped the gas a few times, then turned the engine over. It whined, but didn't start.

"You're flooding it," said Sergeant Wu.

"Private, relax," said Jing Yo, walking to the cab. "Take your foot off the gas."

"It always needs a pump."

"You've pumped it plenty already, idiot," said Sergeant Wu.

"Let it rest for a moment," said Jing Yo calmly.

He waited for a full minute, staring at the driver the entire time. The man held his gaze for only a few seconds before turning away.

"Now try. Gently. Do not pump the gas."

The engine caught, ran fitfully for a few moments, then suddenly backfired and gave up.

"Once more," said Jing Yo.

The battery was starting to go. The starter whined as it tried moving the pistons without the proper voltage behind it.

"Now you can pump it," said Jing Yo. "A single tap."

Once again the engine caught, this time solidly. The driver revved it, not entirely trusting it to run on its own. Before Jing Yo could tell him to do so, he put the truck in gear and set off in the direction the others had taken. Sergeant Wu waved the other truck after him.

"Idiot peasants," said Sergeant Wu. "They've never driven. But they're the ones chosen to drive the trucks."

"Which requires more skill, Sergeant? Combat, or driving a truck?" asked Jing Yo.

"Combat, of course."

Jing Yo nodded. "And which is more difficult—fighting an enemy, or delivering supplies?"

"I can't fight without bullets. But I get your point."

Sergeant Wu reached into his pocket for his cigarettes. He shook the pack, then handed it toward Jing Yo. It was the first time he had ever offered one.

"Cigarette, Lieutenant?"

"No thank you."

Wu lit up, then took a long drag from the cigarette. He released a cloud of smoke when he exhaled.

"Brave of you, running over to grab Ai Gua out," said the sergeant. "Considering the way the trucks are rigged with explosives."

"He is my soldier. He should expect nothing less."

Sergeant Wu smiled, amused, though Jing Yo did not quite understand why. It was his duty, as an officer, to look out for his men the way a father would watch his sons.

He hadn't thought of his duty at the moment, just understood it the same way his legs understood how to walk.

"What was that thing you did with your foot?" asked the sergeant. "On the windshield."

"The kick? So we could rig it properly? The

windshield won't matter—it will be blown up in a few hours."

"You're all right, Lieutenant. You're tougher than I thought. And not as stuck-up."

Jing Yo walked over to the side of the road, examining the gouges in the earth. They would not mean anything to anyone, he decided, and could safely be left.

"Uh-oh," said Wu, reading the signal from the lookout. A minute later, Private Po came running up the road.

"Truck coming," he hissed. "Old pickup."

"We'll stop it," said Jing Yo. "We want them alive."

Jing Yo checked his uniform, then reached to his belt to undo the snap holding his pistol in its holster. Wu, rifle in hand, stood two meters away. Po trotted to the side of the road, taking up a position where he could cover the truck.

Headlights appeared in the distance. Jing Yo put up his hand.

The truck began to slow almost immediately. When he was sure it was going to stop, Jing Yo stepped to the side of the road and waited. The driver was a man of about fifty, thin, a wreath of white hair around his head. He reminded Jing Yo of the monks who had taught him as a young boy.

"Where are you going?" Jing Yo demanded in Vietnamese as the man rolled down his window.

"What is the army doing here?"

"We are on official business," said Jing Yo. "Let me see your identification."

The man frowned, then reached into his pocket.

Sergeant Wu, meanwhile, appeared on the other side of the cab.

The man handed out an ID card folded around some papers. Jing Yo opened the card and unfolded the papers, looking at them first. Two were on official letterhead; a third was handwritten.

While the lieutenant had spent several months refining his spoken Vietnamese, his reading ability lagged, and he wasn't sure precisely what the letters said. The man appeared to be a resident of Bo Sai, a village ten kilometers to the south.

Jing Yo knew it well: it was one of the checkpoints for tomorrow night's advance by the main force.

"Why are you going north?" Jing Yo asked, folding the papers.

"As the doctor's letter says. My great-aunt—"

"I'm not interested in aunts, or in sob stories," said Jing Yo sharply. "There is a curfew here. You are not to be driving."

"A curfew?"

"Do you know that you are driving in the direction of China? Our enemy?"

The man tapped his fingers on the steering wheel, apparently a nervous habit.

"I'm not going to China," he said. "My aunt lives with the hill people. She—"

"Have you been over the border recently?" asked Jing Yo sharply.

"Never."

"Have you been there in the last few days?"

"I told you. Never."

Sergeant Wu pulled open the passenger door. For a moment, Jing Yo thought he was going to grab the man; then he realized he was only opening the glove compartment.

The man reached to stop him. Jing Yo grabbed his shoulder.

"Your business is with me," Jing Yo said. "Why are you driving to China?"

"I am not going to China, comrade," said the man. Finally, he was scared. The color drained from his face. His fingers, rather than tapping, were now dancing in a nervous tremor. "My aunt is very sick. She is important to our family. She—"

"Nothing," said Wu, snapping the glove compartment closed.

Wu's Vietnamese was limited, but his accent and tones, especially in very short bursts, were excellent. His brooding manner was a perfect complement, signaling to any who heard him that it would be unwise to question him.

"I have nothing for you," said the driver, turning back to Jing Yo. "But you must be hungry. There will be food in the village. It is just two kilometers ahead."

"You are not going there tonight. Turn around and go back. Move now."

"But—"

"The army has closed the road. And it will be closed until further notice. Tell your friends and neighbors. But do it tomorrow. Tonight there is a curfew, and anyone who violates it will be shot."

The man pushed the truck into reverse, then backed down the road about twenty meters before making a three-point turn.

"I knew you weren't going to kill him," said Sergeant Wu as the taillights disappeared around the bend. "Just like you wouldn't have killed that man last night."

"Why is that?" said Jing Yo coldly.

"Fan thought it was because you were a coward."

Jing Yo couldn't keep himself from smiling.

"But I see it has to do with your superstitions," said Wu. "You're not a coward, Lieutenant. I'm glad of that."

"Which superstitions?"

"Religion, superstitions—it's your kung fu, right? The dance with your leg."

"Do you know a lot about kung fu, Sergeant?"

Sergeant Wu shook his head.

"I do not kill if it is unnecessary," said Jing Yo. "Nor if the death does not serve some higher purpose. I let him go because he will serve us."

"How does he help us?"

"He will tell everyone he meets tomorrow that he encountered Vietnamese soldiers on the highway leading to China. The word of a plain man is worth ten times the promise of a politician."

Sergeant Wu nodded, and went to check on the men.

* * *

When he was positive that the trucks had gone without leaving stragglers or sentries, Josh pushed himself backward and sat in a little hollow amid the brush. What did the trucks mean? he asked himself. Vietnamese army trucks driving out of China, on a back road without their lights in the dead of night—why?

The two countries were not precisely enemies, but Josh knew from the precursory briefing the U.S. State Department envoy had given him before he left on the trip that they were certainly not friends. Even the two debates he'd witnessed at the UN, theoretically focused on allocating money for the scientific expedition he had joined, had made the tensions clear. Enmity between China and all of its neighbors, with the sometime exception of Russia, had grown exponentially since the dramatic upturn in global climate change.

Something was going on, or maybe there was more to the squabbling than met the eye.

Did this have anything to do with the massacres?

The questions were overwhelming. He couldn't answer them. The important thing at the moment was that he didn't know and couldn't know what the situation was. And therefore, he couldn't trust either the Vietnamese or the Chinese. He couldn't trust anyone. He had to depend on himself.

That was the lesson he had learned as a child. He had to go into survival mode. No more panic—use logic to get himself out of this. Logic. A scientist's tool.

Josh took a deep breath. He had to go south, away from the border, and away from the people who were after him. Eventually, he would find a village where he could find transportation. He would make his way to Hanoi, to the U.S. embassy.

Without help from the Vietnamese authorities. Maybe with no one's help.

Plan made, he leaned to the side and rose, unfolding his frame upward. As the blood rushed from his head, he felt slightly faint. *A by-product of hunger*, he told himself—the potatoes had been less than nutritious.

Josh pushed the low bushes near the tree and stepped out into the dirt road. He could follow it, as long as he was careful. It was his only choice, really—walking in the jungle at night was difficult and time consuming, not to mention dangerous. And he had to travel at night, at least until he figured out what was going on.

He'd hide himself and sleep during the day.

For the first hour as he walked, Josh kept his mind busy by reviewing the route they'd taken to get to the camp, trying to remember different landmarks along the way. But it was difficult to do that while still paying attention to the road and nearby jungle. Eventually, his thoughts drifted away, and his mind filled with the details of what was around him, the smells, the sounds, the shadows of the trees rising on both sides of him, funneling him onward.

Fatigue settled against him in long, modulating

waves; his thighs would feel battered for a while, and lifting them would be almost impossible. He would drag them through the dust for a hundred yards or so, until gradually the fatigue dissipated. They would seem lighter; within a few paces he would be walking normally again—not sprinting along by any means, but making steady progress. Then his shoulders would feel tired, and his eyes. The process would repeat, each part of him taking its own turn at being tired.

After about two hours, Josh's left calf cramped terribly. He stopped and tried kneading it out with his hand, pressing his thumb firmly against the knot just below the muscle's crown. But the cramp grew as if it were a contagious disease. His whole lower leg began to spasm, the muscles in his sole and arch freezing in a jagged tangle of pain.

He knew the cure—he simply had to relax his muscles and the pain would go away. But relaxing was the most difficult thing in the world to do just then; climbing Mount Everest barefoot and without oxygen would have been easier.

It was amazing how much pain the muscles managed to generate. His foot and leg felt as if they were tearing themselves in half. *How much worse would it be if I'd been shot?* Josh asked himself.

The question did nothing to help him relax. The despair he'd chased earlier began to creep back, stealing around him like a fog in late fall. He lowered himself to the ground, flat on his back at the side of the road, eyes closed, willing his muscles to loosen.

As he lay there, trying not to writhe, Josh heard a sound rising over the buzz and peep of the insects. It was a mechanical sound, an engine.

The trucks, he thought, *farther ahead.*

Then he heard something else, not mechanical, something moving at the edge of the road, sideswiping brush. It was only for a moment, but the sound put him back on alert, and gave his mind something else to concentrate on. Its subconscious grapple with his leg muscles eased ever so slightly; Josh held his breath and pushed himself off the road and back into the jungle.

Footsteps approached. Men were walking a few yards away, coming up the road, talking.

He lay in the bushes, trying not to breathe. The men continued by, walking north on the road about twenty more yards before stopping. They spoke in low whispers. Josh couldn't have understood what they were saying in any event, but their voices gave him something to concentrate on. He listened as they turned and started walking back toward him, then past again.

They'd been gone a good seven or eight minutes before he sat back upright. He'd have to stay off the road, he decided, at least for a while. The jungle was comparatively sparse here, easier to move through than what he'd passed earlier in the day.

Though no longer cramped, his leg remained stiff as he slipped through the jungle, pushing the brush away branch by branch. He moved uphill, passing through a stand of waist-high ferns turned silver by the moonlight angling down through the gaps in the trees. Despite the slope, the ground was soggy; an underground stream pooled up nearby, running off toward the road.

The wet ground made a sucking noise as he lifted his boots. He had to walk ever slower to keep quiet.

Finally he managed to get beyond the pool, tracking almost due west, walking away from where he thought the road was. But soon the sounds of the trucks he'd heard were closer, straight ahead—the road, he realized as he stopped and listened, must join with the highway here.

There weren't many highways in this part of Vietnam, and Josh thought this must be the same road the expedition had camped along. If that was true, he could simply follow it and find his way back. It would be a long journey, but doable.

The small burst of optimism faded quickly as he heard voices ahead. They were shouting and arguing.

Josh got down, hiding behind the trees. *If it's my time*, he told himself, *I won't go like a coward. I won't beg for my life.*

A truck engine revved. There were more shouts. Then he heard vehicles moving away.

Finally, with the sound gone, the jungle seemed to move back in as it left, as though the insects and animals had been waiting for the humans to leave.

I'm safe now, Josh thought to himself. *Whoever they were, they're gone.*

I'm safe now. For a little while at least.

That was the last conscious thought he had for several hours, as he slipped off to sleep while sitting against the trees.

15

Beijing, China

Premier Cho Lai folded his arms. Vietnam lay before him, its lush, fertile valleys marked prominently on the large map spread over his desk.

Many centuries had passed since the land had been a Chinese kingdom. Soon it would be one again.

Vietnam's oil, located mostly in the southern coastal waters, would be an immediate prize. Even more important were their rice paddies and fields, so lately favored by the weather. But what Cho Lai truly craved was the accomplishment of cutting down the haughty Vietnamese, leaving them groveling at his feet.

Just a month before, they had rejected the Chinese premier's proposal of a mutual economic zone, an arrangement that, while tilted in China's favor, would have been far better for them and their people than war.

Idiots.

Taking Vietnam would not be difficult. The army had studied the possibilities for years, modeling their present plan partly on America's burst through Iraq in 2003.

The occupation, of course, would be different. The Americans had foolishly tried to use a light hand, where nothing but an iron fist would do the job. That, too, would be easy—anyone who did not like China's benevolent rule could leave the country. As a corpse.

The trick would be keeping the rest of the world on his side long enough to at least prevent a military backlash. China's investments in Europe, the Third World, and most especially the United States were a powerful argument for them not to interfere. But Cho Lai knew blackmail would not suffice. Weak as they were, the Westerners needed to feel as if they were doing the right thing.

Hence tonight's operation. The world would soon be convinced, and remain convinced, that he was acting righteously.

And after that—Japan. Korea. The rest of Indochina. Malaysia would finally be dealt with openly. The Philippines. He'd leave Australia—it was a dowdy, useless country.

The deal Vietnam had rejected would be offered to each of them. They would see the wisdom of agreeing. Or be crushed. And then Cho Lai would be free to concentrate on his real goal: America.

There was a delicious irony in starting here, in Vietnam. He would succeed where the Americans had failed. It would be the first thing historians would notice when they wrote of his exploits in a thousand years.

The premier looked up from the map. His generals stared at him, waiting.

"Give the order to proceed," he said. "And do it quickly, exactly as we have planned."

16

Hanoi

Mara took a nap at the minihotel she'd called Bangkok from, then went back to the Star to shower. As she toweled off she checked the TV and the Internet connection. There was nothing on China, and the only hint she could find on the Google News Asian page—heavily censored, not just in Vietnam but throughout Asia—was a story from China quoting the premier on "outside aggressors," but not mentioning Vietnam specifically.

It was still too early to get breakfast at the Star buffet, or at any restaurant catering to foreigners for that matter. A few blocks from the hotel, Mara found a man with a small cart of breakfast items; better-off locals would stop there on their way to work.

She waited her turn amid the small cluster of men, smiling but politely insisting that they take their turn instead of letting her jump ahead. She wasn't just being polite; she was mentally practicing her Vietnamese.

When it was finally her turn, she repeated what the man before her had ordered. Her pronunciation was a bit stiff, and when the man asked her to repeat what she wanted, Mara simply pointed. She got a piece of meat tucked into a half roll of freshly baked French bread.

The meat looked like chicken but tasted gamy, over-whelming the jamlike sweet sauce spread like mayonnaise around it. Maybe it hadn't been her pronunciation that bothered the vendor, but her choice of food.

Mara walked halfway down the block, then dumped the meat into the gutter. Then she began looking for a taxi.

"Airport?" she asked when she finally flagged one down.

The man looked puzzled.

"*San bay,*" she said in Vietnamese. "I need to go to the airport."

"Yes, airport. I understand," said the man, speaking in English. "But—bags?"

"I have business there," she told him, getting in.

As they drove, Mara opened her pocketbook and took out one of the "clean" SIM cards she'd brought. She pried it into her cell phone and tried calling the scientist again. Once again she got his voice mail.

The UN agency that had sponsored the expedition was located in Brussels. Mara called the liaison officer there, claiming to be a relative trying to get in touch with the scientist. The man who answered had heard nothing from the expedition for more than two weeks. This wasn't unusual, and he gave her the name and number of a Vietnamese government official who was supposed to be in contact with the scientists.

It was still two hours before the government offices would officially open, and though she tried the number, Mara wasn't surprised when the official didn't answer his phone. He didn't have voice mail.

If Fleming was simply a day behind schedule, he'd expect to meet her at the restaurant tonight. In the meantime, she was going to go look for him—and see what was going on up near the Chinese border.

Assuming she could find a way to get up there. Driving would take too long. The distance itself wasn't that far—roughly three hundred kilometers as the bird flew—but the roads were winding and notoriously bad; even with a skilled driver leaving at first light it could easily take all day just to go one way.

Flying was a much better option, but it was bound to be difficult. While Vietnam was no longer the strictly run authoritarian state it had once been, renting a plane or helicopter was still not an easy task. The first problem was language. Generally, this could be overcome by enough money, but while Mara practically cleared out an ATM inside the airport terminal, the thick wad of bills she flashed in front of the man inside the office of Pearl Air Surveying seemed only to confuse him.

"I'm looking for a scientific expedition," she told him, speaking as slowly and as clearly as she could. "They may be in trouble. No one has heard from them. They're west of Sapa."

The man shook his head. "No fly."

"Why?" she asked.

He shrugged instead of answering. If he'd been ordered not to by the Vietnamese, this would be an important piece of information—a possible confirmation of the Chinese charges.

"Please," said Mara, pressing. "They may be in great trouble. I need to get there. Isn't this enough money?"

The man shrugged.

"Do you speak French?" she asked. *"Parlez-vous français?"*

Her own French wasn't that good, and she felt almost relieved when he didn't react to the words.

"Maybe Chinese?" Mara suggested.

"The problem isn't the language."

Mara turned around. A short, dark-skinned man dressed in mechanic's coveralls leaned against the wall near the door, arms folded.

"What's the problem then?" she asked.

"Too far for a helicopter. At least any of the helicopters you could get here."

"It's only three hundred kilometers."

"You have to factor in the altitude. And the linger time."

"Can't it refuel?"

"Not out there. There's also the red tape."

He pushed off from the wall and started speaking in Vietnamese to the man behind the desk. The other man responded in a quick, almost nervous voice, speaking so quickly that Mara had no chance to decipher what he said. She watched the mechanic talk—clearly he had some sort of solution in mind.

But he wasn't going to share it in front of the other man.

"No," he told her finally. "It's not possible with these helicopters. The range is too far."

"Where can I go to find one that has the proper range?" she asked.

"You can't."

"I need to find them," she insisted.

"How badly?"

"Badly."

Their eyes met.

"Twenty thousand, U.S."

Mara laughed. "Not *that* badly."

The mechanic folded his arms.

"Five hundred dollars," she said.

"Five hundred won't even pay for the fuel."

"It will pay for the aircraft as well as the fuel."

"In your dreams. All you Americans think we're stupid. The Vietnamese are poor, so they must be stupid." The man's English had a slightly British accent. Mara guessed it originated in Hong Kong.

"I don't think that. But not all Americans are rich, as many Vietnamese seem to think," she told him. "I can pay you five hundred. Plus fuel. With a card."

"A thousand in cash. With fuel. Plus the landing fee and lunch."

"And lunch. If we're back in time."

"We buy it and eat in the plane."

The man's name was Ky Kieu, and though he was Vietnamese, his grandfather had been an American soldier who abandoned his child—or probably never even knew he had one—after the war. Kieu's father had grown up on the streets, but had managed to save enough money—Kieu didn't say how—to send his son to Hong Kong and Australia, where he learned to fix airplanes.

Most important as far as Mara was concerned, he was a pilot and owned an aircraft—though not the type Mara thought.

"That's not a helicopter," she said when he led her out to the parking area beyond the passenger hangars.

"I explained that a helicopter hasn't the range."

"It's a biplane."

"So?"

"A biplane?"

"It can do just about anything you would want a helicopter to do, except hover. The fact that it's a biplane makes it maneuverable. I can land on a road if I want. If you want to pick up your party, they'll fit. And you're unlikely to find another private aircraft in Hanoi. Your CIA friends generally have to travel to Saigon to lease one."

Mara's expression must have remained doubtful, since he added that there was no other way to get where she wanted to go except by truck.

"It's sturdier than it looks," he said, pounding his fist against the side of the aircraft. "It's been around."

The plane was a Chinese-made Yunshuji-5, a license-made copy of the Russian PZL Mielec An-2 Colt older than its owner. A fat engine sat at its nose, fronting a two-level, fully enclosed cabin. A dozen people could crowd into the passenger space, and the plane could carry roughly five thousand pounds, not quite in the range of a small, two-engined, commercial turboprop, but close.

The cockpit looked as if it hadn't been altered since the day it rolled off the line. The black paint on the metal control panel had been worn down to steel gray in all but a few spots.

"How old is this plane?" Mara asked as she sat in the copilot's seat.

"Age isn't important."

"Do you even have radar?"

"Would it make a difference? Sit for a minute. We have to taxi over for fuel. There's a food stall behind the fuel farm where you can buy our lunch."

The Colt vibrated like an unbalanced washing machine. Its engine missed badly on the way over to the fueling area.

"You sure this thing is going to make it?" Mara asked Kieu.

"It's fine."

"It's running rough."

"It always does in the morning."

The pilot didn't seem to be making a joke. Mara climbed down off the wing, nearly losing her balance because of the wash from the prop. She found the food stall behind an abandoned aircraft tug on the other side of the tank area. An irregular circle of white plastic picnic chairs circled a woman squatting between two large baskets and a pair of hibachi charcoal grills. The woman spoke no English, but Mara's Vietnamese and a little bit of pointing did the job. She fished noodles from a pot, and what looked like potatoes from one of the baskets, placing them in a pair of boxes. Then she added some fried fish and a tangle of greens.

"*Cha ca*," said Kieu when she returned to the plane, which was still being fueled. "Good choice. We eat now. Maybe later we don't have a chance."

"Listen, for real—is this airplane going to make it?"

"Do you think I'd go if it didn't? We don't have parachutes. If you die, I die."

The engine settled down with the full tank of fuel. It roared as Kieu brought it up to takeoff power, pushing from the patchwork concrete at the edge of the ramp to the main runway as soon as he got clearance. It rose immediately, the doubled wings eager to get into the air.

Sapa was a little less than three hundred kilometers away; the Colt cruised around 185 kilometers an hour, or roughly a hundred knots—the speed some planes landed at.

It looked like a handful to fly. The plane was unpressurized, but they stayed relatively low, skimming over the city, rice paddies, and eventually the jungle at a few hundred feet.

"When we get closer, you'll need to wear the mask," the pilot told her after they'd been in the air for a while. Kieu hadn't given her a headset. He had to shout to make himself heard over the engine. "In the mountains. I'll tell you when."

"Is it safe?"

"Plenty safe. Just high. Even in the valleys."

"All right."

"So, why is the CIA interested in scientists?"

She'd let the first reference go as if she hadn't heard it, but now felt compelled to reply.

"I'm not a spy. I'm a journalist. I'm doing a story on the expedition."

Kieu laughed. "You expect me to believe that?"

"I don't care what you believe," said Mara.

"All Americans in Vietnam are spies," said Kieu.

"You don't honestly believe that."

"The government does. And maybe I am a spy myself."

"Maybe you are."

People were always accusing Americans in Asia of being spies. Mara knew from experience that if she offered a reasonable alternative, most people would accept it at face value, repeating it to the authorities if asked. What they truly believed was another story, of course. For some, thinking that they were working with a spy was attractive—they liked the idea of danger, even if it was far removed from reality.

"What are these scientists doing? Looking for more oil?" asked Kieu.

"They're studying climate change."

"Ha! They should cool the sun if they want to be useful."

"I'm sure they would if they could."

"It's always been hot in Vietnam. My grandfather sweated the minute he got off the plane, and he landed in December."

"You're in touch with your grandfather?"

"We've met. It's always hot in Vietnam," he repeated,

changing the subject. "Today is very much like last year, and the year before."

"The average daily temperature in Hanoi was three degrees hotter last year than it was five years ago," she said. Though no expert on climate change, Mara had heard the statistics so many times she knew them by heart.

"Three degrees. Nothing."

"That's for the entire year. A change like that is huge. The changes in the extremes have been even more dramatic. And Vietnam is one of the lucky ones. The changes here haven't been catastrophic. They've helped your country, on the whole."

Kieu waved his hand. "The heat means nothing. Weather, that's all."

"You don't think the climate has changed?"

"Nah. Superstition. Like the old people's warts, and burning incense to pray for rain. It doesn't pay to worry about things we can't control," he added. "Time to put the oxygen on."

There were two large canisters, each with its own separate hose and mask. The flow tickled her nose and upper lip. Kieu showed her how to adjust it, easing the gas until it was almost natural.

Mara had marked out the camp's location on a printed map, having transposed it from the satellite data Lucas had given her before she left. Kieu took the map from his clipboard, examining it closely.

"Very close to the border," he said.

"You told me that before."

"Still, very close to the border."

"Problem?"

"Not today."

A few minutes after they began using the oxygen, Kieu banked the aircraft over a road that cut along the bottom of a valley, paralleling what looked like a narrow stream. Ten minutes later, he turned sharply west, climbing up the side of the hill. The aircraft hugged the treetops; from Mara's vantage it looked as if they were barely clearing the upper branches.

They flew slower and slower as they climbed, until finally it seemed as if they were standing still. Finally, Kieu pitched the nose down and they picked up so much speed so quickly that Mara's stomach seemed to shoot into her mouth. Kieu stared intently out the front of the plane, holding the yoke tightly as they pitched down into another valley. He consulted the map again, frowned, then turned northward.

"Almost there," he grunted.

Mara looked at the road below. From the air, it seemed to twist violently; she wondered if what he'd promised about being able to land was true.

"We're within four or five klicks," said Kieu. He pointed ahead. "The border is there somewhere, eight, ten kilometers from us. The camp should be on the right side, about midway down the wing as we come over."

Mara reached below the seat for Kieu's binoculars. They flew northward very slowly, following the road. As they approached the border—the fence itself was hard to see because of the jungle—the glare of a reflection hit her eyes.

She pulled the glasses up to get a look at the car or truck the light had reflected off. But instead of seeing one vehicle, she saw an entire line of them—troop transports, old ZiLs, the Vietnamese equivalent of American two-and-a-half-ton trucks. There were a dozen lined up on the road within spitting distance of the border checkpoint.

"What's going on down there?"

"I don't know. That's weird."

The terrain was rising to meet them, taking them gradually toward the vehicles. The pilot angled the plane to the right, flying toward the camp.

"It looks like there was a fire," said Mara, adjusting the glasses. She could see a campsite, or maybe the remains of one, black blotches in a haphazard circle.

The trucks straddled the border area, some in China, some in Vietnam. Several had crashed into the fence. All seemed to have been destroyed or disabled.

Kieu banked northward again. Smoke rose from beyond the fence. A long gray cloud furrowed in a long line.

Not smoke—dust.

The troop movements.

"Get closer to the border," Mara told Kieu as he turned south again. "Something is going on."

"Something is very strange," said Kieu. Then he said something in Vietnamese, a loud curse word.

As Mara turned to him, something rattled through

the floorboard. It sounded like bolts springing upward. Only as the plane pitched on its wing did she realize it was a spray of bullets. They were under fire.

Worse. They'd been hit.

MORE INDIAN CITIES ABANDONED

MUMBAI, INDIA (World News Service)—India reported today that a further two hundred square miles of countryside east of Jaipur would be abandoned due to the continuing water shortages there. The largest affected city in the region is Phulera.

As recently as 2009, Phulera boasted a population of roughly 25,000. Nearly a decade of drought, however, had provoked an exodus that left it a virtual shell of its former self. Like many towns in the Indian state of Rajasthan, it has been all but abandoned for the past two years.

Scientists warned that Jaipur will be next. Despite widespread emigration from the area, the city remains home to approximately eight hundred thousand people, many of whom fled homes in the countryside over the past four or five years. Jaipur once supported a population above 3.2 million.

"What we are seeing here is a continuing human crisis," said Kumar Singh, chief scientist for the India Drought Project, a nonprofit scientific group that has monitored India's water shortage and its effect on population since 2005. "Last year, an estimated two and a half million people died because of the water shortages and the famines they caused," he added. "This year, the toll will be even worse."

In the capital, meanwhile, opposition party leaders attempted to blame some of the country's woes on the failure of the prime minister to provide adequate . . .

FAMILY FARM EXPANDS AGAIN

WARWICK, N.Y. (AP–Fox News)—Robert Fleming spent the afternoon plowing his father's living room for a fresh corn crop.

Actually, he plowed his old friend Peter Belding's living room as well. Along with the rest of what had once been the Beldings' house and yard. In all, he plowed the lots along Meadow Avenue that been filled with houses, garages, and pools just a year or two before.

It's become a common occurrence in upstate New York, where the dramatic increase in food prices, coupled with the depressed housing market, have fueled a move to change former suburbs back to rural farmland. While in most areas the changes haven't been quite as dramatic—farmers generally plant around existing houses—in some older communities, the age of the buildings has made it economical to replace them with farmland completely.

"I really took pleasure plowing over Agnes Blanchard's yard," said Fleming. "She used to yell at us every time our football landed there."

Blanchard lost her house to foreclosure in 2009. The building had been vacant ever since.

FORD ANNOUNCES 90-MILES-PER-GALLON HYBRID

HOT ON the heels of Toyota's Prius II, the Ford-Fiat Motor Company today announced that next year's Henry II will get up to 90 miles per gallon of gasoline in highway driving.

There is a catch, however: Top mileage will only be achieved on sunny days, when the solar-roof array will be able to fully augment the battery-and-gasoline-powered motors.

The three-wheel, two-passenger LiteCar is the successor to Ford's wildly popular Henry, first introduced in 2011. The Henry's success helped finance Ford's takeover of Fiat-Chrysler and . . .

Danger

危险

1

Northwestern Vietnam, near the border with China

The machine-gun fire that woke Josh sounded like the steady tapping of a heavy rain against a metal drum. An aircraft passed overhead, its engine a loud rasp. Josh jumped to his feet, but before he took a step to run, he remembered that he'd been very close to the trucks the night before. He lowered himself to his haunches, listening to the gun and airplane as he scanned the jungle around him.

The gun was behind him somewhere, to the north.

The airplane—he didn't hear it anymore.

Trucks were moving in the distance. More vehicles, heavy ones, coming toward him.

Lieutenant Jing Yo tightened his hand on the steel rail at the top of the Chinese ZTZ99 tank, holding on as the tank rolled down the highway, passing the last of the wrecked Vietnamese troop trucks. It was the one that had given them so much trouble after crashing the night before; now its battered fender and windshield fit right in with the rest.

An American surveillance satellite had passed over-head barely an hour before. The optical lens on its camera would have snapped a picture of the line of Vietnamese troops trucks on both sides of the border, poised there, it would seem, following an aborted in-vasion.

The satellite's orbit was common knowledge not only to intelligence agencies but to a small commu-nity of Internet geeks, several of whom would soon be pressing the Americans to release what they knew as rumors of the battle spread. It was all part of the campaign to make China's invasion of its neighbor look justified—or at least justifiable enough to keep others from stepping in.

Jing Yo couldn't have cared less for the international politics involved, but they had nonetheless dictated the schedule of the day's operation. For the drive south had had to wait for the satellite to pass—proper public relations demanded clear and easily discernible "proof." A snapshot of Chinese tanks rushing past the alleged bad guys would have made things unnecessarily com-plicated.

But the delay meant the operation was proceeding in daylight, increasing its danger. Already there had been reports of an aircraft, along with gunfire from units farther back in line.

It was now nearly noon, and it would take at least another hour for the lead elements of the brigade to reach Route 128. From there, it would be another half hour before they made Lai Châu, which sat at the intersection of Routes 127 and 12 farther south.

Lai Châu was a key objective, for there was a small force of Vietnamese soldiers there; they were likely to be China's first real test.

Jing Yo's radio buzzed. It was Colonel Sun, a kilometer or two farther behind in a command car.

"Lieutenant, what's going on up there? Are the tanks moving ahead?"

"Yes, Colonel. Good progress."

"That airplane just now. Did you see it go down?"

"We've heard gunfire but saw nothing. The tanks are so loud—"

"One of the antiaircraft units shot it down moments ago," said Sun. "Go back with your men and find it. Make sure there are no survivors."

"Colonel, if it was shot down, it's no longer a problem. And in any event, its radio would have allowed it to alert the Vietnamese. In daylight, we have no real hope of cover. If I might suggest—"

"What you would suggest is of no interest," said Sun, practically shouting into his microphone. "Do as I tell you!"

"Yes, sir."

"The air force is sending planes. I want that wreckage located so they cannot take credit for once."

The real reason for Sun's order—internal politics. Jing Yo should have guessed it.

"As you wish," he told his commander. "What are the coordinates?"

Northern Vietnam

Mara felt her stomach lurch against her ribs as the biplane pitched hard to the left, its wings shuddering under the violent pressure of the maneuver. The hillside was coming up fast.

"Pull up on the wheel," said Ky Kieu. "Pull with me!"

Mara grabbed the yoke—it looked like a small, slightly squeezed steering wheel—and tried to yank it toward her, mimicking what Ky Kieu was doing. It was like pulling the back bumper of a cement mixer—the pressure against them was immense.

"What's wrong with this?" she said.

"Pull!" yelled Ky Kieu.

Mara put her right leg up against the instrument panel, using it as leverage. The wheel barely budged. She pulled her left foot up and put it against the other side, pushing with all her might.

Treetops loomed in the windscreen.

Goddamn, she thought. *What a place to die.*

"Hold on!" yelled Kieu, adding a string of curses in Vietnamese.

The bottom of the fuselage slapped into the very top of one of the trees, which clawed at the plane like a cat raking its nails on a bird taking flight. There was a loud clunk behind them. The plane shook.

Then the sky in front of them cleared. They'd gone over the summit of the mountain.

"Now easy, easy," said Kieu. "We have to level off. Don't let go. Work with me."

"I'm working with you."

"Work with me. Easy. We turn now."

Mara wasn't sure what she was supposed to do, except not let go. She eased forward as much as she dared, which wasn't very much. The nose of the Yunshuji-5 began to come down.

My head feels light, Mara thought.

She looked down, thinking maybe she had been shot and was losing blood. Then she realized they must be so high over the mountains that the air they were breathing didn't have enough oxygen to sustain them.

She reached for the mask. The plane immediately dipped forward.

"What are you doing?" screamed Ky Kieu.

"I need to breathe," she said. She reached down and fished the mask from her lap, put it on, and opened the valve. Then she reached over to Kieu, who'd left his around his neck. He was exerting so much pressure on the yoke that his blood vessels looked as if they were going to pop.

"Breathe," she told him, opening the oxygen.

Kieu began hyperventilating into the mask. Finally his brain caught up with his body, and the breathing began to slow down, approaching something close to normal.

"We need to find a place to land," Mara told him.

"No shit, CIA."

"I'm not CIA."

Kieu said something in Vietnamese. Mara ignored him, putting her hands back on the wheel to help steady it. The plane still wanted to pitch forward, though the pressure wasn't quite as strong as earlier.

"Do you think you can hold it by yourself for a minute?" asked Kieu.

"I'll try," she said, putting her feet back up and tightening her grip.

The aircraft lurched when he let go, but she was able to keep it from plunging into a dive. In the meantime, Kieu rose and pulled off his belt. Then he rigged a harness to hold the wheel, strapping it to the seats.

"Let go," he told her.

"You sure?"

"Let go."

Mara took her hands off the wheel. Its nose slid down a degree or two, but it remained on course.

"What happened?" Mara asked. She rubbed her arms, which were starting to cramp with fatigue.

"Some of those bullets must have taken out the hydraulic control system."

"Isn't there a backup?"

"Yes—brute strength. Just like in the old days."

The bullets had also presumably chewed up the control surfaces, making even brute strength difficult to apply. Landing safely was now their only goal. Kieu unfolded Mara's map and examined it.

"There's a strip near Cham Chu," he told her. "We're on almost a direct line. But it's about a hundred and seventy-five kilometers away. Very long to fly. More than halfway to Hanoi."

"Can we make it?"

Kieu didn't answer, but evidently he didn't think so, as he continued to study the map.

"We look like we're getting a little closer to the hills," she said.

He handed her the map, then took the yoke again.

"Help adjust the belt," he told her.

They slipped the belt slightly higher and, after a little trial and error, had the plane running perfectly level.

"It's all right," Kieu told her. "We'll aim for Cham Chu. When we get close, we'll decide if we can return all the way to Hanoi."

"What if we can't make Cham Chu?"

"Then we'll look for a road or a field. We don't need too long a stretch. The farther we go, the easier it will be."

Mara decided she should call the desk in Bangkok to tell them something was going on. The trick was doing that without blowing her cover.

"I have a friend who's a pilot in Bangkok," she told Kieu. "Maybe he knows a place where we could land."

"I don't think so."

"Well, I'll call him just in case. I'm not doing anything else."

Mara took her sat phone out of her pocket and called the desk. Jesse DeBiase picked up as soon as the connection went through.

"Jess, how are you?"

"Mara I'm fine—how are you?"

"I'm looking for an airfield in northwestern Vietnam."

"Good God, girl—what have you gotten yourself into now?"

"Still trying to hunt down that scientist I told you about the other day," she said. "But you wouldn't believe what happened to us. There were trucks, and I think some sort of tanks, and they fired at us."

Mara imagined what a real journalist would say in that situation, pretending to be shocked and maybe a little naive. DeBiase caught on, prompting her with questions as if he were simply a concerned friend, while still pumping her for information.

Their conversation didn't last long. She hadn't seen all that much.

"They're over the line then, the Chinese?" asked DeBiase.

"I couldn't really say."

"You mean it's hard for you to talk, right?"

"Yeah, exactly."

"But those were Chinese vehicles firing at you."

"Probably."

"I'm going to get someone to look for an airstrip," he told her. "In the meantime—the NSA detected some radars being turned on near the border." He read from the agency's secure text communications system. "'The radar profile is generally used in searches, usually coordinated with PLA air force aircraft.' You may have company, Mara. I'll get back to you."

"Fantastic."

She pushed the sat phone back into her pocket. One consolation—whatever Fleming knew, it was largely obsolete by now. Connecting with him was no longer important.

"What did your friend say?" asked Kieu.

"He knows someone who knows someone. He's going to call back."

"Soon?"

"Pretty soon."

Kieu nodded. His face looked grimmer than before she had called.

"You want me to take over for you?" she asked.

"No. It's not too bad." He hesitated. "The problem is our fuel. We're losing some out of the tanks. I can't seem to isolate the problem. Each one must be leaking a little."

Mara raised herself in the seat and began looking at the ground for a road. But the thick jungle made it hard to see.

The sat phone buzzed. Mara was so intent on looking for a place to land that it took her a few seconds to grab it from her pocket.

"There's a town called Nam Det," said DeBiase. "Can you find it?"

"Maybe."

"You want to stay away from Lao Cai," he added as she looked. "It's right on the border. We think it will be one of the Chinese's first targets."

Mara unfolded the map and found Nam Det, a small dot in Lao Cai Province, twenty-five or thirty kilometers from the border and off the main roads.

"On the south side of the village, there's a long field. We've uh, been familiar with it in the past," DeBiase told her. "Relatively recently."

"Okay."

"The French used it right after World War II," he added. "Some OSO people took off from there in 1946 on a mission, I'm guessing to China. They used a DC-3. Whatever you're in should be able to land there."

He was telling her that so she could share it with the pilot if he had any doubts. OSO was the Office of Special Operations, the interim agency between OSS and CIA.

"I'm looking at a sat photo," said DeBiase. "There are rice paddies all around it. It stands out. There's a little hamlet next to it; Nam Det is to the north, a kilometer maybe."

"We'll try to stay out of the rice."

"We have another alert from the NSA. There are Chinese MiGs in the air. Our Air Force intel center confirms it. This is the whole shooting match here, Mara. The Chinese are going into that country."

"Great."

"Thought you'd want to know. You want me to stay on the line?"

"We can handle it from here, thanks."

Kieu turned to her as she put her phone back into her pocket.

"So?"

"My friend says there's an old field at Nam Det."

"Nam Det? Where is that?"

She showed him.

"Your friend is sure?"

"His friend was very sure. And he brought an image up on Google Earth. He says a DC-3 could land there."

"DC-3s haven't flown for fifty years," said Kieu. "What is he? Another spy?"

"I'm not a spy."

"A drug smuggler?"

Mara gripped the handhold on the cockpit's windshield pillar, peering down at the ground. According to the map they were a little under fifty kilometers away—maybe twenty minutes.

"Help me with the yoke a minute," said Kieu. "We have to adjust our course to make that airfield."

Mara put both hands back on the yoke. The aircraft didn't seem to be fighting them quite as fiercely as it had before. Kieu tipped the wings very gently, steering the plane toward a beeline for the field. When he got on the proper heading, he reset the belt and told Mara she could take a break.

"If you see anything that looks like it might be big enough to land on, straight enough, let me know," he told her.

"Sure."

"From here, it would look like about two fingers long," added Kieu. "Maybe a little less."

Nothing below looked two fingers long, let alone the occasional squiggles of red and black roads that peered through the jungle canopy. A large portion of western and northern Vietnam had been clear-cut over the past ten years, but from here the terrain looked as thick and jungle-bound as ever.

Kieu's hair, neck, and shirt were soaked with sweat. His cheeks looked as if they'd been sucked inward, and his forehead had furrowed to the point that it looked like a stairway to his scalp. He seemed to have lost about ten pounds and aged ten years in the past half hour. If the flight continues too much longer, Mara thought, he'll shrivel into an old man.

"How's the fuel look?" she asked, leaning over toward his side of the dash.

Kieu nodded back in her direction, indicating that the fuel panel was on the right side of the instrument array. She saw round dials with arrows pointing to the left, though with the symbols written in what looked like Chinese she had no idea what she was looking at.

"I'm sure we'll make it," she said.

Kieu mumbled something in Vietnamese. She didn't quite catch the words, but it didn't sound like "you bet."

"We can do it," Mara told him. "Think positive. Cut back on your speed to save gas."

"The problem is the leak, not the speed," he said. He reached over and flicked a silver switch on the panel. "We're leaking at a constant rate. I have to up the speed. That's our only hope."

"Go ahead."

"The engine is already flat out."

"Don't give up on me, Ky."

He looked at her, utter despair in his face.

"We're going to do it," she told him. "Tell me how I can help."

Mara studied him, hoping for some inspiration that might tell her how to buck up his morale—no matter how dire their situation might be, it would be that much worse if he didn't believe he could deal with it.

"Get the map and let's check our distance," he told her. "I'm going to take it lower."

It wasn't the most optimistic statement in the world, but it was a start. Mara picked up the map and found Nam Det again.

"Show me," said Kieu.

She did.

"Twenty-five kilometers," he declared. "Almost there."

"See?"

He nodded.

Suddenly, they pitched downward. A black cloud passed over the cockpit as Kieu grabbed the yoke.

Mara, recoiling in her seat, caught sight of a dagger-shaped blur crossing past the windscreen.

One of the Chinese MiGs had found them.

Northwestern Vietnam, near the border with China

Jing Yo could not divert the tanks from their primary objective, but reaching the point where the aircraft went down by foot might take an hour or more. So after taking a handful of his best men off the tanks, he waited along the side of the road as the column passed, until finally a Shaanqi SX2190 troop truck approached. Telling Sergeant Wu to block the way, Jing Yo waited by the side of the road for the truck to stop. Then he simply opened the door and got in, shoving the driver over to the empty seat beside him.

"Take the next truck, and follow me," Jing Yo yelled to Wu. The rest of the commandos split themselves into two groups, climbing into the back of the trucks, where they jammed in with a platoon's worth of regular troops.

The truck bucked as Jing Yo threw it into gear. He pulled forward, then made a U-turn, driving past the column of trucks that had stopped behind the Shaanqi.

The change in direction was too much for the unit commander, Captain Wi Lai, who had been sitting in the rear with his men as a halfhearted gesture of camaraderie. While at first cowed by the commando uniforms, now he began pounding on the bulkhead between the driver's and passengers' compartments, demanding to know what was going on.

Jing Yo turned to the driver and smiled. The man, a conscript who looked all of sixteen, didn't smile back.

Three kilometers from where he'd turned around, Jing Yo found a dried streambed that led to the east. He put the Shaanqi into low gear and turned off the highway, descending a shallow drop to the bed.

Sand and very small pebbles marked the first half kilometer or so; Jing Yo found the going easy. But gradually the pebbles gave way to rocks and the potholes in the path became larger. There was no escaping up the banks, either—trees grew on each side, and where there were no trees the boulders and exposed rock made it impossible to pass. Jing Yo steered left and right, wrangling a way through the increasingly treacherous terrain until finally, a kilometer and a half from the highway, he could go no farther.

"Everyone out, let's go," said Sergeant Wu, leaping out as his truck stopped.

By now, Captain Wi Lai was too angry for words. His round pumpkin of a face was red, and as he came out to confront Jing Yo his arms pumped up and down like pistons in a diesel engine at red line.

Jing Yo ignored him, telling Sergeant Wu to divide up the men and fan out in a search pattern.

"Who the hell are you?" sputtered the captain. "Why are you ordering my men? Where are we?"

Jing Yo stared at him for a moment before speaking. The captain was well fed, his belly hanging over his belt.

"I am Lieutenant Jing Yo with the Special Squad. We are looking for an enemy aircraft that has been shot down. It is a crucial mission. You will help us."

"You are a *lieutenant*?"

"I'm with the Special Squad," repeated Jing Yo. "The commandos." He took out his satellite phone, in effect dismissing the captain.

"I don't care if you are with the premier's body-guard," shouted Captain Wi Lai. "You are a *lieutenant*. I am a captain. I have an entire company to care for. The rest of my men—"

"If you care to take it up with my superior, I will let you talk to him when we are done," said Jing Yo.

Sun's communications aide answered the call. There had been no new information on the aircraft; two gunners swore they had seen it crash exactly one kilometer from where Jing Yo was calling from.

A jet boomed in the distance. The air force was closing in. Sun would not be happy if they got there soon enough to somehow take credit for shooting down the plane.

He glanced up and saw the regular army captain glaring at him.

"I have a captain who wishes to talk to Colonel Sun," Jing Yo told the aide. "I borrowed one of his pla-toons and two vehicles. They will be useful in the search."

Captain Wi Lai grabbed the phone and began an-grily demanding to speak to the colonel, complaining that he needed to keep his company intact. He was cut off in midsentence. Jing Yo heard the aide tell him that for the duration of the operation, Lieutenant Jing Yo was in charge and authorized to use his squad as he saw fit.

Still not satisfied—and apparently not smart enough to keep his mouth shut—the captain began to bluster again, demanding to know whom he was speaking to.

"Sergeant Lanna," came the reply. And then Lanna hung up.

"Lieutenants giving captains orders? Sergeants approving it? The army has gone crazy."

Jing Yo took the phone from the captain.

"It will not be painful for you, Captain. If your squad does good work, you will certainly be rewarded. Best to accept reality."

Jing Yo began walking up the streambed. It was not the first time he had seen a regular army officer confront the realities of army politics and the commandos' place in the unwritten order of battle, but usually such confrontations were not as satisfying as this one.

J osh leaned on the fallen tree trunk, watching as the trucks continued to pass. He had kept count in the beginning, more in amazement than with a purpose. He'd never seen battle tanks before, and was amazed not only by how many there were, but at how fast they were able to drive on the road.

He stopped counting when he reached thirty. The tanks gave way to troop and supply trucks, then were replaced by more tanks. He estimated that at least 150 vehicles had gone down the highway in the past half hour, and the procession didn't seem likely to end anytime soon.

The vehicles had characters and small red stars on their sides; some had Chinese flags. The Chinese were invading Vietnam.

This is what a war looks like, Josh told himself. No big set-piece battles, no arrows on a map, no roving video cameras and super-serious television announcers—just vehicles rushing by, machine guns in the distance, soldiers chasing you through the woods.

The Chinese were invading Vietnam. It was the start of World War III. And he had a ringside seat.

Northern Vietnam

Mara grabbed the plane's yoke, trying to help Kieu pull back to climb.

Except that's not what he wanted to do.

"No, we're diving. Push," Kieu told her. "We get low. His radar will not be able to see us. Low."

Mara leaned forward, going with him. The airplane zipped downward, a direction it seemed enthusiastic about trying.

"Look for the airstrip," Kieu said. "It should be close. Or another place to land."

As Mara raised her head, a swarm of bees flew in

front of the windscreen, moving so close together that they looked like inky water coming from a hose. They flashed red as they passed; only then did she realized she was looking at cannon fire.

Her head began to float as Kieu dipped the plane hard onto its right wing.

"Hold on, hold on!" yelled the pilot.

The aircraft began to buck. Mara thought they'd been hit. She started trying to think of the best way to hold her body when they crashed.

"Where's that field?" Kieu yelled. "I can't see it!"

Mara pushed up in her seat. The ground was a blur filling the right side of her window. The left side of the window was blue.

"Steer the plane!" she said.

"I have the plane. I need a place to land."

There was a hole in the trees in the right corner of the window.

"There—try there," yelled Mara, pointing to it.

The plane dropped nearly straight down for a few seconds, then leveled off. She struggled to relocate it, finally spotting it much farther to the left.

The hole was black—a pond, not a field.

"It's water," she told him.

"It'll have to do," said Kieu.

He let the nose slip down again, then pulled up so abruptly that the plane seemed to stutter in the air. Mara took the hand grip with both hands, straining once more to see the terrain. A shadow passed across the trees on the left, cast by the MiG that was pursuing them.

"I think there's a village—wait—can you turn right? Turn right!"

Once more, the plane pitched on its wing. This time, Kieu misjudged either the maneuver or his ability to hold it; the wing spun around and the plane went into an invert, twirling upside down. It began in slow motion, then sped as the yaw turned into something dangerously close to a spin.

By now they were barely a thousand feet above the ground, and Kieu had almost no room to recover..The biplane slid sideways through the air, a hockey puck gliding on ice. As it came over through the invert, Kieu managed to get it level.

Mara, her brain scrambled, threw her hand out against the windscreen.

And there was the field, right next to her thumb.

"The field is there on the right," she told Kieu. "Get us there."

"Okay, Okay. Hold on," the pilot said, though he didn't alter course.

Either thinking the biplane was going to crash or simply not realizing that Kieu would try to land, the pilot in the MiG pursuing them took a lazy turn above.

"Hold on!" yelled Kieu once more, and then he pushed the nose forward, setting up for his landing. But almost immediately he began to curse. The stick pulled and jerked, as if trying to wrestle itself out of his hands. Mara closed her eyes for a second, then decided she didn't want to go out that way, if that's what was going to happen. She bolted upright, facing reality with eyes wide open.

The ground, now mere yards away, was coming at them a lot faster than she had thought possible.

The biplane vibrated madly even before its wheels hit the ground. The first touch sent it bolting back upward. Kieu settled her down, holding the aircraft in a straight line as it ran down the old landing strip. He jammed the brakes. Dust flew everywhere. Pebbles and little rocks spit up so violently against the fuselage that Mara was sure they were being fired at from the air. But the MiG was moving too fast to get a shot in, and passed harmlessly overhead as Kieu finally got the plane to stop about three-quarters of the way down the field.

"I knew you could do it," Mara said.

"Out! We have to get out!" yelled Kieu. He undid his seat restraints and leapt up, running through the cabin to the door.

Mara followed. Kieu waited by the door; when he saw her, he threw the lever and pushed it open.

"Go!" he yelled, pushing her ahead of him.

Mara jumped to the ground. The MiG was starting a run above.

"The trees!" she shouted at him, then bolted forward, running on a diagonal toward the ditch at the end of the field about fifty meters away.

The Chinese fighter began to fire its cannon just as they got there. The 23 mm slugs hit the ground with a thick thud, chewing up the hard-packed dirt like a road cutter drumming through asphalt. Mara jumped on her rump and slid down into the ditch, huddling against the side as Kieu came down facefirst.

The MiG flashed by.

Mara help Kieu get to his feet.

"What did you do to my plane?" he said. "Why are they shooting at me?"

"I didn't do anything. It's the Chinese."

"Look at my plane!" A look of shock come to Kieu's face. He seemed a different man. "I have to save it."

He started toward the airplane before Mara could grab him. She scrambled up the slope, chasing after him as the MiG began another run. Mara lunged just as the Chinese fighter began to fire, catching Kieu by the back of his legs in an open-field tackle that would have done an NFL free safety proud.

The air above them seemed to break in two: one of the tracers had found the biplane's fuel tank, igniting the remaining fuel and vapors. The burst sent a fireball ricocheting upward from the plane, propelling the nose forward as shrapnel flew through the air.

"We have to get out of here," said Mara, getting to her feet and dragging Kieu backward to the ditch.

Blood seeped across the back of his shirt. He began to moan.

Mara reached the ditch, slid down, then tried to hoist Kieu onto her back so she could carry him into the jungle, where they'd be less of a target. But though Kieu was shorter and lighter than most men, and Mara was bigger and stronger than most women, she couldn't get enough leverage to hoist him; she had to duck down and practically wrap him around her upper body before she had a good enough grip to move.

By then, the MiG had banked again. Mara felt the ground start to shake. She ran for a few more yards, then felt Kieu starting to slip. She tried to keep him on her back by going down to her knees, but she stumbled. Her right arm scraped hard against the rocks as she sprawled forward, but she still managed to keep the pilot on top of her.

The MiG passed, rising nearly straight up as it went. Mara pushed back to her feet and staggered a few yards, gaining momentum. The ditch opened into a shallow field on her left; Mara picked up speed as she ran through it, finally reaching the trees and safety.

She let Kieu down off her back slowly. He collapsed like a half-filled sack of potatoes.

"Don't fuckin' die on me," she said, clawing at the back of his shirt to check his wounds.

Blood oozed from two spots. One was below his left shoulder, where it seemed to be just easing out, almost by osmosis. The other pulsed in a small rivulet on the left side of his neck.

Mara ripped his shirt off and wadded it against his neck, pushing as hard as she could.

"Come on, come on," she told him. "Stop bleeding."

Kieu groaned. She took that as a good sign. But when she tried slipping the shirt away a short time later, blood quickly began to ooze out.

Mara twisted her body around so she could apply pressure with her knee and free her hands temporarily. Then she pulled off the rest of Kieu's shirt. She tied it around his neck as a bandage, applying what she hoped was enough pressure to stanch the flow, but not quite enough to choke him.

The bleeding slowed, and he continued to breathe, though the breaths were shallow. Mara shifted her position around, keeping pressure on the wound with her hand while taking her sat phone from her pocket.

DeBiase picked up as soon as the call went through.

"How are you, Mara?" he asked, his usual jaunty tone replaced by a somber seriousness that seemed almost foreign.

"I'm okay. My pilot was hit by shrapnel. We're at Nam Det."

"What kind of shape is your plane in—"

"Pieces. A MiG caught us and destroyed it on the ground. Maybe he was mad that we got away."

"What kind of MiG?"

"I don't know. I don't even know if it was a MiG," confessed Mara. "Is that important?"

"It's all right. Whatever details you can remember, that's all right. If you can't, it's not a problem."

DeBiase was gathering intelligence, thinking about the bulletins he was going to send back to the States—bulletins he might even be sending as they spoke.

She was just thinking of dumb little things, like saving her neck.

"Did he fire missiles?" DeBiase asked.

"No. Machine gun or a cannon."

"Okay. How many planes?"

"One."

"Usually they work in pairs."

"I only saw one, Jess."

"Relax."

"Don't tell me to relax."

"Listen, Mara. I've been in difficult situations myself. I can tell you from experience—"

Mara didn't hear the rest of what DeBiase said, not because it was a lecture about staying calm that she didn't particularly need right now, but because when she looked up in exasperation, she saw four cone-hatted Vietnamese villagers staring down at her from the embankment.

"*Xin châo!*" she said. "Hello."

They didn't answer. She tried thinking of the word for help, but couldn't remember it.

"*Ông, có biết iếng Anh không?*" she said, addressing the oldest man and asking if he could speak English. That, too, brought only stares.

"He's hurt," she said in English, gesturing to Kieu. "*Cáp cúu. Cúu hòa.*"

They didn't move.

"Mara?" said DeBiase.

"There are four Vietnamese farmers, I guess, standing here looking at me."

"You used the word for fire brigade," said DeBiase. "Tell them you need an ambulance. *Xe cáp cú.*"

"You really think they have ambulances out here?" she told him. But she repeated the words.

"Put me on with them," he said. "My Vietnamese is better than yours."

Mara held up the phone and gestured for them to take it. Instead, the men began talking to themselves. Then the youngest turned and began trotting away.

"Mara, what's going on?" asked DeBiase.

"I'm not sure. Stay on the line."

The three men continued to stare at her, their slack-jawed expressions similar to those Mara remembered from a photograph of people watching the collapse of the World Trade Center towers on store televisions. Behind them, Kieu's aircraft had stopped burning; the black smoke that had followed the fire had dissipated. But the burnt smell still hung so thick in the air that Mara could taste it in her mouth.

"The Chinese shot down our plane," Mara told the men. "They're invading your country."

One of the men turned to look behind him. Mara thought he had understood what she'd said, until he pointed and took a few steps away. The man who'd left a few moments ago was returning, with two teenage boys and a stretcher.

"We have to be careful," she said in Vietnamese as they ran down the slope. "Careful."

She put the phone back to her ear. "How do I say he may have a neck injury?" she asked DeBiase.

He gave her the words, then stayed on the line a few minutes more, until they had Kieu up the embankment. Worried that her battery would start to run down—the charger had been in her bag, left in the plane and presumably destroyed—Mara told DeBiase that she would check back with him in a half hour.

Hand pressed against Kieu's neck, she walked next to the stretcher as they climbed up the slope and walked south to a barely discernible path at the edge of the field. The path twisted around thick clumps of trees, the jungle growing darker and darker until it seemed as if the sun had fallen. Finally, a pair of twists brought them to a clearing; a small village was visible at the far end.

The hamlet consisted of a dozen small huts and two farm buildings. All but one of the huts were made of bamboo topped by a thatched roof. The exception was made of scrap metal and wood; some of the slats at the front had originally come from vegetable boxes and still had markings on them. The farm buildings were made of corrugated steel. Yellowish red rust extended in small daggers from most of the screws and bolts holding them together; the roofs' white coating was peeling, and large flakes fluttered in the soft breeze.

They took Kieu to a thatched hut at the very entrance to the settlement. The interior was larger than Mara had expected, and divided into several rooms. The front room functioned as a sitting room, with cushions scattered on the straw floor, and a brand-new Sony portable radio on a small table at the side. As Kieu and his stretcher were lowered, Mara knelt next to him, her hand still pressed against his wound.

An old man came in from one of the back rooms. Gaunt and tall, he had a sparse goatee and a wreath of very fine white hair starting at the temples. He bent over the stretcher, stared for a moment, then retreated without saying a word.

"Is he a doctor?" Mara asked the others, but they continued staring at her as if not yet sure she really existed.

The old man returned with a purple cloth bag. He set it down opposite Mara, then slowly lowered himself next to the stretcher. He took a blue bottle from the bag and opened it; a bitter smell immediately wafted through the room. The next thing he removed from the bag was a gauze pad wrapped in sterile paper; he pulled it open, daubed it with the clear liquid from the bottle, then reached with one hand to Mara's and gently pushed her fingers away from the shirt she'd used as a bandage. He pulled up the shirt, then began to clean the wound, very lightly at first, his strokes gradually growing longer and more forceful.

The wound was nearly two inches long, but very shallow. A black L sat at its center. At first Mara thought it was a bone, but as she looked she realized it must be the piece of shrapnel that had caused all the damage. The old man studied it, both with his eyes and the tips of his fingers, probing ever so gently. Then he took the bottle and tipped a bit of liquid into the wound.

Kieu jerked his body violently. The old man stopped pouring, waiting for him to settle. Then he poured again. Kieu jumped once more.

"You're hurting him," Mara said in Vietnamese.

There was no sign that the old man understood or even heard what she said. He capped the bottle, then opened his bag once more. He took out a small set of forceps.

"You're not going to sterilize it?" asked Mara.

He ignored her. Bending over the wound, he lowered the tips of the forceps, maneuvering the instrument as he sized up how he would remove the metal.

Then he sat back, and once more reached into the bag on his lap. This time he removed a Bic lighter and used it to heat the very end of the forceps.

When the metal glowed red, the old man took a very long breath, the sort one uses when meditating. Then he pointed at Kieu, motioning with his hands.

"You want me to hold him," said Mara, using Vietnamese but miming to make sure she was understood.

The old man nodded. As soon as Mara's hands were on Kieu's shoulders, he scooped the forceps down, retrieving the shrapnel. Kieu screamed and bucked. Mara pushed her weight against his, easily holding him down, though there was no way to stop the awful sound coming from his mouth.

The old man cleaned and inspected the wound, which was bleeding again. He took new gauze, daubed it in his solution, and began soaking up the blood. As he did this with one hand, he reached with the other into his bag and removed a jar and a steel rod not unlike a knitting needle. Once again using his Bic lighter, he fired the edge of the rod and cauterized the wound, Kieu screaming the entire time. After dressing the wound with a large piece of gauze and tape, he moved on to the smaller one at Kieu's back, just cleaning and bandaging this one.

Gesturing with his hand, the old man told Mara to roll Kieu over. The poor pilot screamed even louder, his feet jerking violently.

"Ssssh," said the old man kindly, putting his hand under Kieu's head. "Sssh."

He took another bottle from his bag. He told Kieu

something in Vietnamese that she couldn't understand, then held the bottle to the wounded man's lips. Kieu made a face and backed away. The old man held still for a moment, then pressed the bottle against his lips again. Kieu resisted; the old man tilted the bottle up and forced some of the liquid into his mouth. Then he clamped Kieu's mouth closed, making him swallow.

Mara looked up. The men who had come here with her were gone; the room was empty except for her and the old man.

The old man lowered Kieu's head back to the stretcher, then looked up at Mara. He pointed to her chest.

"What?" she said. Glancing down, she realized her shirt was soaked with blood. "It's all from him. I'm fine."

The old man stared at her, as if he didn't believe what she was saying.

"It is. Look," she said, unbuttoning the top button and pulling her shirt to the side. She didn't feel like giving the old man a peep show, and stopped at her bra strap.

Her satellite phone rang in her pocket; she'd forgotten to call DeBiase back.

"Excuse me," she told the old man, rising.

She was surprised to find a tight circle of children and older women gathered just outside the front door. She slipped through them, then walked the few yards toward the clearing before answering the phone.

"Are you all right?" DeBiase asked.

"I'm hanging in there. There's some sort of local medicine man or doctor, I don't know. He helped Kieu."

The sound of jets streaking nearby split the air. Mara looked upward but couldn't see them.

"What's going on?" asked DeBiase.

"Jets going somewhere. Fighters."

"Chinese?"

"I don't know."

"Do you have any means of transportation there?"

"I just got here, Jess. I don't know."

Mara turned back toward the village. It didn't look like the sort of place where you'd find a car in every garage—especially since there weren't any garages.

Maybe there were farm vehicles in the barns. Worst case, she could walk up to Nam Det.

"How far am I from Hanoi?" she asked.

"Almost two hundred kilometers. But distance isn't the problem. The Chinese have launched a major offensive, Mara. They may be in Hanoi by tomorrow."

"Tomorrow?"

"The way things are going, they may be there now."

Carlisle, Pennsylvania

"R.32.14a—Traditional enemies. Start of the simulation. It's right there." Zeus Murphy tapped the keyboard, scrolling through the rule that allowed the game to start with an attack by "a traditional regional enemy."

"Vietnam would never attack China," said Christian. "That's just not going to happen."

"It's not necessarily China," said Rosen, who was suppressing a grin. "It's Red Force."

"Come on. First of all, the simulation calls for China to attack first—"

"Wait a second—that's not in the rules."

"China always attacks."

"But it's not in the rules. Not specifically."

"A Vietnamese attack would be suicide."

"Not necessarily. And there's plenty of historic precedence," said Zeus. He turned toward Colonel Doner, who was standing at the head of the war room projection table. "Is it allowable?"

Doner furled his eyebrows, then glanced over at General Perry, whose expression mixed anger, frustration, and surprise. Before the general could say anything, Christian leaned back and whispered something to him. Perry shrugged. He was a short, skinny man; Christian towered over him. Still, Christian had adopted so many of his mannerisms that they looked like father and son.

Brow knotted, General Perry glanced over his right shoulder toward the smoked-glass panel of the observation room. The VIP Colonel Doner had mentioned was the assistant national security adviser/Asia, Sara Mai, who'd arrived at the base with three Pentagon handlers and a staff person who looked barely old enough to shave his pimple-filled face. Mai stood stiffly and nodded to Zeus when they were introduced, rather than extending her hand; Zeus guessed that her ice-cold manner had Perry confused.

"Oh, why not start out that way," said the general. "If the young major wants to replay the Vietnam War, why not?"

Actually, the model Zeus had in mind was the 1979 conflict between China and Vietnam, which had ended in a confused stalemate. Not that he modeled his strategy on the conflict, which had seen China attack over the border in retaliation for Vietnam's invasion of Cambodia.

On the contrary, he wanted China to attack in the west. And it did, launching a counterstrike in the tracks of the Vietnamese assault on the northwest border. That led Red to funnel its forces into the northwestern valleys near Cambodia and Laos, precisely what Zeus was counting on.

The situation ratcheted up quickly—Christian had obviously whispered that the Chinese could invade along the former Ho Chi Minh Trail, sweep into southern Vietnam, and force a quick Vietnamese surrender.

Such a strategy made a great deal of strategic sense for Red, since it would position its forces to isolate Blue's ally Thailand and provide a jumping-off point for the Malaysian oil fields, a high-point prize in the simulation.

But Zeus had no intention of letting Red get that far. Having identified several choke points where the Chinese advance could be slowed, he waged a series of campaigns along the Da River. The Vietnamese forces were overwhelmed each time, but Red had to spend considerable resources to gain those victories. Meanwhile, Zeus parceled out his meager American forces—two battalions of Special Forces and some SEALs—leveraging their effect. Fortunately, the rules provided that the special operations units increased in power and influence as the game went on.

The critical point came at Dien Bien Phu, as Red swung west on the open plain. Perry—and probably Christian, who was responsible for most of the general's strategy—was clearly hoping to get the Vietnamese into a set-piece battle there, just as the North Vietnamese rebels had done to the French. Red even sent several units along the same route the French had taken, clearly trying to entice a North Vietnamese counterattack along the lines the great North Vietnamese general Giap had used. The difference, of course, was that the Red army was considerably larger than the force the French had had, and enjoyed overwhelming air superiority as well. Rather than trapping China as the North Vietnamese general had done to the French, the Vietnamese themselves would be swept up and overrun.

It wasn't difficult to foresee this. What was tough was to make it seem as if he hadn't. Zeus had Rosen feint all along the Da River and fall back toward Dien Bien Phu; at the same time, he maneuvered other units to make it seem as if he were rushing reinforcements. Perry attacked in force, and succeeded in taking Dien Bien Phu—but the Vietnamese army turned out to have only a hundred men in the area, and most of them escaped.

Then Zeus went for broke. He used his Special Force troops to lead an attack on Lao Cai, the border city at the head of the Hong River, well east of the Chinese breakthrough into Vietnam. Red began rushing forces south from Gejiu and east from Xin Jie to meet the new threat—only to have them cut off at critical river crossings by SEAL attacks on highway bridges obviously believed too far from Vietnam to warrant guarding. The Red army was now caught in two separate pockets, unable to defend against an all-or-nothing missile attack that used American ATACMS ground-to-ground missiles secretly brought to the Vietnamese in the early rounds of the simulation.

"Where did those friggin' missiles come from?" said Christian as the attack unfolded on the simulation screen.

It was the high point of the session. Zeus didn't have time to look up from the computer to see General

Perry's face, but he knew it wouldn't be smiling. Red Force in Vietnam was now effectively cut off from its supply line; the army would have to be resupplied by air until Red could regain territory. That was doable—Red still had an overwhelming advantage over Vietnam—but it would take time. Enough time under the rules of the simulation that Blue had achieved a military stalemate without Red's achieving any of its goals—in other words, a win for Blue, the first ever recorded in Red Dragon War Simulation Scenario 1.

Zeus expected General Perry to rush from the session before it ended just to miss the handshake that had come to mark the close. That had been Perry's MO as Blue commander—he was a sore sport and sourpuss who hated to lose to a junior officer.

Or so Zeus thought. Not only did Perry stay this morning, but he gripped Zeus's hand strongly, smiled, and congratulated him.

"Good work, Major. Good, good work," he said before sweeping out of the room.

Christian looked like he'd been shot in the gut—a familiar look during the sessions. He shook tepidly, then followed his mentor.

"You got any fingers left?" asked Rosen as they secured their laptops.

"Perry's got a hell of a grip," said Zeus.

"A Mafioso grip. I'd watch my back."

"He almost seemed happy."

"Contemplating his revenge."

"What's he going to do?"

"You'll know when your next assignment takes you to Partial, North Dakota."

Zeus laughed. "Lunch?"

"Thought you'd never ask, sweetheart," said Rosen in his best Humphrey Bogart voice.

His best wasn't very good, but Zeus let it pass. Gear packed, he started out of the room, nearly bumping into Sara Mai.

"Oh, jeez, I'm sorry, ma'am," he said as she jerked backward.

One of her Pentagon escorts stopped short behind her, setting off a chain reaction of aides in the hallway. Under any other circumstances, it would have been hilarious, but Zeus felt the temperature in the entire basement suddenly shoot up.

"That's all right, Major," said Mai, straightening her skirt. Knee length, it was a blue pinstripe that matched her double-breasted top; if she'd had glasses, she would have looked like a stereotypical librarian. "That was quite an interesting performance. How often have you taken Blue's position?"

"First time."

"Interesting. Why focus on Vietnam?"

Zeus shrugged. "I don't know."

"Oh, I think you do, Major. It wasn't an accident." Her voice was harsh; she was scolding him, which made Zeus angry.

"You're right. I considered it carefully." He held her stare. Mai was only a few years older than he, with the slightest hint of wrinkles at the corners of her eyes. She was tall for a woman, five ten, though he still towered over her. "I needed a country China would attack. And one that I could use to stall for time. In that scenario, it's the only way to win."

"People playing the simulation for the first time normally defend Taiwan," said Mai. "You left almost no forces there."

"Yeah."

"Why not?"

"I used what resources I had."

He shrugged again. She was right—but how did she know?

Christian, probably. Trying to show off.

"Besides, China wasn't going to attack there," he said.

"No?"

"Doesn't make strategic sense." Zeus shook his head. "They wouldn't in real life either. They see Taiwan the way they see Hong Kong. Estranged brothers who will return to the fold in time. They attack their enemies. Japan I could see. Vietnam looks weak. They'll go right after Malaysia one of these days. I'm surprised they haven't already."

"So you picked Vietnam completely on your own?"

"What do you mean?"

"Because it was a traditional enemy and could attack?"

"Yeah."

"You've had no access to an outside telephone line since you reported for duty this morning?"

"Huh?"

"Have you made any phone calls, Major?" Mai's tone was sharp, almost dismissive.

"No."

"You haven't used a phone?"

"There are no external lines downstairs because of security." Zeus felt himself getting angry. "Listen—"

"And your cell phone?"

"In my car," he snapped. "Why?"

"I'd like you to come to Washington with me, Major."

"Washington? Why?"

"Because roughly an hour ago, the Chinese invaded Vietnam. From what I've been told, their plan sounds very much like what you did today in the simulation. We leave in ten minutes."

Northwestern Vietnam, near the border with China

With Jing Yo's men at the lead, the soldiers formed about a 250-meter search line and began walking through the jungle. It took them nearly an hour to work their way east into and then beyond the area where the enemy plane had been reported shot down. With no wreckage in sight, Jing Yo waited until they had gone about a kilometer beyond the point marked by Colonel Sun before calling a break. At that point, he conferred with Sergeant Wu and the regular army captain, Captain Lai Wi, to expand the search area.

The captain was still brooding from the way he had been treated, and sulked as Jing Yo went over the area with his handheld GPS device.

"We can move up the hill another half kilometer," said Jing Yo. "At that point, we'll reach a road. One group will pivot around on the north, the other on the south, and work back to the highway."

"Three kilometers," groused the captain.

"You don't have to walk it with your men," Jing Yo told him.

Captain Lai frowned, shook his head, then went off to see his sergeants.

"Bad case of red butt, huh?" said Sergeant Wu.

Jing Yo didn't respond. It wasn't his place to encourage disrespect for another officer, even if the officer was a jerk.

"You think we'll find the plane?" asked Wu.

"If it went down here, we'll find it."

"You don't think it went down here, though. Do you, Lieutenant?"

"I think it'd be fair to say that the coordinates we were given were in error," answered Jing Yo.

Wu smirked.

"Let's continue the search," said Jing Yo, "since those are our orders."

* * *

Sergeant Wu concealed a smile as he hiked back to his men. The lieutenant was a decent sort, not the stiff prig he'd taken him for initially. The decision to get rid of the jackass Fan had not been a fluke. Sergeant Wu appreciated the fact that Jing Yo wouldn't directly comment on orders he didn't like— Sergeant Wu would have done the same with a subordinate. Order had to be maintained.

Of course, that theory barely applied to the stuck-up regular army captain whose troops they had commandeered. The captain wasn't countermanding their orders—he was too much of a wimp to do that—but he wasn't exactly helping the search effort either. He'd told his noncommissioned officers to check with him before carrying out the slightest "request"—his word— from the commandos, meaning that every time Sergeant Wu told them to do something, they had to check back with him. It was more a pain than anything else, since the captain was too cowardly—or realistically worried about his own behind—to do anything but rubber-stamp what Wu said. Still, it was an unnecessary bit of officer bullshit, which annoyed Wu no end.

The regular unit's sergeants were sitting with Corporal Li and Private Ai Gua, sharing a pair of cigarettes that were being passed around commune-style. Ai Gua's wrist, either sprained or broken in the accident the night before, was wrapped in a heavy bandage. The private had bruises up and down his side and leg. But he had not complained, nor asked to be relieved from duty as a regular soldier would have.

Excellent. So they had at least one real commando among the untested greenies in the platoon.

"Hey, are you ready to go?" barked Wu.

"Sergeant, you should hear the stories," said Li, looking up from the log where he was sitting.

Wu put his hands on his hips.

"Their old man's a drunk," added Li.

"All right, that's enough," said Wu. "Lieutenant wants us to move on. Let's do it."

Li rolled his eyes but got up. Wu explained how the forces were to be divided, then sent the army sergeants off to check with their commander.

"Why are you so uptight?" asked Li.

By Wu's light, the corporal had earned the right to question him by serving during the clandestine action two years before in Burma—but only just.

"Be thankful we don't have their captain as our boss," Wu told him.

"All officers are scum."

"Most. Not Jing Yo."

"Hmmmph. We'll see."

"He saved me from the truck," said Ai Gua. "I think he's a good commander."

"That was his duty," said Li. "As an officer. Besides, Granddaddy Wu would have grabbed you."

"Most officers wouldn't have rushed in," said Wu. "They would have thought about it first."

"He's still young yet. We'll see what happens when he's a captain."

* * *

Jing Yo took out his paper map as the troops began their sweep back toward the highway. The most galling thing about their mission wasn't the fact that the plane probably hadn't crashed anywhere near here; it was the fact that Colonel Sun moved them around completely at whim, changing plans that had been prepared months in advance simply because he wanted some friend in the antiaircraft artillery to get credit for shooting down the plane. That was Sun, always playing the politics of the situation, no matter what the costs to anyone else.

Jealousy.

Jing Yo took a slow breath, then hung his head, the reprimand of his mentors echoing in his head as loudly as if the monks were standing over him.

Jing Yo was jealous of Colonel Sun's power. And as understandable as it might be, it was nonetheless an emotion that would cloud his judgment, keeping him from doing his duty.

He would do his duty. It was not his place to judge his superior officers. Doing so would make him just like Sergeant Fan.

Or worse, lead him down the path of dissolution, like the regular army captain.

Jing Yo swung to the south, moving among the regular army men, encouraging them as they walked. They were even less refined than the men whom he had been working with the past few days, though like them they were mostly poor farmers. Drafted from the northwest provinces and given a few weeks of rudimentary training, they were undoubtedly scared and awed by their task. Impressionable, they would follow even a bad leader—like their captain.

"Keep our eyes open, now!" he called as he walked up behind them. "Keep our separation. Good work, Sergeant. There, Private, stay alert!"

He walked back and forth across the line for the next hour, until finally the road was once more in sight. Jing Yo ordered the soldiers to rest, then called Colonel Sun to tell him that the search had not produced a downed plane.

"What are you doing up there still?" said Sun as soon as his communications man put him through. "The air force downed the plane to the east. Get your men back in the line."

"Yes, Colonel."

"Wait, Jing Yo—you have regular troops searching with you?"

"Yes, Colonel."

"Have them continue searching. Just in case. You get your men down to Lai Châu as planned. We're making good time. We need to stay on schedule."

"Yes, sir."

Josh felt both his anger and his hunger grow as the hours went on. In the meantime, it seemed as if all China were flooding over the border. Occasionally he caught glimpses of men on the tanks, but for the most part all he could see was gray and green steel passing. The engines drowned out any sounds he made himself; he felt almost invisible.

But he realized he was in grave danger when two men suddenly materialized a few yards from him. His attention had been fixed on the road to his left, and by the time he saw them push into the woods farther north on his right, they were too close for him to run.

He held his breath as they walked closer, then stopped. For a moment he thought they had spotted him. Then he realized they had only come to relieve themselves. As soon as they were done, they ran back toward the road.

Even as he retreated farther into the jungle, Josh berated himself—he could have tackled them for their guns. He had to start thinking long term if he was going to get back.

He had to get back. He was going to tell the world what the Chinese were doing.

It had been the Chinese who'd massacred the scientists and the village. Josh had realized it as he watched the tanks rolling. The Chinese had probably sent advance units in to make sure there would be no alarm or resistance. Their orders had undoubtedly been to kill anyone they found.

It was the only thing that made sense—even though it didn't make sense at all. But what war did?

He had to get out. That meant he had to find a weapon.

Josh walked away from the road in as straight a line as he could manage. At times he heard small animals running through the brush as he approached, but he never saw any. Even the frogs seemed shy—they quickly leapt away as he approached, showing only glimpses of their legs.

The terrain ran uphill, and after about a half hour he began moving farther south to avoid the hardest climb. Finally he stopped to rest. Without planning to, he fell asleep against a tree.

A spider walking across his hand a few minutes later woke him up. He jumped, shaking his hand furiously, unnerved by the tickling sensation. Body shaking, he grabbed his arms, hugging his chest and looking around to get his bearings. Josh wasn't ordinarily afraid of spiders, and when he finally got hold of himself he laughed—softly—mocking his fear.

Can't eat spiders, he told himself, setting out again.

He'd gone about fifty yards, perhaps a little more, when he heard sounds in the jungle to his left. He couldn't tell what was going on at first—the sounds were too faint. Then he saw brush moving in the distance. He started to back up. Thinking it was an animal coming toward him, he glanced around for something to use as a weapon—this might be a chance at food. He saw a rock about the size of his fist and grabbed it, then continued backward, perpendicular to the animal's path.

What was it? Something green.

A man. A soldier.

Josh froze as he saw the rifle slung over the soldier's shoulder. Slowly he sank to his haunches, watching as the man walked. He was about ten yards away, poking at the brush with a stick as he moved forward. His eyes were fixed on the ground in front of him.

Ten yards was close enough to be seen, but not close enough to attack the man with any guarantee of surprise. Josh remained where he was, willing the man past.

The man whacked at the large leaves in front of him. He was talking to himself, singing maybe, shaking his head, looking at the ground, only occasionally looking up to see where he was going.

Josh looked at the rock, still in his hand. One side was smooth; the other, jagged. It didn't weigh very much.

He could come up behind the soldier, hit him on the head, take his gun, shoot him.

But there must be others. A soldier wouldn't walk alone through the woods.

Josh remained still, seeing himself charging up behind the man. He heard something in the distance— another soldier, walking about ten yards farther south, calling to his companion.

The soldier who'd already passed kept moving without answering.

I can take one of them, Josh told himself. But not both.

The man called out again. He was walking on a diagonal, in Josh's direction.

Maybe this was the man to take.

No. This one was more alert. He wasn't hitting the brush with a stick. He kept looking around.

Josh closed his fist around the rock, then pounded

his other palm with it. He had to think long range. He had to think survival.

Don't be a coward, he told himself. This is your chance. You need a rifle if you're going to survive.

Was it a chance? Or was it suicide?

The man wasn't wearing a helmet. Hit him in the head and he would go down quickly.

He might be one of the men who had killed the villagers. He might be—he was one of the men who had killed his friends, his colleagues, on the expedition.

True or not, it didn't matter. Josh began moving forward. His body shrank slightly, slinking closer to the jungle floor. His legs and arms lengthened, the limbs of a cat, preparing to strike.

"*Nihao?*" said the soldier, asking if anyone was there. "*Nihao?*"

Josh sprang.

The soldier heard the noise behind him. Thinking it was his friend, he started to spin around. The rifle was in his hands, across his chest.

Josh hit him square in the forehead with the rock. It didn't seem to do anything. It did nothing—all his strength and he hadn't even moved the man.

He was going to die. Here, in the middle of the jungle, like an animal, this was how he would die.

His anger exploded. He wasn't a cat now; he was a volcano, he was fire, he was violence itself. Josh smashed the soldier's forehead once, twice, a third time—blood splattered everywhere. He smashed it again. He threw his body forward and he hit hard, harder than he had ever hit anything in his life. Again. Another time. He hit the splatter of blood that had been the man's face. He saw something gray, was sure it was the man's brain spurting out.

Josh punched the man's jaw with his fist, the rock still held tightly in his hand. Then he leapt up, grabbed the rifle, and began to run, sure someone had heard, sure he was going to be shot at any second.

He ran until his breath gave out, then pushed himself for a few more strides until finally he threw his arm out and caught himself around a tree. He had a stitch in his side, a sharp pain from muscles not used to such exertion.

He'd just killed a man. He should feel bad. And yet he didn't. He didn't feel good—he didn't feel anything.

He had the gun. The next thing he needed was food. A map maybe.

What had happened to the other man? Was he following him?

As Josh waited for his breath to become regular again, he looked up at the sky, trying to judge direction by the position of the sun. He needed to go southeast, in the general direction of Hanoi.

Not that he'd be able to walk to Hanoi.

He could if he had to. He would.

Josh gripped the rifle, ready to shoot the man's friend. But no one came. There were no shouts, no alarms, no cries for help. It was as if nothing had happened.

But it had. The gun proved it. And the blood on his clothes.

Josh began walking. He went at a good pace for

another half hour, perhaps forty-five minutes, before starting to tire. He was oblivious of the fatigue at first. Then the rock slipped from his hand. He hadn't even realized he'd still been holding it.

He crouched down, hoping that by doing that he would avoid falling asleep as he had last time. His nose was starting to act up and he debated taking one of his pills. Finally he decided to risk one of the lighter ones and reached into his pocket for the pillbox.

His hand shook as he opened it. He had only four left—one white, small dose, three green ones. He picked the lighter pill out with his thumb and forefinger, but as he reached for his mouth it slipped from his grip.

Then he sneezed, dropping the case.

Josh went down his hands and knees, patting for the pills on the ground. He found only one—a white one, fortunately. He swallowed, ignoring the bitter aftertaste. Then he hunted some more, until finally he realized it was hopeless, and gave up.

He continued up the hill, his steps becoming shorter and more labored. He spotted a waterfall in the distance ahead, and made it his goal. It wasn't until he reached it, some ten or fifteen minutes later, that Josh realized it wasn't a waterfall, or at least it wasn't now. Erosion from the seasonal storms had carved a sluice down the slope, but without a hard, steady rain the stream was dry. There was no water.

To his left, a ravine dropped into a cultivated field; Josh could see its edge through the trees.

If there was a field, there would be a village. He could get food there.

Steal food. He couldn't trust anyone now. He'd check it out once night came.

Josh sat on the rocks that had formed the crest of the waterfall and studied the gun he'd taken. He'd handled plenty of rifles and shotguns on his uncle's farm, but this was unlike anything he'd ever used before. It seemed to be made largely of plastic, which contributed to its odd feel in his hands. Its banana clip was located behind the trigger, bullpup style, something he knew was possible though had never seen. It had a large, M16-like carrying handle at the top, with a lever he surmised was the charging handle beneath it. The ejection port sat at the right side; fortunately he was right-handed.

He put the gun across his lap and peered down into the jungle. The friend of the man he'd killed was still out there somewhere, probably looking for him by now. There were bound to be many others as well.

Josh felt a twinge in his stomach—fear, regret that he had made the wrong choice.

I'll just kill them all, he told himself. That's what I'll do.

The idea floated through his head, something foreign, not too theoretical to take hold.

Captain Lai's frustration had ebbed somewhat since the commandos had left them to conduct the search themselves. He was glad to be rid of the lieutenant and his smart-mouthed sergeant; they were a clear threat to his authority. The search mission had seemed like a waste of time from the beginning, but it was a relatively easy task; he didn't have to worry too much about his men, who he knew had been poorly trained. That wasn't his fault—he'd joined the unit only a few weeks before—but he would surely catch the blame if they did poorly in battle.

Lai scrolled his arms together, trying to ward off the thirst that was always with him. He had not had alcohol for over two months, and he knew he would not have it now—he had made very sure not to bring any with him. But the urge was extremely strong, a desire beyond emotion that rose from every part of his body.

He craved the warm honey of the first sip as it spread from his mouth to every muscle and organ. He could taste the wholeness it brought, the way the alcohol—any alcohol, at this point—filled the other half of his soul, a complementary yin.

But he would not have any today, or any day for that matter. He would get through today, and the next one, as his counselor advised.

It was torture.

Lai turned abruptly, realizing that one of his sergeants was staring at him.

"Captain, the units are too spread out. We have many stragglers."

"Then get them together," said Lai.

"We'll have to stop the search, sir."

Lai waved dismissively. "Do it," he said.

The sergeant bowed his head, and moved to spread the word.

Lai took his satellite radio from his belt and called division headquarters. Instead of getting the communications clerk, he was connected immediately to Major Wang, the chief of staff. He explained the situation, saying that he would need transportation when the search was completed.

"You should have stayed away from the commando," said the major. "I told you earlier, once you are attached to anything Colonel Sun does, you are as good as dead to us."

"I did try to," said Lai. "I told him I had other orders. But he wouldn't listen."

"You're an idiot if you think that is enough."

Wang asked about transport.

"Did Sun release you?" asked Wang.

"I need to talk to him?"

"Did he release you?"

Lai was forced to answer that he had not.

"Then you will continue on the mission until you hear from me. I will see what I can do." *But don't count on miracles*, suggested Wang's voice. "Really, the best thing you must do, from now on—is to stay away from the commando. From any commando."

Wonderful advice, thought Lai as he returned the radio to his belt. But he wasn't the one who had placed his unit so close to the spearhead of the attack in the first place.

"I'm going to scout up the way here," he said aloud, though none of his men were nearby. "I'm going to find a good place for a command post."

He hated the army. But it was his penance—if he

had not drunk so much as a young man, his father would never have insisted that he join. He would be working now in the company with his brother.

The army could be a terrific opportunity for the right man. The right man could make use of the power and connections it afforded to advance. Even now, with the hard economic times, the right man in the army had less trouble than most.

Lai, however, wasn't the right man.

Perhaps he could be. If he got through today.

The captain walked slowly uphill through the jungle, picking his way through the trees as they began to thin out. The vegetation amazed him. Much of southern China, where he'd spent the last lonely year and a half, was arid wasteland. Yet here, only a few kilometers over the border, plants of all sorts grew with abandon.

It was as if there were a curse on Chinese land. Or maybe the Americans and their agents had poisoned the Chinese countryside secretly, perhaps years or even decades before. The American war with Vietnam could easily have been just a pretext; while the two countries pretended to be at arm's length now, everyone knew the Vietnamese were simply monkeys in the West's employ. That was the way the Americans operated—lazy themselves, they got someone else to do the work for them.

As he started picking his way around the rocks, the captain heard a pair of voices talking in the distance below. Their voices were hushed—so soft, in fact, that at first he thought he was imagining them. He held his breath, listening as carefully as he could.

They were real voices, he decided: men talking about something back at home, talking about a son, a newborn, a child he had had to leave.

Lai took a tentative step in their direction, moving quietly. As far as he knew, there were no other units in the area. But the men had to be Chinese—they were speaking Chinese.

Right until the moment he saw them, sitting on the ground against a large rock not twenty yards from where he had climbed up, the captain refused to believe that they were his soldiers. His entire unit should have been in front of him, stretched out through the jungle conducting the search. To find two men huddled here, far from where they were supposed to be and goofing off besides—the idea did not even seem possible.

And yet it was. They were so engrossed in their own conversation and the cigarettes they were smoking that they didn't hear him until he was only a meter or two away. By then it was too late—the captain pushed aside a large fern and stood two arm's lengths away.

"Captain!" said the man on the right, jumping up.

Startled, his companion jerked to his feet as well. As he did, he dropped a phone he'd been holding.

Incensed, Lai reached to his belt and took out his pistol.

"You have disobeyed your orders," he told them, struggling to control his emotions. The words sputtered from his mouth, his anger twisting his tongue. "What are you doing here?"

"Captain, we needed a rest and—"

"Silence!" Lai pointed the pistol at them. "You rest when you are given the order to rest. What's that mobile phone doing?"

Neither man spoke. Mobile phones and other communications devices were strictly prohibited to most of the Chinese army; even an officer like Lai was not allowed a personal phone and had to account strictly for his use of the satellite radio.

"The cell phone!" repeated Lai. He pointed the gun at the man who had dropped it.

"Captain, it is a satellite phone," stuttered the man. "It doesn't—it-it—." He cut himself off in midsentence and dropped to his knees, begging for his life.

The captain's anger only grew. He extended his arm, the pressure growing in his finger to fire. Finally, he did—and only a last-second force of will pushed the aim of the barrel straight up, sending the bullet harmlessly into the sky.

"Why do you have the phone?" said Lai after the shot finished echoing against the hillside.

The man on his knees could not respond, so Lai looked at his companion.

"We—we found it, c-clearing the d-dead with the commandos. Y-yesterday. It doesn't work, Captain. There is a code—it won't come to life. He just wanted to talk to his wife about his n-new son."

"The commandos took satellite phones?"

For a brief moment, Lai's spirit soared—here was

something he could use to get back not just at the up-pity lieutenant who had commandeered his men, but at Colonel Sun himself. But the look on the private's face quickly brought him back to earth.

"They d-d-didn't see," answered the private. "We—"

"Weren't you ordered not to take anything?" asked the captain, not quite ready to give up the possibility of revenge.

"Y-y-yes."

"Get down the hill both of you," Lai told them. "Find your sergeant and find your right places in the search. Go. Go now! Before I change my mind!"

The man who had fallen to his knees now dropped on his face, tears flowing from his eyes in gratitude. He began to babble about his son—the newborn they had apparently been speaking of earlier—and how the captain's name would be added to the child's.

"*Go!*" said Lai sharply.

The other man dragged him down the hill.

Lai waited until they were out of his sight, then picked up the phone. His first thought was to chuck it into the trees. But someone might find it there, and it would easily be traced back to his unit. If he was go-ing to dispose of it, he would have to find a much bet-ter place.

Maybe there was still a way to use it to discredit the commandos. Perhaps an idea would occur to him. He tucked it into his belt and began walking back to the crest of the hill.

Lai would have been fully within his rights as captain to execute both men. If anything, it was his decision to show the men mercy that might be questioned. They had not only disobeyed his orders for conducting the search, but disobeyed general orders in possessing the phone—a much graver matter.

He was fairly certain that neither man would speak of the incident, but if they did, Lai might get the reputation of being a "soft" commander, and one who did not care whether his orders were followed or not.

Being a drunk was not necessarily something that would bar one's promotion; being soft was.

He hated the army.

Josh had been sitting on the rock for nearly an hour when he heard the soldier making his way up through the jungle toward him. His first thought was that he had been surrounded, and that the man below was trying to flush him out. Then he realized that was unlikely. Whoever he was hearing was moving slowly, not walking directly toward him but following the channel the water had made.

Josh slipped off the rock and moved to a nearby cluster of chest-high bushes, ducking behind them.

The soldier's head appeared above the rocks. He climbed up onto the rock where Josh had been sitting, then leaned back, resting.

Josh sprang forward. He started to bring the rifle up to use as a club, but the man began turning in his direction.

Josh lowered the rifle and slid his finger into the trigger.

He saw the surprise on the man's face, then the little geysers of dust rising from the rock next to the soldier, then from the soldier himself.

Gray dust from the rock. Red from the soldier.

The man looked up into his face and started to say something, his chubby lips opening into a question. Then he fell back into the dried streambed.

Josh ran to him, and stared down at his face. There was no expression on it now, just a kind of numb emptiness, the eyes staring without comprehension.

The man had had a satellite phone in his hand. As he picked it up, Josh realized it was an AsiaSat2 unit, the same type that the expedition had used.

Josh's anger erupted. He went back to the body and stomped on the dead man's face with his heel, fury unleashed in a violent surge that left him physically drained after only a few seconds. Still he kept stomping, kicking the man for what seemed like hours.

When he stopped, he didn't feel any pleasure; he felt no satisfaction or even justification. He felt only trembling exhaustion.

The gunshot would have been heard for several miles, and others would be reacting. He wasn't going to be lucky like he had been before. This man had an insignia—he was an officer. People would care about him. They would look for him, and want revenge.

Josh had to get out of here—*now*.

He bent down to see if the man had anything useful.

There was a pistol on his belt, and a canteen—Josh jerked the canteen free and drained about a quarter of it in a single gulp. Coughing, he stopped and caught his breath, then took another drink, slower, more measured—the water had a metal taste, though not nearly bad enough to make him spit it out.

Capping the steel bottle, he stood silently for a moment, listening.

There was nothing. It was as if he and the Chinese soldier had been the only two people in the world, and now it was just him.

A dangerous illusion. They would be running to see what the shots were. He had to get as far away from here as he could. Then he could use the phone to call for help.

Josh put the water bottle in his left pocket, then hiked his jeans and tucked the pistol into the front of his waistband. Glancing at his battered boots, he started climbing back over the ridge, rifle ready.

Bangkok

Peter Lucas leaned back in the chair, reaching for his bottle of water as the Air Force intelligence officer began reviewing the satellite data on the Chinese attack for the rest of the participants in the videoconference. Lucas had seen most of this intelligence an hour ago. Gathered from a pair of electronic "ferret" or signal eavesdropping satellites that had been moved into the area, the data indicated a huge jump in traffic on bands associated with a cross section of the Chinese military. In layman's terms: the Chinese were streaming over the border like lava from a volcano.

An admiral from PACOM spoke next, saying that the Navy had no ships closer than a full day's sail from the coast of Vietnam, and it would take several days to get anything bigger than a destroyer there. A P-3 Orion had been scrambled to cover the coast, looking for Chinese submarines, but at the moment that was the extent of the Navy's effort in the area. If American citizens were going to be evacuated from Vietnam—

"My God, we don't want photos like that," blurted Harold Park. As the CIA's director of operations or DDO, he was the number two man in the agency. He was a good DDO, and an even better agency politician.

Which was good for Lucas, unless he somehow ended up as designated scapegoat if things went terribly wrong.

People escaping from the roof of the U.S. embassy would qualify. But so would a lot of other things— most of which they probably couldn't think of.

"At the rate the Chinese are moving, they'll reach Lai Châu by nightfall," said Sara Mai, the deputy national security director for South Asia. She was speaking from a plane, and while the connection was clear, there was a low hum whenever she spoke, the noise-canceling gear not quite successful in cutting out the sound of the engines.

"That's if they don't turn east and go to the river," said the chief of staff, Army General Clayton Fisk. "Which they can also reach by then."

"We don't believe they'll turn east," said Mai.

"Really? You have data to back that up?"

"We're working on a theory—"

"Data," repeated Fisk, using the tone he would have used to browbeat an underling. Lucas always pictured Fisk chewing on a cigar—he had the jowls of a bulldog, and that pretty much described his manner.

"We're looking at the same intelligence you are," answered Mai sharply.

Walter Jackson, the national security adviser and Mai's boss, stepped in to quash the argument before it started.

"Tom, do you have anything new for us?" he said, talking to Thomas Mengzi, the deputy head of the CIA's Chinese station. Mengzi was sitting in for Michael Dalton, who'd flown to Russia two days before and was still in Moscow.

"Just more of what I said at the top," Mengzi told Jackson. "The Chinese say they were attacked. They claim there's plenty of evidence. Rumor has it we caught it on satellite."

"We do have some images," said the Air Force analyst. "There were troop trucks. Hard to tell at this moment if they were Vietnamese, though they seem to have come out of the country."

Has to be a setup, thought Lucas, though he didn't say it.

"All right. Thank you all for the update," said Jackson, who as national security adviser had chaired the session. "We'll reconvene for a fresh update at 2100 Washington time."

Lucas stayed on the line, waiting for Park to come back.

"You wanted a word, Peter?" asked the DDO, his face flashing on the screen. Either the camera or the technology subtly altered the shape of his face, making it even rounder than it was in person.

"One of my people was in a plane that was shot at by the Chinese air force and forced to land," said Lucas. "She's okay. But she's stranded up near the border."

"I see."

"I'd like to take her out."

"How?"

"I haven't settled on the exact plan."

"She? Who is it?"

"Mara Duncan. The PM who was reassigned out of Malaysia. I needed someone clean to contact our Belgian friend. He didn't show. She went looking for him."

"The wrong place at the wrong time."

"I guess it depends on your perspective. She's the one that first told us the Chinese were definitely over the border. Her information came at least an hour before the satellites picked anything up."

Park wasn't impressed. "Where exactly is she?"

"Nam Det. We ran that operation into Xin Jie, China, from there a few months ago."

Park nodded but said nothing.

"I'm pretty confident we can get an airplane onto the field," said Lucas when the silence grew too long.

"Not under these circumstances."

"I can't leave her there."

Park didn't answer. He didn't have to.

"All right," said Lucas finally. "That's all I have right now."

The screen blanked. Lucas took a swig from his water, then unlocked the door and went outside to the small lounge area, grabbing a cup of coffee before proceeding down the hall to Secure Room 1, where Jesse DeBiase was coordinating the efforts to wring as much intelligence as possible from the various sponges and stones the CIA had planted throughout Southeast Asia over the past decade.

"How we doing, Million Dollar Man?" asked Lucas.

"We're doing. Very slowly. Nothing real to report. The Vietnamese still don't know what the hell's going on."

"That's the assessment there?"

"That's my assessment. I don't trust Hanoi. But yes, when you pick through what they said."

DeBiase knew all about the situation there. He was, in fact, Lucas's first choice to become the new station chief—though he clearly didn't want the job.

"And what do our people say?"

"They think the real attack is going to come in the

east. Probably that's the majority view of the government as well. Like I say, they're so confused they don't know which way is up." DeBiase wheeled his seat forward a few inches. "Who's going for Mara?"

Lucas grimaced, and pulled over a chair.

"We're leaving her there?" said DeBiase.

"I don't know what we're doing. Park doesn't want us sending anyone into the area."

"We can't leave her."

"Just because she's a woman, Jesse, doesn't mean she can't take care of herself."

Lucas turned the screen on the computer next to DeBiase, and started paging through the recent communications.

"Seriously, what are we going to do?" asked DeBiase.

"Seriously, I don't know. I've been told we're not allowed to run any operations in Vietnam." Lucas kept his eyes fixed on the screen, partly in hopes of reading something that would give him an idea of what precisely he should do.

"Peter, we can't leave her on her own up there. Her Vietnamese is patchy. She has no equipment. God knows how banged up she is after the plane crash. She was never supposed to be in that area in the first place. If the Chinese find her, she'll be taken prisoner. The Vietnamese will do the same thing."

Lucas continued paging through the data, which was an unfiltered hodgepodge of reports, ranging from NSA intercept summaries to second- and thirdhand accounts sent via instant message to CIA officers around the world. The real trick wasn't getting information—there was tons of it here. It was organizing it into a coherent shape. And the more there was, the harder that became.

"It doesn't look like they're heading in her direction," Lucas said finally. "It looks from this that they're going directly south."

"She's not all that far from Lao Cai."

"Far enough."

"Peter, we can't leave her there."

"I'll talk to her," said Lucas. "Then I'll figure out how we'll get her."

"She's supposed to call in another hour."

"I don't want to wait. Call her now."

"She turned her phone off to conserve the batteries."

"Sounds like Mara," said Lucas. "Always thinking ahead."

Northwestern Vietnam, near the border with China

Josh crossed over the ridge and walked for at least an hour before taking the satellite phone from his pocket. The delay was an act of will, a test to see if he could withstand temptation—to demonstrate to himself that he had the mental toughness he needed to survive. Because to survive, he could not give in to temptation, and he suspected that there would be many more instances of temptation before he reached safety. So he left the phone in his pocket as he walked south, skirting the edge of the fields he'd seen earlier, moving parallel to the hilltops until finding a dry streambed gouged into the hill.

A cluster of half a dozen houses sat in the lap of two hills between the terraced fields. Josh skirted it, walking deeper into the jungle. He'd have to stay away from the settlements, at least during the day; anyone pursuing him would search there first. With water and a gun, he could wait until nightfall to get food.

He *would* wait. He would do what he had to do to survive.

South of the village, surrounded by thick jungle, Josh finally allowed himself to examine the phone. There were no markings on it, but he was convinced it was one of the team's. It looked exactly like his—so much so that only when his personal ID didn't unlock it was he sure it wasn't.

The model was designed so that it wouldn't turn on unless its owner's identification code was entered properly. But it came from the factory with a default code. Josh wondered if maybe its owner hadn't changed it. Most people, he'd heard, didn't bother.

But what had the code been? He seemed to remember that it had been four similar digits. He tried the

0's, then 1's. Neither worked. 2's, 3's—he went through all of the digits without unlocking it.

It had to be one of those. Maybe if he took the battery out, the memory would die and the code would reset.

Josh tried it, then hit 0-0-0-0. Again he got a PIN failed message. He tried 1-1-1-1.

"Locked," flashed on the screen.

He snapped the red Off button, angry.

Stay in control, he told himself. With or without the phone, you'll get out of here. With or without it.

Sliding the phone into his pocket, he began walking again. It was starting to get dark. He had trouble seeing until he stumbled onto a narrow dirt trail, nearly falling as he pushed past some brush. He took a quick step back, looking left and right to make sure no one was nearby. Not trusting his eyes, he remained motionless a while longer, listening for any sound. Finally satisfied, he turned to the left and began walking along the edge of the path, moving as quietly as he could.

The trail seemed to meander almost without purpose or direction. He began stopping at every turn, peeking forward around a tree or thick bush, sure he was going to spot a village just ahead. But there was nothing.

Gradually, Josh began to relax. He picked up his pace. Finally, perhaps two kilometers after starting on the path, he smelled the faint odor of a fire in the distance. A few minutes later, he smelled food.

I'll stop here now, he told himself. I'll find a place

to hide until nightfall. Then I'll go and see what I can find of use in the village.

Food.

He didn't want to get too close to whatever village the food was being cooked at—if he was too close, his hunger might take over and he would do something stupid. He walked for a good ten minutes before finding a good place to stop, a low niche in an embankment formed by large tree roots along the side of the trail. The shadows would hide him completely, yet he'd still be able to see the trail. He climbed into the spot, a bird stealing another's nest.

Josh took a sip of water. The sky had been clear; once the moon came out, there would be plenty of light to see by. Sneaking into the village would be easy. Getting inside one of the huts might be a little harder— he'd have to do it without being heard, difficult in their small houses.

Was that what had happened in the village he'd been in? Maybe the Chinese hadn't killed the people at all—maybe it had been someone as desperate to survive as he was.

No. The entire village had not only been killed; they'd been buried. He knew what he had seen, and he had the proof in his pocket.

Josh arched his back, slipping his hand into his pocket for the satellite phone. He turned it on again, different number combinations running through his head.

As the device powered up, a message flashed briefly on the screen: EMERGENCY SERVICE ONLY. The phone was set to dial an emergency number, whether its account was open or not.

Yes! But what was it? 7-0-7? 1-1-2?

God, he couldn't remember. He could picture the session in Tokyo where Dr. Renaldo's assistant Tracey told them how to use the phones, but he couldn't remember the number.

God, she was beautiful.

She'd gone only as far as Tokyo. He remembered wishing she was coming; now he was glad she hadn't.

Josh tried the first combination that came into his head.

CONNECTED.

Connected!

He stared at the phone, not quite believing it. By the time he got it to his ear, the operator was asking what the nature of his call was.

The man had a British-Malaysian accent.

"My name is Josh MacArthur. Dr. Joshua MacArthur," he said, using the honorific though he had not been given the degree yet, hoping it would make him sound more important. "I am working for the UN. I'm in Vietnam. The Chinese have just invaded across the border. They attacked us. They killed everyone in the expedition. I'm a few kilometers, no more than ten, from the base camp. Maybe less than ten. I don't know. There was a village nearby. They attacked it. Murdered civilians. I have video. It's—it's pretty disgusting."

Josh stopped speaking. The operator hadn't said anything, not even "Go on" or "Yes" or "You're out of your mind." He listened for a moment, trying to hear breathing on the other side.

"Are you there?" asked Josh.

There was no answer.

"Are you there? I'm with the UN. We need help."

Josh fought to keep the desperation from his voice, but it was impossible.

"Are you there? Operator? This is an emergency. Operator?"

The phone claimed it was connected, but Josh couldn't hear anything. It was as if the line had been cut.

Had there really been an operator? Or had he imagined it?

"Hello? Hello?" he repeated. "I'll hang up and dial again."

He hesitated, then pressed the red button.

Don't panic, he told himself. But his fingers trembled as he redialed.

The word CONNECTED came on the screen again. But this time, there was no answer from the operator, just more quiet.

"This is Josh MacArthur. I'm with the UN. We've been attacked in northwestern Vietnam. We need help. Can you hear me? Hello? Hello? . . ."

There was nothing in response, not even a signal telling him he had misdialed. The line didn't even seem dead. It was more like a vacuum, sucking sound away: a static-free limbo.

Josh hit the End Call button.

Whom else could he call?

His uncle in Iowa.

He punched in the numbers and hit Send. But this time the phone didn't connect at all—it was still in emergency mode.

Whatever was going on must be affecting the phones. Dejected, Josh stuck the phone in his pocket and gazed back at the trail, struggling to separate the shadows into those that were real, and those his mind invented.

9

Northern Vietnam

The settlement where Mara and the wounded Vietnamese pilot Kieu had been taken was so small that there were no televisions; the nearest was in the marginally larger Nam Det, about two kilometers up the road. With Kieu resting and seemingly in good care, Mara decided to go there and see if she could get news from the wider world. One of the young men who had carried the stretcher was appointed to be her guide, and they set out just as it was turning dark.

The Vietnamese knew that something serious was happening. They'd seen the MiG overhead and heard the gunfire that had led to the crash and explosion. But they didn't seem overly curious about the situation. They made no attempt to ask Mara what was going on. She supposed curiosity was not a good characteristic in a dictatorship. Still, she knew no good ever came from closing one's eyes to trouble, and found herself asking her escort what he thought was going on as they walked to Nam Det.

He didn't answer. Mara wasn't sure whether he didn't understand what she was saying—she was still struggling with the language's tones and accent—or whether he had been instructed not to say anything. She tried again, a little louder, pretending there was a possibility that he hadn't heard.

Again he said nothing.

"Am I saying the words wrong?" she said.

"Your pronunciation need work," said the young man in English.

"You speak English," replied Mara, also in English.

"We learn in school."

"So what do you think?"

"Think?"

"About the Chinese attack. Aren't you curious? Do you think it's true?"

"If you say those were Chinese planes, why wouldn't I believe you?" He seemed genuinely surprised that she would think he didn't.

"Are you going to defend your country?"

"I am not in the army."

"Are you going to join?"

"If the government tells me to join, then I will be in the army."

"I would think—I know if America was attacked, I would want to join the army."

"You are not in the army?"

"I'm a journalist," said Mara, reverting to her cover story.

The young man nodded, but he didn't seem convinced. Probably like Kieu, he assumed she worked for the CIA.

"What do you do now?" Mara asked. "What work?"

"We farm."

"You?"

"Me, yes."

"And you still go to school? You studied English— are you going to move to Hanoi or Saigon when you graduate?"

The young man explained that the school was more like an American grammar school, and that students there learned French and English by the time they were twelve. At that time, they also generally went to work in their village, which was what he had done. He had not been in a schoolroom for several years.

"It is not like in the south," said the young man, who still hadn't volunteered his name. "Some of the older people—many of the older people—don't think we should learn English. But it is a necessary language."

"What about Chinese?"

The young man smiled, reeling off a few Chinese phrases so quickly Mara couldn't decipher them all, though her Chinese was somewhat better than her

Vietnamese. It seemed amazing that someone with what amounted to a middle-school education could speak four different languages, but the young man assured her it was not unusual. The Vietnamese people were willing to work hard, he said, to "advance in knowledge."

The young man took her to a house that belonged to his uncle, who was one of the village elders. It was larger than the hut where she'd left Kieu, with more furniture and possessions, but there was no mistaking it for a rich man's home. The only signs of prosperity—indeed, the only things in the house that would not have been there fifty years before—were a refrigerator, which stood against the wall in the front room, and the television, which stood opposite it. The TV and refrigerator could not be on at the same time; her interpreter's uncle ordered the refrigerator cord pulled from the wall before plugging in the television. The two lights in the room blinked as the set was turned on.

Mara waited while the picture came up. A picture of dancers dressed in elaborate costumes appeared; they twirled their skirts across the screen.

"A cultural show," said the young man.

The uncle changed the channel. An Indian movie, dubbed into Vietnamese, appeared.

"Is there a news channel?" Mara asked.

They put on the "official" government station—the others, though heavily censored and owned by the government, were officially "unofficial."

It was showing a travelogue on Ho Chi Minh City.

"There has to be some news," said Mara. She asked how the signal came to the sets and learned it was supplied by a satellite. "Can we change the orientation? To get signals from other stations?"

The uncle's face grew tense as soon as his nephew explained what Mara wanted to do. The signal came from a satellite dish that he had applied for a license to use. When he was issued the license, he had also been given a descrambler to pick up the allowed signal—and only the allowed signal.

"The device blocks other signals," the young man told Mara. "He's not saying that, but everyone knows it's true. And there is a wire on the dish mechanism—if it's moved, the authorities will find out."

"A wire? It reports back?"

"It's more like a lock."

"He can put it back and make it seem as if it hasn't been touched," said Mara. "They won't find out."

But the uncle would not be persuaded.

"Tell him the Chinese are attacking your country," said Mara. "Tell him it's important to find out what's going on, before you are killed."

"I tried. He said the government will let us know what needs to be done. We will not be defeated by the Chinese."

Frustrated, Mara walked outside for some fresh air. She still had a few minutes before it was time to check in with Bangkok. Rather than calling early, she began walking up the street, looking to see if there were any vehicles she might borrow or, more likely, buy. She could use one to scout around the local roads, checking on the Chinese advance, before whatever Bangkok arranged to get her out.

Or just drive south to Hanoi and bug out on her own.

A flatbed truck was parked in a front yard two houses down, so close to the house that the bumper nearly touched the wall. Mara decided she wanted something else—the people here would need it if they had to flee.

"My uncle doesn't believe there is a war," said her translator, jogging up to join her as she stood looking at the truck.

"Where does he think the MiG came from?"

"It must have been a government plane, he says, and you are some sort of pirate."

"Did he see the markings? It was clearly Chinese."

"He couldn't see the plane from here."

"You saw the plane?"

The young man nodded. "Everyone in my village did. My uncle did, too, I'm sure. He's just stubborn."

"What's your name?"

"Tom Khiaw."

They shook hands, as if meeting for the first time.

"One of the village leaders was a mechanic for the air force in the American war, and knows the markings," explained Tom. "But to my uncle, claiming that you are a pirate makes more sense than China being at war with us. You are American."

"What will happen tomorrow when the government announces that you are at war?" asked Mara.

"I don't know."

"You're not that far from the border. The road network is bad, but still."

"I think—we will wait and do as the government says. The old people will listen for what Uncle Ho tells them."

Uncle Ho was Ho Chi Minh—Vietnam's legendary leader, dead now many years. Tom—the name was pronounced as if it had two o's—saw Mara's confused expression and tried to explain.

"Uncle Ho is still with us in a way," said the young man. "His spirit lives on."

He meant that literally; many in Vietnam and in Asia believed that a person, especially one as important as Ho Chi Minh had been, continued to look after people following his death. Having saved the country from both the French and the Americans, he would undoubtedly do the same against the Chinese, who were more ancient enemies.

There was no sense debating religion. Mara pointed at the truck.

"Is there something smaller than that? Maybe a motorcycle that I could drive to Hanoi?"

"I know two people who have motorbikes. They're at the other end of this street."

"I have to make a phone call. You go there. I'll follow."

Mara waited until he was a little ways up the street before taking out her phone. Larry Hammer had taken over for DeBiase, and answered in his undertaker voice.

"How's it going?" he asked.

"All right, considering." Mara gave him a quick update. "How long before you can get a plane up here? I want to get Kieu out—if the Chinese find him, they'll probably arrest him."

"Why would they arrest him?"

"For the same reason they tried to shoot us down," she said. "They just will. All these people are in trouble, but they don't seem to realize it. Or maybe they do and they don't want to face it."

"Listen, Lucas wants to talk to you," said Hammer suddenly. "Here he is."

"Hey, boss, how's it hanging?"

"Mara, we have to talk." His tone was dead-dirt serious, nearly always a sign of big trouble.

"Fire away."

"It's going to be a while before we get you out," said Lucas.

"How long?"

"I don't know. Maybe not until tomorrow or the next night. Maybe longer. At the moment I'm under orders to sit tight."

"Things are that bad here?"

"They're that confused. We should know a little more by the morning. I want you to stay in touch."

She resisted the impulse to give him a wise-ass response. "Tell me where the Chinese are," she said evenly.

Lucas sighed. Mara realized he couldn't—if she somehow fell into Chinese hands, or even Vietnamese, and told them what she knew of the Chinese advance and when she knew it, she would pass on valuable information about the U.S.'s intelligence-gathering capabilities.

Which meant the Chinese must be very close. Damn close.

"Should I go back to Hanoi?"

Lucas hesitated. "I can't tell you to do that. It may be too dangerous."

"More dangerous than here?"

"Things are moving very quickly. Their intentions are not entirely clear, and our reconnaissance—" He stopped himself, leaving her to guess what he had decided was too sensitive to share. "All I'm asking is for you to sit tight for now," said Lucas. "I'll figure something out."

"Like?"

"I don't know. I will get you. You can count on that."

"Uh-huh."

"It's not like Malaysia. I'm *not* Croton."

"Hey, boss, I never said you were. And as far as Croton goes—we all work with what we got, right?"

"Mara, I promise—"

"I'm worried about the phone's battery, boss. I'll sign back on at 0600 tomorrow. Sayonara until then."

Peter Lucas handed the communications headset back to Hammer.

"How'd she take it?" asked Hammer.

"About what I expected."

"She's going to stay put?"

"Probably," said Lucas.

"If she can get down to Saigon, she can get out," said Hammer. "Even Hanoi."

"She's okay where she is for now. Farther south, she may run into the Chinese. Until we know exactly where they're going, I can't tell her to leave. I may be sending her right into a trap."

"She's in one already if they send more troops through Lao Cai."

"Hey, Peter, you may want to look at this NSA summary," said Gina DiMarco, who was monitoring the National Security bulletins at a nearby workstation. Gina was a cryptography clerk Lucas had pressed into service to help keep up with the data flow.

"What am I looking at?" he asked, dropping down to one knee to look at her screen.

"The Chinese started selectively blocking satellite phone communications from the area satellite phone services a few hours ago. AsiaSat2, Iridium—they've all been hit. The system is pretty sophisticated—there's technical information on what exactly they're doing back in this tab here."

She rolled the cursor up and tapped one of the windows. A screen dense with words appeared.

"Do I need to know how this all works?" Lucas asked.

"No," she said, clearly disappointed.

A strong scent stung Lucas's nose.

"What'd you have for dinner?" he asked.

"*Som tam.*" Papaya salad—with chilies. "My breath bad?"

"It's sharp, Gina."

"Sorry, boss. About an hour ago, a member of a UN science team tried calling out on the emergency line. The Chinese blocked the other side of the transmission shortly after it began. Then they blocked it completely, but he still continued to talk."

"He didn't realize it was blocked?"

"Apparently you can only tell that you don't hear someone responding."

"They can do that?"

"They're using a type of ferret satellite." Gina rolled the cursor arrow back toward the window with the technical data. "It's kind of fascinating. They lock onto the bands the commercial satellite is using, and then selectively—"

"You can explain it to me when we're past all this," Lucas said, starting to read the transcript.

10

Northwestern Vietnam, near the border with China

Among the important first-night targets for the Chinese invaders was an army barracks just north of Lai Châu city. The two companies stationed there represented the only substantial Vietnamese force in the spearhead's path. Defeating it was therefore important both tactically and psychologically, and Jing Yo's platoon had been assigned to help secure the victory.

After being transported into the area with the main force, the commandos would leapfrog the defenses, sabotaging telephone and electric lines as they proceeded to a point southwest of the city where Highways 12 and 6 split. They would secure a small culvert bridge on Route 12 just south of that intersection, holding it to cut off any retreat by the Vietnamese.

The plan called for them to meet with three platoons of paratroopers, who were to have landed about five kilometers south and proceeded north along the highway. Because of the paratroopers—together the force amounted to about a hundred men—Jing Yo had been given only one of his squads, amounting to eight men, not counting him. The other was assigned to provide protection at the force headquarters, basically operating as bodyguards for Colonel Sun, who was traveling with the main body.

Jing Yo hadn't protested when the orders were first drawn up; the paratroopers were well trained, and the force was more than sufficient to hold the bridge. But while racing to rejoin the tanks, the paratroopers had not been able to take off due to problems with their aircraft. That meant he and his eight men, initially assigned as little more than advance scouts, were now expected to do the work of one hundred.

Colonel Sun, of course, had not mentioned any of this when ordering him to rejoin the force. Jing

Yo could only wonder if the colonel was purposely sabotaging him with an eye toward taking him down a peg or two.

Or maybe he was hoping he'd be killed when his unit was overrun.

Getting south past the column of rapidly advancing armor and trucks on the narrow Vietnamese highways wasn't easy. In many cases the two lanes of Chinese traffic completely blocked the road, including the narrow shoulder. So by the time Jing Yo managed to meet up with the vanguard of the assault, they were almost within sight of the barracks' perimeter. The infantry troops riding with the tanks had already dismounted, preparing for the attack.

"Through the field, quickly," Jing Yo told Private Ai Gua, who was driving.

They veered across the ditch that ran along the highway. The land, tropical forest only a few years before, had been plowed under and turned into a wheat field. It was fallow at the moment; the season's planting wouldn't take place for another few months.

While the moon was very strong, it was difficult to see obstructions in the field without turning their headlights on. Twice Ai Gua barely missed large rocks. When he came to what looked like a path between the fields but turned out to be an irrigation ditch, he was going too fast to stop in time. He tried plunging across. He made it to the other side of the embankment, but then stalled the engine. Jing Yo leapt from the cab and ran to the back, where Sergeant Wu was already mustering the men in an attempt to push the vehicle forward.

There was only a small trickle of water in the bottom of the ditch, but its shallow sides were soft mud, and it took several minutes before the truck's wheels finally caught enough hard earth to move forward. Ai Gua revved the engine, spattering mud over everyone, including Jing Yo, as he made it back onto solid ground.

"Let's go!" yelled the lieutenant, racing back to the cab.

He heard gunshots in the distance, the low crack of rifle fire. The assault had already begun.

"Turn on the headlights," he told Ai Gua. "Let's go."

Fifty meters farther on, they came to a dirt road that led back in the direction of the highway. They turned onto it, Ai Gua stomping the gas pedal for all he was worth. But the lane soon angled southward, away from the highway.

"We need to go west," Jing Yo told Ai Gua. "Cut across the field."

The private did as he was told. The vehicle jerked unevenly, climbing in the direction of the highway.

"Another ditch ahead, Lieutenant," said Ai Gua.

"Try south. Turn left."

They did, but it was obvious that the ditch blocking their way wasn't going to end anytime soon. Jing Yo checked his GPS. According to the device, the nearest road back to the highway was two kilometers farther south.

"Stop here," he told Ai Gua. He jerked open the door and ran to the back. "Take as much ammunition as you can," he told his squad. "Leave the rucks. Let's go, let's go—we run from here."

Sergeant Wu began mustering the men. Jing Yo told Ai Gua to take the truck alone, find the road, and come back north.

"Just me?"

"Just you, Private. I know you can do it."

Ai Gua nodded. Jing Yo slapped the fender and he put it in gear, spitting up large clods of dirt as he drove away.

"Could've just left the truck," said Sergeant Wu.

"I don't want to lose it," said Jing Yo. "And we can get there faster without the backpacks. He'll be okay." He raised his voice to what they had called in officers' training a commanding shout. "Come on, men. The road is this way! We run together."

The squad fell in behind him, moving at a good pace over the field. The night had cooled, and after the long ride the sensation of blood and adrenaline pumping through his veins felt good. Jing Yo ran at about three-quarters pace up the gradual rise, until he came to a three-strand barbed-wire fence whose black wires stood out against the moon-painted silver ground beyond.

He stopped and turned around, waiting as his men caught up. Sergeant Wu, the oldest of the squad—not to mention the heaviest smoker—took up the rear, wheezing as he ran. It would have been a better idea to let him take the truck, thought Jing Yo, but it is too late now.

Private Chin removed a small pair of wire cutters

from his tactical vest and cut the wires, which fell lazily against the ground. Jing Yo plunged back into the lead, running a little faster, until he began to tire and wondered where the road was. Finally the dark slick of macadam appeared ahead. He slowed to a jog, extending his hands to alert the others. Then he raced ahead to the drainage ditch flanking the road, flopping down against the side.

There was enough moonlight to see the road, but the glasses' magnification allowed him to see down it for about a kilometer. Once he was sure there were no snipers on the other side, he rose and ran to the edge, pausing to make sure he was still clear. Then he leapt across the road, landing on the opposite shoulder in two giant bounds. He slid into the ditch that ran along that side, once more making sure they weren't running their way into an ambush.

When he didn't spot anyone, he stood and whistled; his team double-timed across the highway.

"Where's the bridge?" asked Wu, out of breath.

"This is Route 6. We've got to go across that field, then up to our right," said Jing Yo. "It should be less than a hundred meters."

"All right."

Jing Yo paused, listening. The gunfire he'd heard earlier had stopped.

That didn't make any sense. The assault should be well under way by now.

Maybe the Vietnamese had thrown down their weapons and were fleeing. In which case, Jing Yo had best get his men into position quickly.

"Let's go," he told his men, and once more began to run.

Running always reminded Jing Yo of the days before being formally accepted for training as a *Ch'an* novitiate, when he and the other boys under the monks' care had had to prepare their bodies for the order's grueling physical tests. The early-morning and late-evening sessions cleared his head and made his body work with his mind in a way that couldn't be entirely explained in words; it was as if the exercise created new pathways between his muscles and his brain. Even now, running relaxed him, and though there were many things Jing Yo could have thought or worried about—whether the Vietnamese had wired the bridge for explosives, whether a unit had been assigned to protect it—his mind was an easy blank, filled only with the idea and sensation of running.

The field climbed upward toward a small copse. Jing Yo ordered his men to rest as they reached it, planning to use the trees as a vantage point to scout for the road. But before he could climb one, Private Chin shouted.

"There! The road is there, through the trees."

Their target was less than fifty meters away.

"Chin, Bo, with me," said Jing Yo, already starting back in motion. "Sergeant, stay with the others and cover us until we are sure it is clear."

Jing Yo's right boot hit the pavement as the sky to the north turned white. An instant later, the first big shell from the tanks exploded as it hit one of the Vietnamese positions; a dozen or more followed in rapid succession. Even Jing Yo, who had been in combat several times before as a "mercenary" in Malaysia, stopped, his attention momentarily drawn to the thunderous assault a few kilometers away.

But only for a moment.

"The bridge is that way. Go!" he yelled. Then he turned back to Sergeant Wu, signaling for him to follow as he and the other two men ran north.

Jing Yo sprinted until he saw the low white arch at the side of the road ahead. The bridge seemed much smaller in real life than on the map they had used to prepare—so much smaller that when he reached it he took two GPS readings to make sure he had the right place. It rose barely three meters over a small, rocky stream, and extended for only ten or twelve meters.

"This is it?" asked Sergeant Wu, as always arriving at the rear of the pack.

"According to the GPS," said Jing Yo.

"We should send someone north to make sure."

Jing Yo agreed, and chose Chin and Bo, telling them to make sure they weren't seen by anyone. Then he inspected the area, looking for a place to defend the bridge from if they were attacked. A cluster of trees sat on the bank at the northwestern side; otherwise there was no cover at all, except for the bridge walls.

"No explosives," said Sergeant Wu. "They weren't expecting us."

They divided up the men, posting two in the trees and the rest in spots under the bridge, where they had decent firing lines on the road. Jing Yo called the division headquarters, announcing that they had reached their objective. He stayed on the bridge with Sergeant Wu, waiting for the two men whom they'd sent up the road, and watching the flashes on the horizon.

"I'd hate to be those bastards," said Wu as a succession of explosions shook the ground. "Going against tanks at night. You never know what the hell hit you."

The Vietnamese had faced tanks before, Jing Yo thought, when they fought the Americans and French. They had quickly become experts on antitank tactics and weapons; indeed, he had studied some of the Vietnamese tactics while training to be a commando, and used a few in Malaysia, though there the biggest vehicle he had fought against was an armored car.

"You think this is going to last long, Lieutenant?" asked Wu.

Jing Yo shrugged. He hadn't really given it much thought.

"I think it will be over inside a week," said Wu. "They'll quit before we reach Saigon."

"I would imagine the Americans thought the same way."

Sergeant Wu laughed. "Yes, but we're not the Americans."

One of the men below hissed. Someone was running up the road.

"Hold your fire. It's Bo and Chin," said Jing Yo, recognizing the shadows. "Report."

"The Vietnamese are coming," said Chin breathlessly. "They have armored cars."

"Shit," said Wu, a little too loudly for Jing Yo's taste. "Here comes hell."

"Get your grenade launchers ready," shouted Jing Yo. "Wait until they are very close!"

He took a step to run off the bridge, then realized that his men were watching and might misinterpret his haste. So he moved at a slow, almost relaxed pace up to the copse. Corporal Linn had already zeroed his shoulder-launched Type 2010 rocket-propelled grenade launcher on the road when he arrived.

In its basic design, the Type 2010 was very similar to the RPG-7 model the Vietcong used much farther south against the Americans in the 1960s war. But in the particulars—charge and propellant—it was much better. The shaped charge could get past all but the largest main battle tanks; even then, a charge fired at the right angle and in the right spot could disable a Russian tank. Jing Yo knew this for a fact, since he had seen it done.

The vehicles they were up against were not nearly so well protected. But they were not tin crates either. French-made Panhard Sagaie 1's, they mounted 90 mm guns on their low-slung turrets. The trucks had wheels rather than traditional tank treads, which allowed them to move relatively quickly—Jing Yo estimated they were doing at least thirty kilometers an hour as they rounded the last bend before the bridge, about eighty meters from the trees.

"Aim for the lead car," he told Linn. "The ones behind it will crash."

Linn waited another half second, then fired. The rocket spit across the night, its whistle thin against the sounds of the battle in the distance.

The nose of the armored car flashed white and it stopped dead in its tracks. As Jing Yo had predicted, the second vehicle ran into the rear of the first with a tremendous smash.

A second grenade, this one fired by one of the men near the bridge, hit the lead vehicle just below the turret's muzzle. The charge penetrated the metal, and turned the inside of the tank red hot in an instant, not merely frying the occupants but setting off several of the thirty-odd charges for the gun. A fireball leapt from the open hatch at the top of the car, its red light cascading across the night sky.

Remarkably, the second car was able to back away from the wreck. As it moved, its gun began to rotate in the direction of the trees.

"Take it," Jing Yo told Linn.

But the private was having trouble reloading his weapon and wasn't ready. The muzzle of the armored car flashed, and Jing Yo felt his breath involuntarily catch in his chest.

It has missed, he thought, if I can feel this.

The shell *had* missed, whizzing through the trees several meters above them. The gunner in the armored car immediately began to correct; his next shell passed only a few centimeters away.

Linn's grenade hit the front corner of the truck before he could get another one off.

The grenade happened to strike at a bad angle for penetration, and rather than sinking into the armor, it exploded outside of the vehicle, pushing it a few feet back but doing comparatively little damage. The explosion did throw off the gunner's aim, shoving the muzzle upward as it fired.

Jing Yo leapt from behind the tree and ran toward the road. It was not a logical thing to do, nor was it entirely prudent. Yet he knew instinctively that he had to do it.

Racing across the road, he took one of the grenades from his tac vest and thumbed off the tape holding the fuse closed. He circled around the front of the burning armored car, swerving to avoid the flames as they shot out from under the turret. As he did, the gun on the second car swung in the direction of his men on the hill. Jing Yo grabbed the thick iron rail at the rear of the car's body and leapt onto the Panhard, feet sprawling over the rear. Then he rolled upward and climbed to the top of the turret just as the car's commander popped through the hatch and reached for the machine gun.

Jing Yo had not expected to have such an easy chance, and for the briefest moment—a fraction of a fraction of a second—he hesitated. Then he dropped the grenade through the opening. With his left hand, he grabbed the Vietnamese soldier and pulled him with him as he leapt back off the armored car. The grenade exploded with a dull thud, the vehicle rocking and then hissing as smoke rose from the open hatch.

Jing Yo dragged the Panhard commander across the road. The man was dazed, unable to comprehend what was going on, let alone resist. By the time Jing Yo's men came up to help him, Jing Yo had already taken his pistol and trussed his hands behind his back with a thick plastic zip cord.

"You took quite a risk," said Wu.

The launcher at the base of the bridge had not had a clear shot at the second tank, and it would have taken Linn nearly another minute to fire a third grenade, during which time the armored car's gunner would surely have found his target.

Did he have to explain that to Wu? What was the point?

"What needed to be done, I did," he said. "There was no other option."

Sergeant Wu laughed softly, shaking his head.

The Vietnamese armored car commander was a sergeant, who was either too shell-shocked to say anything useful, or a very good actor. Jing Yo brought him under the bridge, removing the man's boots. He used the laces to bind his feet.

"If you try to leave, my man will shoot you," Jing Yo warned, first in Vietnamese and then in Chinese. "You're not worth the trouble of chasing."

Back up on the road, Sergeant Wu had climbed into the second armored car. With help from Linn, he cleared it of its dead crew, restarted it, and managed to back it up off the road. The main gun seemed to have been damaged during the fight, but the machine gun at the top was still working, a fact Sergeant Wu demonstrated with a few bursts in the direction of the curve to the north.

"We'll catch them by surprise," said the sergeant.

"If our tanks arrive, the surprise will be on us," Jing Yo told him. He sent Private Chin back up the road to act as a lookout, then checked in with division to see how the assault was progressing.

Communications were coordinated at the divisional headquarters, a legacy of decades of Communist top-down military philosophy as well as the political need to keep tight control on the army. The headquarters was actually a mobile unit only a few kilometers behind the lead element of the assault; still, it was clear that they were having a difficult time sorting through the various reports and coordinating support on the fly.

Jing Yo was told to hold his ground; the tanks would be arriving shortly.

"We have disabled two enemy vehicles," he repeated, sure that the specialist on the other side of the radio did not fully comprehend what he had just been told. "I don't want the tanks to fire at us."

"Yes, Captain, I understand."

Under other circumstances, the unintended promotion might have amused Jing Yo, but it only made him even more wary.

"As soon as you see our units, get off the armored car and run away from it," Jing Yo told Wu. "Take no chances."

"You're a fine one to talk about chances."

"Don't compare yourself to me, Sergeant. Simply do your duty."

Jing Yo checked on each of his men, trotting to them in turn. Then he went over to the Vietnamese sergeant. The man was hunkered by the side of the stream, shivering.

It was such a pathetic sight that Jing Yo thought of putting him out of his misery: the man would face a life of shame as a prisoner of war, even after he was released. But he would have to face his fate; Jing Yo could not help him escape it.

The Panhard's machine gun started firing. Jing Yo raced up the embankment and saw that several Vietnamese soldiers had come up through the field near the trees, apparently getting to the road before being spotted. Sergeant Wu had killed all but one; the survivor, having retreated to the ditch at the edge of the road, was firing back with an AK-47. His shots dinged harmlessly off the armored car. But the man was equally protected by his hiding place; Sergeant Wu couldn't manage to silence him.

The firefight had an almost surreal quality, as if it were a practice exercise rather than an actual conflict. Wu would fire several rounds, temporarily silencing the Vietnamese soldier. Then, just as it seemed as if the man were dead, he would start firing from a slightly different position. Wu would respond, and the exchange would continue.

Finally, Wu tossed a hand grenade into the ditch. The AK-47 stopped firing.

A minute later, more trucks appeared on the road. These were pickup trucks, filled with Vietnamese soldiers who hung over the cab and off the back willy-nilly.

Sergeant Wu caught the first truck in the radiator,

the machine gun's bullets slicing into the engine block after passing through the narrow fins. Wu's gun jammed as he swung it toward the second truck just to its left. Cursing, he fired a burst from his own rifle, then climbed out of the armored car and ran back toward the bridge.

By then, everyone else in the squad was emptying their rifles at the rest of the trucks. The Vietnamese threw themselves over the side, desperate to escape the hail of bullets as the vehicles knotted on the road.

"Stop wasting your ammunition!" yelled Jing Yo when he saw they were having little effect on the Vietnamese soldiers. "Let them bunch up! Linn, get ready to take it with a grenade."

The lack of squad radios—a handicap he hadn't had in Malaysia—hurt Jing Yo immensely. He couldn't be sure his men heard what he was saying.

The hell with the army's rules, he decided. He would find a way to procure squad radios as soon as possible.

Jing Yo heard one of the Vietnamese officers yelling something at his men, directing them one way or another—probably away from the truck, though he couldn't quite be sure.

"Fire, Linn!" yelled Jing Yo, worried that they would soon lose their easy target. "Fire!"

Linn may or may not have heard him—they were separated by roughly forty meters—but if not, he read the situation as well as Jing Yo did. The grenade popped from its launcher, rocketing across the darkness in a fiery red flash like a meteorite plunging into the earth's atmosphere. It hit the cab of the truck and exploded, sending shrapnel and debris into the small crowd of soldiers behind it. Panicked, the men began to retreat, only to be caught by Chin, who worked them over with his assault rifle.

The darkness, the confusion of battle, and most of all the inexperience of the Vietnamese soldiers had given the commandos a serious advantage against a numerically superior and more heavily armed foe. But Jing Yo realized that those were nebulous and fleeting qualities in war. His small force could easily be overmatched by the sheer number of Vietnamese soldiers trying to retreat down the road.

The first sign of this danger came a minute or so later, when he saw flashes in the field beyond the trees to his right. The Vietnamese had finally realized they didn't have to use the road to advance.

"Chin! Drop back to the bridge, to the ravine!" Jing Yo ordered. He shouted, then had to resort to using his flashlight to send the message up the road.

Chin acknowledged, and began making his way back.

Had their instructions not been to hold the bridge, now would have been the time to retreat. The commandos had stalled the retreat, killed a large number of enemy soldiers, and not taken any casualties. An artillery strike zeroed in on the destroyed vehicles and then gradually expanding would safely eliminate a sizable portion of the enemy, and provide ample cover for Jing Yo and his men to get away.

But such a strike would almost surely damage the bridge as well, and besides, his instructions were to take and hold the span. It didn't matter that the original plan had called for another three companies to be there to help, or that the bridge seemed, in Jing Yo's opinion, considerably less important than the planners had believed. It mattered that those were his orders, and he knew better than to try and get them changed.

Having Chin retreat saved the private, who could easily have been overrun, but it also allowed the Vietnamese to advance without opposition. Jing Yo could partially compensate for this by having someone flank them from the east; it turned out that Sergeant Wu had already thought of this, and tracers began whipping through the brush and high grass.

A whistle sounded from the Vietnamese line. Jing Yo braced for an all-out attack, then realized that the Vietnamese commander was calling for a retreat.

"Hold your fire," he ordered.

Undoubtedly it would be only a temporary respite. The enemy would regroup quickly.

Jing Yo called division again, to get a read on the location of the vanguard and to tell them that they were under heavy fire at the bridge. The major who was coordinating the attack communications told him that the vanguard was on Highway 12 and would soon be in his area.

"How close are they?" Jing Yo asked. "Can you give me a GPS point?"

"We don't have specific data points," said the major. "Things are in flux, Lieutenant."

"We have a sizable number of enemy in front of us."

"Then you have much opportunity. I must move on; there are many things happening."

Judging only by the sound of explosions in the distance, the battle at the Lai Châu barracks had begun to wind down. But there was no way of knowing how close the tanks and infantry at the leading edge of the assault were. Nor could Jing Yo communicate directly with them.

Colonel Sun could. Jing Yo punched in the colonel's command line. Sun surprised him by answering himself. His voice was nearly drowned out by the sound of explosions.

"Sun."

"Colonel, we are holding the objective on Route 12," said Jing Yo quickly. "We have a large force in front of us."

"Good."

"We have held off two assaults, one by armored cars. The force opposing us is mustering for a fresh attack. We've used about half of our ammunition," said Jing Yo, laying out the problem in its starkest terms. "If they continue to press, we will run out of ammunition."

"Hold your position," snapped Sun.

"If I could get a read from the vanguard—"

"Hold your position."

The colonel snapped off the line.

"On the road!" yelled Sergeant Wu.

"Let them get a little closer," said Jing Yo. "Wait until I fire. Sergeant, watch the right flank—this may just be to get our attention."

Nearly two dozen Vietnamese came up the road, crouching along the sides in the thickest part of the shadows. Jing Yo waited until they were parallel with his position before starting to fire. The others quickly followed, cutting down about half of the attackers within a few seconds. The rest of the enemy fired back erratically, some at the copse, some at the bridge.

A second wave, another two dozen strong, came up behind them. There was no sense waiting this time; the commandos began firing as soon as the enemy was in range, and once again cut down about half the squad. But they took their first casualty as well: Private Bo got hit in the shoulder, and was temporarily out of action.

"Use the grenade launchers!" shouted Jing Yo, and almost immediately three of the small bombs exploded near the burned-out truck and the roadside. Unlike the rocket-propelled weapons, the 40 mm grenades were antipersonnel weapons, modeled on the grenades American infantrymen typically had mounted to their gun barrels. The Chinese version was roughly as dangerous, but they were in very short supply. The commandos had three launchers, with only four rounds apiece.

Gunfire erupted to the far right of the bridge, nearly a hundred meters away. One of the Vietnamese soldiers had been spooked in the dark, and he and his companions fired for thirty or forty seconds before their commander took nearly half a minute to get them under control. There were at least a dozen of them in the field, aiming to come up the flank against the commandos.

As the gunfire petered out, Wu decided to restoke it with a fresh round of grenades, hoping to get the Vietnamese to waste as much of their ammunition as possible. The night became an arc of red light, the gunfire so steady that for a few moments there seemed to be a solid wall of bullets.

Jing Yo ordered the sergeant to fall back, yelling his command and then signaling with the light. Wu acknowledged with a single blink.

Jing Yo and the two privates near him began firing, attracting the Vietnamese soldiers' attention. When the answering fire began to peter out, Jing Yo got up and led the others down the hill, hustling through the trees and then staying low in the field until they reached the ravine. They slid in and moved up to the bridge quickly, reorienting themselves.

They'd have no hope against a concerted attack down the ravine; the enemy would have clear lines of fire to the bridge.

There was a whistle from the woods. This time it was a signal for an attack, and the Vietnamese began firing and rushing forward.

"Lai, Kim, back to the rocks," he said, pointing to a set of low boulders on the bank. "I'll cover from here."

Jing Yo's words were drowned out by two grenades, both of which exploded a short distance away. The Vietnamese were now advancing in front of them and to their side. There were at least several dozen men, maybe a hundred.

Jing Yo tossed a hand grenade, then emptied his gun's magazine, pulled out the box, and slid in the mate he had taped to it. Within seconds he was through that one too, firing too fast, but there were so many bullets flying at him from so many directions that it was impossible to take his time. He hardly had to aim—there were flashes and bodies running toward him everywhere he looked.

He fumbled reloading, his fingers wet with sweat. He fired so quickly that he missed the incendiary round signaling he was near the end of the box, and was surprised when his gun clicked empty.

Jing Yo pushed a replacement into place and started firing again. Grenades exploded in a crescendo. Then something screeched behind the ravine, and suddenly the bullets stopped flying from that direction. Sergeant Wu had begun a counterattack, striking with several grenades into the heart of the Vietnamese force. The enemy was caught in the V of the dried-out stream, where Wu's grenades found easy targets.

Jing Yo turned his attention back to the road. The Vietnamese were very close—all around the burned-out armored cars. He emptied his gun, then threw his last hand grenade.

Jing Yo pressed himself against the dirt, expecting to die now; the only question was whether he would run out of ammunition first.

Another whistle sounded. The enemy gunfire ceased. The Vietnamese commander had called for another retreat.

Jing Yo started to get up to look after his two men, then stopped—they hadn't left his side.

That was a fatal decision for Lai; he'd been shot through the forehead.

Jing Yo took Lai's gun and spare ammo. He'd been down to his last two boxes when he died.

"What ammunition do you have left?" Jing Yo asked Kim.

Kim held up his rifle. Jing Yo gave him Lai's mags.

"Back to the bridge," Jing Yo said.

Kim scrambled up from the streambed and ran toward the nearest dead body, hoping to get his gun and ammunition. It was a good idea, but a very dangerous one—before Jing Yo could warn him, gunfire from the highway shoulder near the burned-out armored car cut the private down. The bullets blew away a good portion of the private's head, leaving no doubt he was dead.

Jing Yo fired in anger, unable to control himself. There was no answering fire, but it was impossible to tell whether he had killed Kim's executioner or merely convinced him to take cover.

He made his way back to the ravine below the bridge. Wu was already there, tending to Chin. The private had been shot in the leg and groin. His blood flowed freely despite the bandage that Wu had placed; Jing Yo took a look at his face and knew he was going to die.

To lose so many men for an insignificant bridge—what would his mentors say?

That he had done his duty.

"Give him morphine," Jing Yo told Wu as Chin began to scream in pain.

"Already did."

Jing Yo opened his med pouch and took out his syringe. He pulled off the plastic protector and plunged it into Chin's leg.

"Something's coming," said Wu. "A truck."

Jing Yo turned to the north, then realized the vehicle was coming from the south.

Ai Gua.

He ran up onto the road. The vehicle did not have its lights on, and at the last moment Jing Yo felt a pang of indecision—what if this wasn't Ai Gua? But then he recognized the shape of the cab.

"Sorry it took so long," said the private, jerking to a stop.

"Pull off the road near the bridge," said Jing Yo. "No—go over the bridge."

Jing Yo leapt onto the running board as Ai Gua put the truck in gear and raced forward. They stopped a few yards beyond the stone pillars. Both men jumped out, ran to the back, and began pulling gear from the back. They managed two trips back to the stream before the Vietnamese began firing at them again.

Their ammunition had been replenished, but the odds were still overwhelming. They were down to six men, counting the wounded Bo.

"We could drop back off the bridge, let them come over, then retake it," suggested Wu as Jing Yo caught his breath. "They're just going to want to get the hell out of here. If we hit them hard enough, they'll run."

Jing Yo frowned.

"Who's gonna know?" said Wu. "And what difference will a hundred Vietnamese make in the end?"

"I'll know," said Jing Yo, rising.

"Trucks coming down the road," said Ai Gua as the sound of the vehicles rose above the cries of the wounded Vietnamese.

"There's going to be another mad rush," said Wu. "We'll be massacred."

"Take your three men and go up to the copse," Jing Yo told him. "Wait until you hear me fire."

Wu frowned, but then waved to the others and began cutting down the streambed to circle into the trees.

Jing Yo told Ai Gua and Bo to move up the ravine to the right and cover him.

"If they begin firing to your right, retreat back to those rocks," Jing Yo told them. He gave them two grenades from the store he'd pulled out of the truck to use to cover the withdrawal.

"Where are you going, Lieutenant?" asked Ai Gua.

"I'm going to rig one of the demolition kits in the truck."

Jing Yo crawled up the side of the streambed, moving across to the pavement on his belly for about ten meters before deciding to risk running the rest of the way. No one fired at him as he leapt into the back of the truck.

It was too dark to see. He got to his knees and began feeling around for metal boxes where the demolition kits were stored. He started to open one, then realized it was a med kit. Finally he found one of the boxes with a double latch. Undoing them, he pulled up the top and reached inside for one of the briefcase-like kits.

The plastic explosives inside were relatively easy to handle. The charges were prewired and set with a small primer package at the side; intended to be put together as modular units and adjusted to the size of the target, they were activated either by a radio signal or, as a backup, wire current.

Radio was the much better option, but it required coding the control and charge units, a safety precaution to keep them from being exploded accidentally or by the enemy. With no time to do that, Jing Yo had to opt for the old-fashioned wire. He took the reel from the side of the case and clipped the leads in place. Then he put the explosive pack back into the storage box, tucked the control unit under his arm, and took the wire, stringing a good bit as he moved to the tailgate.

As he dropped down from the truck, he realized he had left his gun in the back. Cursing, he started to go back, then hit the ground as someone began firing at him. With bullets chewing through the macadam, Jing Yo crawled to the side of the road, stringing the wire out behind him.

He made it to the side of the road without being hit. Once in the ditch, he was no longer a target, and the shooter lost interest. Jing Yo crawled back to the streambed, trailing the wire.

"They're coming!" yelled Ai Gua as engines began revving around the road.

Either forgetting his order or seeing an opportunity too good to pass up, Sergeant Wu's team began firing. The Vietnamese began firing back.

Jing Yo curled himself around the detonator, wrapping the first lead around the metal post. A memory shot into his head—the last time he had done this under fire, in Malaysia. They'd snuck into an oil dump to sabotage some of the tanks, but had been surprised before the work could be completed. His two companions had been killed; he had escaped unscathed.

Luck had been his companion that night. Perhaps it would return.

Jing Yo finished attaching the wire, then unhooked the small hand crank at the side of the device. As he cranked it, he raised his head and peered over the side of the embankment.

Guns were blazing in earnest now—an armored personnel carrier rounded the curve, heading toward the armored cars. Bullets pinged off its side.

"Hold your fire!" yelled Jing Yo. "Wu! Stop firing! Stop! Stop!"

Wu couldn't hear him and continued firing. But the bulk of the Vietnamese were moving with the armored car or along the other side of the road, trying to bypass Wu's position and reach the bridge.

The APC—it appeared to be a captured American relic—rambled to the first armored car. Rather than continuing past, it pushed it off the roadway. A second APC came up behind it as it succeeded in getting the car off the pavement. It took on the second armored car, pushing it to the right.

A troop truck appeared behind it. Jing Yo felt his breath starting to get shallow and forced himself to breathe slowly and deeply.

The first APC approached the truck with the demolitions, aiming to push it out of the way.

Chin's body was between it and the truck. The APC ran over it.

Not yet, Jing Yo told himself.

It would be best if he could get both APCs—he had to get both of them. But the other was ten meters away.

No time.

As the APC's fender smacked up against the truck's cab, Jing Yo pressed the detonator.

Nothing happened.

Jing Yo's fingers flew down to the screws. He checked the connections, retightening them. Then he cranked up the charge again. The truck was screeching on the pavement, pushed sideways toward the edge of the road.

Jing Yo pulled up on the plunger, tugged to make sure it was engaged all the way, then slammed his hand down.

The truck seemed to implode in a flash of light. A crack and deep rumble followed, the explosion so fierce that the wind first pushed and then sucked at Jing Yo's body, trying to pull him into the vaporizing truck.

The explosions and gunfire throughout the battle

had steadily eroded Jing Yo's hearing, but this was so loud it clapped him into hushed silence.

Caught by surprise, the Vietnamese APCs were heavily damaged. The front of the first, which took most of the force, sheared back in a distorted crumple. The other lost its treads and stopped dead. Maybe a dozen infantrymen had come around the bend behind the two APCs; at least half were killed by the explosion.

Nothing moved for a moment, not even Jing Yo's heart. Then there were flashes on the right side of their position—Sergeant Wu and the others had caught sight of a second Vietnamese force off the road, coming up from the rear.

Wu did not have a perfect angle, and a number of the Vietnamese soldiers were able to push past. They reached the streambed to Jing Yo's left. His hearing returned with the stutter of a machine gun, which began firing down in the direction of the bridge from his right.

The tanks were either going to make it to them now, he thought, or they were going to die. It was as simple as that.

He pressed himself against the side of the streambed below the bridge, trying to think of a way to get the machine gun.

The gunfire was too heavy for him to move. Dirt replaced the asphalt taste in his mouth as he pushed closer to the earth. He could hear everything now, wails as well as explosions, the cries of disembodied souls fleeing lifeless bones and skin.

A grenade—Sergeant Wu's last one—took out the

machine gun. Jing Yo heard his men calling to him.

Now was his chance to retreat. He could run down the streambed, cross over, order everyone back.

But he had his orders.

Jing Yo looked around him for his rifle before remembering he'd left it in the truck. He pulled his pistol out, then scrambled up the side of the streambed, deciding he would die on the bridge.

The ground shook with a heavy thud, then another. A black geyser of dirt rose through the moonlight near the curve.

The tanks had arrived.

"Pull back! Pull back to the other side of the bridge!" yelled Jing Yo, his voice hoarse. "The tanks are here. Be careful not to fire at our own men."

11

Northern Vietnam

Mara's conversation with Lucas convinced her of two things: One, the Chinese were moving through Vietnam at a lightning pace, so quickly that it would soon be too late to slip out. And two, it was highly unlikely Lucas would be able to put a plan together anytime soon.

It made absolutely no sense for her to stay in the town, especially if she couldn't provide any useful information. The only question was where to go.

Her best choice was Hanoi. Transportation out of the country would be much easier from there; she might even be able to arrange it herself. She would also be in a much better position to do something if Lucas needed her to.

There was an outside possibility that the scientists, if they weren't already in Chinese custody, had made their way there as well. So Hanoi was the destination.

And there was no sense waiting.

"Let's see this motorbike," she told Tom.

"Two bikes," he said, starting up the road.

"I don't think my friend is going to be up to traveling tonight."

"No. I go with you."

"I don't think so."

"Yes, yes. You need a guide."

"I'm going pretty far." She didn't want to tell him where.

"More reason to come." He stopped and turned to her. "You go to Hanoi, yes?"

"Hanoi?"

He laughed.

"I was thinking of Ho Chi Minh City," she lied.

"Saigon. Better. But first go through Hanoi. I go all the way. I am your guide."

Mara started walking, unsure what else to say. Obviously, a guide would be valuable—but why was he volunteering? For excitement? Or because he was some sort of government agent?

Maybe the villagers hadn't rallied to her because

one of the older men recognized the airplane as belonging to an ancient enemy. Maybe this was a way to get her to Hanoi, and jail, with a minimum of hassle.

And yet, if that were the case, wouldn't the uncle have pretended to help her?

The owner of the motorcycles seemed skeptical, which somehow reassured Mara. Tom convinced him to let them see the bikes, which were parked in a small shed behind his house. The hinges on the door had rusted into nothingness ages ago, and to open it the owner had to grasp the end and pick it up, pivoting it to the side as if it were still connected to the frame.

A two- or three-year-old Honda sat just beyond the threshold. Moonlight gleamed off the handlebars and glossy gas tank. The owner went to it and wheeled it from the shed.

"How much does he want?" Mara asked.

"It's not that bike," said Tom.

The bikes that were for sale—or might be—sat at the back of the shed. These were decidedly older, battered and dirty but not, as far as she could tell, rusted. They were Hondas, though not models she was familiar with from the States, or anywhere else for that matter.

"These work?" said Mara.

Not waiting for Tom to translate—her skepticism was evident—the owner seated himself on one of the bikes and kicked at the starter. It started on the second try, oily smoke pumping from the exhaust.

"It doesn't have a light," said Mara.

"That one does," said Tom.

The owner left the bike running and went to the second. This one took several tries before it coughed to life. It stalled as soon as the owner tried revving the engine, and refused to start again.

"How much does he want for this one?" Mara asked, pointing at the one that had run.

"It's a package deal," said Tom. "Two or none."

"That's not what he said, Tom."

"Your Vietnamese is not very good."

"I can ask him myself."

She tried, but the owner either didn't understand what she was saying, or was too busy fiddling with the bike's engine to pay attention. After a few minutes of coaxing and gentle cursing, the bike revved to life.

"Good Honda, yes?" said the owner, a broad smile on his face.

"Does the light work?"

Tom translated, and the owner flicked it on. The beam grew stronger and weaker in rough sync with the uneven engine.

"How much?" asked Mara.

The two men began negotiating in Vietnamese. Finally Tom turned to her and said, "He'll rent both for two hundred American."

"I want to buy. And just one."

"He won't sell. Rent."

"Tell him it's unlikely I'll be back."

"He's not going to sell."

"Tell him. Tell him the Chinese are coming."

"He won't believe that."

"I'll tell him."

Tom turned back to the owner and began explaining that she wouldn't be able to get back—or at least Mara thought that's what he was saying; she couldn't keep up with the words as they flew back and forth.

"He will rent both for one seventy-five. Last offer."

"I want to buy them," Mara insisted.

"Not going to happen." He smiled, obviously proud that he knew an appropriate piece of American slang.

"I just want one."

"If I come with you, I can find someone to drive the motorcycle back," said Tom. "This is cheaper than buying, no? And you need a guide."

"All right," said Mara finally. "I need to go back to the village to get the money."

She didn't have that much cash, but figured she could borrow it from Kieu. Tom, nearly ecstatic, began negotiating for gasoline. His tone was even more enthusiastic than before, and the two men appeared close to arguing before Mara finally cut them off.

"We'll take his price, his last price," she said. "I don't want to be here all night."

Kieu was sleeping soundly when she returned. Mara felt guilty as she went through his pants, now folded and placed carefully on his shoes at the side of the bed. The money she'd given him earlier was clipped in a wedge in his hip pocket, apparently untouched by the man looking after him, though Mara guessed it was more money than he would see in a year. His honesty made her feel even more guilty, and after counting out the bills—along with a little extra to help her get to Hanoi—she decided she would write out an IOU to make it clear that she intended to return the cash. The only paper she could find was the credit card receipt for the fuel; she tucked it into the wedge of bills and pushed it back into his pocket, folding the clothes at the edge of the bed.

"Someone will be back for you, if it's not me," she told him, though he hadn't stirred. "We'll pay for the plane."

She saw the village doctor standing by the door as she tiptoed out.

"I'm going to pay him back," she said. "I gave him the money in the first place."

He didn't answer.

"How long before he can travel?" she said, ignoring his stern look of disapproval.

"Four or five days. The pain will be greatest tomorrow."

"I'll be back," said Mara, but her cracking voice didn't even convince herself.

12

Bangkok

Peter Lucas massaged his forehead, trying to rub away the fatigue.

"You think this guy is real?" he asked DeBiase.

"There is a MacArthur on the team. Who would go to the trouble of faking this?"

"The Chinese maybe. The Vietnamese."

"Why?"

"I don't know."

"The satellite phone number belongs to the team."

"Somebody could have found it. The Chinese."

"What would they have to gain by this?"

"Yeah."

Still, Lucas didn't like it. It was too enticing somehow, a big prize that had dropped into his lap.

Or *maybe* a prize. The guy could easily be dead by now.

"Best way to find out is to try calling the number," said DeBiase. "It will go through our system, bypassing the jammed satellite. You have nothing to lose."

The Chinese wouldn't be able to jam the incoming call, but because Josh was using a commercial phone, the call could not be encrypted. If the Chinese happened to pick up the frequency—not a certainty, but a definite possibility—they'd hear everything.

But there was no other alternative—what the scientist had said was too enticing to pass up.

"Let's give it a try," Lucas told DeBiase. Then he leaned back against the console, waiting.

A thousand miles away in Vietnam, Josh McArthur had come to the end of his energy. Embedded in his small hollow near the side of the road, he stopped fighting fatigue and let his eyes close.

His mind began drifting. Different thoughts floated through his consciousness. Suddenly he was talking to his uncle, explaining what was going on.

Except it wasn't his uncle. And he was no longer dreaming.

"Everyone at the science camp was killed?" said the voice.

"What's your name?"

"Peter. My name is Peter. You're sure of what you saw?"

"Everyone was killed. And in the village."

"Could you find the village on a map?"

"Yeah."

"I don't want you to tell me where it is," added the voice quickly. "Okay?"

"Okay." Josh had only a rough idea now anyway. "I have video."

"Video?"

"Yeah."

"Okay."

Was he sleeping? Josh realized he was awake—

truly awake. The phone had rung and he'd answered
it still mostly asleep, with his brain working on automatic.

They're going to rescue me. This is real.

He pushed out of his niche, standing on the road.
The air seemed cool.

"Can you get me out of here?" he asked.

"Yeah. Yeah. We will. It's not going to be easy."

"I know that. Are you going to get me out?"

"Yes."

"When?"

"Soon. For the time being, stay where you are."

That's impossible, thought Josh. But he didn't want
to disappoint the man, who might be his only chance
for help.

Lucas rubbed his eyes as he looked at the map,
pinpointing Josh MacArthur's location with the
help of the data DeBiase had gotten from the satellite.
It was about ten kilometers from the science camp,
very close to the Chinese border.

Very, very close.

Where was Mara?

Eighty-five kilometers away.

Far, even if the country wasn't at war. And she'd
have to cross into the area under Chinese control.

He couldn't send just her. He'd need more people, a
full team.

The hostage rescue unit. Or SEAL Team 2.

Either way, he needed his boss to sign off. But he

would. This was big—a video of atrocities, an eyewitness.

"Josh, are you still with me?" he asked.

"Yes. I'm here."

"I need you to—" Lucas stopped short. He was on an open line; he couldn't say anything.

Probably the Chinese weren't listening. They had so much else to do.

"What do you need?" asked Josh.

"I need you to . . . I need you to hide for a while."

"I *am* hiding. When are you going to get me?"

"Can we play it by ear?" Lucas asked. "I have a few—"

"No. I want to get out of here."

"We'll get you out." Lucas winced, remembering he'd said the same thing to Mara a short while before. "I just need time to work out the details."

"How long?"

"It will take a while. At least a day."

"*A day?*"

"Maybe even longer." He had to be honest. "A few days. Can you make it?"

Josh didn't answer at first. When he did, he sounded resigned. Not distraught, just resigned. "I can last a few days. Longer if I have to."

"Just a few days. I'll call you back."

"When?"

Lucas bit his lip, trying to think what to say, and worried that he had already given away too much. He didn't want to make it obvious that he knew the Chinese were blocking calls. He also didn't want to give a specific time, which would make it easier to intercept his transmission.

Or even jam it, if they figured out how he was able to get around their gear.

"I'm moving around," he told Josh finally. "I'm hard to get. But I can call you. At noon, I'll call you."

"Noon tomorrow?"

"Yes. Can you make it until then?"

"Of course."

"Good."

"Good."

"All right then," said Lucas. "I'm going to hang up."

But Josh MacArthur had already killed the line.

13

Washington, D.C.

President Greene began swinging back and forth ever so slightly in the chair, a nervous habit he had picked up as a young pilot. If he cared to, he could probably have recalled the exact moment it started—a preflight briefing before a bombing mission up the Ho Chi Minh Trail.

The irony would have struck him as extremely amusing—but this was not a moment for either irony or amusement.

"The Vietnamese aren't saying anything officially."

Secretary of State Knox paused to rub his chin. He seemed genuinely insulted by the Vietnamese government's reluctance to acknowledge they were in very deep trouble. "It's possible that they simply don't understand what's going on. It's all moving very quickly. Very quickly."

"They've put troops in Lang Son, Bac Giang, and Quang Ninh provinces on alert in the last hour," said Walter Jackson, the national security director. "They appear to believe the main thrust will come from the northeast."

"Don't you?" asked Knox.

"No. Admittedly they have troops there. But my Southeastern Asian expert thinks this is their main attack. The intelligence is still inconclusive."

"There are a hell of a lot of troops in southeast China," said Knox. "More than three times what Vietnam can field in the region. And they've made a show of moving there over the past several hours."

"Exactly," said Jackson. "They want them to be seen."

"The units in that area are all undermanned," said Frost, the CIA director. "And there's no armor to speak of."

"They attacked sooner than we thought," said Knox. "And they're moving faster. Frankly, we've been underestimating them."

You have, thought Greene. The rest of us haven't. I haven't.

Greene's thoughts flew back to his year in the Vietnamese POW camp, and then to the day of his release at the very end of the war. He could feel the hot tears that welled in his eyes—the first tears that he'd cried since the early days of torture. Tears of relief—and the vow that he would one day get revenge.

This was his opportunity, wasn't it? Yet his duty demanded precisely the opposite.

Irony.

"Will they let us help them?" Greene said abruptly, turning to the secretary of state.

"I honestly don't know," said Knox.

"What did you have in mind?" asked Jackson.

"Intelligence for starters," said the president. "Let them at least know what they're dealing with."

Greene rose. He had too much energy, physical as well as mental, to stay still when considering a problem. "We can't just let the Chinese roll through Vietnam," he added.

"Putting American troops into Vietnam—even I know that's political suicide," said Knox.

"We'd never get anything there beyond a token force anyway," admitted Jackson. "And that's if the Vietnamese even accepted our help."

But the problem *wasn't* Vietnam, it was China. Greene had known for years this day would come: the moment when China decided it no longer needed to play by the rest of the world's rules. He hated parallels to the past, and was especially wary of comparisons to the years before World War II—they were too easy, too glib.

But if ever a situation looked like a replay of Hitler's invasion of Czechoslovakia, this was it.

Or maybe the annexation of Austria. At least Czechoslovakia had generated some outrage. Early indications were that this would barely draw a yawn at the UN.

And forget about the American public's reaction.

"We can't just let the Chinese roll through Vietnam," insisted Greene. "They must be stopped."

"A weak show of force would be worse than no show of force," said Jackson. "I agree with the Chiefs on that."

"We could talk to the Vietnamese under the guise of preparing the protest to the UN," said the secretary of state. "And give them intelligence that way."

"Good," said Greene. "That's a start."

"The Chinese have been working the justified-strike angle hard already," said Knox. "They're claiming they were attacked first."

"What a bunch of horse shit," said the president.

"The photo intelligence is ambiguous," said Knox. "It's possible—"

"None of the other intelligence backs that up," said Frost. "Besides, the Vietnamese aren't that stupid."

"Enough people will pretend they believe what the Chinese say," said Greene. "That's their goal. Make it hard to pass a resolution condemning them. Keep public opinion on their side, or at least paralyzed."

This was the way war was fought in the twenty-first century, Greene thought—with one eye on world opinion and the other on the battlefield. But hadn't it always been that way? Roosevelt, fighting the most popular war in American history, had worked tirelessly to make sure the voters remained supportive of the war effort. Even George Washington had staged his most famous—and desperate—attacks at Trenton and Princeton to convince his fellow countrymen that the war could be won.

"We just have to prove the Chinese are full of crap," said Jackson.

"Easier said than done," admitted Greene.

14

Bangkok

Peter Lucas bent forward as he rose from his chair, trying to unkink the knots in his back.

"This guy is a witness to a Chinese massacre," Lucas said, addressing the image of his boss, CIA DDO Harold Park, projected on the flat screen in front of him. "He's a scientist. He has a video. A video. That's gold. More than gold. You saw the bulletins coming out of Beijing. They all make it sound as if Hanoi pushed troops over their border. The Europeans will buy it. Because they need peace. They don't want China canceling contracts and withdrawing deposits because they voted the wrong way in the UN. Unless things are so obvious, so criminal, that they have no choice. That's what this guy represents."

The media campaign had started, and it was a good one, with terse reports to the official press, and several off-the-record remarks on the situation to the resident AP and Reuters correspondents, all indicating that Vietnam had unexpectedly crossed the border. Chinese troops were rushing to respond.

Hanoi had yet to comment. If the NSA intercepts were any indication, they had only a vague idea of what was going on. One of the CIA analysts had said they seemed to be in denial about what was happening.

"Where is this guy?"

"His last transmission was about ten kilometers from the science camp, a little more than five kilometers south of the border. We think we know which village he was referring to. It's a Hmong settlement, very small. We've set it up for long-range surveillance by one of the Global Hawks. It looks to be right in the area where the Chinese advanced." Lucas pressed closer to the video camera. "I'm sure this is just the tip of the iceberg, Harry. I've been looking at what the Chinese did in 1979, as they withdrew from Vietnam. They burned everything down. They hate the Vietnamese. You know what the rhetoric is like. I could see them doing this easily."

"I have no doubt," said Park bitterly. "What if the Chinese find your man first?"

"They may."

Park stared at the camera broadcasting his image. It was more scowl than stare; Lucas knew he was working out the different possibilities in his head.

Then suddenly his face relaxed—the sign that he had made his decision.

"What do you need?" Park asked.

"SEAL Team Two."

"Off limits."

"Why?"

"We won't get military personnel in. No U.S. personnel. I won't even bother asking. I'll only be shot down."

"Just—"

"Negative. U.S. military personnel are off limits."

"All right. The hostage rescue team."

"No. Same reason."

"I'll use my own people."

"No American fingerprints, Peter. I don't want anyone else going into that country."

"Not even for this?"

"Especially for this. It's too dangerous."

"All right. The company from Korea we used in southern China last year."

Park was speaking from a secure situation room at Langley; at least four other people were working nearby, though the system prevented Lucas from seeing anything more than shadows. One of them apparently said something to Park off camera. He turned away from the screen for a moment.

"Can you get them into Vietnam?" asked Park when he came back.

"Yes."

"Quickly?"

"Yes."

Lucas wasn't sure how quickly he could get them there—or even if they'd take the job. But uncertainty wasn't the way to win Park over.

"They're expensive," said Park.

"They're worth it. And so is MacArthur. And his video."

"Do it."

"Thanks." Lucas reached for the switch to kill the communication.

Park started to say something, but someone to the right of the screen caught his attention. Lucas watched as he bent over and conferred with an aide whom Lucas didn't recognize. When Park came back on camera, his scowl had deepened.

"The Vietnamese won't be able to remain in denial for very much longer," he told Lucas. "The Chinese have just launched an air attack on the port facilities at Hai Phong."

Northern Vietnam

The spare can of gas Mara had strapped to the seat was only three-quarters full, and the gas sloshed every time the motorcycle hit a bump. The whole can shook and bounced every time she hit a bump, even though she'd stopped twice to make sure it was secure. Now it even bounced on the flat macadam.

Compared to the roads they'd taken out of Nam Det, Highway 2 was a superhighway. Not only was the road well paved—at least by Vietnamese standards—but it was also comparatively straight, which made it much easier to follow Tom. It was only two lanes across, but even during the day the road would have been empty for vast stretches, as it was now.

Mara had given Tom the motorcycle with the headlight, figuring that it made more sense for him to have it, since he was the one who knew where they were going. The problem was that he kept roaring ahead, and she had trouble staying with him. When they went through Vin Tuy—a small village on the outskirts of the Cham Chu Nature Reserve—she nearly missed the turn the highway took in the middle of town, guessing the way only after stopping and realizing the more logical choice was asphalt, not hard-pressed dirt.

Vin Tuy was tiny and quiet. So was Tân Yên, a slightly larger village about sixty kilometers farther south. The buildings looking like empty movie sets as she roared past.

Mara took the eerie quiet as an ominous sign. From what Lucas had said, the Chinese had launched an all-out invasion. Yet there was no sign of a response. The military and police checkpoints Mara expected were nowhere to be seen. Vietnam seemed to be sleeping through its incoming devastation.

Small farms dotted the jungle on both sides of the

highway as she continued south. The global climate changes that had altered Vietnam's rainfall patterns had encouraged more farming. This was especially evident in the central highlands and the south, where large swaths of jungle were being reclaimed and smaller plots were being consolidated to accommodate modern farming techniques. In the north, while the ground was just as fertile, the rugged hillside made development more difficult. It might be years before most of the uncultivated land was plowed under for farming.

Mara remembered the fields of her own childhood, paved over rather than plowed up as suburban sprawl marched inexorably across the American landscape. Now it was going back the other way—her uncle, who lived in a distant Philadelphia suburb, had just sold his tract house to a European agribusiness that planned to turn the development into a cornfield.

Roughly twenty minutes south of Tân Yên, tall shadows loomed on Mara's left. For a moment she thought she saw a missile launcher in the black space beyond the road. There were two, five, but no activity around them.

Then she realized she was looking at a strip mine operation, an open pit where bauxite was extracted. She had mistaken the harmless machinery for something much more lethal. They were getting close to Tuyên Quang, a city about seventy-five kilometers north of Hanoi, nestled in the valley between the Con Voi and Tam Dao mountains.

It was also the place where they had arranged to stop and refuel their bikes. Houses began to appear close to the road, in ones and twos at first, then in clumps, then in solid rows. Mara found it harder and harder to keep up with Tom; her bike was slightly less powerful than his, but more important, the shadows and her fatigue ate at her confidence, and she couldn't force herself to drive any faster. Finally she lost sight of his dim red taillight, the road taking a twist before entering town.

This would have been the perfect spot for a military or police sentry, but there was none. Mara slowed, mentally rehearsing the words she would use if she was stopped. But the main street was as deserted as those of the small villages farther north. It was only as she was leaving town—with Tom's brake light finally ahead in the distance—that she saw an army transport. It was parked on a side street. The tailgate was up, but she could see someone moving near it as she passed.

Tom stopped at the side of the road about a kilometer outside of the city limits. He'd already filled his tank and thrown away his gas can when she drove up.

"You turtle," he laughed. "Me hare."

"Don't forget the turtle wins in the end," said Mara.

When she got off the bike, she realized that the rusted top corner of the can had sprung a leak. It was minuscule, but enough gas had spit out to wet the back of her shirt. She squeezed the liquid from her shirt and pants, but the odor seemed to get stronger.

The Clear River bent close to the highway; she could see it as she emptied the gas can into her tank. Some of the smaller tributaries near the road were dry, but there was still a sizable pond a dozen meters from the road. Mara went down to it, stripped off her shoes, and waded in, dunking herself in a vain attempt to rinse the smell away.

"You crazy lady?" asked Tom as she climbed back up to the bike.

"I felt like taking a bath."

"Hanoi two hours," he said, kicking his bike to life. "Less if you drive fast like me."

"Wait!" yelled Mara.

She wanted to go over again how they would deal with anyone who stopped them, emphasizing her status as a journalist, but Tom had already launched his bike. She went to hers, got it going—the kicks got easier with practice—and set off after him.

Route 2 crossed the river near Viet Triv. Fish farms had been built in the delta formed by the river and its tributaries; the pennants that marked the underwater fences fluttered in the moonlight as they passed. The land flattened, with large communal farms gradually giving way to a real city—Vinh Yen, the provincial capital and the headquarters for an infantry division.

The army base lay on the northern side of the city, away from the highway and most of the civilian population. Lulled by her earlier experiences, Mara was surprised to find the road ahead blocked by a pair of jeeplike vehicles. Two soldiers, one with a rifle slung over his shoulder, the other with a set of traffic flags, stood in front of the trucks.

Tom was nowhere in sight. Mara had her passport with her, and a credible cover story, but with only a second or two to make up her mind, she followed the instincts that told her not to stop if she could possibly help it. Hunkering down near the handlebars, she squeezed the throttle and shot by the soldiers.

Her burst of speed made it much harder for her to keep her balance as she ran across a series of bumps a few meters beyond the trucks. The bike vibrated worse than a bronco on a cold Texas night. Easing off the throttle, she saw an army truck up ahead—another checkpoint.

If she was going to avoid one, she was going to avoid them all. Spotting a street to the right, Mara turned down it, nearly ditching the bike as the pavement changed from macadam to dirt.

Mara tucked left with the road, found another intersection, and turned back to the right, following the general direction south and hoping Highway 2 would appear soon. But the road took her into a maze of low-slung apartment buildings, new housing for government workers lucky enough to win selection in the bureaucratic lottery—or more likely, perceptive enough to find the right person to bribe. She went left, then right, then left again, finally running out of roadway and crossing a field rutted by trucks. Seeing what she thought was the road to her left, Mara started to lean and accelerate, only to find herself flying headfirst over the handlebars.

The ground came up too fast for her to react, let alone think. She smashed her nose hard, felt her left shoulder crash and give way. Her body twirled hard left as she slid another six feet.

"Shit, that hurt," said Mara, pushing her hands under her chest and lifting herself up.

Her cheeks had been scraped so badly they felt like they were on fire; her nose felt soft, full of blood. She pushed the dirt away from her eyes, then spun quickly, sure she was about to be grabbed by the soldiers. But there was no one there, only the bike, groaning as it circled in the dust, its rear wheel still engaged and propelling it in a crazy arc.

Mara grabbed the handlebars and pushed it upright, trying to mount as she did. But the throttle had jammed, and the wheel was moving too fast for her. She fell back on her butt, just barely managing to throw the Honda off to the other side as she went down.

"Let's go, let's go," she told herself, willing her body to get itself back on its feet. She grabbed the bike and killed the engine. Back upright, it took only a kick to get it restarted, but the transmission had gotten stuck in fourth gear, and as soon as the clutch engaged, it stalled. She pushed forward to a little hill, started moving downhill, then restarted the engine. The bike jerked and bucked as she let go of the clutch, but didn't stall; she worked the controls and unjammed whatever had tied it up.

Her nose was bleeding. Blood trickled down, a few drops at a time, to the left corner of her mouth. Her cheeks burned where she'd scraped them, and hurt more with the wind as she rode. She didn't dare try to peek in the mirror to see what her face looked like.

It took Mara nearly a half hour of zigging and zagging to find Route 2. There was no sign of Tom on the road; if he'd made it through the checkpoints, he could easily be halfway to Hanoi by now.

Mara drove in dull numbness for the next hour and a half, her mind in a state of semishock. It was far from the most dire situation she'd ever faced—not even in the top three—but still, her body needed to recover from the pounding.

When she spotted the glow of lights from Noi Bai Airport in the distance, Mara examined her options again. The best might be simply to go there, grab a plane—any plane—and get the hell out.

She was too bloody for that; she needed new clothes and a bath.

A long, long bath, in a tub filled with Epsom salts.

And then?

She'd be needed here. She couldn't bug out when there was work to be done.

Expecting that the airport would be a mustering point for the army as well as the air force, Mara took a right onto the first decent-looking road she came to, heading south. She hadn't had much to eat back in the village, and on top of the bruises and cuts, she was beginning to feel faint. She wasn't tired at least—her heart was beating too fast to let her rest.

There were plenty of houses along the road, and Mara slowed, hoping to see one with a clothesline where she could steal a dress. About a mile after turning off the main highway she came to a shantytown of shacks, each seemingly leaning on the other. She decided it would be the perfect place to "shop."

Idling back her engine, Mara eased the bike into the warren of houses, looking down the alleys into the backyards. Rope was strung between the houses for clotheslines, but there were only a few items out; the handful of things she saw that might be close to her size were dresses, and she would have greatly preferred pants. But she was in no position to be too picky, and after leaning the bike against a building across the way, she slipped back through the alley and found a dress and pair of men's pants that looked as if they would fit.

She felt guilty about taking the clothes, which were undoubtedly among the family's few possessions. Her conscience suggested that she leave one of her hundred-dollar bills, but that might be dangerous for the family, since it would inevitably raise questions about where the funds had come from. In the end, she left nothing.

Mara drove back to the highway, then found a narrow lane that led to a fallow field where she could change. The pants came to her calves, but their pockets gave her a place where she could tuck her satellite phone, money, and ID. She hiked the dress—a bit short and tight at the bosom, though ample at the waist—and folded it beneath her thighs so she could ride the bike more easily. Then she set back out for Hanoi, dumping her pants in a ditch before returning to the highway.

Two kilometers later, Mara saw a dim red shadow from a flashing police light beyond the next rise. She pulled over, checking her passport, but decided to avoid the checkpoint by going back to the side streets.

There were still a few hours before dawn, and it would seem more than a little odd to a Vietnamese policeman that a foreigner was driving when almost no one else was.

Her first right took her down a street lined with warehouse buildings, all relatively new. Streetlights lit the intersections, hazes of yellow mist wafting around the lights.

She started to turn left at the first intersection, then pulled back as she caught sight of a line of trucks idling in the road ahead. They looked like troop trucks, but it was dark and she didn't think it wise to stop or get any closer to find out.

Mara wound her way through the industrial park into an apartment complex and then an older residential area, going slowly to soften the noise of her engine. She had only the vaguest idea of where she was in the city, and soon became confused enough that she decided she needed to take a break. Making sure she was alone, she pulled off to the side of the road on a quiet street down the hill from an apartment complex.

Mara decided to check in with Bangkok. She couldn't call from the Star, and whoever was on the communications desk might also be able to point her in the right direction. She was getting low on gas, and admitting she was lost was better than walking.

"It's Mara," she said as the line connected.

"This is Peter."

"Hey, boss."

"I'm glad you checked in. We have a developing situation. That science team—"

"Fleming?"

"Somebody else on the team. He's south of Lao Cai. You think you can get there?"

"Yeah. No problem. He's in the city?"

"No, he's in the jungle somewhere. We're working on getting a real fix—we can track his satellite phone, but only when he transmits. How long will it take you?"

"I have no idea. A day, maybe. I'll have to find better wheels."

Lucas didn't answer for a moment. Then he asked where she was, surprise in his voice.

"That's a good question. I got kind of confused on these side streets—"

"You're in *Hanoi*."

"Right. Somewhere west of the center of town, but I don't—"

"What the hell are you doing there? Didn't I tell you to stay where you were?"

"No, you didn't."

"Bullshit—"

"You told me you didn't know when you could get me out. I figured if I'd stayed there, I'd be behind Chinese lines."

"Goddamn it."

"I didn't know you were going to give me another assignment. You should have told me."

"That's not the point, Mara."

"Don't worry about it. I can get back. There are no checkpoints beyond Vinh Yen. Do these people realize they're at war?"

"You're two hundred friggin' kilometers from where MacArthur is."

"Where is he exactly?"

"You're *not* going back."

"Where is he?"

"I don't know."

"Well, then how do you know he's two hundred friggin' kilometers away? Give me the location of the last transmission."

"Get yourself to the embassy. Get out."

"Like hell. If I go to the embassy, I'm burned for Southeast Asia. Right? The Vietnamese watch the place around the clock. That's the reason you didn't use them for this. Correct?"

"Get your ass to Hanoi."

"I'm in Hanoi."

"I want you out of the country, Mara. Come back to Bangkok."

"Bullshit!" Mara couldn't help herself. "This is what I'm trained to do, Peter—you want this guy? Fine. I'm here. I'm ready. You have a covert fucking mission, it's mine. You know I'm good. You know what I've done. You know this is for me."

"You're supposed to do what you're told," he said, his voice slightly more subdued.

"You did *not* tell me to stay put. And even if you had—which you didn't—if you had, it's up to the officer in the field to make the final call. Lucas—Peter—you always say you don't second-guess. . . . If I were a man, you would *not* be giving me crap over this, Peter. I know you wouldn't. You're treating me like your daughter. And I'm not. I'm a field agent. With experience. Good experience. This is my mission, these scientists."

"I don't think of you as my daughter."

"Then why are you giving me crap? Because of Malaysia?"

"You did fine in Malaysia."

"So it's sex, huh?"

The words weren't coming out the way she wanted them to, but she was too mad to get them into the right order.

"This is what I was trained to do," she repeated. "Don't screw me here, Peter."

"Damn it, Mara, give me a break."

She heard him expel a deep breath, almost a hoarse sigh, as if his whole body were involved in the act of thinking, of making a decision.

Men always claimed that they didn't think about an officer's gender before making a decision on a mission, but Mara and most other women knew that was a crock; it always entered into the equation, whether consciously or not. She was always fighting to overcome the prejudice. Every woman did.

"I'll be back in Nam Det by this time tomorrow," she said. "I'll need a good location by then."

"You're going to need help. The Chinese are all around him."

"So get me help."

Before Lucas could reply, the ground shook as if in an earthquake. The night flashed white, then red. Mara turned around on the bike and saw flames shooting up from the industrial area she'd driven through just before. Flames popped up in a row to the north. There were more explosions, and then antiaircraft guns and sirens began to sound.

"Mara?"

"I'll have to call you back," she told Lucas.

"Mara!"

"Hanoi's on fire. It's being bombed. The whole goddamn city, from the looks of it."

OIL EXPORTS DOWN, REVENUE
UP IN MALAYSIA

KUALA LUMPUR, MALAYSIA (World News Service)—While oil exports dropped due to a decline in production at the Sahah off-shore oil fields, income rose by nearly eighty percent last year due to the continuing increase in energy prices, the oil ministry reported today.

The increase was roughly in line with analysts' projections. Other oil producers, notably Saudi Arabia and Venezuela, have reported similar increases over the past week.

UN BEGS FRESH RELIEF EFFORT
IN SOUTH AMERICA

BUENOS AIRES (World News Service)—UN Secretary General Cyrus Bapoto today called on Western governments to increase funding to aid countries in South America devastated by climate change.

Bapoto recited now all-too-familiar statistics detailing the devastation of agriculture in South American economies, including the virtual evaporation of Argentina's beef production.

Until recently, Argentina accounted for approximately eight percent of world beef exports. A combination of decline in purchasing power of its traditional markets and widespread drought in the Pampa Húmeda region have provided a double whammy to Argentina. The country's economic crisis is even worse than 1999–2002, with the GDP expected to decline roughly twenty percent this year. The decline comes on top of a fifteen percent decline over the last six months of 2013.

NON-RICE PADDY RICE SCIENTISTS' DREAM

GIVERNEY, FRANCE (Reuters–Gannet News Service)—Here in the bucolic town that once inspired some of the world's most beautiful Impressionist painters, a French scientist is working on hybrid plants that he hopes will one day solve the world's famine crisis.

His goal: rice that can be grown on dry land.

Professor Pierre Valois, 52, has already successfully bred several versions of the plant that require only about half the rainfall of the mainstream variants. He cautions, however, that he may be "five or six years" from finding a "waterless rice," and that it may take ten years beyond that to prepare seeds for farmers in sufficient numbers to make production worthwhile.

More promising is a salt-water variety, which Valois says can be grown in ocean areas. The crop's yield so far has been disappointing—merely one-tenth of a normal rice paddy—still, the scientist thinks rice may be grown in sea farms by the beginning of the next decade . . .

Chaos

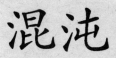

1

Northwestern Vietnam, near the border with China

Josh opened his eyes into a gray stillness.

His chest and legs ached; his hip felt bruised. His neck, stiff from sleep, felt cold.

It was still dark, at least an hour if not more before dawn.

Slowly, he pushed himself from his side to his belly, then raised his head and chest. Gripping the pistol, he crawled from his hiding spot and slipped down to the path, rifle in his hand. There he turned around in a slow circle, pausing every few degrees to listen as best as he could to the jungle, trying to detect any sound made by machines.

When he was sure no one was nearby, Josh went back to the niche where he'd slept and took a drink of water from the soldier's bottle. He slipped the pistol into his pocket. He did the same with the satellite phone, sliding it next to the video camera in his left pocket.

The satellite phone's software lock made it impossible to check the calls-received list. But he knew the call hadn't been a dream. Someone was going to help him.

In the meantime, he had to find some food. And a real place to hide.

Josh decided he would wait for the dawn, but after only a few minutes he found himself walking. It was impossible to stand still, he realized, and maybe even dangerous. When he came to a Y in the path, he turned left, believing it led south.

The farther south he was, the easier it would be for his rescuers, Josh thought. Here, he was too close to the Chinese border.

About fifteen minutes after starting, still before light, Josh smelled something burning. Immediately, he felt disappointed, almost depressed—smoke meant the people who lived in whatever village was nearby were awake already, which would make it hard for him to sneak in and find food. But he kept walking, slowing as he neared curves and pausing every so often to listen in case someone was coming.

The village had been built on the hillside above the path. The trail skirted around it, just at the edge of the jungle, coming no closer than a hundred meters. Josh didn't realize this until he had gone about halfway around the settlement. He backtracked to a spot where his approach would be hidden by bushes, and began sneaking closer to the hamlet.

The sun was just about to rise; the trees and bushes in front of him seemed to have turned a light shade of blue, standing out from the gray.

The scent of tea wafted down the hill. Josh's stomach began to rumble.

He was incredibly hungry. Should he show himself?

Josh heard voices. He lowered himself to his knees, trying to see who was talking. When he found he couldn't, he began moving up the hill again, this time crawling on his hands and knees. He heard the light singsong of voices, but saw nothing until he came to a low fence or wall made of logs stacked two high and laid out on the edge of the slope.

Something moved just beyond the fence, shadows, people.

Men in uniform.

He stared through the trees. He could see only their legs, but he was convinced they were Chinese.

Josh began moving backward. Each sound he made seemed to echo around him, and with each push he thought the soldiers would finally hear him and rush down the hill to kill him.

Finally, he reached the trail again. He took a small sip of water and considered what to do.

Part of him wanted to go back and kill as many of the bastards as possible. The emotion, his anger, surprised him. He wasn't sure where it came from. He should be afraid, petrified.

He *was* afraid. But he also wanted revenge. And maybe just to stop the ordeal.

Going back was suicide, and he wasn't ready for that. He didn't need it—he was getting out. And he was going to help the world fight these bastards.

He started walking again, quietly but quickly, aiming to get around the village and away from the troops as soon as he could. After a few steps, he realized the sun was coming up over his right shoulder: he was headed north.

Josh changed course, heading back toward the split in the path he'd taken earlier.

Near Hanoi

A wave of missiles hit the north side of Hanoi just as Mara got the motorcycle started. The explosions were no closer than a mile away, but they shook the ground so fiercely that Mara nearly lost control of the bike.

A bright meteor flew overhead—the tail end of a malfunctioning missile arcing in the direction of the old city. Antiaircraft batteries north and east of the city began to fire. Geysers of yellow smoke shot up a few hundred yards ahead, foaming across the sky. A black streak passed through the top of the cloud, then several more; explosions shook the ground.

Ten minutes before, no one in the city seemed to be awake. Now everyone was up and running into the streets. Mara turned onto an avenue flanked by five- and six-story apartment buildings and found herself surrounded by people, many in their nightclothes, who surged to the middle of the road and stared at the sky above. She had to brake hard to avoid hitting an elderly man dressed in pajama bottoms and holding a broomstick in his hand. He turned and looked at her, brandishing the broom as if it were a halberd.

The next block was just as crowded, with people running back and forth or staring in disbelief at the sky. Antiaircraft tracers sprayed in furious streaks while the ground jumped up and down with fresh explosions. The entire northern horizon was red. Sirens began wailing above the explosions. Here and there a woman or child screamed, but most of the people in the streets were quiet, shocked into silence.

Turning down a side street, Mara found her path blocked by a small delivery van, which itself had been blocked by two other cars. It was nearly impossible to squeeze through the people jamming into the street around the vehicles. Mara had to inch forward with her feet on the ground. People began to take hold of her, clinging to her as if she were some good luck charm. They pulled her left and right, making it harder and harder for her to keep her balance.

"Sister, you must help us," pleaded an older woman in Vietnamese, curling herself around her arm.

"Yes," answered Mara, unsure what to say.

They walked together for a minute more, both silent. The woman saw someone and began to pull away, tugging for Mara to come with her.

"I'm sorry, I can't," said Mara, using English this time.

She unhooked her arm and pushed the motorcycle forward, hitting the horn. The sharp, drawn-out squeal had no effect on the people in front of her; they seemed to drift rather than move, clotting like blood from a minor wound.

The air raid sirens began to shriek louder. Someone on the street yelled at the people to get inside, to find shelter, but everyone remained more or less where they were, locked in the middle of the street. Mara managed to reached the end of the block, where she found the cross street was nearly deserted. After a few more zigzags, she got to Hoang Hoa Tham, one of the major east-west roads in the city. But the police had blocked the road to nonemergency traffic. Head down, trying to look as nondescript as possible, she funneled on the side streets toward Ho Tay Lake with the rest of the traffic, bicycles mostly, their worried riders unsure whether they truly had destinations to go to. Anxiety drove them at a good pace, and Mara was able to move ahead as gaps opened in the flood.

Police and military vehicles were parked in front of the luxury hotels and fancy houses that filled the lakeshore area. Spotlights had been set up on the causeway that divided the larger lake from Truch Bac Lake; they wagged back and forth across the sky, illuminating only a few wispy clouds that seemed to struggle to stay out of their grasp.

So far, Mara hadn't seen any destruction up close. But cutting south toward the Star Hotel she passed into an area of older houses, several of which were on fire. The tops of three roofs burned almost as one, flames licking up the sides as black smoke curled from under the eaves. The black looked like bunting, underlining the red and yellow dancing above. Since the buildings themselves hadn't been damaged, Mara guessed that the fires had been set by antiaircraft shells falling to earth. But that wouldn't matter much to the people whose houses they were. There were no fire trucks nearby, no hoses or even bucket brigades; the residents stood on one side of the street, watching as the flames fed on the dry wood.

The Citadel and the surrounding area were blocked off, heavily though somewhat haphazardly guarded by soldiers. Many of the men were not in full uniform. Mara kept her head down as she rode with the traffic detouring away.

A few blocks from the hotel, the motorcycle began pulling back, as if it had lost its will to continue. The problem was purely physical—Mara had nearly run it out of gas. She tried moving to the side of the street as it stalled out, but there were too many bicycles and people closely together. Seeing a small opening, she pulled right, only to be nearly flattened by a bus that had tried cutting out from several car lengths behind.

Mara coasted to a stop on the sidewalk. She was going to dump the motorbike there, but as she started to slip off she realized it might be her only means of leaving the city. She picked it back up and began walking, looking for a safe place to leave it.

Bicyclists passed on both sides. She was right next to the curb, but that didn't seem to have an effect on which direction they took. Sometimes they would jump up onto the narrow sidewalk, ducking through and sometimes into the crowd there, then cut back directly in front of her. Several bumped up against her. Mara looked in the face of one of the riders after he poked his elbow into her side. His eyes were dazed, his mouth slack. He wasn't even worth cursing at.

Two soldiers with automatic rifles were standing in front of the Star Hotel. Several uniformed security people were just inside the lobby door. Unsure whether the soldiers were there for protection or to keep foreigners from leaving, Mara walked her bike past, continuing down the street.

She found the intersection blocked off with sawhorses and a pair of police motorcycles. She turned back around, mixing in with a group of Vietnamese workers, some on bikes, some on foot, and went back in the direction of the hotel.

As she neared it, she decided that the soldiers had probably been posed there in case the locals decided that the foreigners were somehow involved in the bombings. But she didn't want to take the chance of becoming a prisoner there, not even for the sake of a warm, perfumed bath, so she kept walking.

The crowd took her in the direction of the Hien Lam, the hotel where the Belgian scientist was supposed to have been staying. When she didn't see any soldiers or policemen outside, Mara decided the Hien Lam would be as good as any other hotel. She wheeled her bike down the alley at the back, where she found a small lean-to about half filled with other motorcycles, scooters, and bicycles. She propped hers against the wall, then went inside.

The sole clerk on duty stood on the steps in front of the hotel door, a small pile of cigarettes on the concrete next to him. He stared at the sky, seemingly oblivious to everything around him. Mara had to wave her hand in front of his face to get his attention.

"I need a room," she told him.

He shook his head.

"I know you have vacancies."

"Too early, lady. Come back two p.m."

Mara reached up and under her dress for some of the cash in her pocket. She did it without thinking—she was after all wearing pants—but it had more of an effect on the clerk than her hundred-dollar bribe. His face flushed, then flushed again as she pressed the bill into his hand.

"No business here."

"I'm not interested in business," she told him. "Get me a room."

He looked at the hundred-dollar bill. It revived him.

"Room, yes," he said, leading her back inside.

Shown to her room, Mara went straight to the bathroom, not even bothering to check for bugs—without her electronic detector, she could never be sure a room like this was clean.

Her face was filthy and scratched, though not as badly as she had feared. The blood was clotted on one side of her nose. Her hair, though short, was a tangled, frizzled mess: a werewolf would have been proud.

She washed up as best she could, then went to find a place to call Bangkok from.

3

Washington, D.C.

Zeus Murphy's head felt as if it were going to spin itself right off his shoulders. So much had happened—*was happening*—in the past few hours that his brain couldn't process anything anymore.

But here he was, standing in the national security adviser's smaller-than-he'd-expected office in the White House West Wing, telling him and the president's chief of staff, Dickson Theodore, how and why China was tearing through western Vietnam.

"If I were running the operation"—it was important to keep adding a disclaimer to make it clear that he wasn't clairvoyant—"I'd sweep in under Hanoi, cut the north off, then go for the south. Once I'm into the middle of the country, I have highways, I have infrastructure—I'll have an easy time of it. It won't really matter how I got there. I don't want to bother with Hanoi if I don't have to. That's where their defenses are. If I had come down the east coast, where everyone expected—say Route 1—I'd have much better roads, but I'd also have to deal with half the Vietnamese army. Out here, my main problem is traffic control."

"I wouldn't make light of that," said the national security adviser, Walter Jackson. "Logistics are the key to any battle."

Murphy fought to keep a smile from forming on his lips. It was always amusing when civilians tried to talk about military theory with a few chestnuts they'd picked up from PowerPoint lectures. The problem was they couldn't quite get those chestnuts into the proper context.

"If the Chinese were battling us, or even the Russians," he told Jackson, "then they'd have to be worried—very worried. But they're not fighting us. They're fighting Vietnam. It has a small and largely unprepared army. There's a lot of margin for error."

"Whose error? The Chinese? Or ours?" came a voice behind him.

Murphy turned, then immediately jumped to his feet.

"Mr. President."

"At ease, Major." Greene looked at Jackson and Theodore. "I wanted to hear this for myself. Where's Ms. Mai?"

"She's down the hall on the phone with the Pentagon," said Jackson. "She heard all this already. That's why she brought him back with her."

The president leaned back against the wall and folded his arms in front of his chest. He looked like a college professor quizzing a young freshman.

And Murphy felt like that freshman, and not a particularly cocky one, as he continued explaining what he thought the Chinese had in mind—a lightning strike to sweep around the Vietnamese capital, then a second phase to the attack to take the rest of the country.

"I could see them going through Laos. Or landing somewhere in the south. Maybe both."

He pointed to the map on Jackson's desk, jabbing his finger at the yellow amoeba in the center that represented Hanoi.

"In three or four days, maybe even less, they can be down in Quang Tri Province. From there, the country is effectively cut in half. Then they can take their time. My guess is that they save Hanoi for last. All of the Vietnamese troops are concentrated up here, on their border at the northeast. The Vietnamese might be able to pull them down to Hanoi, but never to Saigon. Excuse me, Ho Chi Minh City."

"Saigon is fine," said Greene. "Even the Vietnamese call it that among themselves."

"The south is what they really want," said Zeus. "Because of the agriculture and the oil off the coast. But they have to take Hanoi eventually. They could even offer a deal. Your lives for tribute. Something like that."

"How do you stop them?" asked the president.

"I'm not sure you can," admitted Zeus. "I haven't seen the intelligence, Mr. President."

Zeus did have a few ideas, starting with immediately destroying the road network in and around Quang Tri Province—including Highway 28 in Laos. Shifting forces south immediately by aircraft and ship, rather than waiting for an attack that would never come, might also help.

The president nodded as he spoke.

"All of this might only slow them down," said Zeus.

"But, uh, from our point of view, that's probably the best we could hope for. You know, kind of a diplomatic opening?"

"Slow them down." Greene pushed himself off the wall and bent over the map. "How long can they hold out without help?"

"I wouldn't want to guess."

"How long did they hold out in the simulation you ran?" asked Jackson.

"Well, we, uh, we won that. So I guess you'd say they held out forever."

The others exchanged glances. President Greene looked as if he was trying to suppress a smile.

He looked shorter in person than he did on TV, and thinner, but only a little less intense.

"Usually, any side opposing China loses," added Zeus. "It's, uh, I guess the odds are pretty much against you."

"Major, how did you happen to pick Vietnam to war-game for?" asked Greene.

"It's kind of a long story, sir, but basically I was told that was the force I was to play for. So I followed orders."

"You think you could win if you were the Chinese?"

"Oh, that's not a problem, sir. I can always figure something out."

"Good." Greene turned to his chief of staff. "Get him on the task force, get him out there. It's all right— I'll call the chief of staff myself. I'm sure she'll see it my way."

Zeus knew his future had just been decided for him—dramatically decided. He started to stammer a thank-you.

"It wasn't my idea," the president told him. "I agree with it, but the head of the task force asked for you personally."

"Uh, who—"

"Harland Perry," said Greene. "I believe you already know the general. He's an old friend of mine. I think you'll get along with him pretty well."

4

Beijing

For all his education, the French ambassador had never taken the time to learn Chinese. They had to conduct the interview in French. Cho Lai, rising from the red couch where he had received him, looked at him now in contempt.

"What you say is certainly important," said the Chinese premier. "But Vietnam has been the aggressor, and we must defend our territory. It would be the same if a part of France were attacked. You would not react lightly—or you would find yourself in the situation you were in when the German tanks came in 1940."

"This is not 1940," said the ambassador quietly.

"Very true. And we will not allow it to become a replay of that time. We are not enemies," added Cho Lai, softening his tone. "The Chinese are very large investors in France. Just last week, we were awarded two new seats on the board of Groupe Caisse d'Epargne. I received a framed cycling shirt as a souvenir. *Très bien, eh*?"

Groupe Caisse d'Epargne was one of the largest banking groups in France. China had been "awarded" the seats in exchange for not pulling out its deposits—a move that would not only have sent the firm into bankruptcy, but undoubtedly crashed the French economy.

"Of course," said the ambassador. "But aggression—"

"This is not aggression. I've shown you proof." Cho Lai waved his hand, and returned to the couch. "A resolution in the Security Council condemning China would not be helpful to our interests. Or to yours, in the long run."

The ambassador hesitated, but then said the words Cho Lai had been waiting to hear.

"We would veto any resolution condemning our good friend China," said the ambassador. "So long as the situation is as you say."

Clearly, he was following his government's wishes, not his own—but that was of no consequence.

"Then there is no problem for any of us," said Cho Lai. "This entire matter will pass in a week or two. The Vietnamese will come to their senses, and everything will be finished. *Fine*. Let me call for tea."

5

Western Vietnam

With Lai Châu taken, the Chinese army began concentrating on its next major target farther south, the Na San airbase. Trucks and tanks raced nonstop down Route 107 to Route 6 in broad daylight, moving into position. Temporary forward airbases—little more than landing pads bulldozed from farm fields—were constructed to help support the assault.

Na San had played a critical role in Vietnam's liberation from the French. Attacked by Giap during the campaign that led to the Battle of Dien Bien Phu, it was ultimately held by the French after considerable bloodshed. But the French misinterpreted their victory there, and made the grave mistake of using the Na San victory as a model for their defense of Dien Bien Phu. It was an error on par with the Germans' decision to take and then hold Stalingrad, with similar results.

Jing Yo had considered the Na San and Dien Bien Phu battles carefully. His unit's job—much more critical than at Lai Châu—was to seize the control tower at the Na San airport, and use it to direct the large assault group into the base. The defenses ringing the airport, while not extensive, would now be on high alert. Jing Yo had to bypass them, sneak into the tower, then hold on while all hell broke lose.

The easiest way to do this would have been to get onto the airport grounds before the invasion was launched; the team would have then had an easy time overcoming the guards and getting into the tower. And indeed this had been the original plan. But the assignment of the other tasks had made this impossible, and so Jing Yo had adapted.

Shortly after the battle for Lai Châu ended, a small helicopter skimmed in over the tree-lined streets, heading for a spot on the road just north of the bridge Jing Yo and his men had managed to hold. The helicopter was a warhorse from another era—a Bell Huey UH-1, the same type that the American army had used to great effect farther south some fifty years before.

This particular chopper had not seen action in the Vietnam-American war, and until roughly six months earlier it had been rusting forgotten in a boneyard in the Philippines. The men who had renovated it had found its Lycoming engine dilapidated beyond repair, and had replaced the power plant with a Harbin design nearly twice as powerful, though it had a considerable distance to go before it could prove itself as dependable as the venerable Lycoming. They had also chipped away all of the rust, replaced the rodent-chewed wires with new ones, and given the pilots an avionics system that would have seemed like something out of *Star Trek* to the helicopter's early crews.

Most important, they had dressed the helicopter in the dull gray camouflaged tones favored by the transport division of the Vietnamese air force, topping the image off with a yellow star in a red circle and bar field used by the Vietnamese air force. The helicopter looked exactly like the two old Hueys still used by the Vietnamese air force in the area to the south.

After picking up Jing Yo and his squad, the helicopter flew south to the Ta Sua Nature Preserve, settling down in an isolated clearing several kilometers from the nearest road. The idea was that Jing Yo and his men would get some rest while the main assault elements got closer to the objective.

But sleep didn't come easy to the young lieutenant. The attack on the scientists' camp and the ferocious battle at Lai Châu had unsettled his internal balance. He knew from experience that he could restore it only through meditation, and so, after urging his men to rest, he walked a short distance up a nearby hill and began to meditate. Legs folded, he began to breathe slowly and deeply, pushing up from his diaphragm. His mind hesitated, still filled with distractions. Jing Yo concentrated on the muscles in his stomach, pushing his mind into the tendons as he had been taught at age sixteen. Then he lifted his hands to the sides of his body, moving them upward in a circular motion.

Ego was a stubborn master. His mind remained distracted. Images of the battle passed back and forth in his head. The sensations of doubt, of weakness, of dishonor, drifted through his consciousness.

He and his men had done well; their objectives had been met. Yet the ego would not be satisfied. The ego wished perfection, wanted glory and accolades so overwhelming that no mortal man could hope to enjoy them.

Ego had always been his problem, from the very moment the monks took him in. "Stubbornness," his first mentor called it.

Stubbornness.

But the universe was around him, and so long as he could breathe, he could find balance. So long as he could feel the muscles in his chest expand and contract, the toxins infecting his mind would drift back into the void.

Jing Yo lost track of time.

That was the first sign. He felt the warm breeze tickling his tongue; that was the second.

And then there were no signs, no thoughts, only breathing, and finally, balance.

The wind blew lightly through the trees to the east, rustling through the branches like whispers drifting down a hallway. Jing Yo let the wind push into his lungs, its energy rekindling his.

Gradually, he became aware of another presence nearby, watching him through the long blades of grass on the slope from the wooded area. The rising sun made it hard for him to see, the sharp rays blurring and glaring as they struck the green slope.

It was black, dark, moving toward him slowly.

Striped orange. A tiger.

Jing Yo could feel each shift of the animal's weight against the ground, the slow dance toward him.

Jing Yo rose from where he was sitting. He had faced the tiger many times in his training. It was the spirit of his fears—the enemy within.

As a young trainee, Jing Yo had been exhorted to

face the tiger as the dragon—to assume the power of water, endlessly mutable, energy ready to be channeled at a moment's notice.

The tiger saw him and stopped.

"What are my fears today?" Jing Yo said to it. "Failure. Disgrace. Ego fears—fears of the temporary. I am of the eternal. I am the dragon. You are only a creature of the earthly moment."

The animal moved its head, warning him to retreat. But that was just a tactic—show the slightest weakness, give even an inch to fear, and it would overwhelm you.

Jing Yo spread his fingers and pulled back his arms. His muscles flexed, then stiffened, ready for the attack.

Confronting the tiger did not guarantee victory. But it was nonetheless the necessary course.

"Ha-ah!" said Jing Yo, moving his right foot forward as he brought his arms up into attack position.

The tiger growled. Its shoulders pushed back, gathering strength for a pounce.

"Ha-*ah*!" said Jing Yo again.

The tiger growled, lower this time, then leaned to its left. In an instant, all of its weight shifted—and it slunk backward through the grass, retreating.

Fear could be controlled; that was the lesson today. It was a lesson he had learned many years before, and had relearned many times since. It was a lesson he would learn many times in the years to come.

A voice shook Jing Yo from his meditation.

"Incredible—you scared the damn tiger away!"

Jing Yo turned to find Sergeant Wu squatting on the ground, a few feet away. Wu rose slowly, trembling.

"I thought one of us—I thought one of us was going to be its breakfast," said Wu. "You stared him down. I can't believe it."

"Why are you without your weapon?"

"I came looking for you," said the sergeant. "Colonel Sun wants to talk to you."

"Check on the sentries," said Jing Yo, walking back up the hill. "Make sure they are aware there is a tiger in the jungle."

"Of course."

One of the helicopter's crewmen was waiting with the chopper's secure radio. Jing Yo took the handset and held it to his ear.

"What are you doing, Lieutenant?" snapped Colonel Sun. "Sleeping?"

"Meditating."

"Do your meditation later. The attack time is moved up. The tower must be taken within the hour."

"Yes, Colonel."

"Don't fail in this, Lieutenant."

You are a fearful man, thought Jing Yo as he handed the handset back.

The men were groggy but did not complain when Jing Yo woke them. They donned their fake Vietnamese uniforms and filed toward the helicopter at a deliberate pace; no one ran, and no one lagged behind. They were veterans now, Jing Yo thought; they were just beginning to understand who they were.

It took three battles to test a man. His action in the first could not be counted for anything. War was too confusing to be sorted into categories the first time it was experienced; keeping your balance amid the blows was impossible until you understood where those blows might come from, let alone how much they hurt.

The second battle was almost always a reaction to the first. A man who had frozen might do the opposite, making a grave mistake. A person who had acted like a hero might be filled with the dread he had ignored during his first battle and be overwhelmed. There was no predicting.

So the third battle was the real test. By the third battle, the sound of gunfire, the rumble of the earth as a bomb went off—neither of these things was new. The soldier had survived two encounters, as a hero or a coward, or more likely as something in between. Stripped of his illusions, a man would face himself.

Jing Yo's third battle had come long ago. So had Wu's—a good sergeant, competent and loyal, in his way, Jing Yo decided. For most of the rest of the squad, this would be only the second.

Much room for error.

"We are being queried by their air traffic controller," said the pilot five minutes after they were airborne.

"Very good." Jing Yo turned to his men. "Be ready."

They were quiet. He couldn't read their faces in the shadow-laced interior, but he didn't have to; he knew their expressions would mix fear, anticipation, and even joy. He gripped the hand strap on the metal framework between the cockpit and crew compartment and began breathing slowly, pushing his ribs against the armored vest, easing it outward and then pulling it inward. The pit of his stomach was empty.

"They've accepted us," said the pilot. "Three minutes to the airport."

Jing Yo looked over and caught Sergeant Wu's eye. He nodded.

"Prepare!" yelled the sergeant.

The commandos rose as one from the benches. Weapons were readied, belts cinched.

Jing Yo saw the airport runway through the window as they began to bank into a landing pattern. A pair of MiGs—probably inoperable, according to the premission briefing—were parked in a tarmac apron area at the far end. A civilian aircraft was on the opposite taxiway, waiting to take off.

There was a helicopter nearby. And a second one.

Were they being sucked into a trap?

Two helicopters? There was generally only one—it was a bit of deception they were counting on.

Did the Vietnamese know they were imposters?

Jing Yo twisted around and leaned into the space between the two pilots.

"There are two helicopters at the airport," he said. "Did they ask questions?"

"No," said the copilot. He was a Vietnamese language specialist, chosen specifically because he sounded like a native.

Or had he been chosen because he was someone's

nephew? In China, one could never be absolutely sure, and Jing Yo's Vietnamese wasn't sufficient for him to judge the man's abilities.

"Lieutenant, we are almost over the runway," said the pilot.

"Proceed as planned," said Jing Yo. He reached into his pocket for his earplugs, slipping them into his ears as he joined his men.

The helicopter skimmed forward, exactly as it would do if landing on an ordinary flight. It then began to veer to the left, toward the designated parking area near the civilian terminal. At the last second, the pilot flexed his control, jolting the chopper upward. They flew another three hundred meters, hopping over the terminal building, past the security gate, and right next to the small parking area flanking the tower.

When they'd rehearsed the landing, the lot had always been filled with cars. Today it was empty. That allowed the helicopter pilot to put down closer to the tower than planned, shaving precious seconds off the timetable. But as he hit the pavement, Jing Yo realized the lack of cars might mean there were no workers— it might really be the trap he feared.

Too late.

"Go! Go! Go!" shouted Sergeant Wu.

One team raced for the building; a second, headed by Wu, ran to the auxiliary shack next door, taking out the phone lines that connected the base with the outside world. When that was accomplished, the second team would split up, half providing security at the base of the tower and the other half circling around the far side of the runway, aiming to take out two antiaircraft guns there.

The point man for the tower group, Private Han, and Corporal Chen were already at the tower door. They had it open—no locks, no need for explosives.

It must be a trap.

"Move! Move!" shouted Jing Yo, the last one out of the chopper.

The helicopter was already up. If it was a trap, they were doomed.

The smell of burning metal hit Jing Yo's nose as he pushed into the building. He hadn't heard any gunfire yet, but he could smell that too as he started up the metal steps that led to the control area. The building, opened only within the past year, was basically a staircase topped by a large glass-enclosed room where the flight controllers worked. There were no security checks at each landing, just more steps.

Jing Yo slung his feet on the metal treads, jogging upward. He kept his head up, eyes darting. There were shouts above, but still he hadn't heard gunfire.

The earplugs were good, but not *that* good.

Have I gone deaf? he asked himself. Did someone throw one of the loud grenades, a flash-bang, to get into the control room?

No—he heard the voices around him, barely muffled by the plugs. And he heard his own steps, the slight rasp on the metal.

The steps came up into the middle of the control

room. Jing Yo saw the rail as he approached and put out his arm. Accelerating, he leapt upward, vaulting over the pipe and landing only a few feet from the console area.

Three men lay on the floor, blood pooling around their heads. All Vietnamese. One of their pistols lay on the floor; the others hadn't managed to unholster their weapons.

"The tower is ours," said Corporal Chen.

Jing Yo scanned the consoles quickly. They seemed to be working.

"Geijui, get to the radio," Jing Yo told the corporal who had been trained as an air controller. He was to use the Vietnamese circuits·to broadcast to the incoming flights.

A body lay in front of the console where Geijui was to work. He hesitated, his face pale.

"Bring the bodies downstairs," Jing Yo told Chen. "Put them below the steps. Quickly. Then make sure there are no charges set anywhere inside."

As the squad got to work, there was an explosion outside. Jing Yo pushed up on the console and craned his neck to see if it had been the auxiliary shed, but all he could see was the shack's black sloped roof.

Sergeant Wu ran up the stairs a few moments later.

"Pin and Fushan are at the door," said Wu. "The rest of the team is going for the antiair gun at the southeast."

"Good," said Jing Yo.

"Now comes the fun part," added Wu.

Jing Yo picked up a pair of binoculars from the shelf below the window and began scanning the airstrip. The Vietnamese unit responsible for providing security to the base had not yet reacted; no troops were pouring from the barracks, no messengers running frantically from the headquarters building.

Jing Yo pulled out his radio and sent the prearranged signal that the tower had been taken: "The ostrich has been beheaded."

Before he could return the radio to its pocket in his vest, a cloud of black smoke appeared beyond the runway. The bombardment had begun.

"Direct the fire," Wu told Chen, handing over the radio. "Tell them they have a good hit."

Jing Yo went to the door at the side of the room, which opened onto a metal catwalk that surrounded the tower. Privates Ai Gua and Han were already there, lining up their rocket-grenade launchers on the mobile antiaircraft emplacements at the northern side of the field.

The flak guns were four-barreled ZSU-23 cannons mounted on tank chassis. Though old, they were devastating weapons against slow-moving aircraft, helicopters especially.

The back of Ai Gua's launcher flared as his grenade shot out. A second later, white smoke enveloped the farthest truck. Han fired next, scoring a direct hit on the gun next to the one Ai had hit.

The other antiair unit began firing at the tower a few seconds later. The barrage was thick but at first missed the tower completely, shooting wildly high and well off to the side. The swarm of bullets moved toward them slowly, slamming into the tower almost directly below where Jing Yo was standing before moving across.

Ai Gua cursed—he could not get his launcher loaded correctly.

Han fired, but his grenade flew wide, exploding harmlessly on the runway in front of the ZSU-23-4. The antiaircraft gun raked the tower a second time, this time shattering the glass above them.

Ai Gua continued to curse. Han fired again. His grenade hit the front of the antiaircraft truck, just below the turret. The gunfire stopped.

They had only a few seconds to catch their breath. The two track-mounted ZSU-23-4's at the far end of the runway swung their guns in the tower's direction and began firing. Tracers flew through the air wildly, well above the tower and several degrees left and right, but Jing Yo realized it would take only a few moments for the gunners to adjust.

The ground team wasn't close enough to get the trucks yet. They'd have to take them from here with the RPGs.

Jing Yo went to Ai Gua just as the private finally managed to get his grenade inserted. He stopped short, waiting for the customary hiss as the rocket shot from the launcher.

He didn't hear it. The weapon began to smoke, but the grenade remained attached.

"Throw it down," yelled Jing Yo.

Ai Gua remained in his firing position, stunned. Jing Yo reached for the barrel of the weapon. His hand seemed to catch on fire—the propellant was burning and the barrel hot—but by the time the sensation of pain had reached his brain the launcher had struck the ground and exploded.

Han fired again, hitting the antiaircraft gun on the left straight on. The other one stopped firing.

"Help Han," Jing Yo told Ai Gua, who was staring at him.

"Your hand."

"Help Han."

Ai Gua jumped up, scooping his ammo case along as he went to his comrade.

A second later, a fresh rocket flew from the tower, knocking out the last antiaircraft truck.

"Remain vigilant," Jing Yo told the two privates before going back inside.

"Force is on its way," Wu told him. "Leading helicopters are about ten minutes off."

"The antiair guns have been disabled."

"What the hell happened to your hand?"

Jing Yo held out his right hand, looking at it. It was bright red. The left seemed unscathed, its throbs duller.

"The weapon misfired," he said. "How far away are our troops?"

"Someone get the lieutenant a burn kit. He needs attention."

"How far away are the troops?" Jing Yo asked.

"Twenty minutes."

"The fighters should have been here by now."

"They're always late," said Wu.

Jing Yo wrapped his hand with ointment, gauze, and a pair of cold packs, diminishing the pain. By the time the bandages had been taped, the control tower had come under small arms fire from the north. Bullets flew through the now battered windows and ripped into the metal below. The area around the control room just below the window was armored, so they were not in immediate danger. But it was impossible to return fire from inside.

"Aircraft inbound!" announced the controller.

"About time," said Wu. "Damn air force is *always* late."

The aircraft were a pair of MiGs assigned to shoot up the defenses.

"Make sure they know we took out the antiaircraft guns," said Jing Yo. "Tell them to concentrate on the barracks."

There was a flurry of gunfire outside. The Vietnamese had launched a counterattack against the tower.

Ignoring the pain in his hand, Jing Yo went back out on the catwalk. He got about two steps from the door before a hail of bullets forced him to dive facefirst on the grillwork.

"Grenade!" yelled Han.

Jing Yo wasn't sure whether he was warning about an incoming grenade, or one he was dropping. An explosion settled it—the private had targeted a knot of Vietnamese soldiers below.

Jing Yo's bandages made it impossible to hold a gun in his right hand, but he could drop grenades easily enough with his left. He pulled one of his Type 82-2 grenades from his vest. Holding it against his chest, he slid his finger up the seam, undid the tape that held the plunger, and with the pin out and grenade armed, dropped it over the side.

There was a small explosion, followed by a much larger one, then a second and a third—incoming artillery shells, fired by their own forces. The last was so strong it pitched Jing Yo back against the rail; he just barely managed to keep his balance before turning and racing inside.

"Those are ours!" shouted Wu.

"Tell them to stop firing at us!" Jing Yo screamed.

"I'm working on it," said Chen. He was on his hands and knees, talking on the sat radio with division. Chen unleashed a string of curses at whoever was on the other end of the line.

The shelling continued for a few more rounds, then began retreating to the west. Jing Yo heard the first helicopters approaching. Down on the far end of the runway, the team that had been tasked to hit the anti-aircraft guns went to work on their secondary mission, marking the landing zone with red smoke, indicating that the helicopters would be landing under fire.

The pain in Jing Yo's right hand flared. He tried to force it away as he went back to the door. He stopped short at the threshold—the walkway had broken and was hanging down off the tower to the left.

He leaned out to look for his two men, then threw himself back into the control room as bullets began hitting into the side wall.

"We're going to have to close that door," said Sergeant Wu. "They get a grenade in here, we're done."

There was no panic in Wu's voice. There was no emotion at all. Closing the door meant stranding the two men outside, but Wu was right—unless the armor-paneled door was put back in place, they were all vulnerable. More important, their goal of keeping the tower intact would fail.

Jing Yo went to the door and closed it himself.

Red smoke drifted upward from the runway. The first helicopter was landing.

The tower shook violently. There was an explosion below—inside the tower.

"They're coming up!" someone yelled.

Jing Yo bit the bandage holding the ice packs onto his burned hand and then tore it off. One of the large windows shattered. The tower smelled as if it was on fire, the stench a sickly mix of metal and tar or very heavy plastic.

Where was his rifle? Someone had taken it from him earlier, but he couldn't remember where they had put it.

Jing Yo saw a gun on the floor. He grabbed it, fingers screaming with pain, then ran to the stairwell.

Wu leaned over the rail, firing madly.

"I see the little bastards," yelled the sergeant. "Watch out for their grenades."

Wu fired a fresh burst. There didn't seem to be any

return fire, though it was difficult to tell with the rattle of the bullets striking the outside of the building. Unlike the control area, the stairway section was not reinforced with armor, and the bullets punctured the thin aluminum as if it were paper.

Wu reached for a grenade from his vest.

Jing Yo grabbed his arm. "What if our men are down there?"

"They're dead by now, Lieutenant."

They stared into each other's eyes for the briefest of moments, though it was an eternity under the circumstances.

"Do it," Jing Yo said.

Behind him, Chen crouched at the console, using the satcom radio to talk with a communications aircraft above. Every so often he would raise his head, peeking at what was going on outside before ducking back and continuing his conversation. Private Wing, trained to watch the radar and report to Chen and Geijui, had his hand over his forehead, shading himself from the glare—though it looked as if he was actually trying to avoid looking at what was going on outside.

Corporal Chen was on the satcom, talking to the division communicator, who in turn was speaking with the commander of the troops now hitting the field. Geijui half kneeled, half crouched at the console, watching what was going on in the field and describing where the Vietnamese forces were, using their circuits to talk to the Chinese air force.

Ignoring the bullets still sporadically flying through the window, Jing Yo climbed onto the console shelf, gripping one of the CRTs as he scanned the airport. Four helicopters disgorged troops at the southern end of the runway. The men ran off into the grass, disappearing from view momentarily before emerging on the far taxiway. Vietnamese soldiers were scattered around the airport grounds in small knots. Their resistance did not seem coordinated—a concentrated attack on the runway might have caught the helicopters on the ground or at least contained the troops there. But there was plenty of gunfire, and Jing Yo knew the battle's outcome was far from determined.

Black smoke rose in a tight curl from a small transformer shed near the far end of the runway. Jing Yo's men were supposed to move into that area after laying down the smoke, but he couldn't see if they were there or not.

The artillery shelling had stopped to allow the helicopters to land. As soon as the first wave of choppers was off, it began again, concentrating on the barracks area and the defensive positions near the highway. The barrage was intended to make it hard for the Vietnamese to rush their troops over to the runway area, preventing them from reinforcing the men who were protecting the hangars and the aircraft. But the firing was less than precise, and the main effect of the shells was to add to the monumental sense of chaos and confusion.

A big part of the problem was the lack of team radios and the insistence that all information be funneled through the division communicators, a remnant of old army doctrine modeled on the centralized Soviet concept. In modernizing the Chinese army over the past decade, the general staff had picked the early stages of the second American war in Iraq, the so-called Shock and Awe phase, with its lightning attacks and generous use of tanks and airborne elements. But the generals were reluctant to loosen their grip on the lower commanders, diluting the relative effectiveness of the attack by making it difficult to coordinate its elements.

"They're coming again!" yelled Wu from near the stairs. "I need more grenades!"

Jing Yo jumped from the console and took a grenade from his vest with his left hand. He hopped down the two steps to Wu, put his right hand around his shoulder, then dropped the grenade. As soon as it left his hand, he pulled backward, yanking the sergeant back as well.

The grenade bounced down the steps, rebounded off the wall, then exploded in the stairwell. The firing below immediately stopped.

Jing Yo felt Wu's weight as he rolled off him. The sergeant grunted, then helped him up.

"They're concentrating their attack here," said Wu. "If we don't get some relief, we'll run out of ammunition eventually."

They had practiced the operation countless times. Jing Yo always understood that his men would be hard-pressed if the assault did not go well. But he had also believed that once the helicopters were landing, the enemy would either concentrate on them or retreat, leaving the tower alone.

He'd been wrong.

The problem was to pressure their attackers some-how. He needed someone to hit them from the side or behind, take their attention away.

Jing Yo hoisted himself back up onto the console. The assault team was fanning out at the southern end of the complex. There were several knots of Vietnam-ese between them and the tower; he could not expect them to reach him very quickly.

They would have to supply the counterattack them-selves.

"Private Wing, help Sergeant Wu," said Jing Yo. He opened the med kit on the floor and rewrapped his burned hand in gauze and tape, leaving his finger free to fire.

"What are you going to do?" Wu asked.

"Provide a diversion. Open the door to the catwalk for me."

Wu frowned, but followed him to the side and put his hand on the handle.

"I hope you aren't thinking of jumping," said Wu.

"Not today."

Rifle slung over his shoulder, Jing Yo put his left hand on the side of the frame and steadied himself. If he'd had two good hands, he would have climbed up-ward and used the roof as a vantage point. But with only his left hand really able to grip, he could only work with gravity, not against it. He swung his weight to the side, then let go of the frame.

The catwalk gave way as Jing Yo landed, swinging down as it tore two more of its anchors. He grabbed hold of the rail with his left hand and the trigger finger of his right, scrambling forward and up. Jing Yo managed to push along the grate for about three meters before reaching part of the deck that was still level. Then he crawled toward the ladder that ran down the side of the tower.

As he neared it, a head popped out from around the bend. Thinking the Vietnamese had come up with roughly the same idea he had, Jing Yo swung his rifle up to fire. He stopped at the last second, recognizing Ai Gua.

"Private!"

"Lieutenant!"

"Where is Han?"

Ai Gua pointed up toward the roof. After the catwalk had failed, the two men had climbed up onto the roof, trying to hold off the Vietnamese from there. Seeing that wasn't working well, Ai Gua had just climbed down the work ladder, hoping to attack the Vietnamese from the side.

"Good idea," Jing Yo told him. "Come on."

"Your hand."

"I'm fine. Let's go."

As they started for the ladder, the tower rocked with a pair of small explosions. Han had tossed a pair of grenades down to the ground, hoping to give them some cover.

Any relief the explosions had provided was temporary—bullets began slicing into the tower skin when Jing Yo was about halfway down the side.

It was too high even for Jing Yo to jump. He continued downward, another four or five rungs before one of the bullets caught him in the back, slamming into his bulletproof vest.

While the vest absorbed the bullet and much of the impact, the force felt like a horse's kick in the ribs. Jing Yo's grip loosened on the rungs. Feeling himself falling, he pushed out with his legs, centering his balance as he plummeted the last twelve feet to the ground. He hit evenly, legs and spine loose as he had been taught, and rolled off to the side, tumbling over and coming up on his knee.

Ai Gua was in the grass nearby, firing toward the other side of the parking lot. Shaking off the shock of the impact, Jing Yo got up and ran to him. He tapped him on the head, indicating he should follow, then ran to the side of the tower, beginning to circle around toward the door area.

An armored personnel carrier moved down the access road toward the tower. Jing Yo fired a few shots at it, trying to hit the gunner sitting in the upper hatchway. His aim was off, and all he succeeded in doing was drawing the gunner's attention—the man swung his heavy machine gun around.

As the first bullets began to rake the concrete, white smoke blossomed from the gun. There was a white flash, followed by a volcanic eruption of fire—Han had hit the APC with a rocket-propelled grenade from above.

Jing Yo took two steps out from around the side of

the building. Men lay everywhere. A few moved. Others were frozen in position, dead.

On the access road, soldiers filed beyond the APC, two abreast, trotting toward the building. He laced them with bullets, sweeping his automatic rifle front to back. The men twirled and fell like rag dolls, caught completely unaware.

As the APC smoldered, Jing Yo ran to it, crouching at the side as he fired into the small wedge of men near the door to the tower. One or two managed to get off shots at him as they fell; most simply went down. He tossed his magazine and continued to fire until no one moved.

Ai Gua ran up behind him.

"Two more APCs coming up the road," said the private.

The two vehicles crossed through a field of high grass. Their machine guns were already zeroed in on the tower.

"Come on," he told Ai Gua, jumping up. "Quickly."

They made it across the parking lot without being shot at. Once in the grass, Jing Yo began circling to the left of the approaching armored vehicles. The soldiers who had been mounting the attack on the tower knew they were there and, apparently realizing what they were up to, began firing into the field. But the grass hid Jing Yo and Ai Gua well enough that they realized it was a waste of ammunition.

The APCs, meanwhile, continued in a long arc designed to take them around to the Vietnamese; once there, they would undoubtedly lead another attack on the building. Both vehicles were only equipped with heavy machine guns, but they would provide plenty of cover for a new charge.

Jing Yo got to within twenty meters of the lead carrier when he spotted a soldier running alongside it. The lieutenant stopped in the grass, watching as other soldiers appeared—there were at least a half dozen, moving alongside the vehicles.

"What do we do?" whispered Ai Gua.

"Go that way." Jing Yo pointed to his left. "Get around to the other side that they're taking. In sixty seconds, I'll begin firing."

"Against all those men?"

"We only have to slow them down until the landing teams can fight their way here," said Jing Yo. "We just have to get their attention."

Ai Gua looked dubious.

"Go!" Jing Yo reached out his arm and pushed the private. "Go."

Ai Gua shoved away, crouching as he ran. Jing Yo hoped to get the Vietnamese in a crossfire, but even if he succeeded, he and his private were badly outnumbered. They were down to their last rounds, without any more grenades.

The most they could hope for was to delay the APCs. Every minute they won would increase the odds that the men in the tower would survive.

Jing Yo moved slowly, paralleling the vehicles. He began counting softly to himself, measuring Ai Gua's pace, waiting for him to get into position.

When he reached one hundred, he raised his rifle and fired.

The soldiers near the APCs, at least those he could see, went down.

But the vehicles didn't stop moving.

Bullets began flying around him. Jing Yo hugged the ground, then began squirming around to his left.

Maybe he could sneak up on one of the Vietnamese soldiers, take his grenades, then force open the hatch.

The idea formed in his head, not yet a plan. He rose to all fours and changed course, thinking he might have an easier time taking one of the men from the rear. As he got up, a long, shrill whistle vibrated at the back of his skull. Jing Yo threw himself forward instinctually, his muscles reacting before his brain could give the command.

Incoming!

The first artillery shell landed almost directly on the APC. A second and third bracketed it, spraying clods of grass and dirt through the air.

The shells began to fall in a thick rain. Some of the Vietnamese soldiers who had been with the vehicles began to run back in the direction they'd come, trying to escape. Jing Yo watched as they ran through the steady downpour of bombs. For a few seconds, it appeared as if they might escape the onslaught. Then a shell struck near the lead runner. A swirl of dirt enveloped him, and he disappeared like a magician escaping in a cloud sent by heaven. The man closest to him continued to run, apparently unharmed.

Then the next shell hit. This time, the air seemed to

turn red. Four men fell. Another flew into the air, tumbling over like an acrobat as a series of explosions pummeled his lifeless body.

The artillery fire increased. Belatedly, Jing Yo realized he was in just as much danger as the Vietnamese. He began backing away through the grass, staying as low as possible as the shells continued to fall.

Several of the Vietnamese soldiers who'd been waiting for the APCs to appear were mesmerized by the shells. They stood watching them land in the field, oblivious to the gunfire a few hundred meters away.

He had only one magazine left, the one in his gun. Shooting them was a waste of bullets—they were out of the battle, out of the war. They were useless as soldiers, little more than dead men waited to be buried.

Jing Yo almost wanted to warn them, to tell them to get down. One by one, they started to go down. At first, Jing Yo thought they had been caught by stray bullets. Then he saw Han firing from the top of the tower, squeezing off single bullets.

A Vietnamese soldier lying in the field a few dozen meters away rose, bringing up his gun to target Han. Jing Yo aimed his own weapon, taking the enemy soldier in the side of the head.

Blood spurted as the bone shattered like a piece of overripe fruit.

The shelling stopped so abruptly that Jing Yo didn't realize at first what had happened. He turned back, disoriented. Then he remembered Ai Gua. Fearing the worst, he began moving cautiously in the direction where he'd last seen him.

Someone shouted to him on his left.

"Halt!"

The command was in Chinese.

Jing Yo turned. Four men, guns ready, were standing ten yards away.

"I am Lieutenant Jing Yo," he said loudly. "Chinese commandos."

"Lieutenant!" Ai Gua rose and waved on his right.

The four soldiers eyed him warily.

"We have taken the tower," he told the men. "Get your commander—the tower is secure."

Bangkok

Peter Lucas had met Jimmy Choi only once, and then for only a few minutes in an airport lounge, but the meeting had burned an indelible image of the South Korean mercenary into his brain. He saw him now as Jimmy spoke over the phone, his voice a sharp rasp, his English clipped and slangy. In Lucas's mind's eye, Jimmy had a gold buzz cut, a day-old beard, a gold chain dangling over the dragon's claw tattoo at the apex of his breastbone. He was dressed in a precisely tailored black suit, with an open white shirt, tails out. He was slouching and grinning.

Jimmy *was* chewing something—probably a cigar,

given his affection for Habanos. He was drinking something too—Lucas had finally tracked him down in a bar in Mandalay, Myanmar.

"Pete—what can I do to the CIA today?" asked Jimmy.

"I need help in Vietnam."

"Bad place to be right now," said Jimmy.

"What are you drinking, Jimmy?"

"Shirley Temple. Yes?" The mercenary laughed.

"I have somebody I need to get out. They're far north, near the border."

"Ho-ho—very expensive proposition."

"Can you do it?"

"Where we go?"

"Up near the Chinese border. Somewhere near Lao Cai. I don't know exactly where yet. I'll have the information in the next twenty-four hours."

Jimmy didn't answer for a second. Lucas heard the ice in his glass clinking.

"Lao Cai very interesting place," said Jimmy, exhaling as he smoked his cigar. "Too much interest for me."

"The person I need to get is not in Lao Cai. He's in the area near there."

"Even *more* interesting. Ho-ho, Uncle Pete, you have one very expensive problem on your hand."

Lucas decided to try a different tack. You couldn't threaten a man like Jimmy Choi directly; he would surely stand up to anyone who seemed to bully him. But you could hint that his future would become, as

Jimmy liked to put it, "interesting" if he didn't do what you wanted.

"What are you doing, Jimmy? Working for that drug dealer again?"

"Ho-ho, I am on vacation."

"Yeah, right. Mandalay is quite the vacation spot. Who were you hired to assassinate?"

"Ha-ha, Uncle Pete, you are so funny. You should come here and keep me company. The tables are hot."

"Since when do you gamble?"

"I gamble every day. Not with money." Jimmy laughed at his joke and took another draw on his cigar, a long one. Lucas saw him smiling.

"I can get a plane to meet you in Laos," offered Lucas.

"Ho-ho, no thank you. I do my own transportation. I own two planes now."

"Business is that good, huh?"

"Oh, you pay for it. Always pay."

He might have added, *through the nose.* When they got to the point, it turned out Jimmy wanted five million dollars.

Park had authorized five hundred thousand.

"I might be able to swing one million," said Lucas. "But I don't know."

"One million—ha! I cannot find Vietnam on a map for one million dollar. Let alone Lao Cai."

"What if we paid it to one of your Chinese bank accounts?" said Lucas. "Denoted in Chinese currency?"

"China money not very good. Much inflation. Maybe we try euro?"

"Inflation is never a problem for a man like you, Jimmy—you spend it before you get it. The equivalent of one million dollars, in yuan, ten percent up front, the rest on delivery."

Jimmy Choi laughed. "You hack into account and steal it when we done?"

"If I did that, Jimmy, you'd never let me sleep in peace."

"You got that right, buster." Jimmy laughed.

They negotiated a bit more—the mercenary wanted the money figured in euros and deposited in a South African bank, not even admitting that he had accounts in China. He was not particular what currency the transaction originated in, as long as the fee was sufficient to cover any currency charges.

"And expenses," said Jimmy just as Lucas was about to conclude that they had a deal.

"Screw you. Your expenses come out of your share."

"Gas very expensive today," said Jimmy. "I see markets going crazy as we speak. We work out compromise. You give Jimmy your credit card number and everyone relaxes."

Convincing Park to okay the one million dollars wasn't easy. Lucas wasn't sure whether he was really worried about the money—which would have been uncharacteristic—or if he was having second thoughts on the whole enterprise. Finally, his boss agreed.

"But no results, no money."

"That's why I'm only paying him ten percent up front," said Lucas.

"What's going on in Hanoi?" asked Park.

Two of the agency's three officers were in Saigon; the other was filing reports every half hour. Their status—more specifically, the question of who was leaking information to the Vietnamese—had been put on hold temporarily. But Lucas was still being very careful about what information they would receive: they hadn't been told about the mission, and wouldn't be.

"I expect that they'll find out at some point," Lucas told his boss. "We may never really know the entire story there."

Park said nothing. Lucas knew he was in the process of setting up an elaborate and time-consuming trap to test each officer; it could take weeks or even months to figure out what was really going on. The alternative was to flush all three careers, which Park clearly didn't want to do.

"What's going on in the city?" he asked. "The airport is completely out of commission?"

"There were still fires burning there fifteen minutes ago. Power is still on, there and down in the capital, but the landlines are down. The cell system is still up; the military is using it as an alternative. They've shut down all the servers they know about—the last independent blogger went offline just before I called."

"Do you think they can stop China?"

"How do you stop the ocean?" said Lucas.

7

Northwestern Vietnam, near the border with China

Josh stayed on the trail for another hour, following it as it twisted up and down the mountainside southward. Finally he spotted some thatched roofs through the woods, peeking between the foliage. Moving off the trail, he made his way slowly toward them, at times walking, at other times dropping to all fours and crawling through the grass.

The trail swung down a shallow hill and then across a narrow valley to come into the village about a half mile from where he'd first spotted it. Two bamboo huts, both with well-weathered walls and roofs, shouldered against the trail. Beyond them sat three much newer houses made of painted brick and some sort of cement stucco, with metal saltbox roofs slanting backward amid the fronds.

No one seemed to be in any of the buildings. Josh was ready to step out and have a closer look when a girl of six or seven darted between the houses, running as if she was being chased. He froze, gripping his rifle, expecting to see soldiers chasing her. When none appeared after a minute or so, he realized it was more likely she was playing a game, running from another child. Whatever she was doing, she had moved on, beyond the nearby houses; he could no longer see her.

Josh crawled forward, driven almost unconsciously by his hunger, a vibrating pit in his stomach and chest. He moved out of the jungle like a tiger, head close to the ground, sneaking toward its prey. He listened for the girl and her playmates, but heard nothing as he stalked to one of the brick structures.

The walls were painted blue, the color of the sky on a cloudless summer day, so bright that they looked as if they were plastic. Josh rose, holding his breath as he listened to hear if someone was inside. The wall he was near stretched maybe twelve feet. It had a door but no window; small air vents lined the top where a soffit would have been on an American home.

Josh started to sidle around to the corner, but then decided not to bother—he could be seen from the other house and the clearing beyond, and if he was going to go inside, he was best off going quickly.

The door had a simple knob without a lock. Josh turned it slowly, then pushed in carefully, pressing himself into the house as his eyes adjusted to the dark.

It was humid, almost dank, even more than outside. He gripped the gun tightly. A table sat immediately in front of him, anchoring a kitchen area, with a small, simple refrigerator and a stove. Immediately beyond this were mats, piled along the floor. There were no other rooms in the house.

Sure the house was empty, Josh pulled the door closed behind him. Light filtered in around and through paper shades on a pair of windows to the left, and once more his eyes needed a moment to adjust to the dimness. When they did, he went to the refrigerator.

His hunger was conscious now, and so overwhelming that everything was blocked out. He pulled open the door to the fridge. There was no light, and when he dropped to his knees he felt barely a chill from the appliance.

Two bottles of citrus juice sat on the middle shelf. Above them was a covered bowl of some sort of noodle dish; below sat a box of oranges. Josh grabbed two of the oranges and sat down, pulling at the skin, frustrated when it refused to give way in large pieces.

As soon as he had a hole big enough for his mouth he bit into it. Juice streamed from his mouth. The perfume overwhelmed him; he devoured the orange, turning it inside out as he ate. Slightly overripe, it nonetheless seemed the most delicious thing he had ever eaten.

He ate the second one just as quickly, almost drunk with it. He got up and tried the noodle dish. It had a sharp, spicy smell, but there was no holding back—he scooped the noodles with his fingers and ate greedily.

Done, he put the bowl back and took out one of the bottles. The liquid had a putrid fish scent. He quickly lowered it from his mouth and recapped the bottle. He tried another bottle; the smell was even worse.

Yet he felt an urge to drink it.

Josh's hands trembled as he put it back. He had to keep control.

Clothes were folded neatly on small shelves at the side of the room. There were different piles, most with only two or three items. He found a man's shirt, a long peasant-style shirt that fell to his knees, and put it on over his own, which by now was torn and muddy.

Judging from the piles, five people lived here—two women, a man, two children.

The guess comforted him somehow, as if he'd made some sort of connection with the people, as if they were helping him.

Judging from the sparse furnishings, the family was poor, but they had a solid, new house. Possibly it had been built by an international aid agency. People like that would be happy to help others. They wouldn't begrudge him the food and shirt.

And if they did, so what?

The thought seemed ugly, almost foreign, but there was truth in it—he would have to do what he needed to survive. Surviving wasn't only in his best interests. It would help the Vietnamese, ultimately. He would tell the world about what the Chinese were doing.

Was that why he had to survive? Or was it just that he didn't want to die?

Both.

Which was more important?

"Neither," he said aloud. But then he realized that he could not, must not, lie to himself. "Living is most important. For now."

Josh went back and cracked open the door, peeking through the narrow slit to make sure there was no one watching. When he didn't see anyone, he pulled it open just barely enough to slip through.

Josh worked his way over to the older houses,

which lay near the road. There were no signs of life; even the little girl had completely disappeared. Again, he found the first door he tried unlocked. Salvaged wood boards of different sizes and shapes were piled inside the building.

He was on his way to check the other when he heard a truck approaching.

Josh reached the woods just as the vehicle came into the clearing near the two older huts. It was a troop truck. Men in uniform jumped out, but at first he wasn't sure whether they were Vietnamese or Chinese. He listened as someone barked orders.

Chinese.

Realizing that they would probably fan out into the nearby jungle after searching the huts, Josh began slipping deeper in the woods. Two soldiers trotted toward the path; Josh quietly circled in the opposite direction, only to find himself hemmed in by the road.

A field lined with young fruit trees sat on the other side of the road. Josh paralleled the road, moving away from the village downhill, hoping he could find a point where he could easily get across without being seen. He'd gone only a few yards when a big truck began laboring up the other side of the hill. Moving back, he crouched down and waited for it to pass.

It was a tractor cab pulling a low-rider trailer. On the trailer sat two large bulldozers. The truck stopped in the middle of the road, and the two men in the cab got out and began lowering the ramps at the rear of the trailer. Another truck appeared behind it, also with two dozers. A third truck brought a large excavator. A minute or so later, a pair of gray vans pulled into the field and disgorged the operators; within ten minutes a crew was at work leveling the field. They worked methodically, knocking the trees down, pushing them aside, and running over and over the field.

Josh watched with fascination, absorbed in curiosity though not forgetting that he was in danger. He could hear other trucks arriving farther up the road. Soon a chain saw started up, then two more; within a few minutes the saws were so many and so loud that he could have shouted and he wouldn't have been heard.

The Chinese were building a base.

The realization satisfied his curiosity, and he turned to leave. As he did, he saw a pair of eyes framed by some tree fronds nearby.

His heart froze in his chest. His throat grew so thick he couldn't breathe, let alone swallow.

The eyes moved, and he saw they were part of a small face—the girl he'd seen earlier.

Josh put up his hand but she darted off to the right, moving quickly away.

Worried that she might tell someone about him, he started in her direction. But after a few steps he realized he'd never catch her.

Josh went back along the road, skirting the area where the men were clearing the fields. A fire had been started to burn some of the brush. A pair of soldiers, rifles under their arms, patrolled along the road.

There were wide spaces between the trees, and Josh had little trouble weaving his way south, keeping a good distance from the road. There was a lot of traffic on it; big trucks or tanks kept rolling past every few minutes.

About an hour after leaving the village, Josh sat down to rest on a downed tree trunk. He leaned his head forward, chin supported by his hands and arms, which in turn were propped on his thighs. He stared at the ground, his mind taking a temporary respite.

Something moved just out of his range of sight. It rustled through the brush, moving slowly. It was quiet, somewhat softer than the chain saws and earthmoving equipment two or three kilometers away.

It sounded like an animal, a Vietnamese deer maybe. *Food.*

He'd make a fire. That wasn't a problem: he still had the matches he'd found the other day, and a lighter. There was plenty of wood.

He got up slowly, barely daring to breathe, and brought his rifle up.

Josh waited. His nose began to twitch—he felt a sneeze coming on. He reached his hand up, squeezing the nostrils to stifle it.

His prey was only a few feet away. Josh steadied the gun with his right hand, waiting.

Brown fur appeared, then gray. He pitched the rifle down to aim, letting go of his nose.

Not fur—hair. A person.

A girl.

The girl he'd seen earlier.

She turned and saw him. Shock was in her face, surprise.

Fear.

Then he sneezed.

The girl bolted and ran into the woods at her right.

He'd never seen anything so frightened. That must have been the way he'd looked when the police found him those many years ago. Maybe it was even the way he looked now.

"Hey," he said in a stage whisper, not daring to talk much louder even though he was a good distance from the road. "It's okay. *Xin chào.* Hello. *Xin lỗi.* Sorry."

It was the most polite, nonthreatening thing he knew how to say in Vietnamese, though given his extremely limited vocabulary, there wasn't much of a choice. But the little girl either did not hear him or wasn't persuaded. She continued to run.

Josh followed her for a short distance, but quickly realized it was hopeless. Even if she didn't know the jungle here, she would be pretty good at hiding, and was unlikely to make the mistake of dropping her guard again.

"I wasn't going to hurt you," he said softly, hitching his pants and walking again.

Northern Vietnam

It turned out to be ridiculously easy for Mara to find a truck; it even came filled with gasoline.

It did belong to the Vietnamese army, but that could be considered a plus—civilian-style vehicles were more likely to draw attention from the soldiers she was bound to meet on the way.

The truck, along with two others, was sitting at a curb near an intersection a mile from Mara's Hanoi hotel. The building next to the curb was on fire.

It was far from the only one. City officials, after some confusion, were shepherding their limited resources to protect the government areas. It was likely that the soldiers who had parked the trucks here had done so thinking they'd be safe, but the shifting winds had been spreading the fires throughout the morning and early afternoon.

Mara pulled her motorcycle over, hopped into the truck, and pressed the starter. The engine cranked to life.

She didn't want to give up the motorcycle, so she pulled forward a few feet, then got back out and wheeled the bike around to the back. Jumping up on the tailgate of the truck to lower it, she saw that she had an audience—two young teenage boys were standing across the street, watching her.

"Help me," she told them in Vietnamese. She motioned to the bike, then switched to French. "I need to get the truck—we have to take the truck from the flames. Do you understand? Fire."

The young men looked at each other. Neither one moved to help her—but they didn't try to stop her either, which was her real concern. Mara jumped back down and grabbed the bike. It was heavier than she'd thought. She could barely get it off the ground; there was no way she could lift it high enough to get into the truck.

She put it back down, took a breath, then decided to try again. As she strained, the two teenagers came over and helped.

"Can you drive?" she asked them, switching to English. "The trucks—we have to get them down the road to the police."

The teens shook their head. She repeated it in Vietnamese.

"*Di thẳng.* Go straight," she told them, pretending she thought they had understood. Mara slammed the tailgate shut, then waved at them to take the other trucks. "We're going to the police. I can talk to you there."

Mara didn't bother looking back as she got in. Most likely, she thought, she hadn't fooled them. But the soldiers would be looking for their truck soon anyway.

She ran her hand through her hair as she drove through Hanoi, pushing it back on her head. She really needed a uniform, but it didn't appear that the truck's rightful owners had left one.

A few minutes later she came to a roadblock. Several bicyclists were stopped while soldiers went through their papers.

There was no place to turn around. Mara considered jumping and running, then noticed a church steeple and got an idea.

Rolling down the window, she climbed halfway out the cab and leaned on the horn.

"I need to get to the bridge!" she shouted, first in English, then in French, and finally in Vietnamese. "We have to get soldiers to the hospital! Men are dying."

The bicyclists turned and stared. The two soldiers looked over at her as if she were crazy.

Which was not the worst assessment they could make.

"We need to move. The bridge!" she repeated.

One of the soldiers strutted over. Mara began explaining that she was a nun—she reached beneath her shirt and pulled out her cross, holding it up as evidence.

The majority of Vietnamese, especially those in the north, were not Catholics, but the Catholic orders had a long history of charity and relief work, and nuns were generally viewed favorably. Elsewhere, Mara might not have looked very nunnish, but the paucity of Westerners in the region helped her cover story.

Her cross was small, but her manner was emphatic, and after a few minutes of being harangued, the soldier decided to pass the buck to his companion. He pointed at the other soldier and told her to talk to him.

Mara, naturally, completely misinterpreted this as an okay to proceed—and made sure the other soldier did as well, smiling and waving at him as she drove past.

"Sister Jean, pray for my soul," said Mara, offering up both prayer and apology to one of her old teachers as she escaped down the street.

The cover of an aid worker was too good to pass up, and Mara quickly set about shoring up the image. Soon after reaching Route 32—there were soldiers along the highway, but they weren't stopping military vehicles—Mara spotted a complex built around a Buddhist monastery. She explained to the monks that she was bringing emergency supplies to Son Tay, a city on the Red River to the west. She offered to take the monks with her, and for a moment worried that one of the kindly brothers might actually take her up on the offer. But the monks were already tending to a number of people left wounded and homeless from the attacks, and instead they offered her some bandages, blankets, and bedsheets.

Her next stop was in a town about five miles away. Parking the truck, she found a small shop and bought several pairs of men's clothes and a cap for her hair. She also got two peasant-style dresses, and a basket for lunch. She had just gotten the basket filled and climbed back in the cab when the satellite phone buzzed.

"Hey, Bangkok, how we doing?" she asked, holding

the phone against her ear with her shoulder as she put the truck in gear.

"How are you doing, Mara?"

"DeBiase! They have you back on the communications desk, Million Dollar Man?"

"I requested it specifically so I could talk to you," DeBiase told her. "Where are you exactly?"

"You're not tracking me?"

"You have to transmit for thirty seconds," he told her. "But yes, we are. It was mostly a figure of speech, like hello."

"Hello. I'm near Hoa Binh," she told him. "I want to stay south of the Red River for a few miles. I think there are more troops on that side of the river."

"How far north can you be by tonight?"

"China if I have to be."

"Pick a place farther south, and hopefully a little safer."

"I was thinking of Nam Det, if there aren't many troops in the way."

"Hmmm."

"Are you looking at the satellites? What do they say?"

"The latest satellite says there are no troops there. The Chinese still haven't come across the border at Lao Cai."

"Maybe they won't."

"Don't bet on it. Nam Det . . . You'd have to go up Route 70."

"I'd planned on it—if there aren't a lot of checkpoints."

DeBiase began clicking through information screens on the computer in front of him. Besides satellite data, the U.S. now had Global Hawk UAVs patrolling to provide real-time information on what was going on.

"There are two points I'd steer you around, darling. One is Phan Luong, which the Vietnamese are using as a mustering point for their reserves in Tuyên Quang. The other is farther north, near the Thac Ba Reservoir. That one's the problem—there are no alternate roads unless you go through Yen Bar."

"I can do that."

"I don't think so—the Chinese are bombing it right now. The analysts seem to think they'll attack and occupy it tonight."

Mara tried visualizing Vietnam in her head. The rivers that cut southward were flanked by mountains; her route back to Nam Det was in the shadow of the Con Voi Mountains, between the Chay River and the Hong. The Da River valley, farther to the west—and on the other side of the Hoang Lien Son Mountains—was the main route of the Chinese advance, though no one expected them to stay there very long.

"I think my best bet will be to BS my way past the checkpoint at Tuyên Quang," she told him. "The question is when."

She looked at her watch. Assuming she could keep her speed of fifty kilometers an hour—an iffy proposition, admittedly—she'd be at the checkpoint no later than five p.m., just as dusk was falling.

"Can you get past?" asked DeBiase.

"Sure. I've gotten by two already. I just tell them I'm a nun."

"That works?"

"They don't know me very well."

Mara asked DeBiase if he could arrange an equipment drop; she needed a backup radio, batteries, and most of all ammunition. DeBiase told her he'd have to work on it. Two hours later, he called back to tell her Lucas had wangled an unmanned aerial vehicle to drop the gear on the field at Nam Det just before dawn.

Assuming she could get there.

"We'll know in an hour," Mara told DeBiase. "If that roadblock at Tuyên Quang is still there."

"It is. The Vietnamese are telling people in some of the villages near the Chinese border to leave and go south. You'll be running into refugees soon."

"I'll try not to hit them."

"Yeah."

"That was a joke, Jess. You're losing your sense of humor."

"I know."

Figuring she would be stopped at Tuyên Quang, Mara decided to try and polish her image. She used a needle and thread to sew a makeshift cross out of sheets on the top of the truck, but didn't have enough left over for the sides. She had only a few boxes of supplies—a pathetic effort if she really was working for a relief group. Mara rearranged a few things, but there was only so much she could do, and when she climbed back into the cab and put the truck in gear, she felt even less confident than before.

A half hour later, Mara saw the first refugees walking along the road. They were a family of four, a mother and father with two children around seven and nine, a boy and a girl. Each carried a big bundle on his or her back. They didn't look at her as she passed.

Mara thought they were an anomaly—the area had so far missed the fighting—but within a few minutes she saw more people, bunches of them, groups of ten and twelve. Most were on the side of the road, but here and there a group strayed onto the asphalt. Bicyclists were scattered among the walkers, most pedaling slowly and glumly alongside relatives or friends. By the time she'd gone another kilometer, the highway was flooded with people—old people, middle aged, children, some pulling carts, a few dragging bundles placed on pieces of wood and poles.

Another kilometer farther on and the road was almost impassable.

A few of the refugees stared at her as she drove, slowly, pressing forward against the tide. But most didn't look at her at all; they looked at nothing but the black tar of the road, oozing up in the late-afternoon heat.

The steady flood of people overwhelmed a small village that straddled the highway. They seemed like ants climbing through the remains of a dead animal, moving forward. A few of the inhabitants stood in their door-ways, jaws slack, unable to entirely comprehend what was going on.

North of the village, Mara found she could go fast-est by straddling the edge of the highway and shoulder. People would move off the road more easily there, and she managed to get the truck to twenty kilometers an hour for several stretches. But she was constantly slow-ing down, often hitting the brake as an old person got stubborn in front of her, or a child didn't pay enough attention. By the time she got close enough to Tuyên Quang to see the checkpoint, the sun had set.

Mara had wondered why she hadn't seen any auto-mobiles on the way up; she had assumed that it was because the area was so poor. Now she saw that the authorities were seizing all motor vehicles—cars, trucks, and motorbikes—at the checkpoint. Once stripped of their vehicle, the refugees were then literally pushed onto the road, told to go south. The entire area had ap-parently been ordered evacuated shortly after Mara set out from Hanoi.

Her truck was the only vehicle heading north, and at first as she drove up Mara thought she would just get right through, without even being stopped—the soldiers were focused on the cars and the refugees. But as she passed into the bright glow of the spotlight il-luminating the checkpoint area, an officer turned from the other lane and put up his hand.

Mara thought of ignoring him and simply driving on. But when she saw two soldiers step from the shadows ahead and shoulder their rifles, she downshifted and stopped.

"I have medicine for the orphanage at Nam Det," she told the captain when he strode over. She used English, deciding that what she needed to say was too complicated for her Vietnamese. "I am with the Sisters of Charity. We have to get the children out safely."

The captain either didn't understand her English or didn't care to soil his tongue with it.

"Why are you driving an army truck?" he asked in Vietnamese.

"General Tho gave it to us," Mara said, switching to Vietnamese as well. "The soldiers who were supposed to guard me would go only as far as Vinh Yên. They left me on my own. They had to join the fighting. Maybe you could have some of your men assist me. There are many people who need help with the evacuation there. The little children—"

"Out of the truck!"

When Mara hesitated, the captain took out his pistol and pointed it at her. His two soldiers did the same with their rifles.

"I can get out," said Mara, raising her hands and reaching for the door handle.

The captain pulled the door open.

"I'm a nun," she said, holding up the cross.

The captain yanked her from the truck, throwing her on the ground.

If it had been just he and she, even with the gun, even with her cover story of being a nun, she would have jumped from the ground and thrown herself into his chest. He was a little rooster of a man, probably fifty pounds lighter than she was, and no match for her, especially if caught off guard.

He had a rooster face as well as body, a sharp nose that jutted prominently from his face—a target just waiting to be kicked in.

But he had the two soldiers nearby, and there were many others close by. Even if she escaped at first, she'd stand out in the city, and beyond.

What would a real nun do?

Pray to God to strike the bastard down.

And maybe cry, depending on the nun.

Mara had never been the weepy sort, but she forced herself to simper now, protesting about "God's little children" who needed to be saved. The captain ignored her, ordering his men to search the truck.

Pushed aside, Mara tried calculating an escape route. There were too many soldiers around to give her good odds, though.

She could grab Rooster Face's pistol and use him as a hostage.

Satisfying, but ultimately counterproductive. Best to keep with the cover story, play it through. Worst case they were going to send her south with the refugees. She might miss tonight's drop, but that could be rescheduled.

No, worst case she could be arrested. That was a possibility, but probably a complication Rooster Face wouldn't want to deal with.

Worst case was even worse than that. But she kept

such possibilities locked off in a different part of her brain. No need to examine them now.

"Where are your orders?" the captain demanded as his men finished searching the cab, signaling with their hands that they had not found anything.

"Orders?"

"The general who gave you permission. Where are his orders?"

Mara had some trouble with the words and his accent. She thought at first that he simply meant her papers; she gave him her "safe" EU passport, which identified her as an Irish citizen. Mara had already rehearsed an excuse about why the passport didn't call her "sister"—she was a prenovice, a special category of nuns in training who had not yet joined the novitiate.

"My passport," she said, pushing it into the captain's hands.

"Where are your *orders*?" repeated the captain, throwing the passport on the ground.

"The general did not give me orders. He gave me guards," said Mara. "Soldiers."

"And where are they?"

"They left me. I didn't think it was my place to question them. I am a nun, not a soldier."

"You are a foreign bloodsucker."

Among the many sisters Mara had known growing up, one in particular had been stubborn and strong. A strict disciplinarian, Sister Jean Marie had been the scourge of the parochial school Mara attended until sixth grade. Mara imagined she was her now—a massive, if necessary, leap of imagination, but one that gave her a map to follow.

"I suck no blood," she said, raising her head as she stiffened her spine, both literally and figuratively. "I am doing God's work for the least fortunate."

"God is a fairy tale," answered the captain, adding several words that would probably have made Sister Jean Marie blush.

"The orphans are not fairy tales, and they do not care who feeds them. God or fairy tale," said Mara. The Vietnamese words sprang into her head as she played the role, her confidence gaining. "These are poor children who must be saved from the Chinese devils."

While the captain was not impressed by Mara's religious claims, much less her pose as a nun, his two soldiers were clearly uncomfortable, shifting back and forth behind him. One of them looked particularly embarrassed, frowning and looking down at the ground whenever she glanced in his direction.

"We will repel the Chinese scum," said the captain.

"I pray that you will." Mara made a point of looking at his soldiers. "I thank God that you have such fine men in your command."

This only made the captain more angry. He spun back to his men. "Have you searched the back of the truck? Get your lazy asses in there. Find out what this she-bitch has. Probably poison for the children."

The soldiers rushed to comply. They opened the tailgate, then hauled the motorbike down. It slipped from their hands and bounced on the ground.

"And what does a nun do with a motorcycle!" thundered the captain.

"I needed a way to get to the general's camp," said Mara easily. She pushed her chin up, just as she imagined Sister Jean Marie would do. "One of our parishioners, a very humble and kind man, took pity on me when I said I would walk, and—"

"Silence! Every word you utter is a lie."

The captain walked over to examine the motorbike. He picked it up, frowned at it, then let it drop back into the dirt. He ordered the soldiers to confiscate it.

Mara sensed a compromise was in the works—he was going to take the bike but let her go. The swap was okay with her—she'd make it up to its owner somehow.

The worst thing to do, though, would be to admit that the unspoken deal was a good one.

"Where are you going with the motorcycle?!" she shouted.

"Nuns have no need for such things," answered the captain.

"It's not ours. It is our parishioner's. It is his only possession."

"Then he should have been more careful with it."

The captain walked away, striding toward a knot of other soldiers, who were interrogating the refugees. Mara waited for a second, then scooped up her passport and jumped in the truck, happy to have gotten off so cheaply.

9

Northwestern Vietnam

By dusk, Josh had walked another five or six kilometers, still roughly paralleling the road. There was a lot of activity on the highway, with trucks passing by at a furious rate. The few glimpses he'd caught convinced him they were all Chinese.

There were aircraft as well—jets high overhead and helicopters in the distance.

He was being followed. He knew it had to be the little girl he'd seen earlier, though she was very careful now about not getting close enough to let him see her. He heard noises in the brush, noises unlike those a deer or other animal would make, or a frog, or even the wind.

Pale green, with overly large black eyes, the frogs sat on the rocks and low plants, looking as if they were trying to decide which insect to pull out of the air next. Their color made them blur into the surroundings, and Josh didn't notice them until one leaped almost into his face as he walked, spooked by the human's approach. After that, the scientist realized the amphibians were all around him, occasionally scattering as he walked, but most often just sitting still, clacking in a low, guttural call, and staring.

It wasn't until night began to fall that he realized he could eat the things.

The first frog he tried to catch hopped away into the brush, escaping easily. The second, which he tried to scoop off the ground in front of him a moment later, leaped up toward his hand, smacked against his open palm, and rebounded down against his leg. The live feel of the thing surprised him. It felt like a wet human biceps slapping against his hand. The webbed feet scratched gently at his flesh, the legs flailing awkwardly as he grabbed for them. The sensation was so odd that Josh stared at his hand as the frog went free.

It should have been easy, considering what he had done to the man whose rifle he had, and yet it was hard, very hard.

He was thrust back into his precollege days, biology class in high school, dissecting a frog. They'd tried injecting adrenaline into the thing to see what it would do to its heart.

One of the girls had complained that they were being cruel to animals. The teacher agreed.

If I think like that, I might just as well lie down and die right now. I'm not a scientist, I'm a survivor.

A few meters farther on, he saw two frogs sitting within two feet of each other at the side of the trail, separated by a pair of leaves from one of the plants. Singling out the frog on the right, Josh lowered himself in front of it.

I'm a survivor.

He raised his hand, then began to extend it. When he was about ten inches from the frog, it leapt to the left, escaping easily. Instead of swatting after it, he turned to catch the other one, spotted it in midair, and swung his hand. Much to his surprise, he grabbed the animal. It started to squirm, pushing its head out of his fist until he held it by only one leg.

Josh tightened his grip, clamping his hand against the squirmy skin. Then he swung his hand down, hammerlike, dashing the frog's head against the ground.

He hadn't meant to kill it, just get it to stop squirming. The blow split the creature's skull. Blood and the gray ooze of brains spilled out.

Josh felt like he was going to get sick—like he *had* to get sick. He twisted around and put his hands on his knees, ready to retch. But nothing came out.

I have to survive, he told himself. *I'm going to survive.*

The next one was easier, and the one after that easier still. He caught ten frogs in all, dashing their brains out and piling them at the end of a small clearing about a hundred meters from the road. He brought some twigs together to make a fire, then decided he was too close to the road. He pulled up his shirt, put the dead frogs in it as if he were a kangaroo, and walked through the jungle until he found another clearing, this one with several clumps of dried grass, which he used to start the fire. With sturdy sticks he roasted the frogs on spits, something he had seen in a movie.

Or thought he'd seen. The boundaries between experience and dream seemed to have eroded.

And nightmare.

The fire threw up sparks as the frogs roasted. He picked at the skin of the first frog's leg, burning the tips of his fingers. He managed to pull the flesh out, then lost it as it slipped to the ground.

He used his teeth on the second leg. The meat was tender, not really like chicken as some people said, unique.

He ate two more, quickly. Then a third and fourth.

He took his time with the fifth, hunger nearly satiated. Josh savored the bites, trying to work out the taste—not really fishlike, yet it seemed closer to that than chicken.

Something rustled in the brush. Two eyes looked at him from the dark shadows, their whites glowing with the reflection of the fire.

The girl.

"Here," said Josh, lifting the half-eaten frog toward her. "I can cook some for you."

She didn't move.

"I'll make a fresh one. Here."

He leaned over and took another frog, holding it away from her as he poked the stick through its mouth and then out its body. Then he put it over the fire.

"They're good," he told the girl. "You have to eat. You need to eat."

She was still staring at him. A good sign. He tried to remember the Vietnamese word for hello, but stress had drained his vocabulary away.

"How old are you?" Josh asked, still speaking English. "Five? Seven? I have a cousin who's eight. I think he's eight. I lose track. Maybe he's ten. I haven't seen him in a while."

He reached and turned the stick, roasting the other side of the frog.

"My name is Josh. I'm a scientist. I study weather. It's a good thing to study these days. A lot of call for it. Because it's changing, you know. And, um, everything changes with it. These frogs, probably. I'll guess they're higher than they used to be. I mean their range. Probably it wasn't up this high. They're adapting, or they will adapt. They're following their food source. I don't know a lot about frogs, but that's not exactly a radical guess. They are frogs."

He stopped speaking and looked down at the animal on the skewer. "I think they're frogs, not toads. Fauna's not my thing."

The girl took a step forward, parting the brush. She wore traditional Vietnamese pajamalike clothes, but her shoes were Western-style sneakers, cheap knockoffs that you could get in most Asian cities. Josh crouched down to her level, trying to make himself look less threatening.

"You can eat," he said.

She launched herself forward, streaking toward him so quickly that his only reaction was to flinch, thinking she was going to bowl into him. Instead, she grabbed the frog and continued past him, escaping into the woods beyond.

"Hey!" he shouted, but she didn't stop.

He jumped up just in time to see her disappear into the jungle. Josh stood for a second, unsure what to do. Then he grabbed his rifle and started after her, worried that she would go all the way out to the highway.

He had lost sight of her, but he could hear her running through the brush. He followed along for thirty or forty meters, falling farther and farther behind. He could see only a few meters through the shadows and the trees; with every step the light seemed to fade further, until at last he could barely see to the tips of his extended hands.

Josh stopped and listened, quieting his breath as best he could so he could hear. She was somewhere ahead, not too far, maybe only a few yards, moving slower than before.

Did it really make sense to try and catch her? It wasn't like he could talk to her. The only reason to grab her was to keep her from telling the Chinese about him if she was captured.

That was the only *logical* reason. He'd followed her—why?

Because he wanted her to be his friend. He wanted her to realize he was on her side, he was one of the good guys.

A poor reason to risk his life. Yet he felt compelled to continue after her.

Six or seven steps farther on, Josh heard the sound of heavy vehicles moving in the distance—Chinese troop trucks, no doubt, coming down the highway. He moved a little faster, threading his way through the thick brush and trees.

Something swiped his face. He rebounded, thinking

it was a snake and then realizing it was just a tree frond he hadn't seen. But his reaction threw him off balance; he stumbled to his left, crashed against a tree, and fell over.

Josh lay facedown in the brush, not thinking, not encouraging himself, not despairing. He got to his knees slowly, listening, in full survival mode, listening and only listening.

There were other sounds ahead, something else moving through the jungle.

Voices.

Chinese.

He focused his eyes on the jungle before him. The brush parted—the girl, running to his left.

Two figures in gray swept across from the right.

Josh's rifle had slipped from his shoulder as he fell. Before he could grab his pistol, the girl and the soldiers disappeared.

Two more figures crashed through the brush, five yards away.

They were nearly next to each other. Two hands on the gun, he fired quickly, taking both down. Then something else took over—Josh leaped up, ran, and without thinking about what he was doing, fired point-blank into the skulls of both fallen soldiers. He swept down, grabbed their rifles, pulling them off the fallen men. He pushed over the bodies, grabbed clips—big banana-style clips. He dropped the pistol—the clip was empty—and left the rifle he'd been using, walking in the direction the other soldiers had taken, moving slowly and as quietly as he could, all of his attention focused on following them. No stray thought, no emotion or feeling, interfered with his eyes or ears.

She will go toward the fire, and they will follow her.

Josh veered left. He began moving sideways, keeping his eyes focused on the direction they had gone, but still moving toward the fire. After five or six yards he stopped and listened—he could hear sounds but not make them out.

The fire was a red glow directly in front of him, thirty yards away.

The girl screamed.

Josh resisted the urge to charge ahead. He walked even slower, sifting through the trees, drifting there as if a leaf being pushed by the gentlest of breezes.

The two soldiers were smacking the girl's face.

Josh brought one of the rifles up and aimed. But at this range, in the dark, with a gun he'd never fired before, he worried that he wasn't a good enough shot to ensure he'd hit just the soldier, not the girl.

He started to sift closer.

One of the men grabbed her from behind and began shaking her.

Do not charge them. Wait. Move forward.

One step, two steps.

The other man yelled something, angry. He looked in Josh's direction.

He'd heard something.

The soldier holding the girl threw her down.

Now!

The gun was set on full automatic. Josh emptied the clip in a quick sweep. Out of bullets, he threw the gun down, grabbed the other off his shoulder left-handed, the trigger wrong, everything wrong except what he was doing, except what he had to do.

One of the soldiers was down. The other staggered to his right.

The rifle jumped in Josh's hand. Some of the bullets went wild. The rest did their work.

The girl was still lying on the ground, dazed, when Josh reached her, sliding on his knee next to her side.

"It's okay," he said. "Okay, okay."

She looked at him, big eyes, no voice.

"Did they shoot you?"

She blinked. There was no blood on her that he could see, no wounds.

"Come on," he said, jumping up. He went to the soldiers, took a pistol, as many mags as he could stuff in his pocket and beltline. His heart was pounding.

The girl was still on the ground.

"We go! We go!" he told her, running back.

He reached down and grabbed her shirt. She winced, injured somewhere he couldn't see.

"Come on, we go, we go," he told her.

He lifted her to her feet. She wasn't crying, but she was more than scared.

"Up, we go," he said, and he bent down and levered her up onto his shoulder before turning and starting off in the forest, away from the fire and dead soldiers.

10

Northern Vietnam

Of all the unmanned aircraft and drones the U.S. military operated, "Gumdrop" was arguably the strangest looking. Roughly the size of an executive's desk, it had a sharply faceted body and two wing surfaces, located almost on top of each other biplane-style, about a third of the way from the nose. The wings changed shape, thanks to gas-filled bladders inside them. It couldn't go very fast, largely because its engine was so small, but the wing arrangement made it extremely maneuverable.

The small engine was a handicap in another way—it could handle only a limited payload, especially when taking off from the ground. Because of this, on many missions, Gumdrop was launched from the wing of a larger aircraft, generally a C-130.

The engine had been specified to keep the aircraft's infrared signal as small as possible. Indeed, the signature was said to be smaller than a Bic lighter at one hundred yards.

The facets in the body, along with radar-absorbing coating, made its radar profile even smaller. The Air Force officer who had first briefed Mara on the aircraft's capabilities—a captain with horrible skin and even worse salami-breath—had bragged that it was smaller than a mosquito at three miles.

Mara didn't care particularly about its radar or infrared profiles, except for the fact that they allowed the aircraft to deliver packages under the most stressed circumstances. She had received several in Malaysia, including one delivered to the top of a burning building surrounded by rebel forces.

By comparison, the drop to the field at Nam Det was child's play.

Nam Det and the small village where she had taken Kieu appeared to have been abandoned. The house where she'd left the injured pilot was empty, the only evidence that he had been there the missing sheets on the bed.

Mara checked her watch. It was five minutes to two. Gumdrop was supposed to arrive exactly on the hour. Rolling up her skirt and holding it against her thighs, she trotted along the edge of the old runway, taking one last look in the ditch to make sure there was no one there. Then she jogged onto the edge of the field. Unfurling the skirt, she counted off her steps until she found the center; she then walked from there to the end and counted off three long steps before looking up at the sky.

Gumdrop—its official designation was R26A Unmanned Drone/Replenishment Profile, or UMDRP—was already descending overhead, coming down through ten thousand feet in a gradually tightening spiral. As it passed ten thousand feet, its remote pilot, sitting in a bunker in Utah, reoriented his long-range infrared sensors to look for heat sources on the ground.

The computer assisting him immediately spotted Mara, informing him that a single subject was standing precisely .012 meters from the target area. The pilot continued scanning the screen, observing the nearby jungle to make sure there was no one else waiting nearby.

The computer spotted Mara's truck, identifying it as a Chinese version of the venerable ZiL, a Russian design older than not only the pilot, but his father. The pilot had been told about the truck, but though it served as an additional recognition point, the Air Force lieutenant was under orders not to take anything for granted on this mission. So he reached with his right hand to a panel above his flight controls and hit one of the presets on the infrared control screen. This initiated a face-recognition routine that compared the infrared portrait of Mara's upturned face to images stored in the unit's library. In Mara's case, the library was particularly rich; besides the standard reference image prepared by the CIA for all of its paramilitary and field officers, there were two dozen training images and nineteen different "mission references," the term used to describe images that had been made and stored during previous operations.

Had the pilot cared to, he could have examined the images personally, noting perhaps that while Mara had recently gained a few pounds, her weight was still down significantly from the training period eighteen months ago. But with a long night ahead of him, the pilot followed standard procedure, taking the computer's word for the final confirmation. He pressed his mike button and told his mission controller that he was on final approach for the drop.

Several thousand miles away in northwestern Vietnam, Mara strained to see the UAV above her. Its black paint and small shape made it hard to pick out in the night sky, and the engine was so quiet that on most drops the first indication that it was overhead was the sound of the parachute deploying.

Tonight, Mara thought she saw a dark shadow sailing overhead. Sure enough, a second later she heard the distinctive *fuuu-lumpk* as the drop chute opened.

To increase accuracy and reduce the chance of last-minute winds taking the dufflebag-size package off course, the package was dropped close to the ground using a chute that allowed a relatively quick descent. On one of her first missions, Mara had made the mistake of running toward it as it fell and nearly gotten knocked out when it came down on her head. Now she knew better. She tensed, waiting as it sailed a few feet away. Only when she heard the *whoosh* of air rushing from the landing cushion did she trot forward to retrieve it.

The first thing she did was swap one of the new batteries into her satellite phone. Then she slung the shoulder pistol holster across her chest, situating the military-style Beretta inside. An AK-47 with a folding metal stock sat at the bottom of the case; she took it out, inserted one of the magazines, and made sure it was ready to fire.

Imagine what Sister Jean would have done with that. No boy would ever have made a face behind her back.

Armed, Mara detached the small parachute, rolling and folding it into a small ball. Tucking it under her arm, she zipped up the bag and carried it to the truck. After activating one of the GPS locators—it sent a signal to a satellite the CIA could use to track her—she took the chute out into the jungle looking for a spot to hide it. She was just wedging it beneath a pair of large rocks when the satellite phone rang; it was Lucas.

"You have the package?" he asked.

"Just got it."

"Why didn't you check in?"

"God, Peter, I was about to." She pushed the rocks in place, then rolled over another one. "So, do you have our friend's location yet?"

"Negative. He's still an hour or so away from the call-in time. In the meantime, your help is on the way. They should be there inside half an hour. You can head west; we'll have his exact location and a contact procedure next time you check in."

"Can I trust these guys, Peter?"

"I trust them."

"Not the same thing."

"They're familiar with Nam Det. They've done some work out of there in the past."

"They parachuting or landing?"

"Mara, these are contract guys. They make their own arrangements," said Lucas. "As far as I'm concerned, if they can get there by flapping their arms, that's fine."

"You don't know?"

"I would assume they're coming by plane and landing."

"You know what ass-ume means, don't you, Peter?"

"I'm not in the mood for jokes tonight, Mara. Especially old ones."

"Is that how we're getting out?"

"Not necessarily. We'll make arrangements. What's the situation there? How close are the Chinese?"

"Haven't seen them."

"Lao Cai is thirty kilometers away. There are reports that they're shelling it. The thinking is they may attack over the border there, and push south down the Hong River valley. You should avoid that area."

"You think?"

Lucas didn't say anything. Mara imagined him grimacing at her sarcasm, probably ready with a comeback but not wanting to use it.

"I'll be okay, Peter. And thanks for the helpers."

"Yeah, all right. Check back in when they're on the ground."

B esides the gun, batteries, and food, Gumdrop's package included a handheld computer that doubled as a GPS device, night glasses, and extrastrong bug repellent. But in some ways the most valuable thing in the pack was a paper map of the area.

Mara had learned in Malaysia that paper maps had several advantages over the computerized ones she'd grown up with. They didn't zap batteries, never crashed, and gave you a much better idea of where you were in a single glance. Scrolling through a small GPS screen made it hard to plan a direct route across the Hong using all of the tiny local roads. The topo maps, which were included in Gumdrop's package, showed she had at most three different choices if she was going to avoid Lao Cai at the north and Pho Rang at the south. The Chinese weren't the concern at Pho Rang—the city was bound to be used by the Vietnamese as a rallying point because it sat at the intersection of the largest north-south and east-west highways in the region.

After working her alternatives out on the map, she connected the handheld computer to her sat phone and used it to access the latest satellite and surveillance images posted in a secure online space for her by Bangkok. The most recent photo, an infrared shot by a Global Hawk surveillance aircraft, showed a small concentration of Vietnamese vehicles in the mines south of Lao Cai—mobile reinforcements, according to the analysts' notes. There were troop trucks parked along Route 151 north of Tang Loong, but it looked like she would have clear sailing south. Reaching 279, she could cross the mountains and go north up 32; at that point, she would have to worry about Chinese troops rather than Vietnamese.

Mara's plan was still somewhat tentative, and would have to remain so until she had a definite location for the scientist. But her basic idea was to get the truck as close to the area as she could, and then hike in on foot to find him. Once she had him, she would cross back over the lines to wherever Lucas arranged the pickup.

Mara used the computer to read the synopses of the analysts' predictions about the Chinese assault, then examined the photos one more time before disconnecting and wiping the computer's memory clean.

She was ready. So where the hell were her "helpers"?

Climbing onto the hood of the truck, Mara put on her night glasses and scanned the night sky. Slightly thicker than prescription sunglasses, which they were modeled to resemble, the glasses had a resolution of 64–721p/mm, with an adjustable brightness gain over 3000/fL/fL—in layman's terms, their magnification and night vision were the equivalent of military-issue Gen III night monocles but much smaller, lighter, and easier to use and conceal.

The sky was empty. Mara leaned back against the window of the truck, the AK-47 in her lap, waiting. Twenty minutes later, she finally heard the drone of a small plane approaching.

"About time," she muttered, slipping to the ground.

The plane was an American-made Cessna, a single-engine Skywagon. Flying at treetop level, it dropped abruptly onto the runway, charging all the way to the end before slowing just enough to turn around. It trundled back and turned once more, prop still turning. The door on the side of the aircraft opened. Four figures emerged, each hauling a pair of rucks. They ran quickly off the end of the field, hunkering down.

Mara flashed her small LED flashlight: two greens.

Someone on the team flashed a response: three greens. The man closest to the runway rose and circled his arm. The plane's engine revved and the Cessna shot down the field, airborne in seconds.

As soon as the plane was away, the men rose and began stalking over. Even though they'd just gotten the all-clear signal—and knew that the plane would have been the first target in an ambush—they nonetheless moved across the field with guns ready, scanning back and forth as they came.

All except the last man, who sauntered over as if he were walking down the boardwalk at Atlantic City after hitting a double jackpot.

"Hey, CIA," said Jimmy Choi. "You must be Mara."

"You're Choi?"

"My friends call me Jimmy."

"What do your enemies call you?"

"Enemies? Enemies all dead."

Jimmy laughed and stuck out his hand. He was tall, and not just for a Korean. He squeezed her hand; she squeezed back.

"So, you find yourself trouble here, huh?" said Jimmy.

"No. I'm getting somebody out of trouble."

"Ho-ho. You don't worry now. Jimmy Choi here. We get you out and gone before you can sneeze."

"Ah-choo."

"Ha-ha, funny, funny. This our truck? Good. Get in. I drive."

"I'll drive, thank you."

"Jimmy good driver."

"No doubt. Who's who here?"

"Eenie, Meanie, Moe," said Jimmy.

"Ha-ha."

Jimmy laughed, but it turned out that two of the mercenaries *were* named Meanie and Moe. Meanie was a short but unusually wide Korean, whose right cheek was intersected by a thick and jagged scar. Moe looked to be a Russian or maybe a Mongol. Neither man said anything when they were introduced, nor did they add their full or real names, which was just as well—Mara really didn't need to know.

The last mercenary was an American, though Mara wouldn't have known for certain had Jimmy not told her he was a countryman. His name was Jeb and he had a chiseled light brown face that made him look even thinner than he was. He had an East Coast accent.

"Where you from?" Mara asked.

"Eritrea."

"What state is that?"

"It's in Africa. My mother's American. Most of my life I grew up in Africa."

"Well, glad to be working with you."

She shook his hand. His grip was soft, barely there.

"We go now," said Jimmy.

"Hold on. I have to run down the situation for you," said Mara.

"I know situation."

"You know where our subject is?"

"General area."

"I've already mapped out a route. Let me show you."

"Show on way. I drive. We're waste of time here," he added in his funky English.

"I drive," said Mara. "Get in."

As soon as the others had their gear in the back, she started out, going as quickly as she dared in the dark. Even with the night glasses, it was hard to see the edges of the road, and she found herself constantly hitting the brakes. It didn't help that Jimmy kept interrupting her as she tried to lay out the game plan.

"Easiest way to get there, we go over border, come back around," he said.

"What border?"

"China."

"That's crazy. We'll never get across," said Mara.

"I cross the border all time. Very, very easy."

"We'll do much better in Vietnam," she insisted. "We go where troops aren't."

"Ho-ho. Suit self."

"I will. And it's yourself."

"Jimmy very suited. Thank you."

Mara drove for roughly an hour, heading southwestward. Jimmy Choi was quiet, occasionally consulting a small clamshell computer. Mara thought it was a GPS unit until Jimmy gave her directions.

"Have to change your road," he said. "Troops on road to south."

"How do you know that?"

"I know where troops are," said Jimmy. He tapped his clamshell.

"That's a computer? What are you looking at? You have your own satellite?"

"Ha-ha, very funny," said Jimmy. But he didn't explain where the image came from. Mara guessed that he was hacking into someone's system, probably the Russians'.

"Can I see that?" she asked, reaching for the computer.

He pulled it back.

"You ask questions, I answer them. You go to 178—"

"I'm not going north. It's too dangerous, and we'll be too far from where our target is," snapped Mara.

"Okay, okay, don't have cow. We go it your way." Jimmy laughed. They could have been deciding on what restaurant to try. "Tell me route. I check."

The route, at least according to Jimmy's photos, was still clear. They made it across the Chay and then the Hong, speeding through the small village of Pho Lu before seeing the first signs of the war—a huge crater that blocked the roadway about a mile out of town. Trees on both sides had been knocked down by the blast.

"Ho-ho. We fix," announced Jimmy Choi. "Quick, quick."

He leaped out of the truck. Seconds later, two chain saws started up. In five minutes, there was enough of a path on the right side for Mara to squeeze past.

"It's going to be light soon," said Jimmy when he

got back into the cab. "We should stop and rest until they have the spot."

"I want to make the Hoang Lien Son Mountains first. We'll be safer there."

"Hour drive. Maybe more."

"We can make it."

"We change into Chinese uniforms there," declared Jimmy. "Closer to their lines than the Vietnamese."

"You have one for me?"

"Ha-ha, we find you one, too." Jimmy took out his little clamshell computer and began fiddling with it. "Turn left at next road."

"Why?"

"Need pit stop. Yes?"

"Yeah, all right."

"There, dirt road."

They were almost on it. Mara had to hit the brakes to make the turn.

"Park here. Quick. Pull off."

Mara pulled onto the shoulder. Jimmy Choi jumped from the truck and ran into the back. Mara climbed down and was surprised to see the mercenaries scrambling into the jungle.

"Hey! *Hey!*" she yelled, charging after them.

The men were moving at a good pace, and Mara felt a stitch start in her right side. She ducked through the trees, gradually losing ground. Finally she stopped. There was no sense chasing them.

"Hey!" she yelled after them. "Jesus, Mary, and Joseph. Crap. Crap, crap, crap."

What the hell was the sense of coming all this way into Vietnam to desert her?

Unless they were setting her up for an ambush.

Mara spun around, then dropped to her knee.

Now what do I do?

Mara took a deep breath, listening. If it was an ambush, the Chinese would have surrounded the truck by now. Not seeing her there, they'd be fanning out in the jungle.

Or maybe they'd just wait for her to come back.

No wonder Jimmy Choi didn't want to show her the satellite images, the bastard.

Mara took the night glasses out of her pocket with her left hand, still holding the rifle ready with her right. Even though it was no longer dark, the glasses were powerful enough for her to see anyone hiding in the nearby brush.

No one. She folded them back in her pocket, then took a half step sideways in the direction of the road. As she did, gunfire began reverberating through the jungle.

11

Northwestern Vietnam

Josh ran until he couldn't breathe. Legs shaking, he sank to his knees. The girl clutched him as tightly as she could, her fingers wrapped into the flesh at the back of his arms.

"I need to rest for a minute," he whispered. "It's okay. I'm not going to leave you."

He gently pried her grip loose.

"It's okay," he repeated. "Just let me get my breath."

He knew she couldn't understand his words, but he hoped his tone might reassure her. As soon as he rose she grabbed his leg, clamping her arms around him.

Josh listened for a moment, trying to hear if the Chinese were following him. If they were, they either were moving very quietly or were a good distance away.

"Come on," he told the girl. "Let's go."

He pushed forward gently, trying to move her. She shuffled back a step, absolutely locked onto him.

"Hold my hand," he told her. He gripped her left hand with his and gently pushed her to the side. It took several strides before she was willing to walk rather than be dragged. Both of her hands were welded to his.

It was like walking with a weight attached to him.

Why did I help her? Why did I think I had to save her?

I didn't think—that was the problem.

I'm in survival mode—I have to save myself, not someone else.

Leave her!

Even as the words formed in his mind, Josh felt repulsed.

He did what he had to do. And what he had to do now, for both their sakes, was to move more quickly. He scooped her up and began trotting again, willing strength into his legs.

Josh went on like that for another half hour, running and walking, trotting and catching his breath, until finally no amount of urging could keep his legs moving forward. He slipped down against a large tree, all but collapsing on the ground. The girl sat beside him, silent, eyes open wide as if they might let in his thoughts.

The sparse overhead canopy allowed most of the early evening's moon rays through. Josh could see between ten and twenty yards all around him.

He'd forgotten to turn his phone back on. Remembering it now, he pulled it from his pocket and turned it on. There were no calls waiting, and no indication that Peter had called. But of course it was still locked, on emergency only.

So how had he gotten the call? Because it had happened; he hadn't imagined it. It was real.

Damn! How had he forgotten?

He pounded the ground, then looked up. The girl was still staring.

"What's your name?" he asked. He struggled to remember the Vietnamese words. "*Tên em là gì?*"

She didn't respond. *Em* was the term you used for a child.

He tried again. The girl squinted, as if she were trying to figure out what he was saying.

"My name is Josh," he said. "*Tên tôi là* Josh. Josh. Josh."

He tapped his chest several times, repeating the Vietnamese words. He wasn't sure of his accent, and most especially the tones, but he'd used the phrase several times, and knew he was at least close.

"*Mạ*," she said finally. "*Tên tôi là* Mạ."

Her name, or nickname, was Mạ. Josh knew the word; it was Vietnamese for seedling.

"A good name," he told her. "A very good name."

The sat phone, still in his hand, began to vibrate.

Josh's fingers trembled as he reached for the Receive button. "Hello?"

"Josh, where have you been?"

"I'm conserving the battery," he said, not wanting to admit that he'd left the phone off. His voice was dry.

"Okay. I can understand that. Listen, I have people on their way to you. They'll be with you by tomorrow night at the latest."

"Where are they meeting me?"

"Josh, we know where you are, and they're going to come get you. Just stay where you are now."

"I can't stay here. I have to move."

"I really wish you wouldn't."

"I can't stay here," he told him.

"All right, Josh. Calm down. We'll work this out."

"Give me a number that I can call. Unlock this phone."

"It's not going to work that way."

"Make it."

"Josh, I can't explain the technicalities right now. And frankly, I don't know all the tech stuff anyway. You have to trust me on this, all right? We'll get you out. All right? Josh? Josh?"

"All right. But we can't stay here."

"What do you mean, we? Who's with you?"

"A girl."

"A girl?"

"The soldiers were going to shoot her. Or something."

"There are soldiers where you are?"

"A couple of miles away. I've been running for a half hour, an hour—"

"Is she there? Can you give her the phone?"

"You don't trust me?"

"You don't speak Vietnamese. I have someone who does, who speaks it very well. I can speak it—"

"How do you know I don't speak Vietnamese?"

There was a slight pause. "It's not on your curriculum vitae."

"What are you, checking up on me?"

"I wanted to make sure I was talking to the real Josh MacArthur, yes. I did research you. Yes."

"You have files on me?"

"Josh, don't get angry with me. I'm trying to help. I know you're going through a lot."

"You have no idea what I'm going through, mister.

No fucking idea." Josh looked over at Mạ. She looked worried, as fearful as he had seen her with the soldiers. "I have to go," he told Lucas. "Call me back in two hours. No, three."

"Will you leave your phone on?"

"It will be on in three hours."

"It would be more helpful—"

Josh slapped the phone off and put it in his pocket.

"Come on, Mạ," he said. "Let's find a better place to hide."

12

Northern Vietnam

Mara ran toward the gunfire, AK-47 poised. The gunfire had a very familiar ring to it—a thick, almost bell-like sound that she associated with the Chinese Type 99 assault rifle, the upgraded bullpup-style gun China had developed and "sold" to the rebels in Malaysia.

Not good.

Her muscles tensed, her vision narrowed. She sprinted from cover to cover, ducking behind large trees, staying as low to the ground as possible. There was another road through the jungle ahead, maybe thirty meters away.

By the time Mara slid in behind the broken trunk of a large tree near the road, the shooting had stopped. She waited there for a moment, ducking her head left and right to see, trying to find an angle that might reveal what was going on.

Nothing.

Mara eased forward, finger edging against the rifle's trigger, resting there ever so lightly.

Something moved on the left. She spun, dropped to her knee—and just barely kept herself from firing.

"Ho-ho, you take time catching up," said Jimmy Choi. "All the excitement done."

"What the hell do you think you're doing?"

Mara's curse only made Jimmy laugh harder.

"What the hell is so funny?" she asked. "I could have shot you!"

"You're a professional. You wouldn't shoot."

"Goddamn it."

"Come on. We have something for you."

Still seething, Mara followed the mercenary out of the jungle onto a hard-packed road. A Chinese EQ2050 Hanma—the Chinese version of the Hummer, also known as a Mengshi or Dongfeng Hanma—sat just off the road. Four Chinese soldiers had been killed in the field. Jimmy's men dragged the dead bodies into the jungle.

"One of us not a good shot," said Jimmy, pointing at a body that was stained with blood. "Bad luck for us. We have only three uniforms."

"You did this for the uniforms? You took off, took all this risk, for the uniforms?"

"Hanma big bonus. Chinese Hummer. Voom, voom."

"Jesus, Mary, and Joseph. No. *No*. You have to tell me what the hell you're doing. Don't you understand? You work for me."

Jimmy Choi laughed.

"*Don't laugh at me*. Damn it—you don't just take off like that."

"We get job done." Jimmy shrugged.

"Sure, if they don't stop us."

"Bad luck for them they stop us." He pointed to one of the bodies. "Those would fit you. You try. We close our eyes."

They took the Chinese Hanma as well as the troop truck, threading their way north with help from Jimmy Choi's images. Except that it squeezed her boobs, the uniform fit fairly well. She didn't look very Chinese, however, and the general strategy was to avoid getting very close to the Chinese army if possible.

Soon after they stole the truck and the uniforms, Lucas called in with another update on the Chinese situation. They were continuing to concentrate their efforts farther south and west; the only units in Mara's area were small scouting parties, probing defenses and looking for resources that might be useful.

He gave her a precise location for the scientist—two miles from a Chinese forward operating base being constructed in Lai Châu Province.

"Well at least he's not in it," she said sarcastically.

"They actually don't have a lot of troops in the area

around the base," said Lucas. "They're focusing their efforts farther south."

Mara knew the troop estimate had come from analysts who were basically making educated guesses from satellite photos. She knew better than to trust them.

Shortly after eleven in the morning, she and Jimmy Choi's team reached the heavy jungle area surrounding the Hoang Lien Son nature preserve. They went up a small streambed, stopping near a small copse about a quarter mile from the road to rest. Twelve kilometers separated them from the spot where Lucas had said the scientist was hiding.

"Hey, glamour girl, we've been waiting for you," said DeBiase, answering a split second after the connection went through. "What's going on?"

"You tell me. Where's our subject?"

"Hiding. We'll contact him as soon as the sun goes down."

"You sure he can last until then?"

"He tells us he's fine."

"This guy's for real, right, Million Dollar Man? Because if he's not, I'm going to be seriously upset."

"We'll have a full brief for you tonight, Mara. We should be able to get you in direct contact with him right before the rendezvous. Okay?"

"Okay."

"Everything going well?"

"As well as could be expected."

"What do you think of Jimmy?"

"He's a nutjob."

"In a good way, I hope."

"Not necessarily."

"He's one of the best," said DeBiase, a little too cheerfully.

"That's damning with faint praise," said Mara. "I'm going to get some sleep. Call me if anything changes."

"You'll be the first to know."

13

Beijing

The news that the Chinese troops had massacred several villages did not surprise Premier Cho Lai. The men were peasants, poorly educated, and raised to believe that all races were inferior to the Chinese. The incitements that their commanders had given them to join the battle had undoubtedly pushed them to believe that their enemy was little more than rats to be eradicated as any exterminator would.

But the implication of the message that his intelligence network had intercepted—that there was a Western witness who had evidence and who might be believed in the UN—was more problematic. While the premier was sure of the Russians, the French assurance was not on very firm ground. If France caved in to

American pressure—and Cho Lai had no illusions about where the U.S. would stand—then the Poles would be next, followed by the Germans. He would have to follow through on his threat to pull the country's deposits from the French banks, thereby weakening the country's investments elsewhere. The situation would be difficult.

At some point he would have to confront the rest of the world, but he greatly preferred to do it later, after Japan if possible.

The real problem was the U.S. president. Cho Lai had believed that he, of all people, would be happy to see the Vietnamese crushed. For a brief time he had even toyed with the idea of inviting the Americans to take part in the feast. But the American was a wily opponent, crafty and sure of himself.

The ancient emperors would have been pleased to take on such a worthy enemy.

But that did not make the problem any less vexing. The scientist had to be dealt with. Immediately and discreetly.

Cho Lai turned to General Lang. "Get me Colonel Sun. I will speak to him personally. No one else."

14

Western Vietnam

Jing Yo didn't expect Colonel Sun to be in too good a mood when he returned to Na San from the division meeting; that would be against his character. Still, given that they had achieved all of their objectives, and that by all reports the Chinese army was advancing at an even quicker pace than expected, he did think his commander would be at least neutral. But the frown on the colonel's face was obvious even from fifty paces as he stepped off the helicopter.

"The camp at Ba Nheu Sang," barked Sun as he strode toward the hangar building that had been commandeered as the commandos' headquarters. "The scientists."

Jing Yo fell in, unsure what the problem was.

"Your hands?" asked the colonel as they walked.

"My right hand was burned but has been treated." He held it up. The bandage covered the palm; the rest was fine. "The wounds are of no matter."

"Good."

Sun snapped off a salute as he passed the two guards at the hangar door. Ordinarily, Jing Yo had no trouble keeping up, but Sun's anger was driving him at a rapid pace, and the colonel reached the door to his office several steps ahead of him. Sun threw the door open and went to his desk, a narrow metal table salvaged from one of the terminal offices. The room itself had been used as a storehouse for parts until the Chinese takeover. The bins, nearly all of them empty, lined the wall behind Sun.

"Close the door," said Sun. "The man you chased— you killed him?"

The question had an accusatory ring to it. Jing Yo's hand lingered on the doorknob as he tried to decide whether to remind Sun of his order or not. In the end, he decided mentioning it would at least put Sun on notice that he knew the full story, not whatever one the colonel was going to adopt.

But of course, it had to be done judiciously. Not to avoid the truth, as his mentors would say, but to make the truth something all could view with calmness.

Calmness being a relative quality in Sun's case.

"He had gone into the water, as I reported at the time," said Jing Yo. "We were told to suspend the search. We were required elsewhere, with a higher priority."

Sun's frown deepened, but he did not explode.

"It may not even have been him," said the colonel. "It probably wasn't. This is what happens when we use general troops. Incompetents. Peasants. This was a job the commandos should have done."

"A problem, Colonel?"

"An incredible problem, Lieutenant." Now Sun's temper flared. "A problem that *must* be rectified. That *you* will rectify."

Jing Yo waited. Given the injuries his unit had sustained, he had expected he and the surviving members would be rotated back home for replenishment and training. That was not a prospect he relished—much better to be in the middle of fighting, he felt—but he knew his men would welcome the rest.

"Here. Look at this." Sun reached into the pocket of his shirt for a piece of paper. Unfolding it, he handed it to Jing Yo. "This is a transmission he has made. An American. Josh MacArthur. A CIA agent, undoubtedly."

Jing Yo took the paper. According to the heading, it was a transcript of a transmission made within the past twenty-four hours by sat phone.

"From this description—"

"The village at Pa Nam. Not the one you responded to that night," said Sun. "They covered it up, but apparently not well. Their commander has been recalled."

Jing Yo nodded.

"Peasants with guns. But we are the ones who have to fix it. Because," Sun added derisively, "we are the only ones who are competent in the Chinese army. Only the commandos can carry out an order without screwing it up."

"Do we have the coordinates of the phone that was used to transmit this?"

"We have an area location. The American spy made a second transmission a few hours ago. You're to meet with an intelligence officer from divisional at Ba Hong forward operating base in an hour to discuss the latest information."

"Yes, Colonel."

Sun folded his arms in front of his chest, shaking his head. Jing Yo stepped back, bowed his head, then prepared to leave. As he reached the door, Sun stopped him.

"Beijing has heard of your fine work," the colonel said. "The premier himself asked about you."

Jing Yo felt his face flush.

"It will be very clear that this problem originated with the regular army," said Sun. "But we must not fail to correct it."

"I will correct it to the best of my ability, Colonel."

Sun nodded, dismissing him.

15

Northwestern Vietnam

The small house and the buildings surrounding it looked normal from the top of the hill, and it was only when Josh and Mạ got a dozen meters away that he realized something was wrong. A pair of goats were braying in the yard between the house and the livestock barn, pleading hungrily for attention. They were standing at the edge of a pond so wide it blocked the way. It looked as if it had been there forever, yet it blocked off not only the yard but the driveway to the road, which easily twisted around several other obstructions on the three-hundred-yard path from the macadam.

Josh guessed what had happened—a Chinese bomb had hit the ground and disturbed an underground spring or well piping. The goats might have been able to swim across, but the pond's sudden appearance baffled and spooked them.

The rear of the house had been hit by another bomb or missile. The explosion had cratered the rear third of the structure. Afraid of what he might find in the house, Josh decided not to scout it by himself; he didn't want the girl to see any dead bodies. So he carried her around the back of the barn to a small saltbox shanty covered in sheets of rusted tin. Putting Mạ down, he knocked on the door, even though the building looked barely big enough to hold a few rakes.

The structure shuddered with his tap.

"Hello," he said. *"Xin chào!"*

No answer.

The door was held in place by its odd angle against the threshold; he had to lift it up and toward him to open it. The interior was empty except for an old shovel and several seed bags of grain.

"Here, come on," he told Mạ, gently pushing her inside. "You stay here. I want to look at the rest of the farm. Stay."

He mimed her sleeping, and pointed to the seed bags on the floor. The girl looked fearful, almost on the verge of tears. Josh dropped to his knees, trying to explain that he would be back. He mimed himself walking around—fingers on his palm—and looking for trouble—hands cupped like binoculars—and then coming back. When he was done, she looked confused rather than reassured, but she stayed when he pressed the door closed.

About ten feet of the side wall of the house had disintegrated, and there was a sizable hole where the floor had been in the back room. Josh squeezed gingerly around the jagged edge, slipping between the leaning interior walls into what had been a children's bedroom. Except for the cracks in the walls and ceiling, it appeared entirely untouched by the chaos. Bedrolls were neatly lined up against one wall. A small shelf above them held a rock collection; stones of all sizes and shapes sat on the linoleum paper surface as if on display. Two dolls, one made of vegetable husks and the other of yarn, flanked the collection, as if they were guarding it.

Josh tucked the yarn doll under his arm and went to explore the rest of the house. It was large and clearly belonged to a relatively well-to-do family. The furniture in the living room looked Western and new. The television was a large LCD screen.

The blue power light was on. Curious, Josh went and pushed the Power button. The TV flicked off. He pushed it again, expecting that he would get a screen of static. Instead, he got a picture—snowy, but visible.

A newscaster was speaking, not in Vietnamese, but in Chinese. Josh couldn't follow what he was saying, but the graphics that flashed on the screen showed an arrow arcing into China, and then arcing back.

Were the Chinese saying that the Vietnamese had attacked first?

The newscaster's face came back, angry, flushed.

He was saying that, wasn't he? Claiming the Vietnamese were getting what they deserved for having attacked first.

But Josh knew they hadn't. He'd lived through it. And he had evidence.

He put his hand on his pocket, touching the digital video recorder.

As he did, something creaked behind him. Panic seized him before he could turn around, before he could grab the rifle hanging from his shoulder. It was so important that he live, and yet here he had gone and let his guard down; he was going to die.

But it was only Mạ.

"You scared me," he told her. "I told you to stay."

She held her hands out to him.

"Look, a doll," he told her, holding out the toy he'd found.

She ignored it, raising her hands up and down emphatically. It was the signal they'd used while walking, indicating she wanted to be carried.

"It's okay. I'm just looking around," said Josh, kneeling to talk to her. "Did you know this house? Did you know these people?"

She didn't answer, just kept pumping her arms.

"Is this your house?" he asked.

He tried to think of a way to put the question into

gestures, looking upward, pointing at her. But she didn't understand. She grabbed hold of his shirt and tugged him toward the window.

"What's up, Má? What's going on?"

She pointed through the window. He pulled the curtain back to see.

There were soldiers in the field, moving toward the building.

16

The Pentagon

Zeus propped his hands on both cheeks, holding his face about four inches from the surface of the conference room table where he'd taped the large-scale map of Vietnam's western provinces. The map's features were a blur of yellow, green, and brown, swirling before his eyes. He needed sleep, real sleep, and if he couldn't get that, he needed coffee, the stronger the better.

"Trying to learn by osmosis?" said Win Christian across the room. The snicker in his voice was anything but subtle.

"I got the map memorized already," Zeus said, lifting his head slightly. "I'm trying to blank out your face."

"Very good, Zeus. Just remember, I'm chief of staff.

Anything you want, from dental floss to a weekend off, goes through me."

"Nice." Zeus knew he wouldn't be getting any free time for the foreseeable future, and he'd already stocked up on dental floss. "I'll tell you what I do need. Real-time access to the satellite data. Can you arrange that? There's no reason we can't have it immediately, not an hour later. I don't need the analysts to tell me what I'm seeing."

"We all need it. Intel is screaming for it."

"They should scream louder."

Zeus stretched his muscles. The Chinese plan to invade Vietnam clearly incorporated American doctrine—lightning strikes away from the main centers of resistance, along with coordinated air and armor movements. Cover a lot of ground, don't let the enemy know precisely what you are up to. It was Shock and Awe, Chinese style.

But the Chinese army wasn't the American army, and it wasn't fighting in a desert, where Shock and Awe had had its proving ground. There were flaws in the strategy—plenty of them, starting with the limited road network in the areas they were attacking, and the decision to keep the flanks lightly protected. The latter had been a feature of the second Gulf War, where the risk was carefully calculated and deemed acceptable. In this case, it seemed like an even greater gamble, though the Vietnamese had yet to make the Chinese pay for it.

Tanks were the keystone of the attack. The Chinese Type 99 main battle tank was a hell of a weapon, a main battle tank that, while not quite on par with the American M1A1, easily overmatched anything the Vietnamese were able to field. It was fast and powerful, capable of moving along the roads at high speed and then overcoming all but the most concentrated defenses. Its most glaring vulnerability was the fact that, like the Russian designs that had inspired it, its extra ammo was kept in the crew compartment, an invitation to disaster if it met a high-powered antitank round.

Had this been a simulation, Zeus could have blunted Red's attacks by making the most of this vulnerability. He'd hit the leading edge of the attacks with old but sturdy A-10A Warthogs, chewing up the leading edge of the invading force. He could mop up with special operations teams deposited near key intersections, who could strike with shoulder-held antitank weapons when the tanks came through.

But in real life, the Vietnamese had no A-10s. Their antitank weapons were either old Russian designs or Chinese-made-for-export missiles that conspicuously lacked the punch to get past the Type 99's skin and explosive reactive armor. Even if they somehow managed to get defensive forces in the right place—a big if at the moment—the Vietnamese weapons were the equivalent of peashooters as far as the tanks were concerned.

That could be partly solved by giving the Vietnamese new weapons. But even if they were flown over immediately from Army stockpiles, there'd be a delay in training and deployment. Several days at the very least, and by then the Chinese would have enough of the country that it wouldn't matter.

So there had to be another way to stop the Chinese. Or at least slow them down.

They'd just taken Na San and were staging there for their next big run. As Zeus saw it, tonight they would zoom down Route 6, probably overrun Moc Chau, and then go on either to Hanoi or farther south, down to the area of Nimh Binh.

Nimh Binh was the far better choice. From there, they had a real road network south. They could cut Hanoi off, take it at their leisure.

Everything they had done so far pointed south. Think of Shock and Awe—the big defenses were initially bypassed, then attacked at a time of the aggressor's choosing. The Chinese would do the same here. The Vietnamese expected the attack around Hanoi— most of their forces were very close to the city, even north of it. So that would be the last place the Chinese would go.

The country would open up after Nimh Binh. There were real highways, and plenty of them. Plus, the satellites had shown some activity on Hai Ham on their last pass. The Chinese island off the Gulf of Bac Bo pointed like a fist to Vietnam's midsection. It was the perfect place to stage an amphibious assault from.

A pincer from both directions, once Hanoi was cut off. The south was the real prize, and it lay nearly unprotected.

So what would I do if this were Red Dragon?

Slow the tanks down. That was the first job. Make

the Chinese take their time. Even if meant steering them directly toward Hanoi. Hanoi was a battle that the Vietnamese were prepared to fight. They might not win, but they at least had defenses in place.

Or send the Chinese into Laos. Easy pickings, but it would upend their timetable. The roads there were even worse than in northwestern Vietnam, especially in rain. Plus, they wouldn't be able to hide behind the PR line that they were invading Vietnam only to ensure their own safety.

As if anyone would believe that anyway. Anyone outside the UN, that is.

He needed a bottleneck, something more than just a road.

"General, I didn't expect you here tonight," said Christian as General Perry came into the room.

"Well, I am. Zeus, how are you?"

As the general walked across the room, Zeus flinched involuntarily. He started to salute, then realized Perry wanted to shake his hand.

"Good to have you aboard, Zeus," added Perry. "Win has filled you in on the details?"

"Yes, sir," said Zeus, though it had sounded more like a statement than a question. "I'm coming up with a strategy for the Vietnamese."

"You have the problem solved yet?"

"If I could get some A-10As over there, sure."

"I'm afraid that's not going to work." Perry's smile disintegrated into a frown.

"No, sir."

Did generals have to turn in their sense of humor

when they took their first star? Or did the promotion board limit its review to candidates who never got a joke?

Christian was smirking behind Perry, as if to say, *You idiot; now you're on my turf.*

That burned Zeus. Really burned him.

"I, uh, did have a little bit of an idea," he told Perry.

"Let's hear it."

Zeus looked down at the map, hoping inspiration would strike.

"They'll come down this way, the main attack, right down Route 6 to Moc Chau. All the intelligence points to it," said Zeus.

Perry looked at the map. Zeus stared at it as well, hoping it would spark his imagination. It didn't.

"How are the Vietnamese defenses there?" Perry asked.

"About on par with their defenses everywhere else except Hanoi," said Zeus. "Almost nonexistent. But I don't think they should take their stand there."

"No?"

"They'd get creamed."

"You're not suggesting they run away, are you?"

"If it would work, definitely. But, uh, what they have to do is, uh, slow the tanks down, try and get some of the momentum back—they have to stop the tanks temporarily and get the Chinese commanders to have to think on their feet. The um, Shock and Awe, which is what they're trying, is predicated on flexibility. Chinese doctrine isn't flexible. It hasn't been. Some units—their commandos are very good. But most of the infantry is very poorly educated and trained. Some of them are just basically farmers and, uh, in some cases criminals."

"How does this help the Vietnamese?" asked Christian. "How do they stop the tanks?"

"What they should do is flood the plain here," Zeus said, the idea coming to him as he saw the red line of the highway curling around the reservoirs at Song Da. "Divert the water from Song Da Lake south, destroy the road right before Routes 6 and 15. If they did a good enough job with the water, blew up the bridges, gutting the road—if they do that, the Chinese would have to stop. They'd have to stop."

The idea blossomed full in Zeus's mind. He saw the strategy now—cede Moc Chau, give up everything down to the Ma River. Using the water from Song Da—the tanks would be forced through a narrow, slow passage. The Chinese might cut a road through the jungle—or they might do the next logical thing and divert eastward, going after Hanoi. In either case, their plan would be thwarted. They'd need days—maybe weeks—to reorganize everything. Time to get help to the Vietnamese.

General Perry said nothing as Zeus fleshed out the plan, possible strategies popping into his mind. It was all a big roll of the dice, but at this point anything the Vietnamese did was a roll of the dice.

"What's to keep the Chinese from just blowing through Laos?" said Christian. There was a sneer in his voice. "They can slam right through there, bypass whatever the Vietnamese try setting up at the reservoir, then turn up in Saigon."

"That's mountainous terrain, mostly jungle, with even fewer roads than where they are now," said Zeus. "I mean, they may try it—it may be an alternative for them, especially if they're not planning an amphibious landing. But getting through those mountains with the tanks—they've done okay so far on paved roads, but Laos is a lot worse. Narrower—you can check the intel and—"

"Amphibious landings are not their forte," said Christian.

"That's right. But intelligence shows a buildup of activity on Hai Ham."

"A landing in Vietnam would give them practice for Taiwan," said Perry drily. "Your thinking is very sound, Major. Do you think the Vietnamese would agree?"

"I couldn't, uh, speak for them, General."

"A rhetorical question, son. You'll come with me to explain it to them. We'll both find out together."

"We're going over to the embassy?"

"We're going to Hanoi," said Perry. "There's an RT-1 waiting for us at Andrews. We'll be there in a few hours. The Vietnamese want our help. Unofficially, of course."

17

Northwestern Vietnam

A sharp pain pinched Josh's chest as he watched the soldiers move across the field. Every muscle froze. He couldn't breathe.

Mạ tugged at his hand.

"Yeah, we have to go. We have to—go," said Josh, forcing the words out. He pushed his legs to move, walking stiffly to the next room, which had a wall facing the front of the house. Halfway to the window, he spotted soldiers outside, up near the road. They were just standing there, but they could easily see the window.

"This way," Josh said, pulling Mạ backward with him. He fought against the panic trying to seize his chest and slipped into the scarred and battered room at the rear corner of the house. The soldiers hadn't reached the rear yard yet.

Josh grabbed Mạ, holding her under his side as he skirted the hole and then climbed over the rubble. As soon as they were out of the building, he threw himself and the girl down to the ground.

"Crawl," he whispered. Then he pulled her up and showed her how to go, on all fours, toward the rough grass and weeds a few yards away.

Mạ needed no urging; staying low to the ground, she scampered ahead and disappeared in the brush.

When he reached the grass, Josh turned back around to try and get a look out at the field and see what the soldiers were doing. He couldn't see much of the barn, or the field in front of the house. He backed up, still on hands and knees, pushing the grass back and forth—a telltale sign, he knew, that someone was hiding there.

Josh froze, then eased his head to the side, looking for a passage where he could crawl without disturbing the vegetation. He spotted one a few feet away. Pressing his stomach into the earth, he moved toward it as wormlike as possible. The earth smelled wet, with a vague manure scent.

His nose started to twitch.

Josh caught the sneeze in the crook of his arm, smothering it. He held his breath, and bit the side of his lip with his mouth. The pain felt almost good, reassuring. It was an easy trade—endure this pinprick of pain in exchange for safety.

But there were no deals to be made with fate. The soldiers began to yell. Once more Josh froze.

Some gunshots.

Mạ!

He started to jump up, rifle poised. He knew exactly what he was going to do: run out to the soldiers, finger pressed on the trigger of the rifle as he ran. He'd get a small measure of revenge before they killed him. He'd release his anger—not just from the assault by the Chinese, but from everything, from the unfair slaughter of his family when he was a child, from everything.

As he started to spring up, a small hand gripped his

side. Mạ's touch was light, but it stopped him. Josh folded forward.

The girl curled herself around him. He pulled Mạ close, expecting the soldiers to run to them at any second.

But they didn't. There were more shouts, a little farther away.

Josh smelled smoke. He let go of the girl and crawled forward a few feet, raising his head.

The barn was made of wood. There were stacks of bamboo near the sides. The soldiers had taken these and set fires.

The door opened. Two figures emerged, coughing. Some of the soldiers nearby began firing. The men fell.

They looked like farmers to him. They definitely weren't soldiers.

There were more shots. From the barn? Josh couldn't tell.

The soldiers were running, moving toward the barn.

Go, now, while everyone's attention was there.

He took out his video camera, fumbling with it. There was about forty-five seconds of memory left, part of the file he'd erased the day before. He pressed the button and began shooting.

Go! Get out of here!

Another figure came out of the barn, hands up. The soldiers cut her down as well.

The memory on the camera was full. He turned it off, slid it back into his pocket.

More gunfire. They were firing into the barn now, blindly.

Mạ was kneeling next to him. Rising into a crouch, Josh poked her to come with him. He started moving through the field, gradually rising, moving so fast that he was tugging the girl.

"Come on," he growled at her beneath his breath. Finally he reached down and pulled her up on his hip, running full speed toward a thick wedge of trees. Just as he reached it, he saw it was bordered by a barbed-wire fence. Afraid he couldn't stop in time, he plunged down to the side, rolling on the ground and then into the wire.

Mạ began to cry.

"Sssh," he said sharply.

One of the barbs had gone into his side. He felt it as he pulled away. He pulled the girl up, checked her—she didn't seem to be hurt, just scared, very scared.

"Through here."

Josh held up a strand of the wire. Mạ didn't move. He leaned down, levering the strands apart so the space was bigger.

"Go," he whispered to Mạ, trying to make his voice sound gentle, knowing that he had to be reassuring even though he felt anything but.

Mạ squeezed through. Josh followed. His stomach hurt as he contorted. His right pants leg caught on one of the barbs, snagged, and ripped as he forced his leg to follow the rest of his body.

Through the wire, he rolled onto the ground, fighting the pain. He forced himself up, then felt a new wave of panic when he didn't see the girl.

"Mạ." Her name sounded like a groan. *"Mạ!"*

He took a step, felt the pain swell in his side. He looked down. There was a black spot on his shirt.

Something moved near him.

"Ma?"

The girl popped out of the brush. "*Kia*," she said, pointing.

He wasn't sure what the word meant, but he pushed himself forward, glad to see her, still half fearing the worst.

A bicycle was leaning next to a tree. It was almost brand new, obviously parked there very recently, maybe by one of the people in the barn as an emergency escape.

They were on a slight rise; ten yards down the hillside a trail wound through the woods.

Josh grabbed the bicycle and walked it down through the trees to the path. The trail was rough but passable. He climbed onto the seat.

The pain in his side wasn't that bad. He could deal with it. He would have to.

"Come on, Ma," he said. She ran over; he started to grab her but she already knew what to do, climbing directly onto the crossbar.

His side seemed to split open with his first push on the pedal. Josh struggled to ignore it, pushing with his left foot, and then his right.

Go, he told himself. *Go!*

After twenty yards, the path met a blacktopped road. Josh veered onto it without really thinking, grateful for the easier pedaling and surer balance. It was only after he'd gone a hundred yards that he realized he was back on the road the Chinese must have used to get to the house. But it was too late to turn back. He leaned forward, his chest touching Mạ's side, putting as much energy into his legs as possible. His torn pants leg flapped against the chain guard, a steady if light drum keeping time as he went.

Another sound rose over it, behind him. A truck.

Several trucks.

Josh veered off the road onto the shoulder. Mạ hopped off; he grabbed the bike and pointed to the trees.

His head was swimming by the time he reached the thick clump of vegetation. He put the bike down and lay down, curling around his wound, trying to get his breath back. Mạ sat next to him, her tiny body on top of his.

The trucks took longer than he expected to arrive. The sound kept building and building. Finally Josh forced himself up to take a look. At first he couldn't see anything. Then a green and brown blur passed by—a camouflaged command vehicle.

Not much.

Another blur, similar in size and shape.

A lot of noise for just two trucks.

And then a gray truck passed by, a two-part troop vehicle. Then another. And another. A whole parade of them, an endless parade.

Josh sank back in despair.

"I should have shot them when I had the chance," he said aloud. "Now there's way too many. Shit. Shit, shit, shit."

Ma looked at him.

"We're not giving up," he told her. He made fists. "We're not."

She looked at him fearfully. Maybe she thought he was crazy, or was lying. Maybe she knew it was hopeless.

Was it hopeless? If he died, what would happen to the girl? What would happen to the world—the evidence of what had really happened here would be lost forever.

The whole damn world was depending on him—he was a witness.

Josh touched his pocket, making sure the camera was still there.

So was the sat phone.

Josh took the phone out and turned it on. It was still locked.

He dialed the emergency number. The line seemed dead. But he knew it wasn't—Peter had heard him.

More trucks passed on the road. And something bigger, heavier.

Tanks.

"Where the hell are you, Peter?" said Josh into the handset. "Get us out of here now. I repeat—get us the hell out of here now. *Now!*"

Northwestern Vietnam, near the border with China

The division intelligence officer wore eyeglasses with lenses thicker than any Jing Yo had ever seen before. The frames were at least a size too big for his small head, and as he spoke, the glasses worked their way toward the edge of his nose, until finally they seemed ready to fall straight off. Had the briefing been any less serious, Jing Yo would have broken out laughing. As it was, he had a hard time concentrating on everything the man said.

The American scientist who had managed to escape the camp had at least one satellite phone and was using it to communicate with the outside world. He had made at least one call on a civilian network even though China had already blocked calls on the network. The intelligence people suspected that he had received calls through a network used by the American military, and were working on detecting and monitoring them.

"We have aircraft operating in this area here," said Owl Eyes, pointing to the map. "You see his transmission was in this area, not very far from FOB number two. We have two aircraft crisscrossing the area, listening for transmissions. The next time he makes a call, we will be able to pinpoint it."

"On the military network or civilian?"

The briefer shook his head. "Civilian definitely. Military maybe. There are a number of factors—we may at least be able to find a transmission. Decrypting it—possibly, but there are no guarantees."

"Good," said Jing Yo.

Not coincidentally, FOB #2 was the forward operating base where they had met the briefer. It was a former orange grove plowed under for use as a helicopter landing field.

"The electronics aircraft are excellent planes. Canadian Twin Otters." Owl Eyes continued, telling how the insides had been gutted and then equipped with electronic devices that were at least as good as anything the Americans were fielding. It was undoubtedly an exaggeration, though how much Jing Yo couldn't tell.

Nor did he really care. He was much more interested in finding a helicopter for his team.

There were plenty outside. The newest ones—Z-10 gunships—were ferocious warplanes but could not carry passengers. For that job they would use Chenyang Stallions, Chinese copies of the Sikorsky S-76. It was a smaller, more maneuverable aircraft than its brother, the more famous S-70 Sikorsky Blackhawk used by America and its NATO allies. The Chinese company that built the helicopters was being sued by Sikorsky for patent violations—a sign to Jing Yo that it had done its work well.

"The American may have several men with him," said Owl Eyes. "If this is a trap, he will be armed with antiaircraft weapons."

"Why do you think that?"

Owl Eyes gave him a blank look. "I think that because, because it makes sense."

"If it is a trap."

"I would not underestimate them."

"I don't."

But neither did Jing Yo overestimate them. The Americans bled like anyone else. He had dealt with a few in Malaysia, generally through proxies. They were very good, most of them, but human.

The intelligence officer started to tell him a few things about the terrain, how large swaths were being developed for farmland because of the effects of climate change, and how the jungle had become even more unruly because of the increased carbon dioxide in the atmosphere, which encouraged growth. Jing Yo already knew a great deal about all this; he'd had to learn it when planning his original mission. But he let Owl Eyes talk, unsure whether the man was authorized to know about those missions or not.

When they were finished, Jing Yo went to the mess tent to get himself some tea and something to eat before tackling his next piece of business—wrestling more men to help in the search. He had only his squad at present. True, he could call on regular army units to help—but they were the cause of the problem in the first place, and he was loath to rely on them.

That was the real difference between the Americans and the Chinese. Surely the Americans did not have to worry about politics and infighting between commands, the logrolling that was necessary to get simple directives fulfilled and enough men recruited for a task. Jing Yo was involved in a mission of considerable importance—or so he was told—yet he had not been assigned enough men to carry it out. Even the helicopters that were to transport him had been given over grudgingly.

How important was the mission, really? Maybe now that Na San had been taken, Sun simply wanted him out of the way.

No. The colonel's anger had been real. And despite that, he had spoken almost kindly to Jing Yo. That could have meant only that this was more than a wild-goose chase.

Owl Eyes rushed into the tent, breathless.

"Lieutenant! We have him! We have a location for you! Six kilometers away! Hurry!"

19

Northwestern Vietnam

It seemed to Mara that she had just begun to drift off when the satellite phone began ringing desperately, its shrill clatter reverberating through the back of the truck.

"Yeah?" she said as she grabbed it.

"Mara, this is Lucas. Are you sleeping?"

"Sleeping?"

"Get up. I have a precise location on MacArthur. He's in trouble. You're only four kilometers away."

Mara jumped up, shaking the fatigue and confusion away. "Give me coordinates," she said. "GPS."

"They're already uploaded. How soon can you get there?"

"I can't get anywhere until I know where they are."

"Open up your system."

Mara slid over to her gear, which she had piled next to her makeshift bed. She grabbed the handheld computer.

It was four kilometers away, all right, but there was a mountain in between. The nearest road would almost double the distance.

"What sort of troops are near there?" she asked Lucas.

"Our latest intelligence is nearly an hour old. We had elements of the Forty-fifth Division sweeping through. They're infantry, light vehicles. There's a small armored unit attached, APCs and armored cars. A handful of tanks. They were probing the area."

"Roadblocks? Checks?"

"None on the latest imagery. We're scrambling to get more real-time data and coverage. You'll probably be there before we get it, though."

"Great." Mara reached down and began pulling on her boots.

"Be careful, Mara. Don't take any unnecessary risks."

You should have told me that before I joined the company, she thought.

Jimmy Choi had taken the first watch himself. His usual smile slipped when Mara told him that their subject was in trouble—but just a bit.

"We pull his fanny from fire, what you say?" The Korean slapped his hands together. "Four kilometers nothing."

"It's more like eight on the roads."

"Four, eight—good round numbers. Very lucky."

Jimmy trotted over to the tented lean-to his men had erected to sleep under. Three minutes later, he had them ready to go. He and Meanie, his fellow Korean, sat together in the Hanma. Moe, the Russian, rode shotgun in the truck with Mara behind the wheel; Jeb, the American-Eritrean, was in the back.

Moe grunted when Mara handed him the paper map. She didn't speak Russian, and if he spoke English he had yet to share a word of it. But he looked vaguely Asian, certainly more so than the fair-skinned Jeb.

And Mara, for that matter. She pulled her soft cap down and pulled up her collar, obscuring but not hiding her European features.

Moe rode with a Chinese rifle locked and loaded upright in his hand. His own FN SCAR, configured for close-quarter combat with a stubby barrel, sat on his lap. He had ammo all around him, and two pistols on the floor. Mara worried about taking the bumps too hard.

The Hanma had the lead. Jimmy took them down the streambed pretty fast, then spun onto the hard-top, pressing the command car for all it was worth.

Mara did the best she could do trying to keep up, but it was definitely a losing battle. The Hanma's engine was nearly the same size as the truck's but had a lot less weight to pull.

"Tell him to slow the hell down," Mara told Moe finally as Jimmy disappeared around a curve. "We have to get there together. And in one piece."

Moe didn't answer. In fact, he made no sign that he had heard.

"Give me the radio," Mara said, holding out her hand. "Radio."

Moe grunted, but apparently not in assent, because he didn't move. Mara slammed on the brakes.

"Radio, damn it."

Moe looked at her, then slowly unhooked his headset and handed it over.

"Choi, where the hell are you?" said Mara, holding the mike up.

"Where you, boss lady?"

"I'm way the hell behind you. Wait for me until I catch up."

"Ho-ho. We're in a hurry, right?"

"We have to get there in one piece."

Jimmy started laughing. Mara put the truck back into gear. She found him waiting two curves ahead.

He didn't adjust his speed all that much. As they came down a hill, they passed out of the jungle and suddenly had a good view of the valley where MacArthur had made his call.

"Wait," Mara said over the radio. She slammed the brakes hard enough to jar Moe, then jumped out of the cab, running to the side of the road with her binoculars.

Lucas had described the surrounding area, saying that there was a farm very close to MacArthur's hiding spot. Mara saw a farm that she thought might be it; smoke was rising from the barn. Roughly two dozen Chinese soldiers were in the field watching as it burned.

"Shit," muttered Mara.

She pulled out her sat phone and called Lucas back. "Peter, can you connect me with the scientist?"

"How close are you?"

"Maybe two miles."

"I'm reluctant to call him right now, Mara. It looks like the Chinese have an ELINT plane in the area. They may be looking for his signal."

"I'm looking at the farm you said was near where he was. The Chinese have surrounded a barn. It's on fire. If he's there, I want to know."

"Shit. Shit."

Mara heard Lucas putting through the connection, then switching her into the line. A thin, tired voice came on.

"Yes?"

"It's Peter, Josh. Are you in the barn?"

"Barn? What—no. No, I'm not."

"Good. Are you safe where you are?"

"No." It was an emphatic no.

"I want you to find a good hiding place, a very good hiding place, and stay there," said Mara. "I'll worry about everything else."

"Who are you?" Josh asked.

"Josh, I want you to find a hiding place near where you are," said Peter. "Don't say anything else. Sign off now."

His line cut out.

"Stand by for the location," Lucas told her. "It's two kilometers to the west of that farm."

Lucas said something else, but his words were drowned out by the heavy drone of approaching helicopters.

"Ho-ho, better get back in the truck," shouted Jimmy Choi from the Hanma. "Those are Z-10's—Chinese versions of the Apache. If they even suspect we're not on their side, they make us wish we were."

Northwestern Vietnam

Mạ didn't weigh much, but in his depleted state, she felt like an anchor as Josh struggled up the hill on the bike, desperately pedaling away from the burning barn. The gun strap kept slipping down his arm. He tried twisting his shoulder up to keep it in place, but the only real solution was to take his hand off the handlebars and move it back. Every time he did, the bike pitched to the left, and he had a hard time keeping his balance.

Sheer adrenaline propelled him, but even adrenaline had its limits. Finally Josh had to stop, the bike nearly dropping out from under him as his strength failed. Mạ jumped off, landing on her bare feet, legs bent and body ready, as if she were a wrestler getting ready for an opponent.

"We'll have to hide," he said.

Josh got off the bike and wheeled it into the jungle beyond the road. Mạ followed as he pushed through the thick bushes. He rammed the bike forward so carelessly that he nearly pushed it into a tree.

He was starting to lose his grip, starting to give in.

I'm in survival mode, he told himself. Stay alert. But the words were more a theory than a command, and far from a plan. What was the plan? To survive long enough for Peter to grab him and get him the hell out of there. Which was hardly a plan at all.

What if they just gave themselves up to the Chinese? Weren't the Chinese America's allies? Or friends, at least. Business partners. America bought Chinese goods, all sorts of goods. China bought American bonds.

The soldiers he'd seen in the field weren't anyone's friends.

Josh rolled the bike under a nearby bush, hiding it. The Chinese would never see it from the road, and they'd have no reason to come here—unless they were looking for them.

What if the man who called himself Peter wasn't working for the CIA at all? What if he wasn't American? What if he was Chinese?

The thick stretch of trees gave way to a sparse patch

of jungle, very lightly wooded. Josh stopped at the edge of this partial clearing, trying to figure out what it was. Rock outcroppings poked from the ground at his right; the terrain seemed too rocky to be a farm field. But maybe that's why it had been abandoned.

Mạ tugged at his arm, then pointed to his side.

"I'm okay," he told her. "I cut myself."

The pain from the wound had slackened. It no longer seemed to be bleeding, though his shirt was stained dark red. He held out his hands, shrugging as if it were nothing. She looked as if she was ready to cry.

"It's okay. Just a cut. A lot of blood, but no real harm," Josh told her. "Okay. It's okay. You understand 'okay'?"

He tried to think of words to use to reassure her, but he couldn't find any. His Vietnamese vocabulary, never large to begin with, had totally deserted him.

"Come on," he said. "Let's find a place to hide."

He walked along the rock outcroppings. There had been a road here not very long ago. The jungle had rushed back in, but it was too soon for thick trees.

Josh spotted the remains of a shack, busted down and overgrown, opposite the rocks. A rusted sign lay half covered with dirt and weeds in his path. He pointed to it, trying to get Mạ to read it, though he wouldn't have understood even if she did.

The loud stutter of an approaching helicopter, of two or three or four helicopters, reverberated through the hills. Josh looked up and decided they needed to find a spot with more cover from above.

"This way," he told Mạ, starting toward what looked like a large rock about twenty yards ahead.

As he came closer, Josh saw it wasn't a rock at all, but the remains of a structure. It was too overgrown and ramshackle to provide any cover. Just beyond it, however, the rocks formed a narrow ledge and a cleft in the hill. He led Mạ to it, and pushed her beneath it. She barely fit, but Josh knew he couldn't leave her alone.

"I'll hide in the trees," he told her, this time remembering to mime. "I'll be right there."

She grabbed hold of his leg and wouldn't let go.

"You're safer here," he said. "They'll come after me. They won't bother you. They won't be expecting a kid."

He hoped he wasn't lying.

As he started to push her back into her spot, he looked up and caught sight of something large beyond the row of rocks, a green hole at the edge of the jungle.

It took a few seconds for him to realize that it was the gaping mouth of a mine shaft, roughly six feet tall and only partly reclaimed by nature.

He tugged Mạ from her hiding place. "Come on," he said. "There's a mine shaft. We'll hide there. We can both hide there. Come on."

21

Northwestern Vietnam

Jing Yo tightened his grip on the handle at the side of the helicopter door, waiting as the aircraft banked toward the small farm on the side of the hill. Thick black smoke curled from the undersides of the tin roof, seething outward as if the barn were a pot with an overcooked stew. He looked back into the compartment and saw Sergeant Wu grinning behind him.

"Did our work for us," yelled the sergeant, leaning toward him. "Now maybe we get some rest."

The helicopter pitched backward slightly as it landed. Jing Yo leapt onto the uneven ground and, head lowered, trotted toward the knot of soldiers standing near the building.

"Who's in charge here?" he yelled.

"Sergeant Wong," replied the private closest to him. The man barely glanced at him.

Ordinarily, Jing Yo didn't stand on ceremony, especially when in a hurry, but the private's attitude could not be ignored.

"Stand at attention when an officer talks to you," he barked.

The private turned and frowned, then complied.

"What is your name?" said Jing Yo.

The soldier finally realized that he might actually

be in trouble. He went ramrod straight, hands to his sides, and snapped out his name, along with the requisite sir and tone of respect.

"Take me to Sergeant Wong," said Jing Yo.

"He's in the house."

"Take me to him. Now."

"Yes, sir."

Jing Yo told Wu and the rest of the team to watch the barn, then went with the private around the back end of the building, circling through a narrow garden and farm yard before reaching the small yard separating the barn and building. A dead goat lay next to the pond bordering the yard. Its head had been chewed up by 5.8 mm bullets. Flies buzzed across the wounds.

Ordinarily a private's attitude toward an officer mimicked that of his squad sergeant, and Jing Yo expected to be met with disrespect from Sergeant Wong. But the sergeant spotted the commando patch on Jing Yo's uniform and was instantly cooperative.

"Lieutenant, a pleasure," said Wong. He held out his hand. "I am Sergeant Wong. How can we help the commandos?"

"You may have a person I'm looking for. Have you searched the house?"

"We are in the process of doing so, Lieutenant."

"You and I must talk. Alone."

"Of course, Lieutenant. A pleasure."

Jing Yo led the sergeant outside. As they walked toward the front of the house, he noticed that no one was standing guard on that part of the property. In fact, the soldiers were poorly organized, clumping around the barn and the house.

"Why haven't you secured this property?" Jing Yo asked.

"It is secure, Lieutenant."

"You have no guards along the road, or on this side of the house."

"Who would we be guarding the house from?"

"Before you search an area, you secure it."

"We weren't searching it, Lieutenant. We were moving through. Our job is to probe Viet defenses. We found three snipers in the barn," he added. "We smoked them out."

"Where are they?"

"In the field, not far from where we shot them."

"Take me to them. Make sure the area is secured and searched. My men will search as well."

The people who had run from the barn were lying faceup about thirty meters from the still-smoldering structure. Their eyes gaped at the blue sky; they wore puzzled expressions on their faces, as if they couldn't yet believe they had passed on.

Two men, both Vietnamese.

"Why were they shot?" Jing Yo asked the sergeant.

"They were snipers."

"Where are their weapons?"

"We haven't searched the barn yet. No sense risking our own necks, eh, Lieutenant?"

Jing Yo knelt down to check if either of the men had identification cards. Neither one did.

"You know these Vietnamese," continued Wong.

"They're all trained killers. They were guerrillas during the war with the Americans. They see a uniform and it gets them excited. Blood to a shark."

"These were the only two men at the farm?" asked Jing Yo.

"We're still searching."

"Why didn't you search before you set the barn on fire?"

"We were just in the process when we came under fire," said the sergeant.

He answered quickly, his voice high. Jing Yo concluded that he was lying. Most likely one of his own men had begun to shoot out of panic, perhaps even before the fire had been set. It wasn't important; finding the American was.

"Sergeant Wu, send someone up to the house to help the search. You and I will look in the barn."

22

Bangkok

Peter Lucas stared at the computer screen, waiting for the refresh to take effect. The image was coming from a Global Hawk 2 unmanned reconnaissance aircraft, which was flying over Laos. Flying at just over 120,000 feet, the plane used a special lens to get a sideways view into Vietnam without actually going over the territory.

The camera showed incredible detail: if someone stood on the ground with a pair of coins in his hand, an expert could tell the difference between the penny and the quarter. But it wasn't good enough for Lucas—it didn't show him where MacArthur was.

Had he gone to the farm? Or was he running from it when he called?

"You can let the computer refresh on its own," said DeBiase, standing next to him. "It's not going to go any quicker if you do it manually."

"It gives me something to do."

The screen flashed and the image began redrawing itself. The barn was still on fire. The two helicopters, which had been at the edge of the frame on the last shot, were now on the ground.

"Those helicopters are a bad sign," said DeBiase. "They wouldn't have sent them unless they were there for something important."

"Mmmm."

"You could call him."

"Ringer might give him away. If he's hiding there."

"They'll find him sooner or later. Mara's awful close. The Chinese may find her instead of him."

Lucas tapped his fingers on the console. DeBiase was right. He reached to the keyboard, selected the dialer, and called.

T he phone started to ring as Josh neared the entrance to the mine. He stopped, then took a step toward the cave, then decided to answer the phone.

"What?" he said.

"Josh, it's Peter."

"Are you who you say you are?"

"Josh, listen—"

Mạ tugged at him. The helicopters were practically overhead.

"Go to hell," said Josh. He hit the Kill button and shoved the phone in his pocket as he ran toward the cave, his finger moving to the trigger of his gun.

Mara studied the Chinese helicopters from the cab of the truck. She'd never seen the gunships before. They looked a lot like American Apaches, but with faceted sides and a thick cowling over the engine. These were features designed to make the chopper stealthier, though in their present configuration, with thick air-to-ground missiles and gun pods on their stubby winglets, they didn't look like they were in much of a mood to pass by unnoticed.

"What we doin', boss?" asked Jimmy Choi over the squad radio.

"We're waiting until we get a positive location," said Mara. She still had the Russian's headset.

"And what we do if it's on the barn?"

"What do you suggest we do?"

"Ho-ho. I suggest we blow through the Chinese army." Jimmy laughed. "If you get rid of the helicopters. No helicopters, we're in like Flynn, babe."

"I'm glad you can laugh at a time like this."

"Better than crying, right?"

"Seriously."

"Serious—helicopters a problem but we have grenades. We can take down two or three. But maybe kill your scientist, too."

Mara picked up the sat phone to call Lucas and find out if he had a location, but he beat her to it. She hit the Talk button as the phone started to ring.

"It's Mara. Go ahead, Bangkok."

"Mara, listen. I'm just beaming you the GPS coordinates. He's on a hill two kilometers southwest of that farm. The helicopters are circling all around the area. But the only ground troops we can see are at the farm."

She picked up the field glasses and scanned the area. The hill was probably the one almost directly to her left, less than a mile away.

"Can you get him?"

"Definitely," she said, digging out her GPS to make sure.

Jing Yo raised his rifle, ready to follow the soldiers into the smoldering barn.

Was the scientist the man he had chased into the water days before? If so, he was a difficult opponent, a man with much luck or many lives, perhaps both. And skill.

His satcom radio buzzed. Jing Yo raised his hand, signaling Wu to wait, and answered the hail. It was the intelligence officer from division who was helping track the scientist.

"I have a new fix for you," said Owl Eyes excitedly. "Not three kilometers away. He's just communicated within the last two minutes. Hurry; he may be trying to escape."

They were airborne two minutes later. Jing Yo stood in the space behind the flight deck between the two pilots, crouching forward so he could see. The GPS coordinates, projected onto a rolling map in the center of the helicopter's control panel as well as on the HUD or heads-up displays in front of the pilots, indicated the scientist was on a small hill to their right as they flew.

"No place to land," said the pilot.

"Land in the road," said Jing Yo.

"Not wide enough. The rotors will clip the trees."

"We have a field half a klick south, right there," said the copilot.

"No. We'll rappel," said Jing Yo. "We'll go down lines into the road."

"As you wish, Lieutenant."

"Who's that?" Jing Yo asked, pointing to a command vehicle and troop truck that were coming up the road toward the hill. The direction was wrong for it to be Wong, whom he'd ordered to finish the search as a precaution.

As they watched, the trucks pulled over by the side of the road and several soldiers got out, sprinting up the hill.

"You sure they're not your people?" the copilot asked.

Had Sun put another unit on the job without telling him? It would be just like the colonel.

But no; Sun didn't have enough resources to waste them in a meaningless competition.

"It doesn't matter. Get us in there."

Mara's heart pounded as she jogged up the incline. She swept her eyes back and forth, dodging the biggest rocks and clumps of brush.

"Josh!" she yelled, nearly out of breath. "Josh! Peter sent us! We're here. Where are you, Josh?"

There was no answer.

"Josh!"

Mara took one last look at the handheld computer's GPS display, then slid it into her pocket in favor of the sat phone.

"Peter—some of us are wearing Chinese uniforms. Tell him it's okay."

"I'm trying to get him, Mara. He's not answering."

"Shit." She kept the phone in her hand and yelled. "Josh! Come out! We need to get you the hell out of here *now*!"

A line of rocks on Mara's left ran up the side of the hill like exposed ribs. She began following them, moving slowly so she could see any possible hiding places.

The vegetation cleared. The ruins of old buildings were scattered around, ghosts from a not-too-distant past.

"Josh!" Mara yelled again.

Jimmy Choi, Moe, and Jeb came up behind her.

"Where is he?" said Jimmy. He wasn't smiling any-more.

"He has to be nearby," said Mara. "Maybe he saw our uniforms and panicked. Search the sides of the woods—I'll take that lean-to or whatever the hell it is."

A helicopter had begun circling above, moving around the hill.

Was it a trap? It had that smell.

"Josh!"

There was a cave near the summit of the hill—no, a mine shaft.

Mara put her phone to her ear. "Peter? Did he go in the mine?"

"He didn't say anything about a mine."

"Are we in the right goddamn place?"

"Mara, I wouldn't let you go to the wrong place. You're about ten feet from where he was when he called—ten feet south of the exact spot."

The exact spot was two or three steps from the entrance to the mine. He must've gone inside.

"Josh!"

Her voice echoed into the darkness. She took her LED key-chain light out of her pocket and held it up. The dim light didn't shine very far into the shaft.

Jimmy Choi ran up outside. "The helicopter is go-ing to land," he told her. "Very bad news."

"Don't let it. I think our guy is in here. I'm going into the cave."

"Ho-ho. You make us earn our money, lady. We see you at the truck."

Jimmy's laugh stayed with her as she stepped forward into the darkness.

J ing Yo glanced down at the road as he reached for the line at the side of the helicopter. They were less than thirty meters from the road surface, hovering within a meter of the nearby trees. He could see the Hanma a few meters away. From the markings, the vehicle looked like it belonged to an artillery scouting team; very possibly they had been diverted from some other chore.

"Let's go!" he yelled over the roar of the rotors, swinging out. Feet in place, he began to slide downward.

Something passed overhead, a bird flashing with incredible speed.

Jing Yo's instincts took over, and though still a few meters from the ground, he released his grip on the line. The rope snapped at him, angry. The sky howled, an angry wind erupting as he fell.

Jing Yo spread his arms, relaxing his muscles as his feet hit the ground. He rolled forward, hitting the ground far harder than he would have under ordinary circumstances, but not so hard that he was in danger of breaking any bones. He rolled forward, falling as he had fallen many times before, swirling upward as he had been trained to do, balanced, perfectly balanced—everything was a matter of balance.

The air exploded. Jing Yo was pushed to the ground. He struggled to get back up, to understand what had happened.

The helicopter was down. The jungle was on fire.

Josh pushed Mạ ahead as the voice echoed through the tunnel, holding and prodding her with his left hand while he felt along the wall with his right. It was pitch-black; he couldn't even see Mạ's hair, let alone the wall or what was ahead.

A set of iron rails ran down the center of the tunnel, but the side where they were walking was smooth. There were hooks in the wall from an old rope guide. Josh started counting them as he went, hoping to use them as a rough gauge when he came back.

He heard his name echoing through the tunnel, distorted by the walls.

It had been a clever trick all along. The Chinese had thought of everything.

Mạ halted. Josh pushed her lightly, then stumbled against her, twisting downward and slipping down against the wall.

They'd come to a barrier. Wooden slats were posted sideways across the passage, cutting it off.

Josh scrambled to his feet and ran his hands along the boards, top to bottom, trying to find an opening. Mạ moved with him, clinging to his leg, as he worked left.

The path was completely cut off. Josh reached his

hands back and forth, then started along the other wall, hoping for an opening.

"Josh!" came the call behind him. They were closing in.

He still had the gun. It was the only way now.

He dropped to his knee, raising the rifle. But then he got another idea—perhaps he could use the barrel as a crowbar, prying off enough of the boards to at least send Mạ through.

He got up and began feeling for a slit big enough to stick the barrel in. Mạ tugged at his pants leg.

"It's okay," he told her.

The sound of someone coming for him grew louder. He chose one of the narrow spaces between the boards and pushed the tip of the barrel against it. The gun slipped from the tiny hole, nearly falling out of his grip.

"Josh," said Mạ, tugging.

He turned and saw a faint bluish light glimmering in the tunnel. It was above his head; he hadn't realized how sloped the tunnel was.

"All right," he said, getting down on his knee again. "I'm sorry. I'm really sorry. I thought we would be safe here."

He tucked her behind him and got ready. There was nothing else to do now. Offering his life in exchange for the girl's was worthless; they'd just kill her after they shot him.

How many were after him? If it was only a couple, he could fire, grab their guns and ammo, maybe make it out of the tunnel.

That was what he was going to do.

"Josh? Are you in here?" said the voice.

It was a woman. She was a decent English speaker, too. The Chinese really had prepared very well.

"Peter sent me. I'm going to get you out of here, but we have to hurry—there are Chinese troops nearby. They have helicopters. Come on, Josh. We have to leave now."

"Oh, you're damn good," muttered Josh.

"It's not a trick."

The light stopped moving.

"Josh—I know you don't trust anybody, but I'm not with the Chinese. I'm an American. I want to get you out. You have important information, don't you? You can tell the UN—the world."

Josh felt his finger cramp against the trigger. The blue light was faint; they must be far away. If he fired now, would he be able to run close enough to grab the fallen soldiers' weapons before their comrades came? How many of them were there?

"Josh—do you hear me? I know you're near. Come on—we have to hurry."

"How many of you are there?"

"Right now there's only me. Outside I have four men. Josh—you can trust me."

"Bullshit!"

Mara stretched to keep the flashlight as high as possible, hoping it would illuminate more of the tunnel. She couldn't see where he was, but it must not be too far away, maybe just a few inches beyond the dark circle ahead.

"Josh? There's nothing to be afraid of." Mara started forward. "I understand why you're worried. I had the same fear myself. But if you were Chinese, you would have shot me by now. And vice versa. If I was trying to trap you, I could have rolled a grenade down the shaft."

"You bastards!" he shouted.

Mara threw herself down, sprawling on the floor of the tunnel a second before Josh fired two bursts in her direction. The bullets were well over her head, but as they flew into the roof of the tunnel they rained splinters down from the ceiling.

The LED had slipped from her hand as she landed, spinning as it hit the floor and sailing toward Josh. She saw a figure crouched against the blackness ahead, starting to rise.

She started to get up, only to throw herself back down as Josh fired again.

Josh felt the rifle click empty. He launched himself forward, desperate, determined to sacrifice himself for the girl. It was the only thing he had now, the only reason for his existence. He flew through the air, aiming at the dark shadow in front of him, his feet barely touching the ground.

He bowled the shadow over, wrestling desperately, struggling. It had more energy than he thought, more power—he hadn't hurt it at all, maybe hadn't even wounded it.

"Stop, you idiot!" it yelled. "Stop. I'm here to help you, damn it."

The shadow flung him around, twisting him to the ground. It jumped on him.

Josh's energy fled. The gash from the barbed wire reopened, shrieking with pain. Everything he'd suffered over the past several days, his lack of food, of sleep, every injury, sapped his strength, left him weak and powerless. He lay on the ground, completely drained, ready for death.

Mara felt the fight go out of him. She gave him a hard smash to the jaw just in case, then pushed backward, rising and starting to pull him with her. As she took a step, something flew into her back—a wild animal, scratching and biting.

"Off!" she yelled, swirling around, unsure what was attacking her.

It was the size of a small bear, with all its fury.

A girl?

"*Em!*" yelled Mara, speaking Vietnamese as she tried to restrain the tornado. "Little sister, stop. I'm your friend. I'm a friend of Josh's. Stop. *Stop!*"

The girl continued to hit her. Mara managed to grab her shirt and push her against the wall, trying not to hurt her yet desperate to stop her so they could leave. Finally the child's fury expired. She deflated, falling against Mara like a rag doll.

"We have to get out of here," said Mara. "Josh— Josh, are you all right?"

He groaned, and pushed himself back against the wall.

"Come on," she told him.

"I don't trust you."

"If I was working with the Chinese, would I have come in here alone? God, you'd be dead by now. Come on."

Mara scooped up her AK-47 and flashlight and began trotting up the mine shaft. Looking back as she reached the first arc of light, she saw Josh following, the girl clutching his side. He'd picked up his gun and held it by the barrel, practically dragging it along.

Mara threw herself down near the mouth of the cave, crawling to the entrance on her hands and knees. It was eerily silent outside.

"Jimmy, where are you?" she asked over the team radio.

There was no response. She moved out of the cave mouth cautiously, worried that the Chinese had overwhelmed Choi's people and had set an ambush. But there was no one there.

"Come on, come on," she said to the others, waving them from the cave. "We have a truck down on the road."

The helicopter had crashed into the trees near the road, lodging itself about ten meters off the ground. The grenade that had hit it started a fire near the engine compartment; within seconds it consumed the entire helicopter.

As Jing Yo ran toward the wreckage, he heard the anguished scream of one of the crewmen stuck in the aircraft.

"Jump!" he yelled, even as threw himself onto a tree trunk below the wreck and began shimmying upward.

Jing Yo got about halfway up when the chopper's fuel tank exploded, shaking him and a good part of the wreckage from the tree. Tumbling, he smacked against another tree, rebounding into a thick bush a few feet from the ground.

He lay twisted in the branches for several minutes, his wits scrambled.

"Lieutenant, are you all right?"

Sergeant Wu's voice roused him like the cold air the monks would let into the dormitories after taking the novices' sheets. Jing Yo pushed to get up.

"Careful, you're about two meters from the ground," said Wu.

Jing Yo brought his feet down, gradually regaining his senses as he slithered through the leaves to the ground. He took a wobbly step, then stopped and forced a deep breath into his lungs.

"You okay, Lieutenant?"

Rather than answering, Jing Yo looked up. Only a third of the helicopter remained in the trees. The rest was a tangled mess, scattered in a haphazard circle around the area.

"There was a crewman," said Jing Yo.

"They're all dead. Come on—our guys are on the road. Let's find who did this."

Sergeant Wu led him back to the shoulder of the road, where the rest of the team had gathered, crouching in a defensive position. Jing Yo took out his satellite radio and gave it to Ai Gua.

"Find out what the situation is," he told the private. "Get division to talk to the helicopters. Where is our enemy?"

"There are soldiers in the jungle near the hill," Ai Gua said a few minutes later. "And near the trucks."

"We take the trucks first," said Jing Yo.

Disoriented and still weak, Josh followed Mara out of the cave. She was a big woman, nearly as tall as he was, and dressed like a Chinese soldier. But what she'd said had to be true—if she was on the Chinese side she'd have killed him by now.

"My people are down by the road," she told him, holding out her hand to stop him as he followed. "Wait."

Josh heard the pop-pop-pop of automatic weapons as he squatted down. Little Mạ clung to his back, her body trembling.

"I'm Mara, by the way," said the CIA officer, holding out her hand. "Mara Duncan."

"Josh MacArthur."

"Yeah, I know. You have video, right?"

A twinge of suspicion came back. He patted his pocket. "Yeah, I got it."

"Who's the girl?"

"Mạ."

"*Who* is she? Was she on the expedition?"

"No, she found me. She was tracking me through the woods, and then the Chinese soldiers grabbed her. They would have killed her."

"You saved her?"

"Yeah, I saved her." Josh felt his face flush. "I haven't eaten or slept that much in a couple of days. Otherwise I would have pounded your head into the ground. You're damn lucky."

"Then you're lucky, too," said Mara mildly. "But I don't know that we have much more luck than that." She looked at the girl. "*Tên em là gì?*"

"Mạ."

"Mara."

She held out her hand, but Mạ wouldn't take it.

"You have bullets in that gun?" she asked Josh.

"It's empty."

Mara put her hand to her ear, cupping an earpiece for her radio.

"Right," she told whoever was on the other end. Then she pulled a pistol from beneath her tac vest. "Take this. I hope you're a better shot in the daylight. Come on. We have to move."

Josh scrambled to follow her as she ran down the trail. He felt angry—she was treating him like he was a jerk, or worse.

She stopped near the road, catching him as he ran up.

"Hold, hold," she said. "Easy."

He flicked her hand away and slid next to a tree, gun ready. When Mạ finally reached them, she threw herself over Josh's back as she had before. It felt somehow reassuring, though his ego was still deeply bruised.

"Our trucks are just up the road. My guys will drive down this way in a second," added Mara. "Take the girl when they come. I'll cover you."

As she said that, gunfire sounded up the road.

Jing Yo split his small squad in two, sending Wu and three others across the road while he worked up the near side with the rest. They came under fire before they were in sight of the trucks, bullets splashing into the macadam and the trees behind them. Chest pressed against the side of the road, Jing Yo caught a glimpse of someone retreating near the command vehicle. He wore black clothes—clearly not a Chinese soldier.

Jing Yo turned to Ai Gua. "Tell the helicopter to destroy the trucks. The troop truck first."

Mara heard the truck rumbling toward her and got ready to launch herself into the road. She glanced to the right, looking at Josh and the girl, Mạ. The girl was another complication, but it was very possible that she would be a valuable one—not only did they have an eyewitness and video footage of China's brutality, but they also had a victim. It would be a PR jackpot.

Assuming she got them back to the UN safe and sound.

Jimmy Choi and one of his men started laying covering fire from across the road. The bumper of the truck appeared as it rounded the bend.

"Let's go," said Mara, starting into the road.

A helicopter's heavy rotor pounded the ground. Mara stopped and turned back, looking for Josh. He was still by the trees, picking up the girl.

"Come on!" yelled Mara. She stepped toward them. "Come on!"

Something flashed behind her. Mara felt herself thrown forward. Then everything went black.

ELECTRONICS GIANT STAI-ON
DECLARES BANKRUPTCY
AMID JAPAN ELECTRONICS DOWNTURN

TOKYO, JAPAN (World News Service)—Japanese conglomerate Stai-On today officially filed for bankruptcy protection.

"This move will allow us to reemerge as a stronger, though smaller company," said Masura Takai, company spokesman. "We expect to continue operations through this difficult period."

The chairman of the company was found dead in his Tokyo apartment last week. Police have not revealed the cause of death. Rumors continue to circulate that he committed suicide in the face of the company's financial crisis.

Stai-On, known for its exports of electronic consumer goods, has been in trouble since worldwide exports declined in 2009. Until then, Stai-On was the number one electronics exporter in Japan, besting the Sony Corporation by about $3 billion in exports annually.

Electronics purchases declined sharply in the U.S. beginning with the 2008–2009 recession. While sales were essentially flat in 2010 and 2011, an even sharper decline in 2012 drove many companies into financial disarray. Among the firms . . .

CONGO BRUSHFIRE SPREADS; SMOKE PLUME TO AFFECT CLIMATE THROUGH REST OF YEAR

BUMBA, DEMOCRATIC REPUBLIC OF CONGO, CENTRAL AFRICA (AP–Fox News)—Firefighters reported today that two wildfires previously thought to have been brought under control have spread past firebreaks and are now racing toward the Congo River.

Approximately five thousand square kilometers of savannah and forest have been burned so far. Smoke from the fire now covers much of western Africa and is expected to linger in the atmosphere for several months.

Joseph Kituba, a local fire warden, said that the spread of the fires was fanned by unexpected winds that reached upwards of sixty kilometers per hour overnight.

"Under normal weather conditions, we would never see something like this," said Kituba. "But the weather that we have had here the past few years has been anything but normal . . ."

Survivor

幸存者

Northwestern Vietnam

The explosion threw Josh forward, tumbling him over Mạ into a heap of dirt at the side of the road.

It was too much, all too much.

For a second he gave up, capitulated to despair. He was dirt, dust—he lay there helpless, ready to let the Chinese take him, let them chew him up like everything else they were chewing up. He gave up completely, utterly.

Then Mạ moved beneath him, whimpering. He heard her, and for a moment he became the boy who'd run from the murderers at roughly her age—the scared, desperate little boy.

And then in the next moment he became the scientist again, and more. He became the man who was going to tell the world what was going on, who was going to help keep people from dying.

Josh pushed himself to his feet, aching, weakened by hunger and fatigue, by a thousand cuts and bruises. Mạ scrambled to her feet beneath him. He saw her face, the question in her eyes she didn't have the words to ask.

"We'll make it," he told her.

He turned around. The truck was on fire. Mara lay

in the road. The explosion had torn into the small rucksack on her back, battering the contents. Josh tore the pack off, looking for wounds. The mangled gear had apparently saved her life, preventing any of the shrapnel from entering her back.

Heavy gunfire ripped through the other side of the road only a few yards away. He bent and put his shoulder into her side, lifting her upward. He staggered under her weight, but made it to the side of the road.

Mạ was waiting.

"Take the gun," he told her, letting go of Mara just long enough to point to the rifle on the ground.

The girl hesitated, then scooped up the weapon from the ground as if it were a piece of poisoned fruit. Josh started up the road, Mara on his back.

She groaned.

"Jesus you're heavy," he complained, still moving, but just barely, as he went up the incline. A few yards past the path to the mine he spotted another old, overgrown road. He kept going, pushing his legs forward despite the burn that spread from his thigh muscles to the rest of his legs. The mine was a trap; the Chinese would look there first.

He continued, moving slower and slower, until he spotted a narrow culvert running under the road. The cement pipe below contained a stream, which ran southward after crossing beneath the roadbed.

Josh veered toward the shallow embankment, heading toward the creek. Within three steps he lost his balance and fell on his side, slipping down into the water and losing Mara in the process.

Mạ ran to him to see if he was all right.

"Yes, yes, I'm all right," he told the girl. "It's okay."

"God," groaned Mara on the ground a few feet away. "Jesus, Mary, and Joseph, what the hell?"

Josh got to his knees and splashed water onto his face. Then he cupped his hands and took a few sips before rubbing the water on his eyes.

Mara remained dazed on the ground. The gunfire continued in the distance. Josh got to his feet and went to her.

"We have to keep moving," he said. "Come on."

"What the hell?" Her voice was a mumble, far away. "My bag? Where's my bag?"

"It got blown up," he said.

"God, my back hurts."

"You'll be all right. You're not even bleeding."

"Yeah."

Josh took the gun from Mạ's hand.

"If you could walk, it would be really good," he told Mara. "I don't think I can carry you anymore."

"Walk," she repeated as he helped her to her feet.

Mara was shaky, but she kept her balance as they started down the stream. Josh took the rear, figuring that was where the threat would come from.

"Where are we going?" asked Mara.

"We're just going," said Josh. "Keep moving. Go!"

2

Northwestern Vietnam

The tracers flying out from the edge of the jungle told Jing Yo several things, the most important of which was that they were not fighting Vietnamese soldiers, or at least not regular soldiers. The gunfire was much more carefully aimed and coordinated, the shots purposeful even when they missed. The tracers weren't being used to help the soldiers aim; rather, the rounds told the gunner he was nearing the end of his box. As he stopped to reload, another took up the fire, so that there was never a break in the gunfire that could be exploited.

The sound of the weapons was also telling—it was tinnier than an AK-47's. Yet it was deeper than the *slish-slish* a SCAR would make—an indication, Jing Yo thought, that these men were not Americans.

Perhaps not, though they had at least one thing in common with the American SEALs Jing Yo had briefly trained with at the start of his career—they were turning an incredibly minute tactical advantage into a commanding position. They had the road completely covered, yet Jing Yo believed they had no more than six men, and most likely only four. They even used the destruction of their vehicles to their advantage, using the covering smoke to launch brief feints to stall a counterattack.

The helicopter gunships were impotent. The enemy force was so close to Jing Yo's men that they couldn't fire their rockets without either exposing themselves to more grenade fire or risking a miss that would kill their own troops.

"Couple of grenades there and we can push whoever's holding that spot back," said Sergeant Wu, crouching near Jing Yo. He pointed left to the north side of the road, where a slight rise gave the enemy just enough of a vantage to keep the commandos in place. "We can gang up on them. Sweep around once we're on that side of the road and beyond their trucks."

"Hmmm."

The gunfire continued, controlled bursts plowing through the jungle anytime Jing Yo's men tried to move.

"We get that side, we can roll them up," said Wu, elaborating on his plan. "We push them back from the road. Helicopters can come in and pick up the wounded from the crash."

Jing Yo didn't answer.

"You want to wait until the reinforcements get here?" Wu asked. Soldiers from the unit that had been at the farm had landed up the road and were marching up the road. "They'll be here in five minutes. That'll work, too."

"Why do you think the enemy is still firing?" Jing Yo asked his sergeant.

"What do you mean?"

"If we were holding that position, we would have moved back by now. We would try to get away before our enemy could bring in many reinforcements. We would expect reinforcements."

"Maybe they don't. Or maybe they're stupid."

"They're not stupid." Jing Yo shifted his rifle. "They are covering a retreat."

"All right. But we can't deal with that until we deal with them."

"Yes."

The soldiers must have gotten the scientist; it was the only reason they could be here.

Which way was he going? Directly behind them? Or somewhere else?

There was no way to know. The safest line of retreat would be behind the defenses. Jing Yo would have to try that way first.

The enemy would naturally expect the attack the sergeant had suggested, since they would know or at least suspect that was the direction the reinforcements would come from. He would therefore pretend to launch the assault there, but instead come up from the other side, the southwestern corner, across the road. The defenders would either retreat immediately, or be caught in place as the reinforcements arrived.

"I will take Ai Gua and Private Kim with me," Jing Yo told Wu, outlining his plan. "We will circle around and launch an attack from the southeast, behind the position at that point in the road."

"The jungle is pretty thick there."

"Yes, they may be counting on that. You will launch

your grenades at the northern point, and make them think we are concentrating on them there."

Sergeant Wu nodded.

"Take the radio from Ai Gua. Have the helicopters take some of the regular troops to the farming area beyond the jungle," Jing Yo told Wu. "And tell them to continue patrolling above. Give us ten minutes to get into position, then launch your attack."

As Jing Yo leaped up, a fresh fusillade of bullets crashed into the jungle near him, forcing him to dive headfirst into the brush to his right. He crawled nearly ten meters on his belly before rising again, running in a crouch as he started to arc into position.

Ai Gua and Kim, meanwhile, withdrew from their spots near the shoulder of the road. They met Jing Yo about fifteen meters from the curve just opposite the enemy's southernmost position. They moved another fifty meters farther west, crossing the road near a stream culvert.

Jing Yo slid down into the crevice cut by the stream. The streambed formed an easy path southward, keeping the brush at bay. He trotted down it for twenty meters, then went up the embankment, leading his men into the jungle at a slow but steady pace. They could hear the enemy gunner firing his rounds, but the vegetation was so thick they couldn't see him.

Both men were on his left, Ai Gua a few yards away, Kim closer to the road. Jing Yo signaled to them to stay put, then began slipping forward through the brush, moving as quietly as he could. Stealth was an animal virtue; he imagined himself a tiger, passing through the stalks and branches with less sound than a raindrop slipping between the leaves of a tree.

The gunfire was very close.

A dark shadow shifted on his left, moving ever so slightly.

The enemy, twelve yards away, temporarily protected by a tree.

Wu's grenades exploded to the north near the road. The gunfire stoked into a thunderstorm.

Jing Yo waited for the shadow he was watching to move. He didn't, nor did he fire.

Very disciplined.

Sergeant Wu's attack continued with a fresh round of grenades. Jing Yo heard the man near him say something, undoubtedly speaking into a radio, and start to move to his right.

Jing Yo raised his rifle, then fired a three-shot burst into the middle of the moving green blur. It didn't stop.

Bulletproof vest.

Jing Yo adjusted his aim lower, but there was so much vegetation and debris that he couldn't be sure of what he was aiming at. The soldier crashed farther into the jungle, moving eastward.

The others were, too. Jing Yo got up to start after them, then realized the danger.

"Down!" he yelled as loud as he could, hoping his voice would reach not just Ai Gua and Kim but Wu and the others. "Down!"

His warning was cut off by a tremendous explosion. The enemy had planted an IED or improvised explosive device at the edge of their position, exploding it to cover their trail.

"Come on!" he yelled to Ai Gua and Kim. "They're running away!"

En route to Thailand

Only a few airports in the world could handle the U.S. Air Force's RT-1, the official designation of the hypersonic transport. None of them were in Vietnam.

The airport at Bangkok in Thailand had a long enough runway and was relatively close to Vietnam, but was known to be under surveillance by Chinese agents. So was the airport at U-Tapao, the Thailand naval air base that doubled as a sparsely used international airport. But U-Tapao's regular military use made it a little easier to camouflage the ultimate destination of the plane's passengers, and so it was chosen as the RT-1's destination.

Zeus Murphy had never been aboard the hypersonic aircraft. Though the outer hull of the plane was large—lengthwise, it rivaled stretched versions of the 747—the interior cabin was about the size of a corporate jet. It was nowhere near as luxurious. While the Air Force used the RT, as everyone called it, exclusively as a VIP transport, Congress had severely limited the amount of money that could be used for the aircraft's amenities. That meant the cabin looked a lot like what would be found in the first-class section of a circa-2000 Boeing 777. Not bad by any means, but not ultrafancy.

The stewards, all male, left something to be desired, but that was another story.

The flight itself was so quick—just over two hours— that Zeus hardly had time to finish his PowerPoint presentation for the Vietnamese. The general's translator, a Vietnamese national on contract to the Defense Department, worked on a translation page by page on a piece of paper next to him as they flew. He hadn't even had a chance to type it into the computer when the steward came back and said they were landing.

"The captain requests that you buckle your seat belts," said the steward. "General? I'm afraid your seat has to be upright for the landing."

"Yes, thank you, Sergeant," said Perry, fixing his seat.

While the RT could fly at roughly ten times the speed of sound, the flight was extremely smooth, without the nosebleed, gut-punching acceleration of a fighter, let alone a spacecraft. For the passengers, taking off felt no different from what they'd experience in a Boeing Dreamliner, and the acceleration was gradual. On most flights, the same might be said of landing. In this case, however, with time at a premium— and no concerns about a sonic boom over the ocean— the landing was relatively abrupt. Zeus felt himself straining against his seat belt as the plane began to drop. The strain continued, increasing as the plane lowered itself toward the runway.

Even so, landing seemed to take forever. The RT lacked windows, so Zeus had no way of knowing how close to the ground they actually were. The noise of the engines continued to increase; inertia kept pushing him against the seat belt. Zeus felt as if he were stuck in a bizarre amusement park ride that would never end.

Finally the plane jerked up, then back down, the tires screeching. Despite huge shock absorbers that dampened the impact, the vibration could be felt throughout the entire craft as it slowed to a stop on the tarmac.

Zeus undid his belt and picked up his briefcase, waiting for General Perry to lead the way out of the cabin. Win Christian studiously avoided his gaze—just fine by Zeus.

General Perry paused in front of the door as the steward cracked it open.

"Smile, you're on *Candid Camera*," said the general, jokingly reminding them that Chinese spies were probably watching. Then Perry stepped quickly out of the plane, practically running down the moving stairway that had been rolled out to meet them. Christian did the same, springing down the steps as if he were jogging toward a reception.

Zeus had never been to Thailand before—in fact, his only tour in Asia had been a very brief temporary duty in South Korea—and he decided that he was going to take his time, savoring the moment and absorbing as much of the scene as possible.

The first thing he absorbed was the tremendous

heat. Everyone said that Southeast Asia was warm and muggy; everyone was right. Zeus felt as if his clothes—he was in his Class A, look-your-best-because-you're-meeting-the-top-brass, dress uniform—absorbed a gallon of water in his first step off the plane.

They'd been directed to a relatively secluded area of the airport, not so much to avoid prying eyes as to stay away from the simply curious. The RT sat at the center of a large expanse of concrete. The nearest buildings were a pair of hangars about a hundred yards away. A U.S. Navy Orion electronic intelligence-gathering, or ELINT, aircraft was being refueled in front of one of them, guarded by several sailors. A small civilian airliner was rolling on a ramp beyond the hangars, passing rows of warehouses and a fenced-off area used for ammunition storage by the Thai Navy.

A pair of large Korean Hyundai sedans stood with their doors open about twenty yards from the aircraft. Flanked by a handful of marines and sandwiched between two Hummers, the limos had their doors open, waiting for the general and his party.

Zeus got into the second car, sitting with the general's administrative assistant, a prim but extremely efficient middle-aged woman with the unfortunate nickname of Candy.

If "Candy" fit any woman in the world, it was surely not this one. For Zeus, the name evoked images of a gum-cracking, lipstick-smearing woman whose clothes were always a size too tight. This Candy wore a skirt that came to her calves and glasses so thickly framed that even a librarian would have found them unfashionable.

Staying on her good side was highly advisable, since practically everything the general did went through her or Christian. And cultivating Christian was not an option.

"Hot, huh?" said Zeus as the doors were closed.

"I expected worse."

"So, how long have you worked for the general?"

Candy turned and gave him a look that implied he had just asked a question requiring code-word clearance.

"A while, huh?" he said when she didn't answer.

"A while."

"Good boss?"

"My boss is the U.S. taxpayer."

"Good answer," offered Zeus, ending his stab at making conversation. Not even Rosen could have charmed this battle-ax.

The procession drove a few hundred yards down the concrete, passing behind an empty military bus before stopping in front of a Thai Navy helicopter. Zeus got out and followed the others into the helicopter. The chopper took off before he even got seated, rising quickly and turning hard.

"Wow," said Zeus as he bumped against Christian, who was seated next to him. Though it was used as a VIP transport, the accommodations on the chopper were cramped and basic. The seat cushion had less foam in it than a cheap throwaway sunshade.

"Antiterrorist tactic, Major," said Perry, who was sitting in front of him. "We're in a war zone. Have to get used to that."

"Yes, sir."

The base didn't look as if it was ramping up for war, particularly. A number of warships—patrol craft sized, mostly—sat tied up at their docks, all nestled together: an easy target for an enemy. And the traffic on the field looked no heavier than what one might see at a base in Alaska on a Sunday afternoon in July.

The port-area industries gave way to jungle as they moved inland. Suddenly the helo tipped hard to the right. The trees seemed to part, and a large green field appeared. They put down quickly, then scrambled out the door to another waiting chopper, this one a Sikorsky with no markings. In seconds they were airborne, and rushing to the northeast.

Their destination was Korat, a Thai air force base where a Korean Airlines jet waited on the tarmac for them. The jet was an actual Korean Airlines plane, leased by the U.S. so the arrival in Vietnam would be low-key. The pilots were U.S. Air Force captains, and shortly after takeoff they called General Perry into the cockpit to brief him on their flight plan.

Perry had Christian and Zeus go up with him. The cockpit was cramped, tighter than Zeus had imagined it would be—it was the first time he'd ever been in a cockpit of anything other than a C-130 or a helicopter.

Originally, they had planned to land in Da Nang—

the old U.S. Marine base was now a Vietnamese airport—since it was one of the few airports in the country that had not been damaged by Chinese bombing. But the Vietnamese had done some emergency repairs to the Hanoi airport, and had passed the word that they preferred the delegation to land there.

"That's where we're landing then," said Perry.

"It's still very vulnerable to a Chinese attack," said Christian. "And it's got to be in their crosshairs."

"We're not going to score any points by landing in Da Nang," said Perry. "And we're going to need all the points we can get. We're here to help them, but make no mistake, gentlemen: from their point of view, we're the ones who aren't to be trusted."

That was the end of the conversation.

While the holes on the runway had been patched, the damage to the airport was considerable. There were still fires burning as the jet prepared to land, and much of Zeus's view of the city and nearby countryside was obscured by coils of thick black smoke. The landing was so bumpy he was sure they were going to crash.

A Vietnamese army captain met them on the tarmac. The officer's low rank could have been interpreted as a snub, but Perry took it in stride. Nor did he balk at riding in the open jeep waiting for him.

Except for Captain Ford—Perry's personal bodyguard and the head of the security detail—the rest of the small delegation had to follow in a bus. Christian started grumbling about the lack of proper protocol

as soon as they were moving. Zeus was more concerned by the amount of damage he saw as they headed
toward the city.

When most people thought of the damage wrought
by a bombing, they tended to think in absolutes—
whole cities or at least swaths of them wiped out.
Images from history, especially World War II, reinforced this notion; the mind tended to remember the
images of block after block of rubble.

But the reality of modern warfare was somewhat
different. Smart weapons such as laser- and GPS-guided
missiles were more discreet than the free-falling bombs
dropped by B-17's during World War II. The destruction they wrought, especially in the early stages of a
conflict, tended to be confined to specific places, and
generally these were military targets.

When planners talked about this, they tended to
focus on how desirable it was to limit collateral damage. Civilians, they would say, were not the targets and
should be spared. The main lesson of World War II—
that there are no real noncombatants in a war—was
an inconvenient and irrelevant point.

Zeus looked at the matter differently. Waging a
war was like running a budget. Missiles, GPS bombs,
even unguided iron bombs, were all very expensive.
The side that got the most bang for its buck—pun only
partially intended—usually won. So you didn't waste
your weapons destroying apartment buildings, or killing civilians for that matter. You used them on high-
value targets, targets that played a direct role in your
enemy's ability to wage war.

The airport runways were an example, as were its fuel farms and the hangars where its military aircraft were stored. All had been hit. So had the small industrial parks just outside the airport, which was where most of the fires were still raging. These were of lesser immediate value, especially since few if any made anything related to the military.

But to attack the hotels and apartment buildings lining the highway to Hanoi? Building after building had been torn in half. Some looked as if they had been bitten by a large monster; others were little more than rubble. They hadn't been accidentally targeted, either; too many were in ruins for that.

This told Zeus two things about the men running the war: (1) they were absolutely ruthless, probably determined to kill as many Vietnamese as possible and scare the rest, and (2) they had a large amount of resources at their disposal, much more than Zeus had anticipated.

Much more than the Red Dragon simulation called for. And China was practically unbeatable there.

Zeus kept his conclusions to himself as they drove through the city. They stopped in front of the Sofitel Metropole Hotel, one of the most famous and oldest of the hotels in the city. It had escaped the bombing unscathed.

The American ambassador was waiting for General Perry just outside the door, to the evident discomfort of her security detail. There were no Vietnamese army or police, plainclothes or otherwise, nearby. In fact, the entire street seemed deserted, even though it was the middle of the day.

"General, I'm glad your flight was a good one," said the ambassador, shaking his hand. "A good decision to land in Hanoi."

Ambassador Melanie Behrens was a short woman, barely five feet. A leather pocketbook hung by a strap from her shoulder. She clutched one end of it the way a soldier might hold a gun.

"Is this where they're putting us up?" asked the general.

"No. You'll stay at the embassy. Most of the government buildings were bombed overnight. They've moved some of the operations here."

"Shouldn't they be in bunkers?" asked Christian.

"All of the important operations are. This is where they wanted to meet."

"We're being tested," Perry told Zeus before following the ambassador inside.

Perry's assessment seemed at least partially true, but as the meeting with the assistant deputy in charge of defense began, Zeus got the impression that the Vietnamese had no expectation that the Americans would really help them. This was probably because their memory of the American Vietnam War was still very fresh, even for the men, like the deputy, who were too young to have experienced it firsthand.

The deputy, Hai Ba, was roughly the equivalent of an undersecretary of defense. Only a few years older than Zeus, he moved with a stiff and very formal gait. He also spoke English well enough to dispense with a translator, though one remained discreetly behind him during the meeting.

"We are grateful for your interest," he told Perry and the others after they were shown into a small conference room on the first floor. "It is a difficult time."

"We believe we can help," said Perry. "The president wants you to know that he is extremely interested in assisting Vietnam at this critical point, and that he wishes to help in any way possible. He told me this himself. Personally."

"That is appreciated."

The conversation continued like that for a while, until the ambassador interrupted to say that America was ready to make its goodwill tangible. The president was willing to provide real assistance, including military intelligence, if the Vietnamese wanted it.

"What conditions?" asked the deputy.

"No conditions," said Behrens. "None."

"A man that was held prisoner by us now wants to become our friend?"

"In the president's view, Mr. Deputy, Vietnam is just the first of many states that will be attacked by the Chinese," said Perry. "He wants to stop the attack here."

"It has been a ferocious attack so far," said Ba.

"And it's going to get worse. We have an idea about where the Chinese are going," added the general. "And we have a plan to stop them."

"I see."

Hai Ba listened as Perry and the ambassador outlined what other things American aid would mean—and what it wouldn't mean. No loss of Vietnamese sovereignty, no large formations of American troops on its soil. America would be a guest, a helpful guest, ready to leave when requested.

And in exchange?

"In exchange you stop these bastards here, now," said Perry. "It's a fair deal for us. A very fair deal."

The deputy soon excused himself, presumably to report back to his boss. A succession of army officials joined them for discussions that were basically variations of the one they had had with Ba: generalities, never specifics. Zeus was mostly an observer during these conversations, and an unimportant one at that.

Not one of the Vietnamese asked what sort of plan the Americans thought would stop the Chinese. Perry mentioned several times that he had brought along "experts" who had studied the Chinese tactical situation; each time the Vietnamese nodded politely before moving on to other subjects.

Deputy Ba reappeared about two hours later. Zeus noticed for the first time that he was walking with a limp. Looking at his leg, Zeus realized that there was a bandage or a brace on it.

"The premier would be pleased if you could see him," Ba said.

"It would be my pleasure."

The jeep and bus were waiting out front.

"Nothing like treating VIPs in style," said Christian.

A police car had been added to the convoy. Its siren rebounded off the buildings as they sped through the center of town. Whole blocks had been wiped out, reduced to nothing but rubble, while the next street appeared completely unscathed.

"They'll get the rest tonight," said Christian. "Hopefully we'll be out of here by then."

The Vietnamese took them a few miles south of the city, past a suburban section to an area of farms. They passed a large military base, where soldiers were mustering into trucks and armored vehicles; they sped by so fast Zeus didn't get a good enough look to guesstimate how big the unit was.

Two miles farther down, they veered off the highway onto a dirt road. It looked like a mistake—the area ahead was an open field. Two motorcycles raced out of nowhere, overtaking them as if they were standing still. Two more appeared, slowing and flanking the military vehicles at the front of the convoy. As the land dipped down, a wall topped by barbed wire came into view. There were warning signs in front of the wall: the area was mined. The wall itself was lined with soldiers and flanked by two tanks, both of them ancient T-54's.

Passing through a pair of gates, the convoy swerved slowly in an S pattern around a set of concrete barriers designed to slow a would-be suicide bomber. A second wall, this one much higher and also topped by barbed wire, sat beyond the first. A pair of men held open the gate at its center.

Zeus counted more than thirty men standing on his side of the road after they passed through the gate. Mobile antiair missiles and guns were positioned around a wide dirt courtyard. A half dozen small, low-slung buildings sat in the middle of the dust.

The structures were entrances to an underground

bunker complex. Far from elaborate, they consisted of large concrete slabs that sheltered wide stairways. These steps, about twice as wide as the bus Perry's party had taken, ended in a narrow hall that had a passage at the side leading downward. The passage was so narrow only one person could go down at a time.

A pair of guards waited at the bottom of the ramp. Each one of the Americans was checked for weapons with a detector rod.

"Your communication devices will not work here," Hai Ba told them, watching as the checks were completed. "Just so you know."

"Of course," said Perry.

"The nonessential members of your party should stay behind," added the deputy minister, glancing at the four Delta Force sergeants who were part of the security team. Perry told Ford that only officers would accompany him to the meeting. Ford nodded without comment; the order meant that only he would stay with Perry.

While Perry was still making all of the expected diplomatic noises, Zeus could tell the general was starting to get a little annoyed. This was even more obvious at the next security station, which was down another set of steps. Perry held his arms out with a frown Zeus recognized from their war games; he was probably one bad poke away from losing his patience.

The ambassador made a joke that the security was almost as bad as going to a Washington Nationals game. Perry didn't laugh.

They were led to yet another set of stairs, these much wider. The stairwell had low-energy fluorescents that gave it a pure white glow, almost surrealistic under the circumstances.

A tall man dressed in a Western-style business suit met them at the base of the stairs. He was the foreign minister, and after greeting them he began talking to Behrens in Vietnamese. Despite the circumstances, both smiled broadly, chatting as they walked down the hall.

A thin industrial-style carpet covered the floor; the walls and floor of the passage were smooth concrete. A single steel door sat at the far end of the hall. A guard, armed with a Russian-made submachine gun, stood at attention in front of it. He moved to the side as they approached, watching the Americans warily.

The room behind the door looked like a staff room, dominated by two large tables pushed together. Simple wooden chairs were arranged around them; the chairs were slightly askew, as if a meeting had broken up a short while ago and no one had had a chance to put them back in place. There was nothing on the walls: no maps, no charts, no whiteboards or projection equipment. The only thing breaking the monotony of the dull white concrete was two doors on either side of the room. Both were solid steel, gray and featureless.

The foreign minister gestured to one side of the table. General Perry and the ambassador took seats at the center. Zeus, Christian, and Candy sat to their left; Perry's translator and Captain Ford sat to the right. Zeus was closest to the door.

The foreign minister sat opposite them.

"Tell me now why you've come," said the foreign minister. His English was not quite as sharp as the deputy defense minister's, the accent heavy.

Perry repeated basically the same speech that he had given earlier. He was about halfway through when one of the doors behind them opened.

The foreign minister rose; the Americans followed his lead. Zeus turned and saw Vietnam's premier, Lein Thap, shuffling around the side of the room, walking slowly to the Vietnamese side of the table. He was an old man, well past seventy, and his gray hair and stoop made him appear almost ghostlike.

Perry began recounting his offer, this time beginning with the president's pledge. Their translator went to work, putting each of Perry's sentences into Vietnamese. Thap raised his finger after only a few words.

"Yes, sir?" said the general.

"I know of your president, and have met him," said the premier, speaking in Vietnamese. "He was our prisoner during the war."

"Yes, sir," said the general after the words were translated.

"The United States has been China's ally for many years now."

"America is a trading partner with China," interjected the ambassador, first in Vietnamese and then in English. "Just as we are partners with Vietnam. We have no defense or aid agreements with the Chinese."

The premier let the comment pass. Perry continued, laying out what the U.S. could do, gesturing toward

Zeus to say that a series of suggestions had been prepared as well as intelligence.

"The strategy has been extensively gamed," added Perry. "We are confident of its success."

Zeus winced internally at the exaggeration.

"What does "gamed" mean?" asked the Vietnamese foreign minister in English. "The translation is . . . difficult."

"Tested. By computer," said Perry.

The foreign minister leaned close to the premier, whispering the explanation in his ear. If the premier was impressed—or even moved at all—it didn't show on his face.

If the Vietnamese turned down U.S. assistance, what would happen next?

Zeus hadn't even thought that possible. Surely the Vietnamese wanted help. But as he studied the premier's expression, he realized that they might not.

If the Vietnamese were overrun, every other country in Asia would think there was nothing to be gained by opposing the Chinese at all; capitulation would at least spare their people immediate pain.

And then Zeus realized they might be overrun in any event. What happened then?

"It is a strong man who can help those who were once his enemy," said the premier finally. He looked at Zeus. "You will speak to General Trung. If he believes he can use your help, he will do so."

4

Northwestern Vietnam

Josh walked behind Mara and Mạ, urging them on as gently as he could, until finally he decided that they were far enough away from the road and possible pursuers that he could lead the way. He slipped between them, carrying Mạ for a few hundred meters before setting her back down and urging her to keep up.

Pulling Mara away from the burning wreck seemed to have given him new energy. Or maybe it had restored his pride, weakened by the ordeal in the mine shaft. He'd been ready to die there—he hadn't cared anymore.

Despair was the one unforgivable sin, he'd always thought; he hadn't despaired that day long ago when his parents had been murdered. It was the most important lesson he'd gained, a hard-earned one. But now it seemed the line was not precise—one moment of weakness did not eliminate the sum of who he was and what he did. He was a survivor, not a victim, a man who tried to do something rather than giving up. Even when it had seemed hopeless, he had tried to go out with action rather than lying down. And that was a better, more precise measure of real despair.

The jungle closed in as they walked, until the vegetation became so thick that the stream was nearly impossible to see. The water gradually turned from a narrow channel perhaps six inches deep to a mushy, widespread marsh marked by a few rocks and dead trees.

Bugs swarmed thickly over the narrow swamp. Josh had become so used to the insects that usually he barely noticed them, but these swarms were impossible to ignore. They got into his eyes and nose, his mouth when he opened it. Finally, he decided they had no choice but to leave the soggy ground. This wasn't easy—pushing through the weeds and brush felt like pushing through a foam-filled room. A bush would give way to a thicker bush; a momentary hole would lead to a tree trunk. Once they were away from the worst of the insects, Josh tried to move parallel to the stream, but after a while had to give it up and go where the jungle was thinnest.

"We stop here," said Mara when they finally broke into a small clearing around three large intertwined trees. "Rest."

"We have to keep moving," said Josh. "They're probably following."

"We stop and figure out where the hell we are," she told him. "And we need to rest."

Josh looked down at Mạ. She had a vacant expression on her face, a desperate blankness.

"You're right. We should stop," he said.

He crouched next to Mạ and gestured that she should sit. He sat down against the nearby tree, patting the ground next to him, but Mạ remained standing.

Mara leaned against the tree, looking upward. "I think I can climb this," she said.

"I thought you were tired."

She frowned but then started upward, slowly at first but gradually gaining speed.

Josh recognized her type—college jock, probably played soccer, a tomboy who felt like a fish out of water once graduation came around. She'd probably looked into joining the army, then settled on the spy business. Maybe she was gay. Most likely.

Not that it was an issue. He wasn't attracted to her in any event.

He looked at the bushes, examining the leaves. If it had been a different time of year, they'd be full of berries and there'd be nuts on the trees—they'd have something to eat.

"There's a hill about a half mile that way," Mara told him as she slid back down to the ground. "There are a lot of trees. The ground should be a little easier to move through."

"Are they following us?"

"I couldn't see them. Doesn't mean they're not."

"Do you have your phone?"

"That's about all I have."

"Are you going to call for help?" Josh asked.

"The only help we're likely to get was shooting it out with the Chinese back at the road," said Mara. "And if they were homing in on you, they may be able to home in on me. Come on—if they're following us, it will be easy for them to see the trail we cut through the brush."

"We didn't cut a trail."

"The vegetation was pushed to the side. Look—it's pretty easy to see the way we've gone."

She was right. Josh got up and took Mạ by the hand, following as Mara led the way to the hill she'd seen. For a while, the brush was just as thick as before, maybe even thicker. But after nearly twenty minutes they began moving uphill. As the incline steepened, the vegetation began to thin out.

The summit was an uneven saddle framed by a group of young trees. The land to the south had been clear-cut of timber within the past two or three years; rotted carcasses of trees that had been taken down but not harvested dotted the new growth. A rutted logging trail meandered off to the southeast.

Mara climbed another of the trees to try and scout the area, but the thin trunk bent before she was high enough to get much of a view.

"All right. I'll check in," Mara told Josh after she shimmied down. She took out her phone and walked a few yards away.

Josh debated whether to follow her, and decided he should. She frowned but said nothing to him as the call went through.

"Yeah, it's me. A whole shitload of trouble," she told whoever was on the other side of the line. "The Chinese had helicopters. Jimmy's people got mixed up in the firefight. We split up. I have the scientist. He's got a kid with him. What can you do for us?"

Josh folded his arms in front of his chest. He didn't

like the way she'd mentioned Mạ, as if he'd been expected to make a business presentation and had shown up with a kid in tow.

Mara turned to him, apparently in response to a question from whoever was on the line.

"You do have the tape, right?" she asked.

"I got it."

"We're good," she told the phone.

She listened some more.

"All right," she said finally. "We'll try."

"What are we going to try?" asked Josh after she hung up abruptly.

"To stay alive. Come on. That trail leads to a road, and there's a deserted village a mile off it that the Chinese haven't occupied yet."

"How do you know?"

"I just had them look at a satellite image. Come on."

Washington, D.C.

President Greene glanced across the Oval Office at a portrait of one of his predecessors before taking the call. He'd ordered the painting of FDR placed where he could see it a few months before. Never a big Roosevelt admirer, he'd come to appreciate the Democrat more and more over the past year.

"Mrs. Prime Minister, thank you for returning my call," President Greene told Ivory Chatham as he retrieved the British prime minister from hold. "I trust you're well."

"Tolerably well," she told him. "The weather here has been just awful. Even for England."

"I'm sorry to hear." Mandatory chitchat finished, Greene plunged into the reason he'd placed the call. "I've been speaking to both my secretary of state and my national security adviser about your concerns."

"I'm going to save you the embarrassment, George," said the prime minister, cutting him short. "His Majesty's government is not currently in a position to help you on the resolution."

Greene stifled a growl. "Why not?"

"I'm sorry, George. The financial situation is very difficult here."

"You're not going to succumb to blackmail, are you? This is a critical point. Crucial."

"I know. The financial situation is very precarious right now," added Chatham. "And I'm afraid that my government would not be able to sustain a challenge."

"I hadn't realized the situation was so . . . precarious." Greene shifted in his chair. Part of the problem, he believed, was that Chatham faced a no-confidence vote in the Parliament in a few days. She had barely survived the last, and undoubtedly didn't want to do anything to tip more votes against her.

"It's the bonds, George. The Chinese have been very clear that they will withdraw their deposits."

"They've hinted the same to us. It will hurt them more than us. Certainly in the long run."

"You're not in the position I am. And frankly, the Chinese have public sentiment on their side. People think the Vietnamese are getting what they deserve. I'm surprised that's not the case in your country."

It probably was, though Greene had made it a point to avoid looking at any public opinion polls on the matter.

"People have seen the photos the Chinese have spread around," added the prime minister. "I know what you've said about them, but they're very convincing. Very, very convincing."

"What if we had proof that the Chinese staged the entire incident? That the Vietnamese never launched an attack."

"Of course we suspect that."

"But if the public had proof. Would it make a difference to you?"

"Well, if we had public opinion on our side, in that case . . ."

"Then let me ask you a favor. Do nothing. For a few days—take no stand on the resolution."

"You have proof?"

"We're working on it," said Greene.

6

Northwestern Vietnam

Jing Yo had been following the enemy soldiers for nearly ten minutes before he spotted the blood. It was a bright splotch on a long blade of grass. He stopped and crouched, wondering if the enemy had managed to set another ambush nearby. When he saw nothing, he moved forward again, staying as low to the ground as he could.

More blood. A big splotch and a little one.

Two more steps and there were three drops, all very large.

The brush got thicker. More branches were broken as they passed, the enemy's haste making its path easier to follow.

It *might* be a trap. They'd been very clever so far.

Jing Yo moved ahead carefully, his eyes straining to see through the brush. There was a shadow ahead.

Stealthily, he crept toward it. It wasn't until he was three meters away that he was sure it was just a tree.

A few steps beyond the shadow, the scattered splotches of blood became a steady line, thin and narrow, then wider. After a few strides, Jing Yo heard a groan ahead.

He strongly suspected a trap. He circled to his right, moving quietly through a group of trees. The enemy soldier had fallen against a bush and was leaning there, half suspended, facedown.

But he was still alive. His hand was clawing at the ground, as if he were a turtle trying to right itself.

Jing Yo sprang forward, rushing toward the man. The enemy soldier had dropped his rifle on the ground.

The gun was Chinese. He wore Chinese uniform pants and top under a bulletproof vest and a regular-issue camo tac vest.

Was he Chinese? What was going on?

Jing Yo reached him just as the soldier managed to push himself faceup.

He looked Chinese.

"Who are you?" demanded Jing Yo, grabbing him by the shirt and pulling him. "Comrade, what unit are you?"

The man grimaced, clearly in pain. His eyes opened and closed. He was barely conscious.

Jing Yo squatted down. The bulletproof vest was not Chinese; it was cut higher and was thinner. The inserts seemed to be made of a thousand spheres rather than the stiff plates used by the Chinese and most other militaries.

His radio was foreign as well. He had German-made field glasses, unusual in Asia.

Jing Yo's bullets had caught him in the thigh and groin, tearing apart the flesh. Not serious at first, the wound had been made much worse by the soldier's exertions running through the jungle. Blood was now oozing out onto his uniform at a steady pace.

"Who are you?" Jing Yo asked again.

The man groaned.

"Tell me your name. What unit are you with? Or are you with the Vietnamese? *Tên anh là gì?*" he added, switching to Vietnamese as he asked him his name again.

The man didn't respond.

"You're American?" Jing Yo asked. "Are you CIA?"

No answer.

"Where is the scientist?"

The man yelled in anguish. Jing Yo reached to his vest and took out his morphine injector. He removed the cap, then plunged the needle into the man's leg.

"Lieutenant, what's this?" asked Ai Gua, plunging out of the brush.

"Our enemy is wearing our uniform."

Sergeant Wu and three other commandos came up behind Ai Gua. Though the explosion had been fearsome, the IED had wounded only two men, both lightly. Wu had left two of his soldiers to care for them.

"Are they Vietnamese?" asked Wu, looking at the man.

"I don't think so, but it's possible," said Jing Yo. Years of intrigue had taught him not to rule out any possibility; though remote, there was even a chance the man was actually Chinese.

"They must have gotten the uniforms from whoever they stole the trucks from," said Wu.

"Yes," said Jing Yo. "We'll continue to pursue them.

The best odds are that the scientist is with them, or behind them somewhere."

"If they reach the road they'll be gone," said Wu.

"The helicopters will continue to patrol the area," said Jing Yo. "It's the best we can do."

Ai Gua had dressed the man's wounds and checked him for identification. He had none, not even a wallet. But he did have money—nearly a hundred Vietnamese five-hundred-thousand-dong notes were wadded in his pants.

Not a bad amount of cash for a soldier wearing a private's uniform.

"Who are you?" Jing Yo asked the man.

The man began to babble. If he was speaking coherently, it wasn't in a language Jing Yo recognized.

"Stay with him," Jing Yo told Ai Gua. "We'll go after the others. Kim, you're with me."

As Jing Yo started back through the jungle, he tried to visualize where the various forces were. The enemy soldiers had retreated eastward; both he and Wu were moving in the same direction and parallel to each other, separated by about a hundred meters. They covered a wide area, but there was still room to lose their enemy. The jungle to Jing Yo's right was thick, and from the satellite maps was almost impassable farther south. The area where Wu was moving was sparser, and backed into a series of farm fields about a kilometer away. Jing Yo had sent troops there before heading to the area of the mine shaft; they should be in place by now, though they had yet to report any contact.

The jungle pitched upward abruptly at a set of rocks that swung in a diagonal to the north. Jing Yo stopped, examining the ridge carefully. It was a perfect ambush point, with a good line of sight to the north.

Just as he started moving to his right, a gunshot cracked through the jungle. He raced forward, throwing himself against the rocks as the gunfire suddenly thickened.

It took him a few seconds to realize that the firefight was at least a hundred meters away. Wu and his men must be under fire.

Jing Yo told Kim to move left, sending the private sweeping around his flank. Then he climbed up the rocks, digging his fingers into the thick moss and hauling himself through the bushes at the top. He rose and started to trot, jogging forward as the gunfire continued. When he had run nearly a hundred meters, he saw something running to his right. He raised his rifle and fired off a burst, then threw himself down. The answering fire came from two distinct directions, right in front of him and to his right.

The one on the right began to run through the jungle.

The enemy had split up. Most likely the man running was with the scientist.

Assuming the scientist was with them at all.

Jing Yo took a few steps back, then started moving to his right. There was a loud pop, and something flew through the trees.

"Grenade!" he yelled, throwing himself down.

The grenade soared over his head and exploded. Jing Yo started moving again, tamping down the impulse to run. He picked his way through the bushes, trying to stay low.

Something green moved through the trees about fifty meters ahead. Jing Yo went down to his knee and fired two bursts.

There was a scream.

Jing Yo leapt to his feet and ran. There was no need for stealth now, no sense in trying to blend into the jungle. It was a race—he had to get to the man before he recovered enough to shoot back.

He saw him lying on the ground, writhing in pain, half groaning, half screaming. He was dressed in black fatigues—no Chinese uniform.

Something about his agony touched Jing Yo, provoking sympathy. He stopped, suddenly filled with compassion.

The man rolled over onto his back. He had a weapon—an FN 40 mm grenade launcher.

Jing Yo leapt to his right as the grenade fired. The projectile passed so close that he felt the wind rushing past, the breath of a dragon provoked from its lair.

He hit the ground hard, rolling as the grenade exploded in the trees some eighty meters away. Jing Yo got to his feet and, before he took a full breath, killed the man who had tried to kill him, crushing his windpipe with the heel of his foot.

The monks had taught him this lesson long ago—

save your compassion for the appropriate moment. In battle, it is weakness.

The dead man had no ID, but like the other man, he had a considerable bankroll of Vietnamese money. He was out of bullets and had no more grenades. His face, big and gruff looking, seemed European; in any event, he was clearly not a Chinese or Vietnamese native.

Was he the scientist?

He was dressed like a warrior, with combat boots. He looked nothing like the man Jing Yo had seen the first night, or what Jing Yo imagined a scientist would look like. It was much more likely that he was one of the rescuers.

The stutter of automatic weapons interrupted his thoughts. Jing Yo put a fresh magazine in his gun, gazing back to his left. He waited, watching for movement, but there was none. Finally the gunfire stopped.

"Lieutenant!" yelled Wu. "Lieutenant!"

"Here!" answered Jing Yo, finally allowing himself to relax. "It's clear!"

"We got two of them," said Wu when he arrived a few minutes later.

"I have a third," said Jing Yo.

"Only four men held us off?" said Wu. "There must have been more."

Jing Yo said nothing. The soldiers had been very skilled. Certainly there must be more, someone with the scientist. But where?

"The scientist has to be farther along," said Wu. "Should we pursue?"

"Yes," said Jing Yo, but even as the word left his mouth he realized he had made a mistake. The scientist had escaped down the stream; the enemy had distracted him, and he had done the logical thing, pursuing them rather than his target.

Washington, D.C.

The president flipped off the television and turned to his national security director, Walter Jackson.

"I cannot believe such a bald-faced lie can possibly succeed in the General Assembly," said Greene.

"They're scared they'll be next."

"That's an excuse for Malaysia, not Germany."

"It's not the Chinese they're worried about. The Russians want Poland."

"They may get it if the Chinese aren't stopped."

"Vietnam is lost, Ches. The Chinese are pouring armies across the border. The Vietnamese don't know it yet, but they're toast. We have to face that reality."

"We have to help them," Greene told Jackson.

"General Perry should be there shortly. If they take us up on the offer of advisers, we can have people inside the country in a matter of hours."

"That's not enough. They need more than pictures and at-a-boys."

"You want to send troops?" Jackson asked.

"I know I said I wouldn't."

"If you do anything sizable, you'll need an authorization from Congress. They'll never pass one. God, Ches, you'd be lucky to get half of your own party behind it. Especially after what's going on in the UN today."

The phone buzzed, preventing Greene from unleashing his full and candid view of Congress.

"Mr. President, the director of the CIA is on the line."

"Put him through."

Peter Frost always sounded a little hoarse when he began a conversation, as if he'd just come inside the building. "Mr. President, there's something up in Vietnam I think you should know about. Something we've been working on."

"Go on."

"We have a witness who saw the Chinese staging the attack they used as a pretense to invade Vietnam. He has a video showing the massacre of a village by Chinese soldiers the day before the attack," continued Frost. "And he saw the Chinese staging the incursion."

"What?"

The president listened as Frost told him about Josh MacArthur and the scientific team. He told him everything, including the fact that one member of the team—not MacArthur—had been persuaded to spy for the U.S. That fact, if it ever came out, might compromise MacArthur's testimony. But if he had a video, his credibility would be nearly unassailable.

"We've been working on getting him out," said Frost. "But we've run into trouble."

Greene put the call on speaker. He knew Vietnam well enough to know the area Frost was talking about. It was a very long way from the coast, and sufficiently far from the border with Laos to make retrieval from that direction difficult as well.

And then there was the little matter of the Chinese wanting to keep Josh MacArthur for themselves.

"How do we get him out?" asked Greene.

"I have a CIA officer with him, someone who was in the country already. But to get him out, we're going to need to take a bigger risk. We need U.S. personnel. It's the only way now."

"Do you have a plan?"

"It involves a SEAL team."

"Do it," said Greene. "Do it now."

Hanoi

After seeing the spartan bunker where the head of the government was working, Zeus was not surprised to find that General Minh Trung was working in an office that couldn't have been much more than eight feet wide and ten long.

What *was* surprising was that he wasn't in a bunker; instead, his headquarters was in a barracks building in the middle of an army base about a mile from the bunker complex. The general was conferring with several aides when Zeus arrived. The lieutenant who had escorted him from Hanoi directed him to wait in the hallway, then disappeared.

There were no chairs. The door to the office was open, and while the men inside were speaking softly, Zeus could easily hear the discussion. Unfortunately, it was in Vietnamese, and the translator had stayed with General Perry and the ambassador.

Zeus stared at the light gray wall, visualizing a map of Vietnam and the route the Chinese army was taking. The Vietnamese did not have very long to implement his plan; if the Chinese got beyond the reservoir, it wouldn't work.

They might even be there by now. His last intelligence update was before they left Washington, several hours ago.

Zeus began to pace, trying to conjure a follow-up plan. In Red Dragon, he could have bombed the hell out of their supply line and hit their spearhead with medium-range missiles. But that wasn't an option for the Vietnamese. They lacked missiles and a strategic bomber fleet. The few MiGs that they could have used as attack aircraft had been heavily targeted by the Chinese already, and the remainder would undoubtedly be shot down if they attempted an attack.

"Major?"

Zeus looked up. General Trung was standing in the corridor.

"Yes, sir. I'm sorry. Um—I am Major Murphy, sir—"

"I know who you are," said the general. "Come."

The general was thin, like many Vietnamese, and very tall—an inch or two taller than Zeus. His close-cropped hair was gray around his temples, but otherwise he looked youthful, even younger than the fifty-one years Zeus remembered from the briefing paper on Vietnam's military leadership.

"I'm Major Murphy from the U.S.," Zeus told the officers who were crowded into the room. "I, um, I'm afraid I have to use English, because I can't speak Vietnamese. My translator is with General Perry."

Trung nodded.

"I've analyzed the intelligence and I have a presentation on my laptop," said Zeus. As he started to unclasp his briefcase, General Trung put his hand on it to stop him.

"We have no electricity."

"It's a laptop. My battery—"

"Tell us in your own words."

Zeus spotted a map of the country on the wall and walked over to it.

"I admit my intelligence is a few hours old," said Zeus. "From what I heard last, the Chinese took the airport at Na San and were consolidating for a fresh push—we believe toward Ninh Binh and the south."

He stopped for a moment, locating the point on the

map. The Vietnamese characters made it hard to read, but there was only one airstrip in that part of the country. He put his finger on it, then traced a path southeastward, following the mountains and river valleys until he came to the massive reservoir.

"We would recommend breaking the reservoir at Hoa Binh and attempting to block their path," said Zeus. "At that point, they would have to redirect their attack toward Hanoi, and you get a chance to fight them on your own terms. Otherwise they simply take over the rest of the country and bomb Hanoi into submission."

One of the officers in the room, a colonel, said something to General Trung in Vietnamese. The general held out his hand, encouraging him to speak directly to Zeus.

"Why do we want them to attack toward Hanoi?" said the colonel.

"Two reasons. One, it's not their plan, and two, that's where you have your best defenses. If they go south, which is what I believe they're planning to do, you'll be swamped."

"The capital would be destroyed in an all-out attack," said the colonel. "Our job is to protect it."

"It will be subject to bombing in any event," said Zeus. "But you can bottleneck the tanks if you wipe out the reservoir. They'll have a hard time getting over the Da—you can hit the bridges, try piecemeal attacks. Get them a little at a time. And if you can get them to come after you, you'll have a chance to use your dug-in defenses. They're trying to avoid them. They've stayed away from all of your serious troop concentrations. This is a game plan straight out of Shock and Awe—our campaign against the Iraqis. They've been studying it for years."

The general's lieutenants started talking among themselves in Vietnamese. General Trung said nothing. He stood perfectly erect and motionless. While he couldn't have helped hearing what they were saying, he didn't react to it in the slightest way.

"What makes you think we could hold out against the Chinese?" asked another of the officers finally.

"I don't know that you can," said Zeus. "Maybe not without help. But you did hold out against us forty years ago. You won that one."

None of the officers smiled. They continued discussing the idea for a few minutes until, one by one, they stopped and looked at the general.

"I have a question, Major," said Trung. He pointed to the map, running his finger below the reservoir. "The people that die when the reservoir is flooded, the people who live in these villages here—what will I tell their families?"

"They died for Vietnam."

General Trung nodded. Zeus's answer had been automatic. In truth, he hadn't thought of the civilians at all. He just assumed they could be evacuated in time.

Civilians were never a factor in the simulations.

"How soon can you blow up the reservoir?" the general asked.

"Me? The U.S.? I thought your army would—"

"There are no explosives in place, and time is of the essence," said the general. "How soon can you blow it up?"

Western Vietnam

Colonel Sun listened patiently as Jing Yo made the case for adding manpower to his team so he could pursue the scientist. The colonel did not require much persuasion. The premier himself had ordered that the scientist be found, and it would be foolish not to use any resource possible.

But Sun did not think the young lieutenant was heading in the proper direction. He wanted to go south rather than east—away from the path the others had taken, and indirectly toward the Chinese lines.

"You are overthinking this, Jing Yo," he said finally. "You are acting as if you were facing another commando. You are not. The man you are pursuing is a frightened scientist. He can't last in the jungle. You should have no trouble finding him."

"I'm not sure how many people are still helping him," said Jing Yo. "We've killed three and captured one. But there may be more."

"Yes, yes, you said. Of course you can have the

troops. I'll have some assigned." Colonel Sun waved at his aide, who was approaching with a fresh round of dispatches. "But you have to search east."

"I believe—"

"You are thinking too much. Here, let me see my map. He'll head for the nearest village and look for help there. A Hmong village, I would imagine. Let me see from the reports which ones have not been abandoned."

10

Washington, D.C.

President Greene leaned his chin on his hand. Though filled, the White House Situation Room was as quiet and silent as it had ever been during his administration.

"Mr. President?"

Greene looked up at the screen at the other end of the room. General Perry was participating in the videoconference from the ambassador's secure suite at the U.S. embassy in Hanoi.

"You're asking an incredible thing," Greene told the general. "Using our missiles to blow up a Vietnamese dam."

"That's what they've asked us to do, sir. I couldn't believe it myself."

"I have been assured by the foreign minister that it is a serious request," said Ambassador Behrens, who was standing next to Perry. "Time is of the essence, and they don't have the proper munitions in place."

"They can't just put a truckload of dynamite at the base of the dam?" asked the defense secretary.

"I'm told it's more complicated than that," answered Perry. "The engineers have called for a set of exact explosions across the dam area. Translating that into Tomahawk hits, I'm told it would take at least six hits to cause a fissure, and at least eight to do the kind of damage that needs to be done."

Greene leaned back in his seat. Not even in his worst days at the Hanoi Hilton had he contemplated doing something like this. "This is the best military plan we could come up with?"

"Sir, I can call the major over," said Perry. "He's working on the details with some of the Navy staff people. But yes, the answer is, this is his plan. I trust him, sir. If you want to talk to him yourself—"

Greene waved his hand, dismissing the idea. There wasn't time to second-guess the details of the plan. He had to give them either a go or a no-go.

The Vietnamese might very well turn around and use the attack against the U.S. Who would believe that they had requested it themselves? Especially if many of their own people died.

And at least a thousand people lived in the shadow of the dam.

A small number compared to the millions who would die if China continued its onslaught. But still . . .

"I want the area below the dam evacuated," said the president. "That is my condition."

"Sir, to be effective, the attack should be launched immediately. Even then—"

"That is my condition," said Greene. "When it's done, I will personally give the order to fire."

11

Northwestern Vietnam

The logging trail followed a seemingly endless series of switchbacks before arriving at a wide, hard-packed dirt road. The road wound through an area of fields, now temporarily fallow, which had been cleared from the jungle only recently. Within a mile, the view opened up, revealing an emerald green valley stretching for miles in the distance. It was a beautiful sight, so pretty Mara felt as if she were walking into a postcard.

The road was made of soft dirt. Mara glanced down and realized little bits of bright yellow clay were clinging to her boots as she walked. Even Mạ left light impressions in the road.

"We need to get off the road," she told the others, erasing the tracks as best she could before joining them on the shoulder.

After they'd walked for ten minutes, the village came

into view. The tin-roofed buildings glinted in the distance, six of them clustered close to the road at the center of the fields. These were large pole barns, open at the bottoms, used by the community to hold crops, machinery, and tools. The houses sat off to the side, on a small rise beyond a circular orchard of orange trees.

Lucas had told her it was unoccupied, but Mara wasn't about to trust his surveillance. She angled for a wide streambed that ran in a semicircle around the village. Used to irrigate the fields, during the rainy season it was a wide and deep body of water, more a river than a stream. Now, though, the water flowed lazily across the rocks, no deeper than a few inches. Beds of silt were covered with green weeds.

They walked up one of the irrigation ditches toward the field closest to the houses, then crossed into a grove of small orange trees.

Except for a headache, Mara had recovered from the blast. She tried not to think about Jimmy Choi and his people, whom she'd last seen firing at the Chinese from across the road. There was nothing she could do for them now.

The house near the orange grove was small, with a very high-pitched roof. Mara stopped twenty yards away. "Give me your rifle," she told Josh.

"Why?"

"I want to check out the house."

"I'll do it."

"You're a scientist. Give me the gun."

"I can handle a gun."

"Stop being so damn defensive," she told him. "Crap, you'd think I was castrating you."

Josh scowled, then held the rifle out. There were five bullets in the magazine.

"You have an extra mag?" she asked.

He shook his head. His lips were pursed—he was mad, but she didn't have time to play psychologist.

Mara made sure the weapon was selected for single fire, then slipped through the trees and trotted to the back of the house. There was a curtain at the window: she couldn't see inside.

She smashed the window with the rifle butt, ducking down quickly in case someone was hiding inside and fired at her. When nothing happened, she cleared the glass, then cautiously poked the rifle barrel past the curtain and peeked in.

The room was empty. Mara hoisted herself inside, gingerly avoiding the shards of glass still in the window.

The house had been abandoned sometime during the night, quickly, but not in a panic. The beds were undone, but otherwise the place was neat. Its owners had taken many of their possessions with them, but there was some rice in a storage closet in the kitchen. There was no running water in the hut; the only jugs were empty, but Josh found a pump near the orange grove and filled it up.

"I say we boil this if possible," suggested Josh. "The septics smell."

The oven was an old gas stove, modified to use bottled gas. The fire flared when Mara lit the stove. Mạ leapt from the floor and ran out of the hut screaming.

Mara tried adjusting the fire while Josh went after the girl. The knob on the stove was broken; the flame had to be adjusted by the handle on the tank, which itself was very loose and slipped after a few seconds if it wasn't held.

Mara managed to get the water and rice simmering without burning down the house. Josh came back, carrying Mạ in his arms.

"She ran all the way back to the ditch. I wasn't sure I was going to find her," he said, setting her down. "I'm going to go check the other huts. I'll be back."

"Good idea."

He reached over to take the rifle. Mara grabbed it.

"What are you doing?" he asked.

"Leave me the gun."

"Why? You afraid?"

"No," she said, but she didn't let go.

Fear wasn't the reason she wanted the gun. She was the professional, the one trained to use it.

But maybe there was some fear there as well.

He looked like he was going to say something, but didn't, turning to leave instead.

"Thank you for saving me," she told him.

"Yeah. We're even."

Not quite, thought Mara, though the ledger wasn't nearly as unbalanced as before.

* * *

A tirade poured through Josh's head as he stalked to the nearest hut. He hadn't expected the CIA officer who'd come for him to be a nice guy, exactly, but neither had he thought he'd be a complete jerkoff.

Guy.

Maybe that was part of the problem. Mara had a chip on her shoulder because she was a woman.

And she was a spook. What kind of person became a CIA agent? Doing renditions and all that crap? Water torture. She probably pulled that shit herself.

Maybe rescuing him was her punishment.

The way he saw it, she had screwed up. The rescue had been botched big-time.

That wasn't exactly fair; the Chinese had been closing in, and really, it was her people who'd taken the brunt of it. They were probably dead. If not for them, Josh would probably by lying in the back of one of the Chinese trucks right now, zipped up in a body bag.

He stopped at the threshold of the hut, reminding himself that he wasn't on a scientific expedition. People with guns, and a lot of them, were looking for him. He couldn't afford to act like a prima donna; the world really didn't care if a woman got his nose all bent out of joint because she was a jerk. The world cared about what he had seen, and the evidence of it on his little camera.

That *was* like science, wasn't it? Science was the

pursuit of truth, and truth didn't care whether you had a cold or whether you were hunting a grant or hoping for some killing when your patent got approved. Truth was the bottom line, and if you let your ego get in the way, then it was lost.

Damn, he was hungry. That was what was in his way now.

The door had no lock. What kind of place was this where you didn't need a lock?

A poor place.

Josh slipped inside quietly, as if he was afraid of waking someone in the front room. It was empty. Just like the other house, the people who had been here appeared to have taken most of what they had before going; certainly anything that was valuable was gone.

So was the food, if there had been any. There was no rice, and not even a dried leaf in the bins near the basin in what he guessed was the kitchen. The stove was even more primitive than the one in the other house, just a metal box attached to a stovepipe.

The barns would be where the food was.

And maybe a farm truck?

He trotted up the road, convinced that he was going to find something. But the barns had no trucks, and no food. One was used as a furniture workshop; several small chairs and bookcases were in various stages of production. Two of the other buildings were used to store wood. The last had probably held vehicles, but they were gone; the bins for food or maybe seeds were empty. There was a chicken coop at the back, with nothing but feathers and one long-broken egg in the nests. The villagers must have taken the birds with them when they'd fled.

Josh eyed the eggshell hungrily before moving on.

A power line ran from the road up to a shed between the barns; lines went from there to the barns, but not the houses. There was also a power generator in the shed, a backup that stank of kerosene. There was an oil lamp next to it, probably meant as an emergency light for someone troubleshooting in the dark. Josh took the lamp with him and went to the north side of the hamlet, where there were three more huts, along with a good-sized toolshed.

He went to the shed first. Besides the plows and a mower, there were a few rusted hand tools. Josh found a machete with a nicked but sharp blade. He took it, then went to see if there was anything of value in the houses. But all three were like the others, stripped of just about anything useful.

He sat down on a bench in the last house, trying to think of where else he might look. It made sense that they would take the vehicles, but all the food, too?

Maybe they hadn't had all that much.

He kicked at a bed mat, then rolled it back with his foot. The floor of the hut, like the others, was wood.

So was the floor in the toolshed.

Why wasn't it dirt? The floors in the barn were all dirt.

Josh got up from the bed and left the house. He

started back toward the hut where he'd left Mara and Mạ, then altered his course to swing by the tool-shed.

The walls looked all of a piece, though, everything together, fifty or more years old, and worn. There was a rug on the floor, a woven bamboo rug, almost brand-new, beneath one of the plows.

Why use a new rug to protect a plow?

Josh pushed the mower and another plow out of the way. The plow holding the rug in place was heavy, close to a hundred pounds, he guessed. That might account for the rug—they needed something to make it easy to push across the floor.

But as Josh pulled it back, the plow blade hung up on the lip of something.

A trapdoor.

Josh pushed the plows and the mower out of the way, then carefully pulled back the rest of the rug to reveal a cutout. It was difficult to get a grip—there were holes where he thought a handle had been, but no handle. He started to use the machete to help pry it open, then realized he was likely to break the blade. A rusted hoe worked much better. He pried up the door and found a set of steps.

The door covered a large cellar storage area stuffed with crates. It was too dark to see much, even with the lamp, but there were dozens and dozens of boxes stacked down there, along with some clothes and tools.

He decided to go back and tell Mara what he had

found. The idea of food pushed him to run—he was hungry beyond belief.

He'd taken a few steps across the compound when he heard the sound in the distance:

Helicopters.

Mara was tending to the rice when Josh came running into the hut.

"Choppers!" he yelled. "The Chinese are coming!"

"We have to hide in the jungle," she said, turning off the stove.

She grabbed the rice pot, using her shirttail as a pot holder. Then she realized that if any soldiers came inside, they'd see the stove was hot and know someone was hiding nearby. She grabbed the water jug, dousing the burner area. The water sizzled off. By the time they got here it would be cold.

"We gotta get out," Josh told her, grabbing Mạ and leading her outside. "They're coming. Come on."

The helicopters were still some distance off, not yet visible in the sky. Mara pulled the door closed behind her, then started after him.

They'd never make it to the jungle. The irrigation ditches were closer, but what then? There were several helicopters; she could tell from the sound. They'd leave one circling the area, looking.

"We have to find a place to hide," Mara said. "The helicopters are too close."

Josh's face went blank, as if he were having trouble processing the information. For a second, Mara thought he had frozen on her.

"This way then," he said, darting toward the barns. "I know the perfect place."

Northwestern Vietnam

Jing Yo pressed his hands together, folding the tips of his fingers against each other and pulling outward. His biceps tightened; the muscles in his shoulders and neck went taut.

Balance is all. A man who is balanced stands at the center of the ever-changing swirl. A man balanced is unchanged by chaos. He does not know catastrophe. He is the eye of the storm.

"We're landing, Lieutenant," said Wu, standing over him as the helicopter touched down. "We are at the village."

Jing Yo got up from the bench. They had already searched an abandoned hamlet farther north, the Hmong settlement Colonel Sun had directed him to. As soon as he saw that it was empty, he had reboarded the helicopter and directed the bulk of his force here—back south of the creek, contrary to the colonel's orders. It was a gamble, but he thought it justified by the circumstances.

Or at least by his gut sense.

The settlement was a small farming commune, with cottages on either side of a central barn area. Jing Yo sent half of the regular army troops to watch the perimeter, then split the remainder in half, sending one group to search the huts at the north and tasking one group on the huts at the south. He and his commandos went to the barns.

"You seem tired," said Sergeant Wu as they walked toward the first building.

"Just thinking."

"You shouldn't do that."

Jing Yo smiled, thinking it was a joke. Wu was serious.

"If you worry too much about losing men, you can't do your job," he said.

Jing Yo nodded.

"They were good, those people," said Wu.

"Very."

"Mercenaries. Working for the Americans, I would bet. Or Americans themselves. They're a mongrel race. You can never tell where they come from."

The man Jing Yo had wounded was probably back at the medical unit at the forward helicopter base by now. Jing Yo would talk to him eventually. Hopefully after they had apprehended the scientist.

The barn was empty. The commandos moved inside quickly, silently, securing it, then moving on.

"The peasants here make furniture," said Wu dismissively, surveying the interior. "Cheap furniture for Americans, I bet."

Jing Yo walked around the interior perimeter, rechecking the areas his men had already looked at. There were no hiding places; it was a plain, simple building without interior walls or a loft.

The next building was a twin of the first, except that it contained piles of rough wood rather than furniture.

If the scientist wasn't here, then most likely the colonel was right, Jing Yo realized as he surveyed the second barn. He was likely to be cowering in the jungle somewhere, hiding like a scared rabbit.

Overestimating an enemy could be nearly as bad as underestimating him. Because he was an American, Jing Yo was preconditioned to see him as almost a superman, when in reality he was no different from anyone else.

Jing Yo returned to the door. Stepping outside, he caught the scent of burning wood on the wind. He thought for a moment that the village wasn't abandoned after all, that someone was making dinner. Then he turned and saw that one of the cottages had been set on fire.

They've found someone and are smoking him out, he thought.

"This way, quickly," he called to the others, who were just about to go into one of the smaller buildings nearby.

As they ran across the compound, Jing Yo signaled to them to spread out. Then he noticed that the soldiers nearby weren't watching the building, but searching the others.

A soldier lit a bundle of dried weeds and held it to the roof of the nearby cottage.

"What are you doing?" Jing Yo shouted. He ran over and grabbed the man's arm as he tried to light another part of the roof.

"Orders, Lieutenant."

"What orders?"

"The captain's."

"No more fires," said Jing Yo.

The unit captain was surprised when Jing Yo confronted him. "My invasion orders said I was to fire any building that wasn't useful," he said. "So that's what we're doing. What's the problem?"

"Where did those orders come from?"

"Division."

"I don't want the house burned," said Jing Yo. "Don't burn any more."

"The order came from division," said the captain. "That means the general, and your colonel, who's his chief of staff. If you want to ask them to rescind it, that's okay with me. But the general has a reputation, and I don't want to cross him. I'm sure you're on better terms, being a commando as well."

Jing Yo knew he could get the order rescinded, but it would take talking to Sun. If he did that, inevitably he would have to say where he was. The colonel would not like the fact that he had disobeyed his orders on where to search.

What difference did it make if the buildings were burned? The people had already run away.

"My people will finish searching the houses," said Jing Yo. "You take the barns. You can burn them after you've searched—but only when you're certain there's no one inside."

"I'm not a barbarian," said the captain, rounding up his men.

"**W**e're next!" hissed Josh, running over from the door where he'd been watching the troops search the barn buildings. He dodged the two plows Mara had placed near the opening and ducked onto the steps next to her, sliding the rug over the top of the trapdoor.

"Get down," she told him. "One, two, three."

On three, Mara ducked down next to him, closing the door over the space. At the same time, she pulled hard on the rope she had in her hand, dragging the mower over the trapdoor. She had tied a very loose knot, trusting that it would come free as she yanked. The idea was that the mower would roll over the space, making it easy to overlook, just as they had originally.

Except the rope didn't untie. As Mara flattened herself on the stairs, it got hung up beneath the panel, keeping the door open a crack and practically drawing an arrow toward where they were.

"Jesus."

Mara put her shoulder against the top of the door

and pulled. The mower had rolled over the door, and was just heavy enough to make it impossible to move the rope.

"Here," whispered Josh, stepping up to help lift the door.

"Easy. We don't want it to roll off."

"It'll be better than what we've got," he said, pushing with his back. The trapdoor went up an inch and a half. Mara pulled again and the rope came free. But now the rug had fallen into the crack.

"Hold the door up just a little," said Mara, pushing at the rug with her fingers.

"Come on."

"I'm trying."

"Give it a good push," said Josh.

Then he sneezed.

Mara managed to flip the rug out of the space. "Down," she said.

Josh lowered the door into place, sending them into total darkness. Then he sneezed. Though most of the force was muffled by his arm, it was still loud enough to hear.

"This is a very bad time to sneeze," she said.

"No shit."

He sneezed again, then moved down the stairs.

The door to the shed crashed open a few seconds later. The soldiers shouted as they came in, screaming "Surrender or die" in Chinese. Then they went silent, apparently scanning the room.

Mara waited, her finger growing stiff as it hovered above the rifle trigger. The silence extended for ten seconds, twenty, thirty, a full minute. Then there was another shout—a brief, sharp command—and the floorboards vibrated as the soldiers fanned out around and across the room.

How close were they? Directly above?

She could kill the first one, and the second. If she was lucky, she could grab a weapon.

Still, they'd be overcome eventually. It would probably be more prudent to surrender.

That would just be another way to die. Better to have some say in it.

A heavy heel set down a few feet away, pushing the floor with a squeak. It pounded twice, tapping maybe to see if there was a hollow sound.

Now, thought Mara, getting ready.

The heels moved away. Mara couldn't believe it— she thought for sure it was a trick of her hearing, her brain unconsciously guilty of wishful thinking.

There was more talk, muffled, indecipherable. And footsteps toward the door.

They'd missed them.

They'd missed them!

J osh felt as if he were suffocating. He had his nose buried deep in the crook of his arm. He held his breath and bit his lip, doing everything imaginable to stifle his sneeze. But the urge overwhelmed him. He pushed farther into the darkness, past Mạ, hunkering against a crate and the wall and bowing down just as he lost the struggle.

His entire body shuddered with the sneeze. He sneezed again and again, curling his head as far down into his midsection as he could, pressing his arm against his face.

If the door opened now, he'd run up, he'd throw himself at them, he'd do everything he could to try and save the others.

He held his breath again, wiping his nose with his sleeve. He sniffled lightly. As quickly as it had come on, the fit was over.

Ma brushed up against him, then curled herself around his side.

He held her for what seemed like a long while, then got up and went toward the front, looking for Mara.

"Ssshh," she whispered. "I think they left."

"How will we know it's safe to go out?" he asked.

"We won't. We'll just have to wait as long as we can."

"Yes," he started to say, but his nose suddenly began to tickle. He buried his face in his arm a second before sneezing again.

"Are you okay?" Mara asked.

"Smoke," he said as another sneeze erupted. "I smell smoke."

"Jesus, Mary, and Joseph—they're setting the building on fire!"

13

Hanoi

When General Perry offered to let Zeus scout the reservoir, Zeus accepted, not so much because he wanted to get a better understanding of the tactical situation, but because he knew offers from generals were basically orders. In truth, though, Zeus didn't particularly like planes, especially the small ones typically used for scouting missions. He couldn't stand helicopters, either. He felt like one good burst of wind or small-arms fire would take them down.

Larger aircraft didn't bother him, even when he had to jump out of them. Of course, he had closed his eyes on his very first jump, and on every one since. But frankly, he felt a hell of a lot safer under a parachute than in the cockpit of a Blackhawk or, God forbid, a Little Bird.

Of course, as bad as they were, at least they flew relatively slowly. A Navy buddy had once arranged a demonstration flight in an F/A-18 when Zeus was in Special Forces. The idea was to educate the soldier on what pilots did when called in on a ground support mission.

The only education Zeus got had to do with the futility of trying to control certain involuntary bodily movements and reactions, none of them pleasant.

He couldn't imagine what sort of aircraft the Vietnamese air force would be flying at this point. Probably one of those open-cockpit biplanes.

He braced himself as he was driven to the airport. Civilian traffic was now practically nonexistent, and the road was empty though it was the middle of the day. Some of the fires Zeus had seen on the way into the city were still burning.

The driver worked hard trying to keep the jeep—an old American vehicle—from falling into the worst of the craters on the access road to the military hangar area. Zeus's teeth rattled as they careened back and forth across the road, the driver occasionally pushing the jeep into the pockmarked infield in an effort to find a smooth path.

A two-engined Russian transport sat at the far end of the apron area, being fueled. It was an An-26 Curl, a member of the turboprop family sometimes compared to the C-130 Hercules. Zeus consoled himself with the thought that he could have done much worse as the jeep barreled toward the aircraft. He gripped the side of the dashboard, expecting the driver would slam on the brakes any second. But the jeep only picked up speed, until it looked for all the world that they were going to crash into the plane. At the last possible second, he turned the wheel and hit the brakes. The jeep screeched to a stop a few feet from the plane—and maybe inches from the fuel truck next to it.

"Great. Thanks," said Zeus, pulling himself out of the vehicle as quickly as he could. Feet shaking, he grabbed his ruck—he had a sweater and a pair of binoculars as well as several maps—and started toward the plane.

The driver began yelling at him in Vietnamese.

"What?" asked Zeus, gesturing.

The man pointed to the right, beyond the oil truck.

"Isn't this the plane?"

The driver signaled that he had to go farther— around the side of the building.

Zeus turned the corner. An old Cessna sat near the hangar.

It didn't look like it could possibly fly, especially since the rear quarter of the plane was covered with a tarp. Zeus walked over and put his hand on the wing strut.

Was it his imagination, or did the strut give way as he pulled back and forth?

"Lieutenant Murphy?"

Zeus turned to find a man dressed in a pilot's jumper grinning at him.

"I'm Murphy."

"I'm Captain Thieu," said the man, removing one of his hands from his hips to shake. The accent made his English hard to understand. "Headquarters told me you were on your way. You're a little late."

"Sorry."

"We're just about ready to take off. I will give you an orientation brief in the hangar. Then we will fly."

"Okay."

"Nice old plane, eh?" said Thieu, coming over and rapping his knuckles on the Cessna's nose. "Old Bird Dog."

"Yup. It's nice."

"It was American," said the pilot approvingly. "You like these?"

"Uh . . ."

"Very good plane."

"I'm sure. Do I get to wear a parachute?"

"Yes, of course."

At least that was something.

"If we're tight on time, why don't we just take off right now," said Zeus. "You can brief me while we're in the plane."

"It will be easier on the ground," said Thieu. "I have to take a last-minute look at the weather and the other intelligence."

"All right. What about that tarp?"

Thieu gave him a puzzled look. "What about it?"

"When do you take it off?"

"Oh no, no, no, Lieutenant. We are not taking that plane."

"Thank God."

"We're flying the Albatros. You see?" Thieu pointed across the concrete parking area toward a fighter jet that looked nearly as small as the Cessna. "We'll go in and out, very fast. Nothing to fear."

Twenty minutes later, Zeus was wishing he hadn't eaten such a big breakfast that morning.

Or any other meal for the past year.

Gravity squeezed him against the rear seat of the Aero L-39C as Thieu rocketed the plane off the runway, pushing the nose up nearly ninety degrees and then twisting onto the proper flight path.

The L-39C was a Czech-built aircraft, intended primarily as a trainer, though used by some Third World countries as a lightweight attack aircraft. Its single engine—there were scoops on either side of the cockpit, but only one power plant—could take it about 755 kilometers an hour, or 408 knots, not supersonic but not standing still either. When it came from the factory, the Albatros did not carry a machine gun or provisions for other weapons; however, the Vietnamese had added a 23mm twin-barrel cannon to its underside, giving it a limited attack capacity.

"Lieutenant, are you with us?" Thieu asked as they cleared through five thousand meters, roughly fifteen thousand feet.

"I'm here."

"We will be over the reservoir in ten minutes."

Zeus checked his watch. The Tomahawk missiles traveled at roughly 550 knots; the ships they were aboard were about 220 miles away. Once Zeus gave the okay for them to launch, it would take nearly a half hour for them to arrive. Zeus and Thieu would be circling the whole time.

Loads of fun.

Zeus closed his eyes, willing his stomach to behave as they flew. After a couple of deep breaths, he opened them again and forced himself to look outside the cockpit toward the ground.

The fields below were divided into long rectangles intersected by irrigation ditches. Houses clustered on the high spots, a few hundred or so gathered around the roads. They looked like little metal toys, their steel roofs glittering in the afternoon sun.

The clouds thickened, obscuring much of his view. When they cleared, he saw a large body of water and thought they were over the reservoir, but it was just the Hung River. They still had a good distance to go.

"You like flying?" asked Thieu over the interphone or internal radio.

"Not particularly."

The pilot laughed. "I love it," said Thieu. "I learned when I was sixteen. So today I have been flying for half my life. Today is my birthday. Much luck today."

"That's good," said Zeus, struggling to sound enthusiastic. "Happy birthday."

"Look at the mountains. Very pretty. No?"

They looked like green wrinkles in the earth.

Green wrinkles of . . .

Zeus took his maps from the leg pocket of his flight suit and unfolded them, trying to correlate what he saw with the ground below. The Tomahawks had three targets: the hydro plant and dam at Hoa Binh, the dam at Suvui, and the bridge below the dam where Route 6 ran south and connected to Route 15.

The Suvui dam was the most important target. Only a few months old, it had been built with the help of the World Bank, which received a good bit of funding from America. Now American taxpayers were going to spend a few million dollars destroying it.

Zeus's first job was to make sure that the villages

along the southern end of the lake had been evacuated. At twenty thousand feet, he could barely make
out the houses, let alone tell whether they were empty.

"We need to go down," he told the pilot when they
came over Song Da. "Way down."

"Oh yes. We go down."

The aircraft's right wing rolled and the Albatros
began plummeting toward the ground. Murphy's
nausea returned. He clamped his mouth shut beneath
the oxygen mask, holding tight as the pilot pushed the
aircraft through ten thousand feet. Thieu rolled the
plane onto its back, then through an invert, before
pushing into a somewhat shallower dive.

Zeus managed to open his eyes. The reservoir's turquoise blue spread before him. "I need to see the houses
on the south side," he said.

"Oh yes. That's where we are going," said Thieu.

Zeus took out the binoculars and began scanning
the bank of the reservoir as the plane continued to
glide downward. They began slowing down as well,
the airspeed dropping through three hundred knots
until it seemed as if they were standing still.

He could see a hut, and what looked like it might
be a boat, but little else. He followed the road for a
while but saw nothing on it.

"Can you get lower?" Zeus asked.

"Next pass," said Thieu, banking the plane.

They crisscrossed along the southern border of the
reservoir three more times, finally getting down to
within about five hundred feet. Thieu kept cutting

their speed, but paradoxically, the lower they got, the faster they seemed to be flying.

Were the villages empty?

He thought they were. Certainly no one was moving around down there.

As they reached the western end of the reservoir, Zeus saw a reflection of light near the bridge. He asked Thieu to go down and check it. They came back around low and slow, barely at a hundred knots.

It was a Vietnamese troop truck, one of the units that had been charged with getting the villagers out of the area. Three soldiers waved as they plane passed overhead.

"We have to get them off the bridge," said Zeus. "And then I need to talk to my general."

Northwestern Vietnam

Mara felt Josh grab her arm.

"They're trying to burn us out," he told her. "I saw them do it earlier. They wait and shoot when we come out."

"I know."

"You think we have enough air down here?"

"The fire might suck it out."

"Yeah. But if we run out, they'll kill us anyway."

It was a hell of a choice, Mara thought—death by suffocation or by bullet.

Josh moved away, back into the cellar. "Mą, where are you?"

Which was better? she wondered. Lie down in the hole and maybe die? Or face certain death trying to leave the building?

Better to stay. They'd have at least something of a chance.

And yet, everything inside her was pushing for her to run up the steps, get out, and kill the bastards who had done this.

Josh came back, poking her in the ribs as he searched for the wall and the steps.

"Where are you going?" Mara asked.

"I had an idea," he said. "You stay with Mą. I'll run out and surrender. They won't realize you're here."

"That'll never work. They'll search the place for sure then. We'll all die. It's noble of you—but no. It'll do the opposite of what you want."

"I can't stay here and suffocate to death. No way."

"That may not happen. We may have enough oxygen."

"You think we should take the chance?"

"It's a better chance than certain death."

Josh started away. Mara grabbed his shirt.

"You told me what they did," she said. "They're waiting out there for us now."

"Maybe if we both go out," he said, "they won't think of the girl."

"They'll find her and kill her. You saved her once."

Mara waited for him to speak. She could hear noises above them—it sounded like more helicopters.

Was it really hopeless?

"I don't know what to do," said Josh finally.

"Neither do I."

She reached forward and touched his arm. He pressed into her.

"All my life, I've known what to do," he told her. "I've survived."

"I don't know what to do either," she said. "But I think we stay."

Jing Yo trotted disgustedly toward the helicopters. Colonel Sun must be right. The scientist must be somewhere back in the jungle, holed up under some bush.

Very possibly dead.

Hopefully not. An infrared searching device was on its way; they'd have an easier time finding him if he was still alive.

Either way, he'd get him.

"Let's go," Jing Yo told the army captain. His men were already heading for the helicopters.

"You're going to just let the fires burn?" asked Sergeant Wu. "What if they spread?"

Jing Yo turned back. Black smoke billowed from the biggest barn; flames were poking from the others. Most of the houses were already destroyed.

"We'll have the helicopters fly over them. The

downdraft will beat the flames down," he said, climbing into the chopper.

J osh slid down against the stack of boxes, holding Mạ with his right arm and leaning against Mara on his left. Trusting himself to fate was something he'd never been able to do. Completely letting go—it was impossible.

This was a time he should be praying, but it had always seemed the coward's way, or a cop-out. Turning yourself over to God, or at least the unknown.

That was what he liked about science. You could measure the odds of something happening, the probability of a specific weather pattern and how it would intersect with the ecosystem, and you could measure the parameters of your guess. You could look at the possibilities and your models, and decide what to do.

Not that it guaranteed success. There were always a lot of variables. The climate crisis proved that. The outliers on the graph—the possibilities everyone had rejected—had proved to be the accurate predictors.

"Are you still conscious?" Mara whispered.

"Yes. You?"

"Well I wouldn't be talking if I wasn't."

He laughed—quickly, briefly, and not very hard. But it was still a laugh.

"The helicopters sound like they're leaving," said Mara.

"You think they're getting more soldiers?"

"I don't know."

Mara wore a cross around her neck, outside her clothes. Josh thought of asking her about faith—asking what she believed, and whether she was praying. But the ground began to shake, vibrating in sympathy with the rotor of a helicopter as it approached. There was a gust of wind through the basement, and then a pop, as if a balloon had burst. Something crashed above. Josh gripped Mara and Mạ tighter.

The helicopter moved away.

Mạ began to cry.

"It's okay," Josh said, bundling her close to him.

"*Em,*" said Mara. "*Bi. làmasao?*"

"What are you saying?" Josh asked.

"I'm asking her what's wrong."

"It's going to be okay," Josh told the girl. "We're not going to let the bad people hurt you."

"Does she understand any English?"

"She understands that."

Mara reached across him, her hand grazing his chin as she felt for the girl. She found her forehead.

"I think she has a temperature," said Mara. "She seems warm."

"Maybe."

Mara put her hand on his forehead as well. Her hand felt cool, and soft—softer than he would have expected.

"You feel warm too," she said.

"Take two aspirin and call you in the morning, right?" he said.

This time the joke fell flat, and neither one of them laughed.

The air smelled more dank than smoky. Josh's nose burned with the irritants. He leaned over and pressed his face into his shoulder, muffling a sneeze.

"Maybe we should see what's going on," he suggested after it had been quiet for a while. "If we just push the door up a little bit."

"Good idea."

The trapdoor wouldn't budge at first, and Josh had to angle himself against the steps to get more leverage. When it finally started to rise, it made a very loud creak; he gritted his teeth, worried now that they had done the wrong thing.

"Can you see?" he asked Mara.

"Just junk."

She turned and covered her mouth, beginning to cough. Josh leaned forward, pushing to the side to lift the door farther. Suddenly the mower shifted, sliding back with a crash.

He stood on the steps, waiting for the soldiers to run into the battered barn. Light streamed through the left side of the building; part of the wall had collapsed. There were charred beams nearby. A haze of smoke drifted through the interior. But the fire itself seemed to be out.

Where were the soldiers?

Outside, waiting?

It was a trick to make them think they'd gone.

Mạ ran up the steps past him, into the barn.

"Mạ. Wait," he said. He pushed the door all the way open and followed her. But by the time he got to the floor, she had slipped through the plows and fallen debris and disappeared.

"Damn it."

"Are they gone?" asked Mara.

"I don't know," he yelled, rushing toward the door where he figured the girl had gone. It was wide open, scorched but intact.

This is where I'll die, he thought, springing into the open air.

Mạ was standing nearby, gulping the fresh air. The Chinese soldiers were gone.

15

Northwestern Vietnam

Contacting General Perry to give the launch go-ahead proved to be much easier than getting the troops off the bridge. Perry was waiting at a command bunker at the Hanoi airport; as soon as Zeus called in, he passed the order along to launch the Tomahawks.

Thieu's controller, meanwhile, claimed he was in touch with the troops' commanding general, and that the order had been given for them to withdraw. But if so, it had no effect, and after ten minutes, they remained on the bridge, roughly thirty feet from one of the Tomahawk's detonation points. The missiles were just under twenty minutes away.

They spent five more minutes on the radio, trying to contact the unit and its parent themselves. As they banked around the southern end of the reservoir, Zeus saw the soldiers still on the bridge.

"You sure they're not Chinese?" he asked the pilot over the interphone.

"Negative. They are our guys."

"We have to get them out of there."

"Yes. Hold on."

Thieu pitched the plane forward. Zeus's stomach immediately began doing flip-flops.

"What are you doing?" he asked.

"Sending them a telegram," said Thieu.

A second later, the aircraft began reverberating as the pilot sent a few dozen cannon rounds into the bridge.

"That'll get them moving," said the pilot.

Thieu was right: the troops began running toward the other end of the bridge—fortunately toward the southwestern side.

They also started firing at the plane. Zeus saw their muzzle flashes as the plane banked away. "They're trying to shoot us down," he said.

"With those peashooters? Not a worry."

Zeus tightened his restraints.

They climbed back up through fifteen thousand feet, sailing high over the water and nearby ground. The highways faded from thick ribbons to infinitesimal threads, dissolving into the fur of the ground.

The missiles would be coming from the east. Zeus lifted his binoculars, curious about whether he would see them coming. He scanned out of the left side of the cockpit first, then realized the plane was going east and he was looking north; the missiles would be coming from the other direction. As he turned, something caught his attention, a fleeting blur in the corner of his eye. He looked back and saw a silver finger in the air, tiny and small, not quite parallel to them. He thumbed the focus on the binoculars, trying to bring the blur into focus. It separated into two small sticks.

"We have company!" shouted Thieu, his voice reverberating in the helmet. "Chinese MiGs."

16

Northwestern Vietnam

Mara surveyed the damage as she caught her breath. All but one of the houses had been burned to the ground. The exception was a charred ruin with its roof caved and two sides down. Two of the barns were fairly well desiccated, more piles of charred black wood than buildings.

At the other extreme was the chicken coop. It seemed undamaged by the flames. The shed and the last barn were in the middle, badly battered, though largely intact.

"They're definitely gone," said Josh, returning from

a quick check of the groves and nearby fields. Mạ had gone with him, refusing to let go of his leg until he picked her up. "Think they'll be back?"

"I don't know. Not soon."

Mara reached into her pocket for her satellite phone. She hit the Power button, then realized the phone was already on. Either she'd forgotten to turn it off, or somewhere in the scramble the phone had accidentally been switched back on.

The battery was at 20 percent.

"Problem?" asked Josh.

"It's nothing."

She dialed into Bangkok. The Million Dollar Man answered.

"Where are you, darlin'?" he asked.

"You're supposed to tell me."

"Figure of speech. I have the GPS reading right . . . now."

"Good. And where are we?"

"About two miles southwest of the spot where you grabbed MacArthur. What's going on? You missed your check-in."

Mara explained what had happened. "When are we getting out?" she asked.

"We're working on that right now. We should have a plan firmed up in a few hours. It'll be tonight," he added. "I'm just not sure exactly when."

"Or how?"

"How is a good question, too. Do you think you could stay where you are?" he asked. "Is it safe?"

"That's a relative word."

Peter Lucas broke into the line. "Mara?"

"Yes, Peter?"

"We have a plan. It will be in place soon. Right now, we need you to just hang tight. Okay? No more stealing bicycles and riding to Hanoi."

"It wasn't a bicycle."

"Listen, I'm being serious. We may have someone land at that farm."

"A helicopter?"

"No. It's too close to their forward air base. But I may be able to parachute some SEALs in. They can escort you out."

"I don't need escorts, Peter. I need transportation."

"I'll call you back in an hour."

"Wait!"

But the line had gone dead. Mara angrily pushed the phone into her pocket—then retrieved it to turn it off. The battery was now below 7 percent.

"What's up?" asked Josh.

"Nothing."

He glared at her. "You want me to trust you, but you don't trust me."

"They want us to wait here." Mara struggled to get her anger under control.

"Staying here until dark isn't that bad an idea," said Josh. "We can eat the rice."

The rice—she'd left it in the cellar. Her stomach growled in anticipation.

"We can build a fire to cook food," added Josh. "It won't look suspicious."

"I'd rather be moving south."

"Once it's dark, right?"

"Yeah."

He pointed to the rifle. "Maybe we can kill something substantial for dinner."

"I'm not a hunter."

"I hunt a lot," he said, holding his hand out for the gun.

17

Northwestern Vietnam

Thieu turned the Albatros back north—directly in the path of the Chinese planes.

"What are we doing?" asked Zeus.

"We can't outrun them," said the pilot, as if that answered everything.

By heading straight toward the enemy planes, Thieu was making it harder for the MiGs to fire their heat-seeking missiles. All but the newest of the missiles had to home in on a tailpipe to be effective. Thieu's maneuver also surprised the Chinese, who didn't expect a Vietnamese aircraft to take them on.

The enemy aircraft began to separate, preparing to turn as the Albatros approached. They hoped to swing behind Thieu, jerk their throttles to max, then goose off the heat-seekers before he could get away. It was a tactic they had employed countless times in similar situations during training.

But they hadn't encountered Thieu. As the two planes began to separate, he pushed his nose in the direction of the plane on his right and started to climb.

Had either of the MiGs been carrying medium-range homing missiles rather than laser-guided bombs under its wings, he would have been dead meat; the MiG could have lain back and fired, confident that the missiles would be close enough to stay with Thieu as he broke from his maneuver. But then the same could have been said for the Chinese planes had Thieu been equipped with American AMRAAMs or even Sparrows—something the Chinese pilot Thieu targeted clearly knew, since he immediately dropped his bombs so he could climb faster.

As soon as Thieu saw that, he jerked the plane to the left, hoping to get the other MiG to do the same. But this pilot wasn't so easily spooked. He turned his nose in toward Thieu's and accelerated.

The two aircraft closed so quickly that Thieu barely got off a few cannon rounds before he was by him. The MiG pilot immediately turned, hoping to get on his back. But Thieu turned as well, dipping his right wing down and then tipping it over so that he could twist back. The acrobatic moves took him so close to the MiG that if the canopy hadn't been in the way, Zeus could have reached out and grabbed the other plane.

Thieu fired a few cannon rounds, but he was out of position to get a hit and began falling steadily behind as the MiG dumped fuel into his engine in an effort to pick up speed. The MiG headed north; Thieu broke off, turning to the south, running back toward the reservoir.

The MiG that had dumped its bombs earlier had not given up the fight—a fact Zeus didn't realize until tracers shot past the canopy.

"Shit!" said Zeus.

"No worry, Lieutenant. You see."

Thieu pushed the plane into a dive. The MiG, temporarily out of maneuvering energy, headed off farther south.

"The Tomahawks are going to hit any second," said Zeus.

"Good idea!"

Thieu pushed the plane down toward the bridge. Zeus spotted the MiG banking about five thousand feet above them. The Chinese pilot was starting to understand how he had to fight the other plane; he swung out to the east and began a turn, undoubtedly plotting an intercept where he could open up with his cannon as he closed on the Albatros.

Behind him and much farther below, Zeus spotted a black pencil hurtling through the air, barely above the ground. As the MiG closed, the pencil leapt upward. It turned white and grew tenfold—a trick of the sun shining on the Tomahawk's surface.

The MiG pilot didn't know that the bridge was about to be blown up. He had no idea that the Tomahawk was fixing itself on its final target, rising so it could dive down in X-marks-the-spot fashion. All he knew was that a missile had suddenly appeared very close to the rear quarter of his aircraft. He did what any self-respecting pilot would do when taken completely by surprise—he hit his flares and his chaff, turned the plane hard into an evasive maneuver, and prayed to his ancient family gods.

And his dry cleaner.

The Tomahawk hit dead center on the bridge, exploding it. Four seconds later, a second missile arrived, smashing what was left of the northern terminus to smithereens.

In the meantime, the MiG had fled.

"Bridge is down," said Zeus. "Get east—check the dam."

"The dam is gone—look," said Thieu, pointing at the side.

The destruction of the two dams created a wall of water nearly fifty feet high, which rolled down the vast expanse of the lake, gathering strength as it went. From three thousand feet, the man-made tsunami looked like a small, frothing ripple in a puddle, but Zeus had only to look at the sides of the reservoir to judge its real impact. Buildings and trees that had been along the shore disappeared in a gulp as it moved. Both sides of the road where the bridge had been were swamped by the wave. The water continued, flooding the valley.

"Holy shit," said Zeus. "Wow."

"Job done?" asked Thieu.

Zeus pulled up his glasses and looked at Highway 6 north of the bridge. There were trucks on it, driving south.

Not trucks, but tanks. Six of them, with a command vehicle. The vanguard of the Chinese force.

Thieu circled, and they watched as the tanks stopped. Then the lead vehicle lurched forward into the stream, followed by a second and a third.

Five yards from the road, the rear end of the first tank swung east. Within seconds it was drifting in the water. The second tank simply sank. The third stopped on the bank.

Thieu couldn't resist peppering them all with his cannon before heading back to the base.

Northern Vietnam

Josh didn't find any animals big enough to eat in the jungle beyond the fields. Nor did he spend much time looking. Part of the problem was that he didn't want to leave the others for very long, Mạ especially. But mostly it was because his patience had evaporated. He'd spent it all waiting in the shed and now wanted, needed, to move.

To get out of here. Maybe they should just start walking and the hell with waiting for the night, as Mara seemed to feel.

Or help. What more help did they need?

When he got back to the shed Mara was sitting

next to Mạ, listening as the girl spoke. They were so intent that he didn't want to interrupt; instead, he took a seat on the ground next to them. Mara had found more rice and oranges in the basement storage area, and cooked them together in the pot where she'd cooked the rice earlier.

He helped himself to the concoction, listening as the girl spoke, even though he had no idea what she was saying. The words seemed to rush out of her mouth, as if they were pushing against one another. She gestured with her hands, motioning up and down, pointing, mimicking, illustrating her narrative with her emphatic body language. Her eyes were wide and darting, as if she were watching what she was describing, conjuring it from the shadows in the room around them.

"Mạ was born in a small village on the other side of a river or a stream, I'm not sure of the word," explained Mara when the girl finally paused. "It wasn't too far from where you found her, or where she found you."

"Is this what happened to her?"

"Yes."

The soldiers had come at night. They seemed to be Vietnamese, or at least one of them had spoken Vietnamese. But clearly something was wrong. The villagers—about two dozen people lived in the small community, all related to one another through blood or marriage—were taken out of their houses and told to wait near a truck that sat in the middle of the settlement. The soldiers didn't say where they were going.

Mạ was scared. She wanted to bring her blanket

with her—it had been a special blanket that she had had since she was a baby. The soldiers said she could not.

As the people were being marched into line, Mạ decided to go back for it. She snuck away, not think-ing that anyone was watching. But someone was—as she darted toward the house, the soldiers began shouting.

Then firing.

Petrified, Mạ ran into the jungle, dodging and dart-ing through the trees in the darkness, running until she couldn't run anymore. In the meantime, the sol-diers had killed everyone in the line.

She had caused all the deaths. It was her fault that her brothers and sisters, parents and relatives, had all died.

Mạ collapsed in tears. Both Mara and Josh held her, trying to console her.

"It wasn't her fault," said Josh. "Tell her that."

"I don't have all the words," said Mara.

"Tell her."

"I'm trying."

He'd felt the same when his parents died. He still felt that way, deep down, after all these years. It was a deep pit of regret and guilt that could never be filled, even though he knew, logically, that it was the killers' fault, not his.

"Tell her it wasn't her fault," repeated Josh.

Bangkok

"You're going to have to give me a better fucking location than that," growled the stubbled face on the video screen. "I ain't jumping into a six-mile-square box."

"I'll give you a precise location," said Peter Lucas. "You'll have real-time data down to the millimeter when you're in the air."

"I fuckin' better."

Lucas pushed his chair from the console. He liked working with the SEALs because they got results. But there was always a price to be paid in terms of ego. The most easygoing SEAL held anyone who was not another SEAL in contempt.

The man on the screen, Lieutenant Ric Kerfer, was hardly easygoing. Kerfer wasn't civil even to other SEALs.

But he was absolutely the man to rely on in this sort of situation. Lucas had worked with him before, with excellent results. There were even indications that Kerfer *liked* working with him—the high cuss count, for example.

Still, he was one grouchy and disrespectful SOB.

"You arrange exfiltration yet?" Kerfer asked.

"At the moment, you're going to have to walk out," said Lucas.

"Fuck that."

"I can't get a helicopter in there," said Lucas calmly. If he had been able to get a chopper, he wouldn't need the SEALs. "I thought maybe you'd be able to steal local transport."

"You just told me the area was evacuated. What did these people use to get out of there? You think they just left their vehicles parked around? Hell no, they drove. Or fucking walked. What's my solution?"

"I don't know, Kerfer," said Lucas, finally losing his patience. "You tell me what your goddamn solution is."

For the first time since he came on the videoconference line, Kerfer smiled. "Bicycles."

"Bicycles?"

"We ride them out of there. I did something like that in Pakistan," the SEAL lieutenant added. "Almost like a picnic."

Lucas reminded him that there was a little girl with them.

"So we get her a little bike."

"If you think bikes will work," said Lucas, "go for it."

"All right. Get them to the drop area."

"Me?"

"Helicopter picks us off the sub in half an hour, Petey. We fly straight to Okinawa and leave as soon as we get there. You either get the bikes aboard the jet, or get them there yourself. Your call."

"All right. They'll be on the jet."

"I ain't biking all the way to Hanoi. It'd be okay

for me and my boys, but your people are going to crap out. Arrange a truck to meet us somewhere half-way."

"Not a problem."

Maybe he could find a Vietnamese national to leave a truck somewhere. He could use the embassy.

Not that he trusted them worth shit, as Kerfer would have put it.

"We're set, Petey?"

"Yeah, we're set," said Lucas. "And don't fuckin' call me Petey."

"Always a pleasure, Petey," said Kerfer, laughing as he killed the connection on his side.

Northern Vietnam

Jing Yo's unit had to return to the forward air base so the infrared searching gear could be installed. The device itself was relatively small—it fit on a long spar at the side of the helicopter, making it look a little like a catamaran with a rotor on top. The control panel, however, was the size of a small desk. Two had to be loaded into the helicopter, each with its own operator. The gear, less than three months old, was considered so valuable that four soldiers had been sent to guard it. They had insisted on flying in the Sikorsky with the operators. That cramped the small helicopter, forcing Jing Yo to put his men and Sergeant Wu in a second helicopter. It also lowered the size of his assault force, limiting him to just two other regular army soldiers instead of the entire squad he'd had earlier.

The operators were a pair of sergeants from Beijing who went about their work very quietly, communicating with each other rarely, and then mostly by nods and an occasional one-word question. Jing Yo leaned over them, watching as they finished calibrating their equipment.

"We can take off anytime," declared the lead operator as a loud tone sounded from his panel. "We are prepared."

Jing Yo picked up the microphone on the helicopter's interphone headset and told the pilot to take off. Within minutes, the aircraft was pushing forward across the field, tilting slightly to the right as it rose.

The main display screen looked very much like a standard television display, except that everything was shaded blue and red. The color scheme was preset to toggle through several variations, each one keyed to a different range of temperatures. The system automatically notified the operator when it found something within a specified range—in this case, roughly the temperature range of a human body. The operator could then "zoom" in by switching to a more sensitive heat band.

The infrared system was not magic. It had trouble "seeing" through thick jungle canopy, though it was better than most commercially available systems at filtering through the trees and brush, even from a distance. It also couldn't "see" in the rain—a problem shared by all infrared systems.

The forecast called for rain. So far it had held off.

A yellow cursor opened around a red squiggle at the bottom left of the screen. The operator circled it with his index finger, then put the tips of his fingers on the screen and pulled up. The image inside the circle expanded, then changed to a collection of muted greens and blacks.

"What is it?" asked Jing Yo.

"A man," said the operator.

Jing Yo went over and looked out the window toward the ground. The sun was setting, and there were long shadows everywhere. All he could see were the tops of the trees, puffy patches of black punctuated by shadow.

"Is that our target?" he asked.

The operator smiled. "A soldier, having a cigarette by the side of the road," he said. "A half kilometer from the field. He's a guard."

"You're sure?"

The operator double-tapped the screen. The image expanded again, once more changing color, this time to yellowish brown.

Except for the tip of the stick that jutted from the yellow blotch. It flared red, then went back to orange.

"Very good," said Jing Yo. "Let us get to work."

21

Noi Bai Airport, Hanoi

"What do you say we have a beer?" Zeus asked his pilot after they landed and were trundling toward the parking area at Noi Bai Airport.

"I like it," replied Captain Thieu. "You pay."

"You got it."

In the two hours since they had been gone, dozens of antiaircraft guns had been brought onto the airport property and lined up opposite the hangars. There were also two mobile missile batteries out on the edge of the apron area, older Russian ground-to-air missiles that Zeus guessed would not be any more effective than the launchers on the perimeter that had failed to strike the intruders the night before. But the Vietnamese had to do something; a second strike at the airport would almost certainly be launched, and if it was half as devastating as the first, the field would have to shut down indefinitely.

Thieu turned the jet around at the far end of the cement, parking it about thirty yards from another Albatross. That one had holes in its wings, and the tail fin looked as if something had taken a bite out of it.

"Are you coming, Lieutenant?" Thieu asked, popping out of his seat as the canopy rose. "I'm thirsty for my beer."

"Aren't we getting a ladder?"

Thieu laughed, then jumped to the ground. Reluctantly, Zeus unstrapped himself, gathered his gear, and followed.

His binoculars slipped from his vest as he landed. He fumbled for them awkwardly, managing to grab them before they hit the ground.

He dropped them as the pilot slapped his back.

"You did all right for a soldier. Maybe you should learn to be a pilot," said Thieu.

"Thanks."

Zeus scooped up the glasses—fortunately not broken—and followed Thieu toward the hangar. They were still about ten yards from the entrance when a jeep came charging around the corner of the building. General Perry was in the passenger seat.

"About time you got back. I need you, Zeus," said Perry. "Get in."

B y the time Zeus and General Perry arrived at General Trung's headquarters, the U.S. had established a link that allowed real-time satellite data to be displayed on a pair of computer screens. The link came to the barracks via a landline that was strung from the embassy, a precarious arrangement that used up a good portion of the capital area's available fiber-optic cable. But the real challenge was finding power for the two screens. Though they were relatively small and drew very little current, the electric lines to Trung's headquarters were still down. A portable generator had been sent over from the embassy; the computer system taxed it severely. In an attempt to balance the load, the lights in the command room, dim to begin with, were completely shut off. The glow of the screens barely illuminated half of the conference table at the middle of the room, and when the image changed, the room temporarily went black.

Still, seeing the pictures was better than hearing the situation described over a phone. Zeus pressed closer to the screen, looking at the satellite photos of the air base at Na San, and of the now clogged road south. A squadron of A-10As, and he could have wiped out half the Chinese armor in a day.

There would still have been a lot left. Swarms of tanks and men were pouring in over the border to the north.

One of the Global Hawks—there were now three on continuous station overhead, authorized by the Vietnamese—streamed live video from the Da River valley. The video showed that the Chinese had not yet adapted to the problem in front of them. They were moving forces down along Route 6 as if the way south were clear, sending very small teams to the east to either probe or act as pickets in case of attack.

"You can turn these off for a while and pop on the lights," Zeus said after he finished going over the images.

The room plunged into darkness as the gear was unplugged and the lights were reenergized. Zeus felt a little like he was with the American army of 1812, trying to stop the British from ravaging the country while equipped with a thousandth of their resources.

When the lights came on, General Trung nodded at him, encouraging him to continue.

"The Chinese haven't adapted yet. They may try and cross the reservoir. We know that's not going to work," said Zeus. He pointed to the map on the table. "The Chinese are stopped here, for the moment, along Highway 6 before the intersection with 15. They have two choices—they go into Laos, maybe try coming all the way down to Highway 217, or they change their game plan. Which do you want them to do?"

"An attack against our neighbor is always preferable to being attacked ourselves," said Trung soberly. "As lamentable as it is. But if they try that way, they will face much difficulty."

"We have cut off the passes at the border, General," said one of his aides. "It will be a grave for them."

"I would suggest you alert the Laotians," said General Perry.

"It has already been done," said Trung. "The evacuations have begun."

"Eventually, they'll come for Hanoi," said Zeus.

As if on cue, an air raid siren sounded. Zeus gritted his teeth and looked at General Perry. Perry simply folded his arms.

"Continue with your thoughts, please," said Trung.

"Hit them along the road while they're stalled, the more often the better," said Zeus. "Hit and run—Vietnamese style."

Trung smiled broadly. Zeus suspected that the attacks were already being launched, since he had seen some activity on the Vietnamese side of the line in the Global Hawk video.

"What they will probably decide eventually is to use 113 as a conduit for an attack," Zeus said, pointing to the east-west highway south of Na San. "It's the best road in the area, given where their forces are collecting. It's not as narrow as the others."

Trung's staff started talking among themselves. Zeus felt frustrated—Perry's translator had not been allowed into the room, and in fact it was clear that the Vietnamese really didn't care to *discuss* the situation with him; they only wanted him to give them intelligence. Trung tolerates my ideas, he thought, primarily out of politeness.

"General, I have another idea," Zeus told Trung. "The Chinese haven't taken Route 109 behind the airfield at Na San. You could get the hills back, and they'd be sitting ducks down there. Just like the French."

Trung smiled faintly. "Diem lost the battle at Na San."

"Only because the French could bring in reinforcements and supplies from Hanoi and farther south. Look how far the Chinese will have to come. And you could sit in the hills with shoulder-launched SAMs."

Trung nodded. It was hard to tell, though, if he was just being polite.

As the Vietnamese staff's discussion grew louder and more animated, General Perry rose. "General, it would appear that your staff would like to work on these problems without us," Perry told Trung. "Perhaps my major and I could go and get some dinner."

"By all means."

"**P**ut yourself in their position. Would we be taking advice from an old enemy?" Perry asked Zeus as they made their way back to the jeep.

"They already did," said Zeus. "They should hit the airstrip. And cut off 113. They have to harass the enemy, hit his supply lines—"

"One thing I would guess about the Vietnamese," said Perry. "They know how to run that sort of war. They did it before."

"They haven't been on this side of it. And the intelligence is a hell of a lot different now. Communications—"

"War's war, Major." Perry stopped in front of the jeep. "You're a damn bright kid. I wish I was half as smart as you. But I'll tell you something—Trung has the whole thing in his head already. I could see it in his eyes. You have to learn to read people. Especially if you're trying to help them."

A few blocks from the embassy, Zeus saw a red glow to the north of the capital. The Chinese had struck at the airport again, this time starting a fire in the underground fuel storage tanks.

The embassy perimeter was guarded by Vietnamese soldiers as well as American marines, and even though

Perry and Zeus were in uniform, they had to show their IDs to three different people before being cleared into the compound itself. By then Perry was in a bad mood, and Zeus thought he was going to bite the head off the Marine sergeant who came up to the jeep. The marine calmly explained that he was under orders to make a positive, personal identification before allowing anyone through.

"Is this positive enough for you?" asked Perry, leaning from the vehicle and putting his face into the marine's.

The sergeant stepped back and snapped off a salute, waving them in.

Major Christian met them in the vestibule. "General, I need to talk to you."

"Talk."

Christian glared at Zeus, clearly not wanting to say whatever it was he had to say in front of him. Zeus decided he'd hold his ground; he'd had enough of the jackass.

"The CIA has a problem, sir. They need to get a truck up to Tuyên Quang."

"Where's that?" asked Perry.

"I know where it is," said Zeus.

Tuyên Quang was about seventy-five miles north of Hanoi. Still controlled by Vietnam, the city had not been bombed or attacked by the Chinese.

The truck, Christian explained, was needed to rendezvous with a group of SEALs who were helping an American scientist and a CIA officer escape from behind enemy lines. They were supposed to be there by dawn or a little after.

On bicycles.

"Bicycles?" asked Perry.

"Dumbshit SEALs," said Zeus.

The others looked at him.

"I'm sorry, sir. When I was in Special Forces, I mean—they were always pulling some idiotic stunt. Why don't they just take a helicopter? Or motorcycles?"

"We have a truck?" Perry asked.

"We have a panel van," said Christian. "But we don't have a driver. Uh, using one of the locals is a real bad idea."

"What about the marines?" asked Perry.

"There are only six and—"

"I'll drive," said Zeus quickly.

"Actually, I was going to volunteer," said Christian.

Perry wasn't particularly keen on either of them going, even though the city was clearly in Vietnamese control. But Christian had already been asking around. The marines were short of the people they needed for security, and if he—or Zeus—didn't take the van, they'd have to give the job to one of the civilian embassy employees. Or the Vietnamese.

"See the thing is," Christian explained, "this has to be as quiet as possible. They don't want the Vietnamese involved, if possible. Because the person who's coming back has sensitive information. The Vietnamese aren't supposed to know he's out there. Or the CIA agent—they didn't tell even me that much."

"All right," said Perry. "You and Zeus head up there. Report in every half hour."

"Every half hour?" said Zeus.

"Try every fifteen minutes," answered the general.

22

Northern Vietnam

Late that evening, China declared northern Vietnam a no-fly zone for commercial aircraft, complicating the SEALs' game plan. They hastily switched from the original blueprint, which called for a jump from the rear door of a leased 727 flying at thirty-five thousand feet, to a contingency plan using a Hercules MC-130J at very low altitude. Before approaching the Chinese early-warning radars near the Vietnamese border, the Hercules would dip low to the ground, allowing it to escape detection in the ground clutter. As far as the SEALs were concerned, the switch was no big deal.

For everyone else though, it was a hassle. Besides making the flight considerably more difficult for the pilots—even with their automated gear, following the country's ragged terrain was no picnic—it also scrambled the arrangements Lucas had made for the bicycles, since they were originally sent to the commercial airport the SEALs were going to use.

The net result was that the SEAL drop was delayed

for several hours. Mara kept checking in for updates every fifteen minutes, severely depleting the battery in the satcom, until it gave way just after midnight. Crouched near the edge of the large field on the east side of the barn, she opened the battery compartment and reseated it, but that had no effect.

She leaned back, shifting her feet so she was sitting. The night had cooled. She figured it was in the mid-seventies, a perfect temperature under other circumstances. She stared at the clouds moving in. They looked like sheep, trotting across the moon and stars.

She'd hear the MC-130 just before the drop. If it followed the usual pattern, it would approach at something like fifty feet above treetop level, then pop up at the last moment to give the SEALs a little more cushion for the jump. Once they went out the door, they'd hit the ground in a matter of seconds.

She'd made two of those jumps herself, not counting the dozen or so in training. They were tougher than the high-altitude ones, at least in her opinion. When you went out at thirty-five thousand feet, you always felt like you had more time to do things. A low-altitude jump meant you made the right decision right away—or you never made any more.

She liked the challenge. They'd trained by going off bridges. Jump, pull, land. *Bing, bang, boom.*

Who used to say that?

Kevin, the instructor she'd had a crush on at Langley. *Bing, bang, boom.* One of his favorite sayings.

He was a good-looking guy. And sweet, too.

Nothing had come of the attraction. Too many rules about fraternizing with the students.

She would have gone out with him. Definitely.

Josh kind of reminded her of him. Very different guy, though. Josh had a bit more of an edge. Which was surprising, because Kevin had been a Ranger, and those guys were supposed to be all edge.

Maybe it was just that she didn't expect him to have an edge. You heard scientist and immediately you thought, cushy. Egghead.

Not necessarily wimp, but the jury would definitely be out.

Josh had something very tough inside him, though. Not just anger.

He was prejudiced toward action, the way she was.

She admired the way he wanted to protect the little girl. It wasn't just a case of him thinking she was going to tell the world what was going on—she wasn't part of a job. He felt he had to keep her safe.

God, I'm a sucker for the old he-man cliché, she told herself.

Mara sat up with a jolt. She heard an aircraft in the distance. She looked at her watch. Barely ten minutes had passed since the battery died while she was talking to DeBiase. At that point, the SEALs had just taken off.

It wasn't an airplane, it was a helicopter.

The Chinese.

* * *

Trying to keep Mạ occupied and kill his own boredom as they waited, Josh tried teaching the girl to play tic-tac-toe. She seemed familiar with it at first, but kept losing.

"You get three in a row to win," he told her. "You go first."

She took the stick and put an X in the corner. Josh went, she went, then he went, this time leaving an opening for her.

She didn't take it.

"Look, put your X here. You win."

She looked at him blankly.

"You want me to win, is that it?"

Mạ yawned. She didn't want him to win. She just didn't get the point of the game. Not at all.

"Sleep," he said, mimicking a pillow with his hands. "Go ahead."

She curled up around him and started to doze. Josh felt his own eyelids getting heavier. Why not sleep? he thought. We'll be out of here soon. It's just a question of time.

Mara pushed open the door and slipped into the barn. "Kill the lamp," she hissed.

Josh pulled it over and cranked down the wick. Mạ didn't stir. "What's going on?"

"Helicopter," said Mara.

"I thought the SEALs were parachuting in."

"They are."

"Shit. Should we stay here? Are we safe?"

"I don't know."

23

Northern Vietnam

Jing Yo bristled as the infrared operator repeated the scan.

"Looks like it's just embers, Lieutenant. Like I said, you burned it down pretty well."

They were looking at the remains of one of the small settlements they had searched earlier in the day.

"Why are some spots hotter than others?" Jing Yo asked, letting the suggestion that he had burned down the village pass.

"It depends on what burns. Different materials produce different hot spots. We haven't trained with building fires," added the operator, "but the principle is the same."

Jing Yo watched as he switched to a wide view, scanning the fields again. The lieutenant noticed something on the corner of the screen.

"Did that move?" he asked.

"Which?"

"Back here—the building. Inside."

The operator returned the screen to close-up mode of the area. "No. The building's warm. That building is almost intact. A lot more to burn there. We're seeing individual parts of the fire, I believe. Look at these ruins. You can see the shape of the embers. Really hot spots blow out the resolution and we back it down like this."

"Okay," said Jing Yo.

"This looks interesting, though," added the operator, switching back to the earlier screen. "This out in the jungle. If we could get the pilot to change course, I think you might want to get a much closer look at this."

J osh and Mara kept their eyes pointed toward the ceiling as the helicopters moved away.

"What do you think?" asked Josh.

"If they move off, it'll be okay."

They waited. The sound faded but didn't die.

"They're hovering nearby," said Mara. "About a mile. A little more."

"Is that too close for the SEALs to parachute in?"

"Too close."

"Maybe we should go farther east. Take the road."

"The road goes south."

"It's still away from the helicopters. I think we should do it."

Mara looked at her watch. The SEALs should be roughly thirty minutes away, perhaps a little more. "If we move, they won't be able to find us," she told him. "We don't have a phone, remember? The battery is dead."

"We have mine." He dug the sat phone out of his pocket.

"The Chinese can track that. Besides, it's not on the same circuit the SEALs will use."

"It's better than nothing. Peter will hear it. He has before."

"It's a good backup," said Mara. She wasn't sure that Bangkok would still be monitoring the frequency, or how long a delay there would be before Lucas got the information. "I think we should wait and see if they move off."

Jing Yo leapt from the helicopter as it touched down, running quickly to catch up with Sergeant Wu and the rest of the squad. The operator had spotted an overturned truck on a rutted farm road. The engine was slightly warm—an indication that it had been driven or at least turned on within the past three or four hours.

And there was a man, or maybe two, near the side, partly hidden from the scanner by the body of the truck.

Wu saw him coming and waved for him to get down; Jing Yo bent toward the ground but kept coming, sliding on the hard-packed dirt as he slipped in next to his sergeant. They were at the edge of a fallow field; the truck was ahead on the road, which lay just beyond a narrow band of trees.

"Somebody there, definitely," said Wu. "I have Ai Gua going around the side. When he's in position, we can close in."

The truck looked like a hazy gray box in Jing Yo's night goggles. Was that an arm curled around the side of the steering wheel—or part of the dash that had pulled away in the crash?

Jing Yo moved to his right, trying to get a better view through the trees. The front third of the truck was in the shallow ditch at the roadside; the rest of the vehicle angled back on the road. The cab was wedged into some brush, which made it hard to see the top and side.

"One person, maybe two," said Jing Yo. "Close to the side of the truck."

Ai Gua flashed a signal back through the squad members that he was in position across the road. The truck was now surrounded.

"Let's move in," Jing Yo told Wu.

They rose. Guns pointed at the truck, they moved forward.

The brush near the truck rustled.

"Watch out!" yelled Wu.

Jing Yo saw it for only a split second before he fired—the dark shadow of the devil, leaping at him.

The three rounds from his rifle hit the tiger in the head and neck, severing several arteries. But the beast had built up considerable momentum, and it crashed onto the road, still alive, leaping at its target.

Jing Yo stepped to his left, all trained instinct now. He wheeled. The gun became a pointed spear that slammed into the animal's rib cage.

The tiger lashed at him as it fell to the ground. It rolled back, ready to fight, spurred by pain. It shoved its fury forward, teeth bared, claws wide. Jing Yo's rifle smashed the top of its skull, breaking the bone and sending the animal to the ground, gurgling its last breath.

"Lieutenant?" said Wu, standing a few feet away. He seemed to be in shock.

Jing Yo looked at him, then turned his attention back to the truck. He moved quickly around the side, wary.

Ai Gua had heard the commotion and come running through the trees. He was standing a meter from the truck, gazing at the body the tiger had been eating when they arrived. It was a gory mess.

Jing Yo knelt next to it. The animal had mauled the corpse so badly that it was impossible to tell if it belonged to an Asian. The clothes looked Vietnamese.

He'd have to see if there was identification.

"Search the vehicle," Jing Yo told the others. "I'll attend to this."

At least one of the helicopters was in the air north of them, a mile or two. It was too close—the SEAL aircraft would be spotted almost immediately.

She checked her watch. They should be over the area in roughly fifteen minutes.

"If they see the helicopter in the area, will they still parachute?" asked Josh.

"Depends," said Mara. "It'll be up to them."

Most SEALs would. But that wouldn't necessarily

be a good idea. A firefight would be counterproductive. The helicopters would call in reinforcements quickly.

"I wonder if we could walk back to the spot where I was in the preserve," she said. "They could jump near there."

"How far is it?"

"A few kilometers."

"We could make it."

"We could walk by the side of the road and hide from the helicopters," said Mara. "The trees are pretty thick."

Mara tried to picture the area. Was there a place where the SEALs could parachute in?

There had been a field nearby. They could use the highway intersection as a meeting place.

Yes, it was a better plan. But was it worth the risk of using Josh's phone?

Yes.

"Call," she told him. "Then wake up Mạ. We'll meet them near the reserve."

"Let's let her sleep. I'll just carry her."

"It's a couple of miles."

"She needs to rest," he said, handing over the phone after punching the emergency number.

"I can't hear anyone."

"No, you just talk. That's how we've done it. He calls back."

"This town is too crowded. We're going to the place where Jimmy and I slept," said Mara, trying to word the message in a way that would confuse the Chinese. "Tell the Million Dollar Man we'll meet where the devil played."

She clicked off the phone and followed Josh out of the barn.

There was no identification in the dead man's clothes, and while there were papers in the truck, they were in the glove compartment and probably belonged to the truck's owner, not necessarily the driver.

The tiger had eaten a good portion of the man's face, along with much of his torso and legs. Jing Yo thought there was a very good possibility there was another animal nearby, though if so it hadn't shown itself.

The mauling made the men jumpy, and so Jing Yo decided they would bug out as soon as possible. He had Ai Gua fetch a body bag from the helicopters, which were idling in the nearby field. The private looked pale when he returned, clearly not relishing the task.

"We will do it together," said Jing Yo. "It is an act that must be performed."

He remembered the first time he had touched a dead man—Brother Fo, an older member of the monastery who had died in his sleep the night before Jing Yo arrived. Jing Yo had helped another monk remove the body from his cell. Seeing his discomfort, the other man had explained the necessary cycle of all things, how death fit into the cycle. When his training was done, said the monk, he would no longer fear death.

Another monk in the hall overheard them. As they passed out, he whispered to Jing Yo, "For some of us, training never ends."

He meant that among even the most devout, death was never fully accepted. It was a lesson Jing Yo valued greatly, but it was not a story to share with Ai Gua.

They completed their task quickly. Remains packed in the helicopter, they took off, Jing Yo once more in the helicopter with the IR sensors.

The operators were just beginning their recalibration routine when a message came in from division intelligence. "The scientist's cell phone has been active again," said the major relaying the information. "Very close to your position. We have the coordinates."

Even as he transferred them to the GPS, Jing Yo realized they were at the village they had flown over earlier.

24

Northern Vietnam

Zeus and Christian didn't find out that the SEALs' plane had been delayed until an hour after they had arrived at the rendezvous point just north of Tuyên Quang. Christian, who hadn't said much the entire ride, cursed as soon as he put the satcom radio down.

The stinking Navy, he said, could never get anything right.

"It was probably the Air Force," said Zeus. "They fly the planes."

"Whatever. Now we have to sit in this damn truck for another four hours at least."

"We can go back and check out the town."

"Give me a break."

"It didn't look that bad."

"Yeah, for Vietnam. It's not like there was a McDonald's on the edge of town."

"Maybe a little restaurant."

"Hell, Zeus, we went right down Main Street. There was no place open. And I wouldn't have trusted them if they were."

Zeus took out his map. They were roughly 140 miles from the province where the SEALs were going to land; that was nearly ten hours of biking, maybe more, since they'd be going over the mountains. The delay meant that they'd have to do a lot of it during the day.

Not a great idea.

"Maybe we should get closer to where they're going to land," suggested Zeus. "At least get into the mountains there."

"Where?"

"The Con Voi range."

"That close to the Chinese?" said Christian, his voice rising an octave.

"They're not that far south or east."

"You're out of your idiot mind."

Zeus sighed and began folding the map back up.

"You think just because you served in Special Forces that you're Mr. Gung Ho," said Christian. "And that you're a goddamn genius."

"I don't think I'm a genius."

"Perry does. Which is what counts, right?"

Zeus shrugged.

"You better tell them what the hell we're doing," said Christian, starting the truck.

25

Northern Vietnam

They walked along the road, staying on the shoulder and moving as quickly as they could. Mara, in the lead and holding the rifle, had to concentrate to see the path ahead. The clouds had thickened and the night was dark; it was hard to see more than a stride or two ahead.

"Can you hold up a bit?" said Josh.

"You want me to take her?" asked Mara, turning around.

"No, just slow down. She's still sleeping. Kid must be exhausted."

He walked up next to her, his shoulder brushing against hers. "Okay," he said.

"Come on," said Mara, hooking her arm through his. "We'll walk together."

They walked together in silence for a few minutes before Mara asked if Mạ was getting heavy.

"It's all right," he told her.

"That was a hell of a story she told."

"What's going to happen to her?"

"I don't know," said Mara. "They'll probably try and find a relative. When it's all over."

"Might be going on a long time."

Not the way things are going, Mara thought, but she kept that to herself.

"How long can the Vietnamese hold out?" Josh asked.

"I don't know. Watch the curve coming up."

They walked in silence again for a few minutes.

"What was it you said about where the devil played?" asked Josh. "The message was confusing."

"The person I was talking to is a Charlie Daniels fan. We were talking about a song just before I came here. He knows that means a crossroad. At least I hope he does."

"You must know him pretty well."

"Well enough."

"He your boyfriend?"

Mara laughed. "Oh, God no."

"I didn't mean to make you laugh."

"That's okay. If you knew the Million Dollar Man, you wouldn't even ask."

"He's rich?"

Mara explained where the nickname had come from. Josh told her that he had never really followed wrestling.

"Really?" said Mara. "I used to watch it all the time when I was little. My brothers got me hooked. Triple H, Batista, Rey Mysterio, all those guys."

"Why would you watch wrestling?"

"If I have to explain it, you won't understand it."

"Uh-huh."

"What'd you do? Watch *The Magic School Bus*?"

"I loved those shows."

Mara laughed. She'd loved them, too.

"Science was a way for me to deal with the world," said Josh. "It kept things . . . ordered."

"And you wanted that."

"I needed that."

He leaned closer to her. Mara waited for him to explain what he meant, but instead he stopped short.

"Is that the airplane?"

She stopped and listened. For a second, she thought it was. Then the sound became much more distinct.

"The helicopters are coming back," she said. "Let's get into the trees."

The helicopters were ninety seconds from landing when the infrared operator raised his hand, signaling Jing Yo over. "There's something about two kilometers south of the village, near the road but in the jungle. Warm bodies."

Jing Yo leaned down, looking at the blur. He'd already told the pilots to land, and had given up his headset so he could jump quickly from the chopper.

"What is it?"

"We'll have to get closer to find out. It may be another tiger or some other animal. Or a person."

"Not in the village?"

"We're still a little far away."

"Let me see the village."

Jing Yo waited while the technician readjusted his screen. He was starting to feel tired, worn down by the last several days.

If he felt that way, then his men would feel even worse. But they had a mission to complete.

"Here, Lieutenant. This is the village."

The screen looked similar but not exactly the same as it had earlier. The technician explained that the fires, having mostly burned themselves out, were continuing to cool, and so looked different to the sensors.

"Wasn't this building on fire before?" said Jing Yo, pointing to the southernmost barn in the center of the hamlet. It was the one they had searched earlier.

"Uh, I'm not sure."

"It was mostly intact, remember?" said Jing Yo. "There was heat on one side, and you thought the fire was spreading up the wall. But now the wall is not burned down."

"Okay."

"It's cold. Why would that be if there had been a fire there?"

The operator shook his head. Jing Yo went to tell the pilots to change course.

* * *

The jungle was so thick and the night so dark that Josh simply couldn't see where he was going. He carried Mạ with him as he pushed slowly ahead, partly guided by Mara's tug. The helicopters were getting closer.

"Which way are we going?" he asked Mara finally.

"We just have to get distance from the road."

They pushed on, stumbling between the bushes and trees. Mạ, her face pushed tightly into Josh's shoulder, groaned as the branches slapped across her back.

"Once they're on the ground, they'll have a hard time finding us. Even if they have night glasses. Goggles won't be able to see through all of this brush. We'll get in deeper and keep moving toward the drop area. Just be calm."

"I'm calm," he told her. "You stay calm."

"I'm calm," said Mara. Her voice was a tight rasp.

"We're going to be okay," Josh told Mạ. "We just keep moving. We'll make it."

"There!" Mara stopped short.

"What?" asked Josh.

"That sound—hear it? It's the MC-130," she said, pointing to the south. "With the SEALs. Come on, let's go."

Jing Yo grabbed the back of the pilot's seat, steadying himself as the helicopter turned sharply over the jungle.

"The trees are too thick near the road to land on

here," the pilot told him. "The best we can do is the edge of that field a half kilometer away."

"Let's do that."

"Lieutenant—there's a plane—it's just ahead," sputtered the copilot. "A large plane."

"Evasive maneuvers!" yelled the chopper pilot, jerking the aircraft hard to the left.

"Get us down," said Jing Yo. "Get us down *now*!"

26

Northern Vietnam

Ric Kerfer's rucksack hit the ground about a quarter second before he did, telling the SEAL lieutenant he was about to touch down. The warning was *just* enough to relax Kerfer's leg muscles in time to avoid serious injury, but the landing still hurt—he rolled on his right shoulder, hitting at exactly the angle that a linebacker had taken to smack him down in high school some ten years before.

Which hurt.

The linebacker had gone on to the NFL; Kerfer had lost out on a possible athletic scholarship to college and ended up going to Navy ROTC, became an officer, and joined the SEALs. He figured that he had gotten the better end of the exchange. Still, it hurt *goddamnit*, and put him in a lousy mood.

Then as now.

"Come on, you sissy boys," he growled, jumping to his feet and unsnapping his parachute harness. "Stevens, take the point. The Commies are in those choppers there. Move!"

Within seconds, one of his team closer to the road began firing toward the helicopters. Kerfer slipped on his night goggles, then got his bearings. As the last man out of the plane, he had hit farthest from the road; the other seven members of the squad—there were two fire teams—were scattered ahead, between him and the two Chinese helicopters that had been prowling the area.

The helos continued to press. Scumbags weren't easily intimidated.

Which kind of pissed him off.

"Put a frickin' grenade into the bastard," yelled Kerfer. He pulled on his radio and began running forward, his Mk 17 ready under his left arm. The SCAR fired 7.62 mm rounds, nice fat slugs that could stop something rather than just whizzing through it as an M-4's or even an MP-5's bullets sometimes did.

"They're landing!" yelled Eric, up ahead on Kerfer's right.

"Ger-*nay*-dez, *goddamn it*!"

The words were no sooner out of Kerfer's mouth than a 40 mm grenade exploded near the landing zone.

"About frickin' time," said the lieutenant, throwing himself down as a heavy machine gun began playing through the field.

* * *

Jing Yo leapt from the helicopter as the door gunner went to work, pounding the far side of the field with his machine gun. The rest of the commandos were down already, having landed in the first helicopter.

A grenade exploded on the ground nearby. The commandos were returning fire.

Jing Yo tasted the dirt as he hit the ground, tripping on something in the darkness. Tracers ripped from the helicopter's .50-caliber door gun, toward muzzle flashes maybe thirty yards away.

A grenade exploded so close its concussion pushed his head down.

This is hell, thought the lieutenant, zeroing his rifle on a shadow and pressing the trigger.

Mara reached back and grabbed Josh as the gunfire intensified. Bullets crashed into the jungle behind them, but the firefight itself was off to their left, nearly a half kilometer away. If they kept moving, they would be okay.

"Come on," she told Josh, "We can get to the rendezvous point."

"Are those the guys that are helping us?"

"Yes."

"Maybe we should help them."

"Just keep moving," said Mara. "They can take care of themselves."

"Okay."

She pushed through the brush. Josh's wanting to help spoke eloquently about who he was, but the impulse was also foolish—their real job was to get away.

The SEALs would have fallen over laughing if they'd heard him. Not that Mara didn't feel the same impulse.

"This is just getting too thick," said Josh. "We have to get closer to the road."

"You're right," said Mara, changing direction. "We can go right to the road—the SEALs have them tied down."

I f the world were perfect, Kerfer would have been able to swing two or three of his men around the flank of his enemy while his main force engaged them in the field. They'd squeeze and the bad guys would go bye-bye.

But the world wasn't perfect. The Chinese helicopters and their machine guns made it hard to move up through the field. And the bastards on the ground weren't exactly looking the other way either.

The first order of business was to get rid of the helos.

"Little Joe, I want you to put a grenade into that helo's door. You got that, Joey? Just like you were trying to do to that whore you bought last weekend."

Little Joe—the SEAL's real name was actually Riccardo Joseph Crabtree—cursed in response, telling his lieutenant that he could put the grenade in there himself.

Music to Kerfer's ears.

Three seconds later, as the helicopter pivoted around the southern side of the field, the petty officer rose and pumped a 40mm grenade from his EGLM launcher into the open hatchway of the chopper.

"Pretty!" shouted Stevens over the squad radio.

"I thought you were pinned down, point," barked Kerfer in reply.

"I am."

"Well stop gawkin' and get your ass unpinned. Little Joe ain't doin' all the work."

The SEAL responded with a burst of gunfire.

"Jenkins, time for your end around," said Kerfer. "Run to the left. I'm going to be right behind you."

"Good. Copy."

"Any of you assholes frag me, I'm comin' back as your girlfriend in my next life and giving you the clap," said Kerfer, jumping to his feet and running to flank their enemy.

J ing Yo saw the flames shoot from the helicopter as the grenade exploded, and knew instantly that the crew was lost. The helo disappeared into a fireball, sailing over the trees behind them.

The second helicopter immediately backed off, leaving them alone in the field.

These were definitely not Vietnamese soldiers they were fighting; they had to be Americans, come to fetch the scientist. There weren't very many of them—a dozen maybe, or perhaps twenty. But they had his small squad outnumbered and outgunned.

A foe this good would try to hold him in place while they sent men to attack the flanks. He had to withdraw temporarily, pick better terms for battle.

Moving back in the face of a superior foe was not dishonorable, but it nonetheless stung to give the order.

J osh nearly lost his balance as the thick branches gave way to the shoulder of the road. He jogged a few steps, swaying left and right as he struggled to stay upright. When he stopped, Mạ slipped down from his arms but continued to cling to his leg.

She was sobbing.

"Come on now," he told her. "We're going."

"This way," said Mara, a few feet away. "Come on."

Something exploded in the distance, louder than the grenades they'd heard just a few minutes before. Mạ clung tighter to his leg.

"One of the helicopters went down," said Mara.

"We're going to be all right," he told Mạ. "Come on."

Mara picked up the girl. Mạ tried to clutch him tighter, but Josh gently pried off her fingers. Then he put his arm around Mara's back, holding Mạ's neck gently as they began trotting along the road.

"It's beginning to rain," said Josh, feeling the first drops.

"Let's hope it does. It will make it harder for them to find us."

"It'll also make us wet."

Mara laughed.

"I didn't mean it as a joke," said Josh. "People are trying to kill us, and you're laughing."

"Crying isn't going to help," she said, laughing even harder.

Kerfer was almost to the road when he realized that the Chinese had decided to withdraw.

Ordinarily, that would have pissed him off—how dare the mothers run away before he had a chance to properly kick their butts?

But given that his job was to grab the spook and the dweeb with a minimum of fuss, he was *almost* happy to let them go. He told his men to hold their positions while he and Jenkins looked for stragglers or snipers.

"Where the hell are our bicycles?" he asked.

"Blown to pieces, Cap," said Stevens. "I'm standing on them."

"Stinking reds," said Little Joe. "Now we gotta fuckin' walk."

"Walkin's good for you," said Stevens. "Work off your beer gut."

"Hey, Cap, who ordered this rain?" asked Mancho.

"Yeah, his dress is gonna get wet," said Stevens.

"Screw my dress. I'm worried about your perm."

"All right, girls. Cut it," said Kerfer. "Let's get to Baker Point with a minimum of bitchin' and lynchin'."

"What fun would that be?" said Jenkins beside him.

Jenkins was a black guy from Brooklyn, New York, who spoke in a voice so high he sounded like a girl. No one made fun of it though, because he was sensitive about it. Ordinarily that would only have encouraged razzing, but Jenkins stood six ten in his bare feet, and weighed so much it took two guys to balance him in the chopper.

No one made fun of it except Kerfer, that is. He was the only person in the platoon Jenkins wouldn't hit or sit on.

"Come on, Squeaky, I'll race you to the road. Let's see if we can get there before your voice changes."

The rain was torrential by the time they reached the slope below the spot where Mara and the mercenaries had slept. Mara, still holding Mạ, put her right hand over her eyes to shield them from the worst of the downpour. She couldn't remember being this wet, not even in the ocean.

Josh, walking a few feet ahead, stopped.

"Global warming, right?" she said as she caught up.

"Not exactly." He reached out and took Mạ. The girl was so tired she simply couldn't walk on her own. "This is the way it's always rained in Vietnam. The aggregate is different, but if you look at the individual episodes, this is well within parameters."

"I keep forgetting you're a scientist. How long is it going to rain?"

"To know that I'd have to be a meteorologist. Or a fortune-teller."

"Come on," she said, tugging. "The intersection is only a half mile away."

"The infrared can't see through the rain, Kerfer. You know that."

"You Air Farters are always making excuses," Kerfer told the major who was handling the interface between the SEALs and the Global Hawk UAV supplying them with intel. Equipped with a powerful infrared imager, the drone had been flown into position specifically for the mission, but the heavy cloud cover and rain rendered the sensors useless. "If it was a nice day you'd tell me there was too much glare."

"Fug you and the airplane you flew in on."

"Any time, Major. I can always use some R & R. Call me back when you have something to contribute." Kerfer killed the transmission and turned to Stevens. "Are you *sure* this is the intersection?"

"Spooks marked it on the GPS."

"Screw the GPS. Let me see the paper map."

Stevens pulled it from his ruck. He switched on his pocket LED light, crouching low to the ground and cupping his hands to contain the glow.

"Why this intersection and not that one?" Kerfer asked, pointing down the road about half a mile.

"This is the one they marked, skipper."

"Get on the horn with Lucas and find out if he can read a fuckin' map. Little Joe, you're with me. We're going to check out the next bus stop down the line."

Josh pulled the sat phone out and looked at it as it started to ring.

"Answer it," said Mara. "Go ahead."

"Hello?"

"Josh?"

"Yes."

"This is Peter, Josh. Are you where you're supposed to be? Your friends are looking for you."

Josh looked in Mara's direction. They were less than three feet apart, but he could barely see her.

"Are we where we're supposed to be?" he asked her.

"Yes."

"Don't worry," said Lucas. "I have it now."

He hung up.

"The line's dead," said Josh.

"The SEALs must be close," said Mara. "And the Chinese, too."

Kerfer and Little Joe walked along the shoulder of the road, moving as quickly as they could despite the darkness and steady rain. The road had become more stream than highway. The muck sucked at their boots and made it hard to keep their balance. Kerfer, who'd taken point himself, pushed himself to stay ahead of Little Joe—if the big man fell forward on him, it would hurt more than being shot.

A hill rose on their right. The road angled to the left. The intersection was coming up.

He heard something and immediately took a step left, grabbing Little Joe and pulling him into a crouch.

"Think it's them?" asked Little Joe, kneeling next to him.

"Hope so."

Kerfer listened. The rain was falling so hard he couldn't be sure of anything.

"Hey," he said finally, his voice soft. "Goldilocks—this is the Big Bad Wolf. That you?"

M ara's heart jumped when she heard the voice on the road.

"I want the identifier," she said, trying not to drop her guard.

"Fuggit you want ID. I want ID," answered the voice. Then he added, "Lucas sent me. I have a grocery list."

"Is eggplant on it?"

"Who the hell comes up with this bullshit?" said Kerfer. "You guys practice to do this?"

"You're Lieutenant Kerfer?" asked Mara.

"Yeah, I'm Kerfer. What about it?"

Mara started down the hill, sliding on the slick grass. Kerfer and one of his men were standing in the muddy stream that marked the shoulder of the road. He flicked on a small penlight, holding it in her direction as she reached the road.

"I've heard about you," said Mara.

"Yeah, well I never heard anything about you." Kerfer raised the light, shining it toward her face. "Which is my loss."

"You're right."

"They didn't tell me I was rescuing a model," said Kerfer.

"Flatter me all you want, Lieutenant. Your reputation precedes you."

She stuck her hand out to shake, not sure what to expect. She *had* heard about Kerfer. He had a reputation for being difficult to get along with and a serious flirt.

"Glad to meet you," he said, shaking her hand quickly. "You should have some others, right?"

"We're here," said Josh, coming down the slope with Mạ.

"And who are you?" Kerfer asked the girl when she got close. He shone the light in her face; she ducked back behind Josh.

"Her name is Mạ," said Josh. "She's shy."

"I have some candy." Kerfer dug into his pockets and held out an energy bar. Mạ peered out from behind Josh's leg. "Go ahead, you can take it. I ain't gonna bite you. It's candy."

Mạ didn't move. Kerfer told her she could have it in Vietnamese.

The girl peeked out tentatively. He tore the side of the package, unwrapping the bar halfway.

"If you don't eat it, I will," he said, mimicking doing just that before holding the bar out to her again.

Josh took it and handed it to her. She took a bite, then began to devour it.

"You're the scientist, right?" said Kerfer, rising.

"Josh MacArthur." He held his hand out.

"Yeah, let's get going," said Kerfer, not bothering to shake. "We have to get as far away from those Commie bastards as possible before this rain lets up."

Northern Vietnam

The van's windshield wipers slapped frantically at the raindrops, pushing them off the glass with a hard squeak. Zeus squinted and leaned toward the steering wheel, trying to get a good view of the road. He had his high beams on but even so could barely see twenty feet in front of him.

"We're coming to that intersection," said Christian, looking at his GPS. "It's a half mile away."

Zeus backed off on the gas, slowing to almost ten miles an hour. Though asphalt, the road surface was very slippery. He'd nearly gone off the road twice while turning.

"You drive like an old lady," said Christian.

"You're welcome to take my place."

Zeus found the road and turned up it, slipping in the mud as the incline increased.

"This road goes straight up," he told Christian.

"Hey, we're in the mountains, right? You wanted a shortcut. This is it."

The van rattled and slipped, the transmission and the traction control working against each other. The rear end began slipping to the left. Zeus started correcting, but the rear end kept moving up.

He started to think he would have to turn around when the hill abruptly crested. Zeus jammed on the brakes, skidding on the wet pavement. He stopped crosswise in the middle of the hill.

Christian glared at him.

"I didn't do it on purpose. Jesus," Zeus told him. "Like I'm saying, if you want to drive, be my guest."

"You can drive," he said.

"Where the hell are we, anyway?" asked Zeus, not quite ready to start down the steep hill.

They were about three kilometers from Pho Lu, midway across the Con Voi mountain range. The SEALs had jumped in about fifty kilometers to the west. Lao Cai, thirty kilometers north, was still in Vietnamese hands—but feeling increasingly nervous, as the Chinese had continued to mass troops nearby and started shelling the place. The small Vietnamese army contingent there would not be able to hold them off if they crossed the line.

"We can move down to that farm near Pho Lu," said Christian, "and wait for them there."

"It'll take them all night to get to us in the rain," said Zeus.

"Perry said under no circumstance are we to go beyond the river," said Christian.

"Yeah."

The rain pounded on the glass. Zeus put the truck in gear and gingerly began downward. Not trusting the tires, he began pumping the brakes. As soon as they slowed almost to a stop, he let off, built a little speed, then began pumping again.

"I think you got it," said Christian.

"Don't jinx me."

A series of switchbacks began about a half kilometer down. These were easier to navigate, though if anything the road was even more slippery because of accumulating runoff. Zeus angled the van as he made each turn, sliding with the mud but still retaining control.

"Man, you're gonna get us killed," muttered Christian.

"I keep telling you—you want to drive, take the wheel."

The road began curving around the side of a cliff, leveling above a jagged valley. Pho Lu sat somewhere at the left end of the valley, though in the dark and the rain it was impossible to see. Zeus spotted a pull-off to the right and drove into it cautiously, flicking off the lights but leaving the engine on.

"Let's check on them," he told Christian.

"Yeah."

Christian picked up the satcom, punching in the frequency for the Bangkok CIA station coordinating the pickup. Zeus leaned back, trying to stretch out. The long drive had knotted his muscles.

"This is Major Christian. We're near Pho Lu. What's their ETA?"

Zeus watched out of the corner of his eye as Christian listened to the CIA officer in Thailand. The dashboard's glow made his look even more sinister than normal.

"Why? What's going on?" asked Christian.

Zeus pushed upright in the seat.

"We can't wait here all night," said Christian.

"What's going on?" asked Zeus.

"They don't have the bikes. They're walking."

"Walking? What is that, fifty klicks away?"

"As the crow flies, maybe."

"Let me talk to him."

"I can handle this." Christian put up his hand, warding him off. "Tell them we can only wait until dawn. After that—"

"What do you mean, we're only waiting until dawn? Where the hell are they?" Zeus reached for the phone.

"I have this, Major," said Christian.

"Get directions for where they are. Get coordinates."

"I have this."

"Get coordinates."

"Yes, we want coordinates," Christian told the CIA officer in Bangkok. "We're not waiting around here all night."

Christian entered the coordinates into his device, made sure he had the frequency for the SEAL team, then signed off.

"You don't really think we should go there, do you?" he said to Zeus.

"Yeah, I do."

"Perry's going to be pissed."

"What's the alternative?"

"Going home and having a beer," said Christian, pulling his rifle up from the floor of the cab. "We have to take a right about three kilometers down the road."

28

Northern Vietnam

The helicopter had burrowed into the hillside as it crashed. It was unlikely anyone aboard had survived, but to be sure, someone had to get close and check. Jing Yo had seen so much death over the past few days that he would gladly have passed the duty to someone else, but in the end it was he who climbed over the tangled wreckage to see.

The pilot and copilot were strapped in their seats, compressed in the metal wreckage. The rear compartment was so charred and battered it was impossible to see inside.

The rain continued to pour. Jing Yo tried to pry the cockpit door open with his rifle, but it was so mangled that it wouldn't budge. The dead men's removal would have to wait until the rain ended and help arrived.

"I hope this bastard is worth it," said Sergeant Wu when Jing Yo walked back to him.

Unlike its companion, the second chopper had suffered only a few bullet holes in the undercarriage. The pilot and his crew huddled inside out of the rain, waiting in a field about 150 meters from their fallen comrades to hear what Jing Yo wanted to do next.

Back in the belly of the chopper, Jing Yo took out his area map, trying to guess where the Americans would go. They had only two choices—to go back east or south. South would take them into the heart of the Chinese army advance. By contrast, the east, while a much harder trek because of the terrain and vegetation, was wide open.

The rain would slow his enemy down, but still, Jing Yo needed help.

Colonel Sun took the request calmly.

"Lao Cai is being attacked as we speak," the colonel told him. "The troops there will come south along Route 70. I will see what can be spared. Pursue the Americans as tightly as possible."

"Yes, Colonel."

"Do not fail me, Lieutenant."

"Yes, Colonel."

The SEALs formed a cocoon around Josh, Mara, and Mạ as they walked. They'd brought extra rain gear, though by now keeping dry was a fantasy. Josh wrapped Mạ in one of the ponchos, fixing the hood so the girl could see out as he carried her. She was heavy—beyond heavy—but she seemed to want only him to carry her. It made him feel proud, in a way, chosen, though part of him would have been just as happy to give up the honor.

He was dead on his feet. He'd sleep for weeks when he got back.

After telling the world what was going on.

Mara trudged a few steps ahead. He was sure she was just as tired as he was. Her reaction to Kerfer irked him; the Navy lieutenant was a hot dog and an asshole, but women seemed to be attracted to that, even smart women who knew better, like Mara. He imagined that she did know better, from personal experience, but still found his charm irresistible.

He no longer thought she was gay. The way she'd reacted to Kerfer ruled that out.

She wasn't as plain as he'd thought either.

Mara kept wiping her eyes, trying to keep them clear. Even so, her vision was so blurred from the rain that she practically ran into Kerfer when he stopped short on the road to talk to someone on his satcom radio.

"Hey, your boss is looking for you," he said, handing her the unit. About the size of a sat phone, it was more powerful and could use an array of different encryptions.

"This is Mara."

"Hey, beautiful, how are the SEALs treating you?" asked DeBiase.

"Like a million dollars."

"Ha-ha. Listen, we have the van coming to meet you. You have to get down to the road that runs along Ngòi Bo. That's a creek. I just told Kerfer about it and he claims to know where it is."

"If he says he does, he probably does."

"Yeah, emphasis on the word 'probably.' Watch him, Mara. He's slick."

"As slick as you?"

"I wouldn't sleep with him. He'll never respect you in the morning."

"No chance of that," she said. Mara flushed a little. There was no chance of that, now or at any point in the future.

Though he was attractive in a SEAL sort of way.

Josh was attractive, too. But that wasn't happening either.

"It's going to take them an hour to get close," continued DeBiase. "So keep walking. This rain is so heavy, none of the UAVs are getting any intelligence. They're up. As soon as the clouds clear they'll see."

"How long is it going to rain?"

"Half hour, another hour. Probably stop just when the truck meets you."

"Figures," she told him before handing the radio back to Kerfer.

29

Northern Vietnam

Zeus stopped at the edge of the bridge. The van's head-lights showed a steady stream of reflections ahead—the stream had overrun the road.

"How deep you think it is?" he asked Christian.

"Not very."

"I don't see a rail."

"Are you kidding?" answered Christian. "The Vietnamese don't put guardrails on their roads. They don't even pave half of them."

"Go wade out and see how deep it is."

"Why?"

"Because it looks like we're going to get washed away."

Christian grabbed the door handle, pulling it sharply and snapping the door open so hard it flew back and hit his leg. He cursed, then stepped out into the rain. Zeus watched as he walked ahead of the van into the water.

He was right. It barely came to his ankles. Zeus started ahead.

"Satisfied?" said Christian, pulling himself inside as Zeus reached him.

"I just wanted to see you wet."

No sooner had Zeus said that than the water seemed to pick the van up. It moved sideways, drifting with the swollen creek before the wheels caught again at the side of the overpass. Slipping on an angle, nose pointing nearly thirty degrees away from the road, the van lurched and skidded forward, out of the rain.

"So maybe I didn't walk out far enough," said Christian when they reached the other side. "Sue me."

The rain began to slow as Zeus continued passing down the mountain. They slipped across 151, then headed toward the unnumbered road that followed Ngòi Bo, a narrow river that cut across the province's central plain. They passed through two villages. Neither had any lights on, and it was impossible to fell if there were even people in the houses or not.

"We turn left at that intersection," said Christian as the road appeared on the left. "We're halfway there."

As Zeus started to slow down, he spotted a canvas-topped jeep on the other side of the highway. Two soldiers in rain gear were standing near it, guns under their plastic ponchos.

"Poor slobs," muttered Christian.

One of the men put his hand up, signaling that they should stop. Zeus started to pump the brakes, but as soon as his foot touched the pedal the rear end of the van began to skid to the right. He backed off the brake and started to steer into the skid, but the angle increased.

"Shit!" he yelled, yanking at the wheel desperately. The van pulled back suddenly, weaving the other way.

One of the soldiers leveled his gun. Zeus tried correcting but the van whipped out of his control. The man fired, riddling the back of the truck with bullets.

Then he tried jumping out of the way, but he was too late; the rear end of the truck whipped into him, pinning him against the front of the other vehicle. As they rebounded off, Zeus got the van facing back in the right direction on the road. As he started to jump out to see if the man was all right, bullets crashed through the windshield. He leapt onto the ground, rolling on the wet pavement.

"Don't shoot us. We're American!" he yelled, scrambling to his feet. He ran around the side of the van, unholstering his gun. "Stop!" he yelled, turning the corner.

The soldier he'd hit lay crumpled at the foot of the damaged truck. The gunfire was coming from the rear of the truck.

"Zeus!" yelled Christian from inside the van.

"Stay down!"

"No shit—I'm coming out your side. I'll cover you from the front."

"Come on then."

The soldier who was firing at them sent another burst into their windshield, taking out the rest of the glass. Zeus fired a warning shot, then yelled again.

"Stop!" he shouted.

The soldier came around the front of the truck, leveling his rifle at Zeus. Something automatic took over. Zeus squeezed off two shots, striking the man in the head. The soldier stood dead still for a moment, then teetered backward, falling back behind the truck.

Zeus ran to the first man, who'd been hit by the truck. He was still breathing.

"I'm sorry," Zeus told him.

He pulled at the raincoat, which was bunched up around his neck, trying to make him more comfortable. As the top fell open, he saw the man was wearing a uniform different from the ones the soldiers in Hanoi had been wearing.

Very different. It was Chinese.

So was the truck.

"What's going on?" asked Christian, running over.

"These guys are Chinese," said Zeus. "They must be scouting."

"This is a troop truck. Where are the rest of them?"

"They must be along the road somewhere."

"We'd better disable the truck," said Christian. "Then get the hell out of here."

He started to pull the hood open. Zeus stopped him.

"Let's take it."

"We have the van."

"The van is beat to crap. This is better. It's bigger, and probably has six-wheel drive. We can get through the rain a hell of a lot easier."

"I don't know." Christian looked at it doubtfully. "It's Chinese."

"So is half the stuff you buy in America."

Zeus pulled open the door. The cab of the truck, a two-year-old six-by-six Dongfeng transport, was almost identical to those of the German NATO trucks Zeus had been in. It had a diesel engine mounted under the cab, with a five-speed transmission.

He pushed the Start button. It rumbled to life.

"Coming?" he yelled, rolling down the window.

"Go!" yelled Christian, jumping onto the side of the cab. There was no running board; he gripped the rail with his right hand and pushed his legs against the door, hanging off as if he were a monkey.

A bullet slammed into the top of the cab. Zeus struggled to get the truck into reverse. They lurched backward, then stalled.

"Shit!" yelled Christian, raising his rifle and returning fire over the top of the cab.

Zeus hit the starter and the truck grumbled back to life. He overrevved it, spinning and kicking mud as he backed up toward the road. He threw the clutch in, jerked the tranny into first, then overrevved it again. The truck lurched and moved forward very s-l-o-w-l-y.

Low gear was very, very low.

"Get us the hell out of here!" screamed Christian, ducking as fresh bullets hit the vehicle, spitting through the canvas back.

Zeus slammed the shifter into second and then third, grinding the gears. As the truck gained speed, he hit the corner of the van and pushed it out of the way. He continued up the hill, building speed.

"Go! Go! Go!" yelled Christian.

"You think you can do better, come inside and try," muttered Zeus.

Two Chinese soldiers stood at the side of the road, not sure what was going on. Zeus popped on the headlights and saw them. Stepping on the gas, he swerved to the side as he passed, knocking one over and sending the other running for cover.

He strained so hard to see if he'd gotten him that he nearly ran off the road.

"You're going to get us killed," hissed Christian, still hanging on outside.

"Stop whining."

"Stop so I can get in."

"Not until we put some distance between them and us."

"One of these days, Murphy, you're going to get what's coming to you."

"I already have."

Zeus stopped a half mile down the road. Christian climbed in the cab.

"I know what they're doing," Zeus told him. "We blocked them off, so now their flank is vulnerable. They have to come down Route 70, shut off all the little routes west. Their flank is even weaker than I thought. They're adapting."

"Wonderful. Can we get the hell out of here?"

Zeus started moving again, this time beginning in second gear rather than first. It didn't seem to mind.

"The satellites and UAVs probably haven't seen the advance because of all this rain," said Zeus. "Call Perry and tell him what's going on. The Vietnamese may want to pick off some of these units. They should get them now, while they're still weak."

"Are you out of your mind? The first thing he'll do when I tell him that is ask how I know. We're not supposed to be here, remember?"

"Call him."

"No f'in' way. You call him."

"Give me the satcom."

Christian held it out to him. He started to take it, but Christian pulled it back.

"I'll talk to him. You're a pain in the ass, Zeus. You've always been a pain in the ass."

Perry took the news calmly—or at least didn't raise his voice loud enough for Zeus to hear as Christian explained what was going on.

"We're less than a half hour from the pickup, General. Then we're on our way back," he said. "Piece of cake . . . birthday cake . . . Yes, sir. . . . Oh, yes, sir. . . . I will. . . . No, sir. Absolutely not."

"Absolutely not what?" Zeus asked when the radio call was over.

"I told him it was a piece of cake."

"And?"

"He said don't let the Chinese blow the candles out."

Northern Vietnam

Mara was the first to hear the helicopter, and began shunting the others to the side of the road before its search beam came into view. The light seemed to cut physically into the rain, pushing it aside with a burst of steam that fell back as it flew. The chopper passed over the road very slowly, only a few feet over the treetops, moving so slowly an octogenarian could have kept up.

"I got it," said one of the SEALs, loading up the grenade launcher on his gun as they crouched a few feet from the roadway.

"No," said Mara sharply. "If you shoot them down, they'll know exactly where we are. No way."

"The spook's right," said Kerfer. "Hold your fire. Let them pass."

They waited as the floodlight approached.

"You sure about this?" whispered Josh, sidling next to Mara. "They found us before."

"If they were using an infrared system," she answered, "they can't right now because of the rain. See how low they are? They'll pass right by us."

"Okay."

The helicopter seemed to pause as it came closer to them. Mara tucked her elbows in against her sides, holding her breath.

The chopper kept moving. No one said anything for a few minutes. Then Kerfer rose and went out into the road.

"It's heading south," said the SEAL. "Let's get moving. Geek boy, you okay with that kid?"

"Fuck yourself," said Josh.

"Fuck yourself back. Scientists."

J osh's legs ached from his hips to his ankles. He felt as if his bones had been replaced with stiff metal rods, and his muscles were battered rubber bands, overstretched and unable to keep his joints together.

Mạ had grown unbearably heavy. Finally she began to slide down, out of his grip; he leaned forward, barely able to deposit her on the ground before dropping her.

She clung to him, unwilling to walk.

"I can take her," said one of the SEALs.

Mạ grabbed Josh's leg more tightly as the SEAL gently touched her shoulder. Josh felt bad for the sailor.

"It's okay, Mạ," he told her, dropping down. "We're all friends, honey."

She said something in Vietnamese, then buried her head in his leg.

"Her whole village was wiped out by the Chinese," Josh explained. "I think she's just afraid of anybody in a uniform."

"Poor kid. Crap. What bastards."

"Are you coming with us?" barked Kerfer.

"Man, he's a jackass," muttered Josh under his breath. He nudged Mạ, moving his leg to get her to walk with him.

"Ah, his bark's worse than his bite," said the SEAL.

"I heard that, Little Joe," snapped Kerfer. "My bite is worse than my bark. You got that, kid."

"Bite me," said Josh.

The SEALs cracked up. Even Kerfer laughed.

"Good one, geek." He came over and punched Josh's shoulder, nearly knocking him over. "Now keep your ass moving. The Commies are still looking for us."

* * *

"I think I hear the truck," said Mara.

The SEALs peeled off to the side, leaving her in the road. Kerfer took her gun and went by the shoulder, kneeling as he aimed his own weapon at the space in front of her.

"Remember to get out of the way if he doesn't stop," said the SEAL lieutenant. "Get far away, because we'll blow the crap out of him."

"Thanks," said Mara.

"Don't mention it."

Mara turned around. "You okay, Josh? You got the girl?"

"We're fine."

The rain was starting to let up. Mara remembered what DeBiase had told her—it would probably end just as the van came.

A pair of lights appeared around the bend. Mara took a breath, trying to relax herself.

It was their ride. Finally.

"Hey," yelled Kerfer as the truck pulled around the corner. "That's no van. That's a Commie troop truck. Look at the lights."

Mara froze. She didn't know if Kerfer was right, but it was too late to run anyway.

She put up her hand to signal them.

She'd throw herself to the left, roll in the mud. The SEALs would take care of the truck and whoever was in.

The vehicle wasn't stopping.

Damn.

The headlights blinded her.

Mara tensed her legs, swinging her hip to the right to act as a counterbalance. The truck began to skid. The tires screeched as they held, lost their grip, then held again. It stopped about six feet from her.

The driver's-side window rolled down. A man stuck his head out—a big target for the SEALs, Mara hoped.

"Hey!" he yelled. "I hope you're Mara."

"I am!"

"I'm Zeus Murphy, U.S. Army. This is Major Christian. Where the hell are your SEALs?"

"Errp, errp," said Kerfer, stepping from the shadows as his men surrounded the truck, brandishing their weapons. "You're our ride?"

"You got it."

"What do you say we get the hell out of here?"

"Fine with me," answered Zeus. "I have to pay double if it's not back in Beijing by sunrise."

31

Northern Vietnam

Jing Yo folded his arms before his chest, watching the road as the helicopter swung through the valley. They'd been searching now for over an hour; clearly, they were not going to find the scientist like this.

The rain was letting up, but without the infrared detection gear, he and whoever was helping him could easily hide in the jungle when the helicopter passed. But searching on the ground would be almost impossible—there was just too much territory to cover.

He was beaten.

"We have thirty more minutes of fuel, Lieutenant," said the pilot. "What do you want me to do?"

"Keep searching on this road," said Jing Yo. Reaching for the radio, he called into the division headquarters, looking for the intelligence officer who was acting as a liaison. "Have there been any more transmissions from that satellite phone?"

"No," said the officer. "We are monitoring."

"What about other transmissions? American transmissions on their military band?"

"Their radios are very difficult to detect," said the officer.

Then an idea occurred to Jing Yo, so simple that he wondered why he hadn't thought of it before.

"The satellite phone that the scientist used—is there a way to get its number?" he asked.

The more he drove the truck, the more Zeus felt comfortable with it. It wasn't very fast—the speedometer claimed ninety kilometers per hour, but that was clearly wishful thinking. Still, it was very sure-footed, easily moving through the muddy road and deep puddles along the creek. The rain had almost entirely stopped, but the downpour had flooded the waterway, and it overlapped much of the road. Sections of the highway were completely covered by running water, which fought against the wheels as they started up the mountain.

"We're going to need some way around that intersection where we left the van," Zeus told Christian. "Find me some little village or something to get through."

"I'm telling you, there are maybe three roads out that way, and they're all within one kilometer of each other. The mountains block everything off."

"Can we go south on 151?"

"You have to go back almost to the van to get there. You want to risk that?"

"It's either that or we backtrack to the spot where they had that firefight," said Zeus. "You want to do that?"

The SEAL commander had told him everything that had happened. He also assured him that they'd have no trouble rushing past any Chinese soldiers they came across.

Easy for him to say; he was sitting in the back with the others.

"There's some little village here we might be able to get through," said Christian. "A couple of klicks from here. Maybe there's a road through it that isn't on the map."

There were plenty of uncharted roads. The problem was, they generally went nowhere, which was why they were uncharted.

"Maybe. We'll decide when we get there," said Zeus. "Keep watching."

Sitting against the side of the truck, Josh let his body go slack. It was over. He was going home.

It didn't seem so much like a bad dream as like a piece of his imagination. Time had been balled up incredibly, twisted around.

But it was real. He had the digital camera to prove it.

Josh reached into his pocket and took out the camera. Mara jostled against his side. She'd nodded off practically the moment they'd climbed in. Ma, who was tucked around him on the other side, had too.

He flipped the switch to play and watched the screen. There was the village; there were the bodies, and the time stamp. It was all evidence.

They might not believe him. They might think he'd made it up. But this was indisputable.

"What are you looking at?" asked one of the SEALs across from him.

"The Chinese destroyed a village. They murdered everyone there. I got a video. Here, take a look."

Josh's sat phone began to ring as he handed the camera to the SEAL. He reached into his pocket and, without thinking, hit the button to receive the call. "This is Josh."

The person on the other side of the line didn't answer.

"This is Josh," he repeated. "Who is this?"

"What the hell are you doing?" barked Kerfer.

"I just—"

"Turn it off."

Josh hit the Kill switch. Kerfer grabbed the phone, glanced at it for a second, then flung it out of the back of the truck.

The location was near a road and a creek that ran east-west. He was moving, trying to get into the mountains.

Jing Yo did have luck with him after all. He leaned into the space between the two pilots, explaining where he thought their target was.

"We're about ten kilometers from there," said the helicopter pilot. "North of them. We can be overhead in a few minutes."

"Can you make the helicopter quieter?"

"I'm sorry, Lieutenant. There's no way to do that."

"Switch off the light at least."

"You sure? They'll hear us coming anyway."

"Switch it off. Take us higher. Make a pass as if we're not interested, as if we're going somewhere else."

"Why not go around then?"

"I want to see what it looks like. We'll spot it, then we'll set an ambush."

The village Major Christian had spotted on the map turned out to be two farm buildings at the edge of a field. Zeus found a path behind them that led in the proper direction, but after driving down it for two hundred yards, they discovered that the path ended in a pond. He had to back up all the way to the road.

Kerfer jumped from the back as he reached the blacktop.

"What's our sitrep?" asked the SEAL lieutenant, climbing up on the side of the truck.

"I thought we had a shortcut to 151," said Zeus. "But it looks like the only way back is through that intersection where the Chinese were."

"No sweat. We can handle them."

"There may be more troops there by now," said Zeus. "They're moving down the mountain range to make sure their main force doesn't get attacked from the side. There could be a lot of troops there by now."

"The UAVs told you this?"

"No, the clouds are still too thick. There won't be data for another half hour at least."

"So you know that how?"

"I know what they'd do. I've war-gamed it."

"War-gamed it. Shit."

"Hey, screw you, Lieutenant," said Christian. "If it wasn't for us, you'd be walking home."

Kerfer snorted. "Me and one of my guys will ride in the cab," he said. "If there's any trouble, we'll take care of it."

"There's no room," said Christian.

"You ride in the back with the rest of the luggage."

"I'm the navigator."

"He doesn't need a navigator. He's going back the way he came, right? Besides, he's got me."

Chinese troops had burst through Lao Cai and were spreading down the eastern side of the Con Voi mountain range, aiming to prevent the Vietnamese from attacking on the northeastern flank and cutting off supply lines south. Jing Yo could see the first advance groups of vehicles along the road as the helicopter headed eastward. The campaign was going well; the Vietnamese would soon be vanquished.

But the victory would be like eating ashes at a New Year's feast if he did not accomplish his mission.

The clouds were drifting east, allowing the moon and stars to light the ground below. Seeing detail was out of the question, but there was enough light to see vehicles.

"Troop truck," noted the pilot as they came through a valley just below Route 151.

Jing Yo leaned closer, looking out the window.

"One of ours," said the copilot as they passed it. "Probably reinforcing that checkpoint ahead."

"Find a place to land near the checkpoint," said Jing Yo, pulling up his radio to get division to alert the checkpoint to what was going on.

Zeus had a simple plan for getting past anyone he came to—hit the gas, duck down, and pray. And run them over, if possible.

The problem was, he had to make a fairly sharp turn right before he got to the intersection, which meant slowing down.

His fingers tightened on the wheel as he climbed up the hill. The truck's speedometer read thirty, but that felt optimistic.

"Maybe we should stop down the road," he told Kerfer. "You guys go through the field and surprise them."

"Too much trouble. Let's just get across."

"Listen, if they blocked the road—"

"No shit, Major. I talked to the head spook before I came up here. They have their UAVs back on line, and he says the only vehicle there is your shot-up van. So just play through. All right? Fuckin' relax. You're with the Navy now."

Zeus took a breath.

"Intersection in like zero-two minutes," said the other SEAL, studying his GPS.

"Better kill your lights," said Kerfer.

"I can handle it."

"Relax, Major. I've done this before."

"So have I."

Kerfer gave him a skeptical look.

"I was in Afghanistan just last year," said Zeus. "I commanded a Special Forces A team."

"Then untwist your panties, loosen your grip, and get this thing moving a little faster."

* * *

Mara leaned against Josh, half sleeping. It was going to be so good to get back to Bangkok and have a bath, she thought, a real bath.

They hit a hard bump. She lifted her head, then started to lean back.

Sleep would be nice.

As she closed her eyes again, the truck began skidding sharply to the left. She was thrown against Josh, nearly bowling him over.

"I'm sorry," she started to say, when the truck flew back in the other direction and he was thrown on top of her.

"**F**aster!" shouted Kerfer as the two Chinese soldiers came out firing from behind the wrecked van ahead.

Little Joe rose and leaned out the passenger-side window with his gun. He fired a grenade at the van, then began emptying his rifle at the soldiers at the other side of the intersection. Kerfer spun his rifle around and bashed the windshield. The glass crinkled but didn't break.

"Scumbag Chinese," he said, hitting it again in a second spot. "Don't even make a goddamn window right."

This time the glass broke, most of it falling straight down on top of him. He spun his gun around, rose in the seat, and began firing.

Zeus swerved hard to take the turn. Even though the truck was going only about twenty kilometers an hour, it rocked hard on its chassis, nearly leaving its wheels as he turned.

They were past them. Safe.

Almost.

"Watch out in the back!" yelled Kerfer. He pushed up through the windshield, onto the truck, looking toward the rear. Three soldiers came running from the side of the road. He fired at them, but it was impossible to tell whether he had got them or his men in the back had.

The lock on Little Joe's door gave way and the door sprang open. The SEAL flew out with it, then lost his weapon as he scrambled to stay aboard the truck. Kerfer tossed his own gun back in the cab and reached over for his shooter, swinging him back in.

Little Joe howled as his arm was caught against the door frame. Zeus hit the brakes.

"What the hell are you stopping the truck for?" screamed Kerfer.

"Get him in."

"I didn't tell you to stop."

"Just get him the hell in."

The helicopter they'd heard earlier buzzed toward them from the east, its searchlight augering through the darkness toward their hood. Kerfer tilted his gun upward and fired. As he did, the woods on both sides of the truck lit up with gunfire.

J ing Yo, rising from the ditch where he and his men had hidden themselves, zeroed in on the front of the truck as the helicopter came overhead.

The truck suddenly stopped, hesitating for a moment before starting backward.

"Fire! Fire!" yelled Jing Yo.

His men, posted with regular army troops from the scouting group that had occupied the area earlier, began complying. The truck jerked backward, then disappeared in fog.

Smoke. A grenade—several grenades, covering their retreat.

"Keep attacking!" yelled Jing Yo.

The helicopter was above, but not close enough to blow the smoke away. The truck wheeled to the side and crashed into something.

Bullets flew back toward the Chinese troops. A tremendous fury rose from behind the trees. In the confusion, the jungle seemed to be exploding on its own, branches and even trunks flying around as the human enemies emptied their weapons against each other.

"Don't let them get away!" yelled Jing Yo. "They're retreating!"

Across the road, Ai Gua rose. He brought his gun up to fire, then fell, hit by a bullet. Sergeant Wu ran toward him.

"No!" yelled Jing Yo, but it was too late—a grenade launched by the Americans exploded nearly in the sergeant's face.

Jing Yo started toward them. Something hit him hard in the shoulder, spinning him downward. His head lost its weight; he tasted the bitter water of pain and felt the admonishment of his mentors, the stern glance of the monks who had overseen his studies.

"You will try harder," they told him.

Their words seized him, and he struggled to his feet to rejoin the battle.

J osh pulled Mạ beneath him as the truck shot backward. The canvas top above them seemed to disintegrate into flying lead. The SEALs scrambled toward the tailgate, pushing over him, but the truck was still moving, lurching from side to side. It slammed into something hard. Josh and Mạ slipped into someone; before he could react, the truck spun back the other way and jerked down into a ditch.

Josh felt himself being pulled or pushed out. He grabbed hold of Mạ.

"We'll be all right, we'll be all right," he told her, the words an incantation.

"Down, Josh, down!" yelled Mara, pulling him from the truck.

Josh shoved himself out, curling Mạ in his arms as he fell. He clung to her tightly, trying to spin so he would land on his shoulder. To his surprise they landed in water, sinking in a big splash before bottoming out. He jerked upright, then fell back under the surface, once more trying to spin to his side to keep Mạ from getting hurt. This time he was only partly successful, and heard the girl yelp as he pushed back to his knees. The cry reassured him—she was still alive.

"This way, this way!" yelled one of the SEALs.

Josh got to his feet and began following in the

direction of the voice, wading through the calf-deep water.

"Come on," said Mara, taking hold of his side. "Go! Come on!"

"I have Mạ," he said, starting to run.

"I know. Come on."

A light lit above, an illumination flare shot by one of the Chinese ambushers. The gunfire stoked up.

"If I die," Josh told Mara, "take the video to the UN."

"You're not going to die," she said. "Run!"

As soon as Zeus felt the truck going down into the embankment, he knew he'd never get it out. He braced himself, revving the engine but not really in control as the vehicle bounded across the rocks and then wedged itself against a tree and the side of the ditch.

"Get out!" he yelled, but he was the only one left in the cab. Kerfer and Little Joe were already on the road, providing covering fire.

Zeus opened his door and threw himself out of the truck. His left arm hit the door side and he went into the dirt face-first, slamming into the side of the embankment. His legs were in water.

He rolled over. Remembering that he had left his gun in the cab, he pulled himself up and went to grab it. As he did, a grenade or rocket shot through the passenger side of the cab, flying through the missing window and through the thin back panel into the back. Zeus fell backward, rifle in his hand, as it exploded in the jungle behind the truck.

He landed under the water. Sputtering, he pulled himself up and started crawling on his hands and knees away from the truck. Someone had fired a flare, and the sky had become white with its harsh light, casting the jungle in alternating shadows of green and white. One of the SEALs lay on the edge of the road, gun pointing toward the area they'd just left.

"Let's get back," Zeus told him.

The sailor looked at him, then leaned his head forward, collapsing on the road. He'd been shot in several places.

"Shit," said Zeus.

He scooped himself under the man's stomach, wedging himself in so he could lift and carry him. He struggled up, then lost his balance and had to drop to his knees. His right knee hit a rock and the pain shook his entire frame.

"Come on, damn it," said Zeus, pushing back up.

Bullets were flying everywhere. He ran along the road in the direction of the troops they had just driven past.

Mara flung herself down as the SEALs in front of her began firing at the pair of Chinese soldiers in the intersection. The two men seemed bewildered, unsure of what was going on, frozen by the suddenness and ferocity of the fight. They paid for their surprise with their lives; the SEALs quickly cut them down.

"Over there, over there!" yelled Mara, spotting two more soldiers up the road.

Even as she yelled, she began firing. One fell; the other threw himself back into the shadows.

She looked back. Josh was in the ditch, carrying the girl.

"That van!" she yelled to him. "We'll take it!"

J ing Yo felt the truth of the battle in his mind, understanding what was happening without the interpretation of words or logical reasoning. He had taken a gamble, and not entirely won—the Americans had been driven back, but the army soldiers he had alerted for assistance had not been able to rally quickly enough to overcome them. As a consequence, his small force had been overwhelmed.

It was up to him.

He reached into his pocket for the pencil flare, and fired it, signaling the helicopter to pick him up.

Z eus ran down the road, carrying the SEAL on his back. With every step he expected to be hit. Bullets flew everywhere.

Troops were firing from the trees along the road on his right—the rest of the SEALs, he thought, and he started angling toward them.

Only as he reached the water on that side of the

road did he realize the gunfire was coming from Chinese troops, part of the unit they had rushed past a minute earlier. A bullet flashed in his direction.

They had spotted him.

"Son of a bitch," he muttered, starting to his left to get into the ditch for shelter.

As he turned, a gun began roaring behind him. Then the woods erupted as a grenade went off.

"Careful with him," yelled Kerfer in Zeus's ear. "He must be pretty shot up to let you carry him."

"No bull," said Zeus.

"Does that van you left behind still run?" Kerfer asked.

"Damned if I know."

"Let's try it."

"Which way?"

"*East!* No sense having to do this again."

J osh yanked the rear door of the van open and slid inside. The truck was perforated with bullet holes.

Mara was in the driver's seat, trying to get it to turn over.

"You're going to flood it!" he yelled.

"You worry about Mạ!" she yelled back. "I got this."

The SEALs were outside, firing frenetically. One of them yelled something, and all at once the gunfire stopped.

The engine coughed and sputtered. Mara tried again, but the battery whined, too tired to crank.

Suddenly, the van lurched forward.

"They're pushing," yelled Josh. "You gotta pop the clutch!"

"What?"

"The clutch." He left Ma and went to the front, leaning over the seat. "Put it in first, push the clutch in, then let off when they're pushing."

Mara cursed.

"Wait until I say to push!" Josh yelled through the window.

"Go, just go!" one of them yelled back.

The van started to roll forward. Mara let off on the clutch too soon and the van stopped abruptly. She pushed back in, then tried again. The engine caught.

"Put the clutch in. Don't let it stall. Don't let it stall!" yelled Josh.

"Hey, I can drive!" she screamed. "Get the hell out of the way!" she shouted to the SEALs. "I gotta turn it around."

"We're going back that way?" said Josh.

"The whole damn Chinese army is west of us," said Mara. "The only things east are the guys who were firing at us. Once we're past them, we're home free."

Zeus saw the van lurching back and forth in the road, trying to turn around. The SEAL grew heavier and heavier on his back as he ran, pressing him down, until his chest practically touched his knees. One of the sailors finally grabbed him near the vehicle, pulling his injured comrade down and helping Zeus get the man inside the truck.

"Let's go, let's go, let's go!" he yelled, jumping inside.

Then he realized Christian wasn't there. Cursing, he turned and hopped out the back. As he did, a thick arm hit him across the chest just below the neck, practically clotheslining him.

"Where are you going?" said Kerfer.

"I need Major Christian," he said. "We can't leave him behind."

"This bus is leaving," said Kerfer.

"He's too valuable."

"I'm here!" yelled Christian, running up with one of the SEALs.

"Go, let's go!" shouted Kerfer. He jumped onto the top of the van. "Don't stop if I fall off! If anybody falls off—don't stop! Just go. It's the scientist we want. Everybody else walks. It's hell or bust!"

J ing Yo threw himself through the large hatchway into the helicopter, scrambled to his feet, and ran up front to the cockpit.

"They're getting into a van!" yelled the pilots.

It was a stroke of luck.

Jing Yo turned and ran back to the cabin. "Shoot at the van," he told the gunner there. "Shoot it when it comes down the road."

"We have only a few rounds left."

They had gone through a dozen boxes of ammunition during the mission.

"Fire until you're out of bullets. Then use your personal weapons."

Jing Yo raised the rifle in his hand. He too was nearly out of ammunition—one more box of shells besides the one he had in the gun.

"Get us over the van!" he shouted as the helicopter swirled. "Get us close!"

The helicopter circled back, following the van. Jing Yo began to fire. So did the door gunner. Bullets flew back at him. The pilot backed off.

Jing Yo's anger exploded. He leapt to the cockpit. "That van must be stopped. Get closer!"

"I'm as close as I dare."

"You will crash into it if necessary," said Jing Yo.

"No, I won't, Lieutenant."

Jing Yo put the muzzle of his rifle against the pilot's neck. The barrel was still hot, and the pilot yelped with pain.

"Crash into the bastards. It is our duty."

The van jerked out of Mara's control every time they hit water. She had to take her foot off the gas, try and hold the wheel straight, and just wait until the steering came back.

The gunfire seemed to have died down, if not stopped. They were past the Chinese, beyond the worst of it.

The van skidded around the corner. Mara backed off on the gas, pushed into the skid, then corrected, trying not to oversteer. She got onto a patch of dry, smooth road and went straight for a few yards, then came to water and began skidding again. The SEALs on the roof—there were at least three—lurched and slid with the van.

Josh had pushed into the front seat beside her, along with one of the SEALs, who was leaning halfway out the window with his gun.

"The helicopter!" yelled Josh. "It's coming back around."

"Shoot it down!" yelled Mara.

Josh grabbed her gun from the floor. The SEAL began firing. The helicopter arced in front of them, giving whoever was in the cabin a good angle to fire. Mara swerved, trying to stay with the road as it pushed right. The chopper passed overhead.

"Good one!" yelled Josh. "Now go! Get us out of here!"

The road took another sharp turn right. It was rising out of the flooded area. Mara stepped on the gas but quickly went into another skid. She just barely retained control.

"He's coming back!" yelled Josh.

The helicopter swung around in front of them. Everyone in the van seemed to be firing at him, but he was coming in, still firing.

"I think he's going to crash into us!" yelled Josh.

"Hang on!" yelled Mara as the turn came up.

She started to yank the wheel right, to take the switchback, but the wheels of the van kept going straight. She gave up trying to correct it and instead spun the wheel to make the skid worse, spinning into the bend of the road. Mara jammed the brakes, trying to stop as they slid in among the trees. The helicopter passed within a few feet, its undercarriage ripping into the treetops as it shot by.

"Go, go, go!" yelled Josh.

"No fucking kiddin'," growled Mara, pulling out of the jungle and back onto the road.

J ing Yo hurtled toward the open door of the helicopter as the aircraft lurched through the tops of the trees. He saw blackness, then light, and for a moment he believed that he had left the realm of pain and confusion, the world that every devout Buddhist vows to escape. Then his hands slammed against the side of the cabin. They grabbed hold, and he managed to hold himself in the aircraft even though his feet dangled in the void.

The helicopter whirled in a backward circle. Jing Yo clawed at the side of the cabin, pulling himself toward the cockpit.

"The van!" he yelled. "The van!"

The pilots were too busy to hear him. The chopper's engine, hit in a dozen places, had given out. They saw a flat, open space before them—the overflowing creek—and aimed for it.

"Brace for impact!" yelled the copilot.

A half second later, the helicopter crashed into the water.

Northern Vietnam

Mara's hand trembled as they climbed up the second switchback. The helicopter seemed to have disappeared.

"God, this thing is impossible to steer," she said, taking the turn. "Did we lose anyone? Josh—where are the SEALs?"

"Don't worry about us," said the sailor to Josh's right. He turned around, putting his feet on the seat and leaning across what had been the windshield before it was shot out. "Just keep going."

"I'm not leaving any of you behind."

"You aren't." Kerfer leaned over the side, his head at her window. "Just keep going."

"Okay, okay." She downshifted to take the next curve. "I hate manual transmissions."

They crested the hill. There were no lights in front of them, no gun flashes, no explosions.

"I'm going to check on Mạ," said Josh. He left the gun and climbed back.

Mạ was sitting between two of the SEALs, watching as they performed a silent puppet show with their fingers. The girl started laughing as the fingers crashed into each other. They'd finally won her over.

Things are going to be all right, thought Josh.

Then he realized that wasn't quite true. They had escaped, but things weren't all right. They were going to be very messed up for a long time.

Maybe forever, as far as Mạ was concerned.

He had to get back to America. Once there, he'd tell his story. A lot of people weren't going to believe it. They'd see the video, and probably think he'd faked it.

He'd make them believe. This was a world war, bigger than anything the world had confronted in decades.

Bigger. Neither side could wipe out life on the planet then. They sure could now.

"How you doing?" asked Zeus.

"I'm doing okay, Major. Thanks for coming for us."

"You can call me Zeus." He stuck out his hand. "We should be back in a couple of hours. I just talked to my general. Another truck is going to meet us at Tuyên Quang. He's driving it himself."

"Good."

"There are no Chinese troops between us and Hanoi. We're home free."

Josh nodded.

"Hey, cheer up," said Major Christian. "It's over, right?"

"No," said Josh. "It's just beginning."

Turn the page for a preview of

LARRY BOND'S
Red Dragon Rising

EDGE OF WAR

LARRY BOND AND
JIM DeFELICE

Available in November 2010 from
Tom Doherty Associates

A FORGE HARDCOVER   ISBN 978-0-7653-2138-1

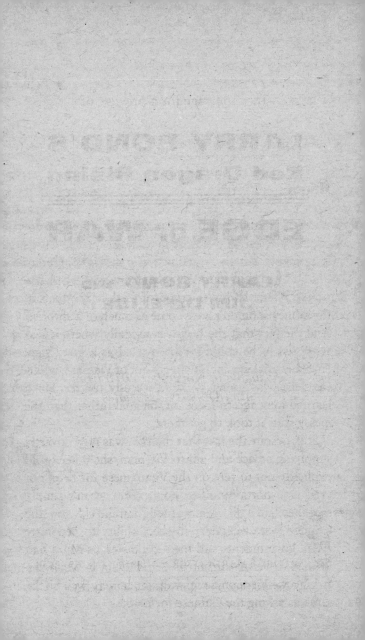

Hanoi

A certain amount of paranoia was absolutely essential to succeed as a covert agent. The problem was figuring out exactly how much was the right amount.

Mara had arrived in Vietnam knowing the CIA station in Hanoi had been compromised, so the theft of the money shouldn't have come as much of a surprise. And the fact that the box was actually where it was supposed to be could be interpreted as a good sign. Since her goal was simply to get out of Vietnam, whatever else was going on didn't really matter. She'd learned long ago to focus on the goal rather than the messy stuff it took to get there.

Still, despite the fact that the U.S. was now covertly supplying advice and aid to Vietnam, she'd been told explicitly not to rely on the Vietnamese for help, not even transportation. The implication wasn't simply that they had a different agenda than the U.S. did: the Chinese were legendary in their ability to penetrate Asian governments and their militaries, as Mara had learned to her detriment time and again in Malaysia. Asking the Vietnamese for help might very well be the same as asking the Chinese for help.

Her suspicions and doubts wrapped themselves tighter and tighter as she drove her scooter over to the shop Phai had mentioned to sell the sat phones. Mara didn't particularly trust Phai, either, even though she knew him from Thailand. She rode around the block twice, making sure she wasn't followed, then parked in an alley about a block away. Even so, she circled around on foot to make sure there wasn't an ambush waiting.

Under other circumstances, Mara might have simply left the sat phones in the city somewhere. But she needed money as well as misdirection.

The fantasies she'd had as a child about being a spy—she'd grown up on *Where in the World Is Carmen Sandiego?*, then graduated to old James Bond movies—didn't involve credit cards or ATM machines. But they turned out to be an agent's best friend in the real world. When they weren't working, life was a hell of a lot harder.

Gold shops were common in the city, combination pawnbrokers and banks as well as jewelers. Like others, the owner of Ha Trung Finest conducted several other businesses on the side concurrently—tourist knickknacks and bottled water were featured in the window, along with handwoven place mats and a rug.

He offered her fifty thousand dong apiece for the two phones—a total of roughly six dollars.

"Be serious," scolded Mara. She was in no mood to bargain.

The proprietor pretended to look at the phones again, then upped his offer to two hundred thousand dong.

"No," said Mara loudly, this time using English. She turned to leave the store.

"Wait, wait, lady," said a woman, rushing from the back room. She spoke in English. "Don't worry about husband. Eels for brains."

Mara showed her the phones impatiently. The woman turned them over, looking at them as if they were pieces of jewelry. She flicked one on.

"These active," said the woman.

"I figured you'd take care of getting new accounts," said Mara.

"Without accounts they're worthless," said the man in Vietnamese.

"You just have to reprogram them," snapped Mara in English. "I know that happens all the time."

What actually happened all the time—and what Mara was counting on—was that the phones would be used on the existing accounts until the phone company finally got around to shutting them off. That could be days if not weeks. Of course, stating that explicitly meant acknowledging that the phones were stolen.

The store owners didn't just suspect the phones were stolen; they were counting on it. But if Mara said that, they wouldn't take them.

The wife looked at her. "Five hundred thousand dong."

"One million dong each."

Mara pushed the phones into the woman's hands. The woman tried to give them back. The man behind the counter harangued her for interfering.

"Eight hundred thousand," said Mara, speaking Vietnamese. "The account is good."

They settled on seven hundred and fifty, with the woman throwing in a sling bag Mara decided she could use for her gun. Once the money changed hands, the man became gracious, insisting on giving Mara a bottle of water. He would have tried selling her the rug if she hadn't left abruptly.

Mara had expected the trains south to be packed, but the station was almost empty when she arrived. Kerfer, Josh, and the others were huddled at the far end of the large room, camped out around a dozen of the light blue chairs. They'd bought some civilian luggage, and used them to stow their weapons and other gear. The SEALs had even found some new clothes and a doll for Mạ. She held the doll in her arms, rocking it gently and humming to it as she leaned against Josh.

"I'm assuming you have some sort of plan," said Kerfer when she arrived. All six of his men—Eric, Little Joe, Stevens, Jenkins, Mancho, and Silvestri— were sprawled nearby.

"Are the trains still running?" Mara asked.

"You sent us here without knowing?"

"They were running this morning," she said defensively.

Kerfer made a face. Mara went over to the ticket stand, a small podium-style desk near the door. The clerk assured her that the full schedule of trains was operating. She asked for tickets for Hai Phong—the cheapest trip available—and tried to pay with her credit card. The clerk told her that they were accepting only cash. She tried to use dongs but he would only take dollars, greatly depleting her supply.

Josh sat on the chair, his head hanging down about midway over his knees. His face looked even whiter than normal, and his eyes were gazing into space. Mạ leaned against him, but he didn't seem to be paying much attention to her.

"You with us, Josh?" Mara asked.

"I'm here."

"He's got some sort of bug," volunteered Little Joe. "He ain't pissing too well."

Great, thought Mara. She had the images Josh had made of massacre, but Washington wanted Josh and the girl as well. There was no substitute for a first-hand story.

She put her hand against his forehead. He seemed a little warm. "You take aspirin?" she asked.

"Eric gave me some. I think it's something I ate," he added.

Hopefully. Otherwise they'd all have it soon.

"Hang in there," Mara told him. Shouldering her backpack and sling bag—her folding-stock AK-47 was in the pack, her pistol in the bag—she pointed to the door out to the tracks. "Our train leaves in ten minutes. Let's go."

Mara walked across to the southbound train. It

wasn't the one she had tickets to, but it was the one she wanted. This train traveled along the coast, with stops at Dong Hoi, Hue, and Da Nang, among others, before heading inland to Saigon. It was a sleeper, and ordinarily would have been at least half full with tourists and businesspeople. But it was empty.

"Hey, they even got TV," said Little Joe, pointing.

They spread out in the cars.

"You gonna give us all tickets?" Kerfer asked.

"They're not for this train," said Mara, handing them out.

"What?"

"They aren't going to collect them," said Mara. "We're not going to be on long anyway."

"What do you mean?"

She shook her head.

"Listen, I gotta know what's going on here," said Kerfer. "I don't like being on a train to begin with."

"Neither do I," said Mara. "I didn't have enough cash for the right train. Besides, we're going to jump out down the line. A friend has arranged to leave some vehicles for us."

"You should have said that before."

"What difference does it make?"

"It makes a difference."

"Well, that's what we're doing. It was a backup plan," she added. "And now we're using it. Because I don't like the fact that the train is so empty. The ones this morning weren't."

Kerfer frowned, then went and gave his men the tickets.

Two minutes later, the train started out of the station. They still hadn't seen a conductor.

Josh slumped against the window. His pelvis felt as if it were burning up. He breathed slowly, trying to dissipate the pain.

He imagined it was something he ate, but had no way of knowing for sure. Maybe it was a urinary infection, but he hadn't had sex in weeks.

Three months now, actually. When he and his girlfriend broke up. So that couldn't be the cause. It must just be something he ate or drank.

"They have bathrooms on these?" he said, feeling the urge to pee.

"Up there," said Mara, pointing.

The small closet reeked of human waste and ammonia. Josh felt his stomach churning and leaned over to retch. But nothing came out.

"Let it all out, man," said Squeaky, who was standing outside. "Just let it go. You'll feel tons better."

"Trying," muttered Josh, steadying himself against the side of the coach as the train began to pick up speed.

The train ran along a highway through the city and immediately south. It chugged along slowly, barely approaching thirty miles an hour. Mara nervously watched the countryside pass by. Knots of Vietnamese troops were parked every quarter mile or so along the road. This was the safest way past the military bunkers where most of the government and army officials had taken shelter to the south, but it took them perversely close to them, as well as to several military installations along the sidings.

Mara left Josh and Mạ in the seat near the back of the car and went up the aisle to the first row, not expecting a conductor but prepared to deal with one if he showed up. A small bribe would be sufficient to take care of any problem about their destination, especially since they weren't going to be on the train for very long.

"So when exactly is it we're getting off?" said Kerfer, settling down beside her. He leaned forward and rested his arm on the seat back of the row in front of him, leaning toward her.

"Soon," she said.

"That ain't good enough, kid."

"You're calling me kid now?"

"I call everybody kid. I figure that's better than lady, right?"

"Mara works."

Kerfer frowned. She could only guess at his age—late twenties, maybe thirties. He had a rough face that seemed made of unpolished stone. His green civilian shirt and blue jeans made him look more military, not less, even though he was unshaven and his hair edged over his ears.

"All right. So Mara—what are we doing?"

"We need to get south of Phú Xuyên," she told him.

"Where's that?"

"Twenty-one miles south of Hanoi. Things are less tense there. We shouldn't have to worry about being stopped."

"I thought Major Murphy said these guys are on our side now."

"I wouldn't trust them for the time of day."

Kerfer frowned again—it seemed to be his basic facial expression—then slowly nodded.

"What about the little girl?" he asked.

"Washington says she can come back with us," said Mara. "That's what you want, right?"

"Hey, I don't care. Better than an orphanage, right?"

Ma had a hell of a story to tell, which was the real reason Washington wanted her back. Still, she could live a far better life in the States than she could here. Regardless of the war.

"When are we getting out?" Kerfer asked.

"I'll tell you in plenty of time."

Kerfer pushed himself back in the seat, extending his legs to relax. "Girl jumping, too?"

"She can come with me. We'll go out uphill. It's like stepping off an escalator."

"I've done it before." He smelled of sweat. "Country's falling apart?"

"Not really," said Mara. "If that was happening, the train would be packed."

"People are afraid to take the train because they know the Chinese will bomb it soon," said Kerfer. "It's an easy target."

"They haven't bombed it yet," said Mara.

"That's because they figured they would waltz right through. They wanted the train. Now that they're starting to slow down, they'll bomb everything in sight. They won't care about how many they kill. They'll just lay it all to waste." He turned to her. "That bother you?"

"It's not my job to be bothered by that."

Kerfer laughed. "You do a good imitation of being a hard-ass," he told her. "I'll give you that."

The train started braking. Mara looked out the window. She wasn't sure where they were, but she knew they couldn't be much more than halfway there; they hadn't even passed Phú yet. She got up and walked to the vestibule of the car.

"Problem?" asked Kerfer, following.

"We shouldn't be stopping," she said, taking a train key from her pocket and opening the door.

"Nice," said Kerfer.

Mara leaned out of the car and saw a contingent of soldiers near the side of the track ahead. They must be the reason the train was stopping.

It was too late to run for it.

"Back in the car. Group together," she told Kerfer. "I do the talking."

"They going to ask us for passports?" said Kerfer.

"Hopefully not."

"We got 'em." The SEALs had prepared civilian covers for this very contingency. They were a soccer team, in the country for an international goodwill tour.

"Hold on to them," said Mara. "The girl is my daughter. I talk. No one else."

Squeaky banged on the door of the restroom. "Come on, come on," he said in his high-pitched whisper.

Josh straightened and took a slow breath. The putrid air of the closet-sized bathroom only made him feel worse. What he needed was fresh air.

"Josh? Stay in there," said Mara outside. "You're all right?"

"Yeah."

"There are soldiers coming onto the car. Stay in the bathroom. Don't come out unless I tell you."

Josh heard her tell Squeaky to stay there as well. He pressed the tap to get some water and wash his hands, but nothing flowed. And then there were Vietnamese voices in the car.

Mara watched the soldiers as they came into the train. They were teenagers, joking about something one of them had done while waiting for the train. The sight of the foreigners silenced them momentarily. They moved into the middle of the car and sat in a clump together, a half dozen of them, all lugging AK-47s and light packs.

Mara had gone back to sit with Mạ. The little girl was tense, sitting stiffly upright. They were two seats from the end of the rear door, just up from the rest-room.

She wouldn't have minded the soldiers at all, except for the fact that she had to jump from the train. She wasn't sure how they were going to react if half a dozen foreigners went off the side.

The train began moving. Mara pretended to be interested in the scenery.

Josh was still in the restroom as the train started to move again. Now that the soldiers were in their seats, Mara decided it was time to get him back out. So she went over and put her head to the door. Squeaky blinked at her, trying to puzzle out what she had in mind.

"Honey, are you okay?" asked Mara. She made her voice just loud enough for the soldiers to hear, guessing that they would know at least a little English.

"I'm okay," said Josh.

"Come out and sit with me," said Mara, her voice softer.

Josh immediately opened the door. Squeaky hesitated for a second, then slipped inside as if he'd been waiting.

"What are we doing?" asked Josh.

"You can have the window," said Mara, gently pushing his side.

He slipped Mạ between them and sat down. A few seconds later, the door at the front of the car opened. Another pair of Vietnamese soldiers entered—a lieutenant and a corporal.

The lieutenant immediately frowned at the foreigners. "Why are you on this train?" he said to Kerfer, who was sitting alone in the seat closest to the door.

"Going to Ho Chi Minh City," said Kerfer. He held his ticket, folded down, in his hand.

The lieutenant shook his head. "You're Americans?" His English was good, his accent by now familiar.

Mara got out of her seat. "We were all here on a visit to Hanoi University," she told the soldier, walking forward. She switched to Vietnamese. "The government advised us to join the rest of our group in Saigon."

"Who?" said the lieutenant, still in English.

Mara used the first name that came into her head—Phú, claiming he was from the education ministry, which had sponsored their soccer visit. The soldier would have no way of checking, and she calculated that if she seemed sure and exact, he would eventually drop the matter.

But she calculated wrongly.

"We will search your bags," said the lieutenant.

"Why?" said Mara, switching to English as well so Kerfer would know what was going on. "Why are you going to search our bags? Do you think we are thieves?"

"Let me see your passport and visa," demanded the lieutenant.

"Okay. Let me get it."

Mara turned and walked to the back, even though her passport was in her pocket. Only one of the soldiers was watching; the others were either listening to MP3 players or reading.

Mara opened her sling bag, poked around quickly—making sure not to expose her pistol—then began patting the pockets of her clothes. She reached inside and pulled out the passport. There was a twenty-dollar bill in it.

The lieutenant opened the passport, keeping the bill in place.

"Is there a problem?" Mara asked him.

"All transportation must be organized by the army," said the lieutenant. "The minister of education is nothing."

Mara saw Kerfer coming down the aisle behind the Vietnamese officer.

Go back to your seat, she thought. We're almost through with this.

"Where in Ho Chi Minh City are you going?" asked the Vietnamese lieutenant, still looking at her passport.

"We're supposed to call when we get to the station," she said. "I would imagine they will send a car. I hope they will send a car, or we will have to walk. We'll do whatever they tell us, of course."

"Whose child?"

"Mine."

"She's not on your passport?"

"That's not necessary in America," she lied.

The lieutenant closed the passport, tapping it against his hand. He seemed to be deciding whether to take the money or not.

Finally he slipped the bill out and handed her the passport back.

"Now let me see your bags," he said.

Kerfer raised his arm, revealing a pistol. Before Mara could say anything, he'd pulled the trigger, putting a bullet through the side of the officer's head.